THE
GAME
OF
HOPE

THE GAME OF HOPE

SANDRA GULLAND

VIKING

VIKING

An imprint of Penguin Random House LLC
375 Hudson Street
New York, New York 10014

First published in the United States of America by Viking,
an imprint of Penguin Random House LLC, 2018

Text copyright © 2018 by Sandra Gulland

Jacket painting by Marie Denise Villers, courtesy of Mr. and Mrs. Isaac D. Fletcher Collection,
Bequest of Isaac D. Fletcher, 1917 | Go to http://bit.ly/Hopecover for more details.

Map by Jean-Claude Dezauche (ca. 1750–1824) / Wikimedia Commons / Public Domain

The Lenormand cards © The Trustees of the British Museum.

LIBRARY OF CONGRESS CATALOGING-IN-PUBLICATION DATA

Names: Gulland, Sandra, author.
Title: The game of hope / Sandra Gulland.
Description: New York : Viking Books for Young Readers, 2018. | Summary: In 1798, fifteen-year-
old Hortense de Beauharnais, Napoleon Bonaparte's stepdaughter, attends an exclusive boarding
school, dreaming of her brother's fellow officer Christophe, unaware of the role she is fated to play.
Identifiers: LCCN 2017058340 (print) | LCCN 2018004014 (ebook)
ISBN 9780425291023 (ebook) | ISBN 9780425291016 (hardback)
Subjects: LCSH: Hortense, Queen, consort of Louis Bonaparte, King of Holland,
1783–1837—Childhood and youth—Juvenile fiction. | France—History—1789–1799—Juvenile
fiction. | CYAC: Hortense, Queen, consort of Louis Bonaparte, King of Holland,
1783–1837—Fiction. | Boarding schools—Fiction. | Schools—Fiction. | Conduct of life—Fiction.
| France—History—1789–1799—Fiction.
Classification: LCC PZ7.1.G874 (ebook) | LCC PZ7.1.G874 Gam 2018 (print) |
DDC [Fic]—dc23
LC record available at https://lccn.loc.gov/2017058340

Printed in U.S.A.

1   3   5   7   9   10   8   6   4   2

For Ellie, Kiki and Estelle,
my Fearsome Threesome

"Secret griefs are more cruel than public calamities."
—VOLTAIRE, FROM *Candide*

THE
GAME
OF
HOPE

CONTENTS

❖

A Historical Note xiii

I: Refuge 1
II: Life Force 47
III: Deceit 83
IV: Transformation 131
V: Happy Times 163
VI: Change 209
VII: New Possibilities 257
VIII: Romantic Fantasies 301

Afterword 347
The Revolutionary Calendar 353
Cast of Characters 354
Glossary 357
Map 364
The Game of Hope 366
Acknowledgements 368

A HISTORICAL NOTE

❖

"It was the best of times, it was the worst of times . . ."

In his novel *A Tale of Two Cities*, Charles Dickens wrote about the French Revolution, a revolution that began in a fever of idealism and goodwill (the *best* of times), and devolved over time into the period known as the Terror (the *worst* of times).

The Terror began when Robespierre—sometimes referred to as "the Tyrant"—gained power. During his rule, thousands of innocent men and women, many of them aristocrats, were imprisoned. Most were subsequently executed, beheaded by a contraption named after Dr. Guillotin, who had invented it as a humanitarian alternative to hanging. He regretted the association of his name with a machine that came to be used with shocking frequency during the Terror.

This was the world of Hortense's childhood. After Robespierre was overthrown and guillotined, many prisoners were released, including Hortense's mother, Josephine, who escaped death by only a day. Her father was not so fortunate.

Although fiction, Hortense's story is based on historical fact. For example, the letters from Maîtresse Campan, the head of her boarding school, are based on letters Campan wrote. Also, the young composer Hyacinthe Jadin was indeed Hortense's teacher. (See the notes at the end of this novel for details.)

The Game of Hope opens in 1798, four years after the end of the Terror. France is in shambles, many grieving the death of someone they loved—especially Hortense, who mourns her beloved father, executed by guillotine.

I

REFUGE

26 Fructidor – Jour du génie, An 6
(12 September – 18 September, 1798)

THE HOUSE CARD: REFUGE

THE DREAM

✤

I saw a man approaching. Cloaked and hooded, he moved with grace in the flickering candlelight.

My heart soared. Father!

He put out one hand, gloved in white leather. Hope was aglow all around him.

But then—as *always*—his hood fell back, and there was only a bloody stump where his head should have been.

I screamed, gasping for air, my heart pounding.

Mouse and Ém tried to calm me, but I only wept all the harder.

What did my father want?

Why was he haunting me?

Maîtresse rushed into our room in rumpled nightclothes, a shawl thrown haphazardly over her shoulders. "Such screaming, angel! You'll terrify the Little Geniuses," she said, putting down her candle. The shadows made her face look like that of a ghoul.

"I'm sorry," I sobbed, slipping the miniature enamel portrait of my father from under my pillow. Father: so handsome, so elegant, to have died like *that*, the crowd cheering as his head fell into a basket of wood shavings.

"It's that same night-fright she always has," Mouse told her aunt, her voice tremulous.

"That scary dream of her father," my cousin Ém said.

I looked into Maîtresse's eyes. She was mistress of our boarding school, quite strict and demanding, yet we all loved her. "With his—" I winced, making a slashing motion across my neck.

"Come here, my sweets," Maîtresse said, opening her arms.

Dragging their blankets, Ém and Mouse huddled in close. I could feel Mouse trembling. We called ourselves the Fearsome Threesome, but in the dead of night, Fearful Threesome might have been more apt.

"Repeat after me," Maîtresse said, pulling the blankets snugly around us. She smelled deliciously of vanilla. "We are safe now."

"We are safe now," we whispered in unison.

Safe now, safe now, safe now.

But were we? It had been four years since the tyrant Robespierre had been executed, bringing an end to the Terror—but what if it were to happen again? Practically every girl in our school was of the nobility. What was to keep us from being hunted down, having our heads cut off?

I bit my lip, recalling the stench of the dead, heaped like garbage in the square.

Maîtresse clasped my shoulder. The strength of her grip brought me back. "You grew up in a violent time," she said, her voice soft. "You witnessed things no child should ever have to see. But memories are like words on a wax tablet: they can be erased. You are smart, and creative, and talented. You can become whatever you wish, but first, you must learn to direct your thoughts—even your dreams." She tucked a stray strand of my hair back up under my nightcap. "Remember: you are safe now."

Safe now.

I woke before dawn, my thoughts in disarray, my heart aching.

Father, must you frighten me so?

Was I the cause of your death?

I whispered my morning devotions curled up under my blankets, praying that I would never have that dream again.

Praying for the safety of my big brother Eugène, who was a soldier now, fighting with our stepfather's army in far-away Egypt.

Praying that my stepfather, General Bonaparte, would somehow disappear from my life, lost to the sands of that barbaric country.

Praying that I would become a better person and not have such evil thoughts.

Praying that my mother would stop trying to find a husband for me.

Praying for a horse of my own.

Praying for one of Maîtresse's delicious chocolate madeleines.

And then, especially heartfelt, praying—sinfully, I know—for the safety of A Certain Someone who was also with the General's army in Egypt.

Dawn breaking, I slipped shivering out of bed and wrapped myself in a shawl. Quietly, so as not to wake Ém and Mouse, I put kindling and a few sticks of wood on the embers in the fireplace, blowing until they caught fire. I heard a rooster crow and tiptoed to the window to unlatch the shutters. It was cold for early fall—there was a shimmer of frost on the courtyard cobbles.

My thick notebooks were stacked to one side on the study table I shared with Ém and Mouse. I'd been away for three months, tending my injured mother. I had missed the Institute so much! I had been enrolled at only twelve, shortly after my father was executed and Maman released from prison. Now I was fifteen, Maman was married to General Bonaparte, and my brother was on the General's staff in Egypt.

Time passed so quickly. And death came quickly, too.

Safe now?

I heard a maid walking the halls, clanging her iron triangle with a metal beater, a grating, high-pitched ringing sound. Six o'clock: time for everyone to wake.

Ém groaned, pulling her covers up over her head.

"Did you sleep, Hortense?" Mouse asked, her voice groggy.

"A bit," I said, yawning. It had taken me time to get back to sleep after the fright of my dream.

Ém chuckled from under her covers. "You kept *me* awake the rest of the night," she said, poking her head out. "Talking *lovey.*"

"No!" I said—yet flushing. I shared everything with Ém and Mouse, everything except one secret, which I'd not had the courage to reveal, knowing how foolish they would find me. Me, fifteen, not pretty, not rich, moonsick for the most handsome of the General's aides. A man I'd only seen a few times and who was now far away in Egypt. A man who hardly knew my name.

"You have a beau?" Mouse asked with that funny little squeak her voice sometimes got.

"I'd tell you if I did," I said, pulling my clothes out of my travel trunk, yet to be unpacked. It wasn't a lie, not really. I didn't have a beau. I only wished I did. One beau in particular.

The triangle sounded a second time, in warning: Get up!

"Your turn to go first, Ém," Mouse said, not wanting to leave the warmth of her bed. Soon we would be on our winter schedule and not have to rise until seven.

Ém, sighing in protest, slipped from under her covers, grabbed her chamber pot and disappeared behind the screen. "Ah me," she said, "the reds."

"Do you have what you need?" I asked.

"There are cloths here," Ém said.

There was a rap at our door. "Citoyenne Hortense, you're back," maid Flor said, surprised to see me.

"She arrived last night," Mouse said from under her covers. "In the *dark*."

"How is your lovely mother?" Flor asked, filling each of our porcelain wash basins with steaming water.

"Improved." *Grâce à Dieu.* "She can stand up now."

As soon as Flor left, the triangle clanged a third time: Get dressed!

Mouse sat up, groping for her spectacles on the table beside her bed.

"It's a bit chilly," I said, slipping on my flannel chemise and a wool school gown over it. The long white dress was starting to feel small for me around the chest. (*Yes.*)

I was arranging my multicolored sash—the sash worn by those of us who had completed all the levels (the Multis, we were called)—when another servant appeared, the country girl who worked in the laundry room. "A frosty morning, girls. Émilie, you will want your lovely shawl. I stitched on your initials and number." She closed the door behind her.

"It's new, Ém?" I asked, passing the shawl over to her. A delicate shade of rose, the thick, luxurious cashmere was well beyond our means.

"It was a gift from her husband," Mouse said with a giggle.

Her husband. That sounded so strange to me. Ém had been introduced to Captain Antoine Lavalette only sixteen days before marrying him, all arranged by the General and my mother. A few days later, Lavalette had left for Egypt, and shortly after that, I had gone south, and I'd not seen my cousin since.

"It's beautiful," I said with envy.

Ém looked stricken, her doe eyes glistening. "I prefer my old one," she said, pulling her moth-eaten, itchy wool shawl out of her trunk.

I caught Mouse's eye. She raised her eyebrows as if to say, *I don't understand either.*

"Don't look like that," Ém said with a flare of surprising emotion. She was usually placid (unlike Mouse and me). "I hate how everyone goes on about me being a married woman."

"But Ém, you *are* a—"

"I'm not," she said, cutting me off. "Not really."

How could she say that? I had been present at the ceremony in our grandparents' house here in Montagne-du-Bon-Air.

"What do you mean, Ém?" Mouse asked, pushing up her heavy glasses.

"It's just that I'm still . . ." Ém flushed.

"Chaste?" I whispered.

Ém answered with a slight nod.

I was surprised. It was common for girls who married young to wait until puberty before consummating their union, but Ém was seventeen, and womanly besides.

CAROLINE

❖

When the seven o'clock triangle sounded, Mouse, Ém and I rushed down the stone stairs to the rooms where the Little Geniuses slept, some of them only four years old. One of our duties as Multis was to help a youngster get washed, dressed and to the dining hall each morning. I hadn't seen my charge, Nelly, since early summer, and I missed her.

Ém and Mouse headed for the first room, and I carried on to the second, a warm south-facing chamber with a good-sized fireplace. The six little beds were lined up along one wall, basins for washing at each foot. On a platform at the end of the room was the tidy bed of the night monitor, Citoyenne Florentine—who was nowhere to be seen.

I waved a greeting to the other Multis, busy with their charges.

"Hortense!" Nelly hugged my legs.

"You're so big now!" She looked irresistibly sweet in her long-sleeved nightdress and cap.

"I'm going to be five," she boasted, holding up one hand, fingers splayed.

Her friend Fru-fru was sitting on the bed next to Nelly's, looking forlorn.

"Where's your helper?" I asked, nodding to three Multis who were already leaving for the dining hall with their charges.

Fru-fru scowled. "I don't know."

"What's her name?"

"Citoyenne Caroline."

Who was Caroline? I didn't know one.

"I can dress myself," Nelly boasted, trying to heft open her trunk. I propped the lid so that it wouldn't crash down on her hands. "Citoyenne Florentine told us to wear our wool smock," she said. "Because it's so cold."

The fire had died down, and I didn't see any wood. "Where is she?" Usually, the monitor was hovering.

"She went to find Caroline," Fru-fru said.

"Petticoat," Nelly demanded, making a shivering motion.

"Petticoat, *please*," I said, checking the contents of Nelly's trunk, making sure that everything was properly labeled: NC (for Nelly Castille) 276 (her student number).

"Petticoat, please," Nelly said, pulling off her night stockings. I slipped a flannel petticoat on over her head. "Somebody saw the ghost last night," she said excitedly.

The ghost? "There is no such thing." Maîtresse warned us against superstitions born of ignorance. My mother believed in ghosts, but she was unschooled.

"There is! It has a beard. A girl upstairs saw it."

"We heard her screaming," Fru-fru said, hugging her pillow.

"That was me," I told them with a laugh.

"*You* saw the ghost with a beard?" Nelly's eyes were round as wagon wheels.

"It wasn't a ghost," I said, fastening Nelly's green school sash. "It was a dream I had that frightened me."

"I want a purple sash," Nelly said.

"You'll get to go up to the Purple level when you know the difference between an M and an N."

"But M and N look the same."

"You'll learn. In three months everyone in the school will take an exam to see who is ready to move up a level. If you don't pass, you can try again three months later. Can you say your letters for me?" I asked, to distract her while I combed out her fine hair, in need of a trim.

She had almost got to L (with help) when Citoyenne Florentine appeared. "Still no sign of Caroline?" she asked Fru-fru.

"Who is Caroline?" I asked. The room was almost empty now.

Florentine snorted with amusement. "General Bonaparte's sister."

"Annunziata? But her name's not Caroline."

"She changed it," Florentine said with an exasperated roll of her eyes.

I shouldn't have been surprised. The Bonapartes, who were from Corsica, seemed to like changing their names. *Buonaparte* had been changed to Bonaparte and *Napoleone* to Napoleon. One of the brothers, *Luciano*, had changed his name twice, first to Brutus and then to Lucien. The General had even made Maman change her name from Rose to Josephine! And now Annunziata had changed to Caroline? How they all kept track was beyond me.

"And this is the fifth time she's been late." Citoyenne Florentine took a notebook and wooden pencil out of her hemp bag and made a notation.

Uh oh. A demerit? "I can help dress Fru-fru." I wondered how many demerits Annunziata-now-Caroline had. Twelve in a month and she would have to eat alone at the Repentance Table. One good mark erased two bad ones, though, so maybe she was in the clear. "Nelly is almost ready."

"Good, I have to get wood for the fire," Florentine said, heading back out.

"I'm ready now." Nelly turned, beaming.

"Not quite." She had put her smock on backward.

As the triangle for breakfast sounded, Annunziata-now-Caroline appeared.

"Where were you?" Fru-fru demanded, pulling on her woolen socks.

"Mind your own business," she said, without an apology for being so late.

"Good morning," I said, forcing a smile. She was, after all, a member of my family now, like it or not. "I'm told you changed your name to Caroline."

"So?" She had a negligent air that seemed almost wanton, in spite of her cherubic appearance, her fat cheeks and rosy complexion.

"It's a pretty name." I didn't know what else to say.

"There you are," Citoyenne Florentine said, a load of firewood in her arms. "Hortense, go ahead to the dining hall with Fru-fru and Nelly," she said, setting the wood down on the hearth. "I need to have a word with Caroline."

The dining hall was a large, cavernous room big enough to seat all the students—over two hundred and seventy of us, at last count. The tables were covered with bright cloths that matched the color of the different levels: green, purple, orange, blue, red, white and multi-colored. An enormous fire was roaring. Scents of freshly baked bread and fried pork filled the air. I'd missed the delicious food at the Institute.

Ém and Mouse were with the Multis by the door to the cellar kitchens. I gave them our silly Fearsome Threesome greeting, wiggling my fingers at my forehead. They wiggled their fingers back, which always made me laugh.

Nelly and Fru-fru made their way to the long, low table covered with a green cloth and stood at their places. "Good girls." I kissed them both and headed for the corner where the Multis stood, ready to serve.

"Hortense, welcome back," the dining hall monitor said, stopping me. "I'd like you to read this morning." She handed me a note with the inspirational reading Maîtresse had chosen for the day.

"Happily," I said, turning toward the lectern at the front of the hall.

The monitor rang a brass bell and all the girls sat down, their chairs making a racket in the cavernous room. Another shake of the bell and everyone bowed their heads.

The Inspiration, as usual, was one Maîtresse had written. This one was about finding the confidence to dream big dreams, and having the courage to fail.

A quiet descended over the room as I read, everyone rapt—until Annunziata-now-Caroline came in, noisily bumping into tables and chairs. Everyone turned to gawk, then titter, as she crashed her way to the small table directly in front of the lectern: the Repentance Table.

Oh no! I thought.

But Caroline didn't seem to care one way or another. With an expression of indifference, she plopped herself into the chair, placing the framed notice of her crimes in front of her, as if she'd won a prize.

I finished the reading, rushing through it. "Life, liberty and equality," everyone responded in a murmur at the end.

"Amen!" Caroline snorted, chewing on a thumbnail.

Flustered, I stepped down from the lectern and joined the Multis. Like clockwork we fanned out, some carrying bowls heaped with warm rolls, others with platters of cheese or cold meats, and some, like me, with pitchers. But for the sound of cutlery and plates, footsteps, whispers and the occasional ill-suppressed giggle, everyone ate in silence.

After serving the girls in White, I headed to the Repentance Table with a pitcher of coffee in one hand and hot milk in the other. *Café au lait?* I gestured silently, holding up the jugs.

"I prefer cognac," Caroline said with a fake innocent smile. "But eau de vie might do—as you and any other drunk would know." This in a voice loud enough to carry.

A pox on your perfect teeth! I thought, walking quickly away, resisting a temptation to upend both pitchers over her head.

As soon as everyone had finished eating (everyone but us servers), the monitor rang her bell. In unison, the girls stood, pushed in their chairs and filed out, beginning with the youngest.

I smiled to see Nelly turn at the door and curtsy. *Well done,* I nodded, and her cheeks blotched pink.

Table by table, in order by level, the girls followed, passing by the Repentance Table, some pausing to read the note listing Caroline's offenses. In the end, she stood and followed them out. At the door, she pulled up her gown and stuck out her naked backside at us.

"Did you see that?" Mouse said, sitting down next to me. Kitchen maids were setting full bowls, platters and pitchers along the length of the two long Multi tables.

"Kind of hard to miss," I said under my breath. We were supposed to eat in silence as well, but the rule was laxer when it was only the Multi servers. "You didn't tell me she changed her name."

"You didn't know?" Mouse said, slathering butter and peach preserves on a roll.

"Is it true she demanded cognac?" Ém asked, helping herself to ham and cheese.

I was near faint with hunger. "*And* she called me a drunkard. What's this about a ghost at school? Both Nelly and Fru-fru were on about it."

Mouse leaned in close. "Someone in Red—"

Ém made a sign of caution: quiet!

I glanced up to see the dining hall monitor headed toward us.

"Hortense, Maîtresse Campan would like to see you."

"Now?" I'd yet to eat a bite.

LA MAÎTRESSE
⚜

Maîtresse Campan's study was my idea of heaven on earth. It even had a smell I loved, leather with a hint of almonds. Book-filled shelves lined the walls and there were stacks of books on every surface: on the windowsills, on the big table she used as a desk and even on the floor. It was different from my mother's house in Paris, where there was hardly a book to be found.

"Welcome back." Maîtresse's housemaid, Claire, hugged me. She was not much taller than a ten-year-old, but round as a hoop. "Maîtresse will be right with you. Would you like a coffee?"

I needed something to perk me up.

A warm cup in hand, I examined Maîtresse's books. Many of the titles were familiar, on subjects I had studied: histories of France, Spain and some other countries, including England (a country we were forever at war with). There was also a new book on Egypt, I noticed. And then there were the texts on meditations, harmonies and fables—I loved those subjects. Geography, Greek literature and mythology. Etiquette and the art of conversation. There was a dense tome, as well, on grammar and logic, and a few religious texts, which surprised me. Maîtresse insisted on our religious education—I had even been confirmed—but she took care not to do so openly. She had had problems with government authorities in the early years of the school and had to close down the chapel (or, rather, disguise it as a storage shed).

I heard the creaking of a hinge and turned to see Maîtresse closing the door behind her. She was dressed simply in black mourning for her husband, who had died the year before. Her face was lined, plain and unpowdered, her eyes radiant.

"Good morning, my angel," she said.

I loved that she called me her angel. She had endearing names for all of us girls, but I was her only angel. It made me feel special.

She enfolded me in her vanilla-scented embrace. "How are you this morning?"

"It's wonderful to be back." I had missed the Institute, and her especially, but of course I was too shy to say so.

"A health spa for the infirm is not a place for a young and lively spirit," she said with a loving smile. "Were you able to get back to sleep last night, after that dream? You don't seem"—she made sparkle-fingers—"your usual effervescent self."

It was impossible to hide my feelings from Maîtresse. She always somehow knew. "It's not that." At least not entirely. "Annunziata got punished this morning. Caroline, I mean. She had to eat at the Repentance Table."

Maîtresse let out an exasperated sigh. "I know."

"But she was a bit—well, she acted horribly toward me, and then she did something offensive to the Multis." I told her what had happened.

"That girl," she said. "She's like a wild creature, feral almost. If only I knew what she wanted. Do you know? Does she ever say?"

"We don't exactly have conversations." To say the least.

"I appreciate that you try." She gestured to the divan by the crackling fire. "I sent for you because I think it time we talked about this dream you keep having," she said, arranging the down pillows to make us comfortable. She sat down, patting the place beside her.

I settled in—a little apprehensively, in truth. I had had many a talk with Maîtresse on that blue damask divan, most rather tearful.

It was there she'd informed me that my mother had married General Bonaparte, a man so stern and humorless he frightened me to death. Not long after, Maîtresse had broken the news to me that Maman had gone to Italy to be with the General, and that I wouldn't see her for a very long time. *If ever.*

"You woke some of the young ones last night," Maîtresse said, refilling my cup with coffee. "Sugar?" She put in two heaping spoonfuls. "They thought you saw a ghost," she added with a smile.

"Nelly and Fru-fru told me." Although they had talked of "the" ghost—not "a" ghost.

"Foolishness, of course," Maîtresse said.

"Of course," I echoed, although seeing my father in that dream had been rather like seeing a ghost—or so I imagined it might be, having never actually seen one. *Not* that ghosts existed.

I was about to ask if anything curious had happened at the Institute while I was away, something that might have prompted the girls to imagine a ghost, when Maîtresse asked, "Have I ever told you I once met your father?"

"No. Really?"

"I was thinking of it this morning, because of these." She propped her feet up on the tapestry footstool, displaying red silk slippers, exquisitely embroidered with gold thread.

So rare. So *elegant.*

"They were a gift to me from the Queen."

I glanced up at the portrait of Queen Marie Antoinette on the wall. She had been one of the first to be beheaded. Maîtresse had been her trusted attendant up until the end. It was a miracle she had survived the slaughter.

"That painting does not do Her Majesty justice," Maîtresse observed. "It fails to capture her wit, her vivacious spirit. Actually, you remind me of her," she said, giving me a playful nudge. "I'm writing a memoir about my years at Court, and wearing these slippers brings it all back. This morning I recalled seeing your father dance at a magnificent ball. This was long before the Revolution, before you were born. Your father had the honor of dancing with the Queen."

Why did I not know about this?

"They opened the ball with a minuet."

Ah, the minuet! I would have loved to have seen that. The minuet was my favorite because it was so elegant, every move precise. It was rare to see it danced well anymore, or even danced at all. It took years of schooling to perform properly.

"And this was a traditional minuet, which could last for over an hour. The rare times we see a minuet danced today, it's far shorter. Your father was the best dancer in Paris. That's why you dance so exquisitely, no doubt."

The awful dream image suddenly came back to me, my father's white-gloved hand, his hood falling back. I put my cup down with a clatter.

"Calm," Maîtresse said, her hand on my back.

I took three deep breaths, as she had taught me. "I'm fine," I said, swallowing.

Safe now?

"Did you have this dream while you were away?"

"Twice," I replied, then paused. Someone had begun to play the pianoforte.

"And it's always the same?" Maîtresse asked.

Always.

"It might help to write down memories of your father."

"Maman says I shouldn't think about him because it disturbs me so much." Yet the dream persisted.

"How is she doing?"

"She's recovering well. At first, I had to feed her like a baby. She couldn't hold a spoon."

"But she's walking now?"

"Yes, although . . ." Whoever was playing the pianoforte was playing it exquisitely, passionately, yet with a light touch. *If only I could play like that*, I thought. "Although with difficulty."

"News of the General's victories must have cheered her—the capturing of Malta, the landing at Alexandria, the triumphant Battle of the Pyramids."

"Yes. And yet the celebrations were a strain on her." And *me*. So boring.

"Any news of your charming brother?"

I grimaced. "Eugène is a negligent letter-writer." It didn't sound quite like the pianoforte, but what else could it be?

"You must worry."

"I do," I burst out. Eugène was two years older than me, yet I had somehow always felt older, coaching him on lessons and helping him prepare for exams. And now he was far away, fighting savages in a land of plague. I got weak with fear thinking about it. "Who is that playing?" I asked, changing the subject. The music had a fragile elusiveness.

"That's our new music instructor, Citoyen Hyacinthe Jadin. He's young, only twenty-two."

"I don't recognize the piece."

"It's one of his newer compositions."

"He's a composer?" I couldn't imagine anything more amazing than creating a piece of music.

"And a genius, in my opinion," Maîtresse said. "I don't use that word lightly, believe me. He teaches girls at the Conservatory in Paris, but I persuaded him to come out here now and again to give private lessons. He's penniless, so he agreed. I told him he could have use of our piano, which was another incentive."

"The pianoforte, you mean?"

"Ah! But of course—you weren't here. Our generous benefactor, Citoyen Rudé, donated a piano to the school. So very kind of him."

"A *piano*?"

"It's similar to a pianoforte, but with a broader range. It can reach to seven octaves." She paused, a finger raised. "Hear that?"

I *did*. Also, the tone was more fluid.

"It has eighty-eight keys, twenty-two more than a pianoforte. I'm told that both Haydn and Beethoven have begun to compose on one."

The music stopped and started, stopped and started, as if he was repeating a measure, trying to perfect it.

"I've been reserving a place in his teaching schedule for you," she said.

"Maîtresse Campan, I'm afraid that—I can't, at least right now." Private lessons cost extra. "My mother is short of funds, because of all her medical expenses." The truth was that my stepfather had arranged for his brother Joseph to give Maman an allowance while he was away, but Joseph refused to cover her medical expenses, claiming that her treatments were not the family's responsibility. *So mean.*

"Your mother and I will sort it out when she gets back to Paris. It's only that . . ." Maîtresse put her hand on my shoulder. "Music is one of your talents, angel, and Jadin is the best teacher in the country. I'll introduce you to him once you're settled."

The pendulum clock chimed the hour and the music stopped. "Goodness! I neglected to offer you something to eat. You must be starved."

I *was*.

She rang the service bell and Claire appeared holding a serving platter.

Chocolate madeleines? My prayer had been answered.

———

I was finishing my fifth chocolate madeleine when there was a rap on the door. I brushed the crumbs off my bodice. It was the woman who looked after the office on the ground floor. Citoyenne Hawk, we students called her, for she patrolled who came and went.

"Three government inspectors are here," she told Maîtresse, her voice timorous.

Aïe. A jolt of fear went through me. Anything to do with government officials brought back unpleasant memories.

"They showed up unexpectedly," Hawk said, adjusting her wooden false teeth, which tended to slip.

"As they are wont to do," Maîtresse said, ringing her service bell. "Bring me my garden smock," she told Claire when she reappeared. "And leather boots," she added, glancing down at her aristocratic slippers.

She stood and turned the portrait of the Queen to the wall. On the backside was a copy of the *Declaration of the Rights of Man and Citizen.* I smiled at her clever ruse. "What about—?" I pointed to the books on religion.

"*And* there's a new student, Maîtresse Campan," Hawk went on, throwing up her hands. "I've put her in the accounts office. Her name is Eliza Monroe."

"Ah, the daughter of the American ambassador," Maîtresse said, scooping up the religious texts. "I was expecting her and her mother this afternoon." She slid back a wall panel to reveal a hidden compartment.

"The mother sent her regrets."

Maîtresse slid the panel closed. One would never have guessed that it wasn't part of the wall. "Hortense, angel? Would you mind showing the new girl around while I see to the inspectors?"

I curtsied and took my leave, remembering not to bound down the stairs two at a time. I would be sixteen in the spring: I needed to learn to act like a lady.

HENRY AND ELIZA

❧

The accounts office was a musty closet on the ground floor, crammed with papers and ledgers. The door had to be forcefully opened, its rusty hinges creaking.

"I am Mademoiselle Eliza Monroe," the new girl said in stilted French, closing a ledger and jumping up to make a perfunctory curtsy. Her hair was russet and her pinched face was covered with freckles. She had a missing front tooth. "And this is Henry," she said, clutching a ratty stuffed animal.

Henry looked like a cat. Maybe.

I glanced back toward the foyer. No sign of the inspectors. "Welcome to the Institute. I'm pleased to meet you."

"I am the equivalent." Eliza frowned. "Enraptured? Beguiled?"

Her French vocabulary was somewhat archaic.

"I am Citoyenne Hortense Beauharnais," I said. "I'm to show you around and explain the rules."

"I am seven and three-quarters and two days of age," Eliza prattled on, sucking the tip of one of her long braids. "I am from America. The New World."

"You should know that we don't say *mademoiselle* here anymore," I said, refraining from taking the braid out of her mouth. Her hair would have to be cut short. We weren't allowed to grow our hair long until we were twelve years of age. That way the roots remained strong and our hair wouldn't fall out with an attack of fever. "We say *citoyenne*." As a Multi, my role was to instruct younger ones on proper etiquette.

"What if I declare in an erroneous manner?"

"We chop off your head." And then I felt simply *terrible*. She was a child, after all. What had come over me? "I'm sorry! That was a jest." Although it wasn't funny, not funny at all.

We began with the privies (of which Eliza expressed an urgent need, due to the rather long carriage ride out from Paris), followed by the eleven classrooms. They were all in use, so we didn't go in.

"This edifice is analogous to a citadel," Eliza said with a shiver. The stone halls were cold, in summer.

"It's a château that used to be owned by a wealthy family." I wondered where Maîtresse and the inspectors were. "We even have a ballroom and a theater." And a chapel, disguised as a storeroom. I hoped the inspectors wouldn't discover it. They could shut down a school for the slightest of reasons. "It's hundreds of years old." And in a state of disrepair, like everything.

"In America, all is new," Eliza said, noting a shattered window that had been boarded over.

The door to the Blue class swung open and students filed out, chattering but orderly, walking two by two.

"Hortense," several girls called out.

"Is it true you saw the ghost?" one asked.

Eliza clutched her stuffed cat. "In America, we do not have ghosts. We have witches."

"It wasn't a ghost," I assured her. "And we don't have ghosts *or* witches here. Everyone, this is Citoyenne Eliza Monroe. She's from America."

"Ooooh, America."

"I am pleased to meet you, Miss Eliza," a girl said slowly, in English.

"Salutations," Eliza responded. "But I am *Citoyenne*."

"Eliza's French is quite good," I said. Sort of. In an odd way.

"Hortense!"

Mouse and Ém were coming down the hall. I introduced them both to Eliza, explaining who she was.

"And this is Henry," Eliza said.

"To meet you pleased," Ém said in rather poor English.

"You will love it here," Mouse said, pushing up her glasses, which tended to slip down to the tip of her nose.

"Indubitably," Eliza said, swinging Henry by his tail.

"Everyone does," Ém assured her. (Everyone except Caroline, I thought with chagrin.) "Hortense, there's a letter from Maîtresse to the Multis on the notice board."

"We have to decide on a virtue," Mouse said.

"*And* a fault," Ém said, rolling her big eyes.

"Multis?" Eliza rolled her eyes up, as if searching her brain.

"We're Multis," I explained. "See how our sashes are multicolored?"

A triangle sounded. "Speaking of virtues, we must not be late for Latin," Mouse said, and she and Ém rushed off.

"Rodent is a singular name," Eliza observed in the silence that followed.

"Her real name is Adèle Auguié," I said, heading toward the north wing. "She's Maîtresse Campan's niece." And my dearest friend.

"You mean Mrs. Campan, the boss of this school?" Eliza asked in English.

It took me a moment to recall that the English word "boss" likely meant "master." "*Maîtresse* Campan," I corrected her, "and yes, this is her school." Maîtresse was much more than a "boss," as I understood the word to mean. The Institute was entirely her creation. "And Mouse is her niece. The other girl, Émilie—"

"The beauteous one?"

"She's my cousin." Ém had always been known as "the

beautiful one," especially when compared to me. "She's seventeen, and married—"

Eliza screwed up her nose in such horror I had to laugh.

"Her husband is with the army in Egypt," I explained. "She lives at school because she doesn't have a family."

"No *family?*"

"Well—no mother and father, to live with, anyway." It was hard to explain. "Her father fled France during the Revolution." Fled for his life. Poor Ém didn't know if he was alive. "And her mother is . . . away." That was a tactful way of saying that Ém's mother had lost her wits in prison, and that she and her new husband (her former prison guard) wanted little to do with her.

"We correspondingly had a revolution in America," Eliza said, taking care not to step on the lines between the floor tiles.

"Yes, but ours turned violent during a phase called the Terror, and a lot of people were executed." I heard children singing.

"Is that a joke also?"

"It's not," I said, my throat tight. It sounded like the Red class. "So, consequently, girls who don't have a family live at the Institute all year, even during the holidays."

The Chosen we called them. Ém was part Chosen because she sometimes stayed with Maman and me, and sometimes with our grandparents here in Montagne-du-Bon-Air. I was sort of part-Chosen too, because my father was dead and Maman was usually somewhere far away with the General. In two and a half years, she'd only been back home for four months, which was why the Institute was really my home (and why Maîtresse was kind of a mother to me).

The Reds began to sing "La Marseillaise," the patriotic Revolutionary song. Ah—to impress the inspectors, no doubt.

"This is the dining hall," I said, crossing to the doors that led to the cellars. "And this is the way down to the kitchens." Government officials made me uneasy. I couldn't help but remember the night they had taken Maman to jail.

"Kitchens?"

"You need to see them because we're taught how to cook."

Eliza stopped on the landing, holding Henry by the neck (strangling him). "Slaves do not perform that function?"

"We have a cook, but Maîtresse Campan believes it's important that we learn to look after ourselves. We make our own beds and tidy our rooms, sew our own smocks and sashes, cook—"

"In America, slaves perform all that," Eliza informed me with a somewhat snobbish tone. As if we in France weren't as advanced.

"Slavery is against the law here," I said.

Her eyes went wide. "No *slaves?*"

"Not since the Revolution. We believe in equality."

"In America, likewise!"

"Equality for *all*," I said, swinging open the heavy door.

"Well, look who's here," Berthe, the head cook, called out, turning from the cooking range set into the massive fireplace. Mounds of dough had been set to rise on a table beside her, ready for baking once the big ovens were stoked. The scent of roast chicken made me hungry again, in spite of the five chocolate madeleines I'd just eaten.

"Citoyenne Hortense?" The scullery girl was holding a heavy enameled kettle in one hand and a laden baking tray in the other. "We heard you were back."

A lanky boy looked up from scrubbing down roasting pans, his hands black. He turned from his task to grin.

"We were talking about you yesterday," the scullery girl said.

"We've decided we're going to vote for you to get the next Rose of Virtue," Berthe said.

"*Again*," said the scullery maid, grinning gap-toothed.

"You're all too kind." Although of course I was delighted. "But the vote won't be for three months. That gives me plenty of time to disappoint you," I said, and they laughed.

Eliza was standing beside me, staring.

"I'd like to introduce you all to the newest addition to the Institute. This is Citoyenne Eliza Monroe." I leaned down to whisper in Eliza's ear, "Curtsy."

"But she is a Negro," she said, indicating Berthe.

"Do as I say!" I murmured, one hand forcefully on her thin shoulder.

She made a little dip. The kitchen staff returned the courtesy with welcoming smiles, unaware of our exchange.

"We must be moving on," I said, mortified. I gathered that in America civilities weren't granted to someone like Berthe.

"What is the Flower of Righteousness?" Eliza demanded, stomping up the stairs.

"The Rose of Virtue?" I paused before explaining, listening. All was quiet. "It's a silk rose, a prize for—well, for just being a worthy person. It's awarded every three months to a student in each level. Everyone votes—all the students, the teachers, and the staff." There was no sign of the inspectors, *grâce à Dieu*.

"Have you acquired it yet? This flower?"

"Twice." If I won the prize again, I would get a beautiful porcelain vase embossed with my name and the date.

"I aspire to attain it," Eliza declared, pressing Henry to her heart.

"That's good, Eliza." I spotted Maîtresse's letter to the Multis in the upper right corner of the notice board. "But you will have to be respectful to everyone—even the servants," I said, taking her hand and setting off. Maîtresse's letter was long. I would come back later.

"The cook?"

"Especially the cook," I said, then stopped so abruptly that Eliza bumped into me.

Aïe. Standing by the fountain in the foyer were Maîtresse and the three inspectors.

"Ah, Hortense," Maîtresse called out before I could turn around. She looked charming in her garden smock and work boots. "Citoyens," she said, addressing the men, "I'd like you to meet one of my best students, General Bonaparte's stepdaughter, Citoyenne Hortense Beauharnais."

"The illustrious General Bonaparte!" the portly one of the three exclaimed.

"And this is Miss Eliza Monroe, daughter of the American ambassador James Monroe," Maîtresse said.

"Ah," the men said, in unison, for America, the land of revolutionary freedom and equality, was much admired.

"My father is going to be President of the United States," Eliza boasted. (An absurd declaration!) "And I am *Citoyenne*, not *Miss*," she added. "If you say *Miss* they will chop off your head."

"A jest, Citoyens!" I said, tugging on Eliza's hand. "We must be going. I hope you continue to enjoy your visit."

"Your father is the boundless general?" Eliza demanded as I dragged her away.

"*Step*father," I said, opening the door to Hawk's office, and closing it behind us.

Safe now.

MEETING
OF THE VOWS

❦

28 Fructidor, An 6
The Institute
Dear Multis,

Please do me the honor of joining me for breakfast tomorrow. I think coffee with cream and pastries is what generally pleases you most.

Many of you are coming to the end of your studies, and this last year of work, accompanied by useful reflections, will be more fruitful than five years of childhood, those years when one studies by force, reprimands and threats.

I therefore invite you to let me know your thoughts regarding the useful employment you will make of this time ahead. Tell me sincerely what fault you would like to correct, and what talent you wish to acquire to a higher degree.

I predict—without possessing the art of soothsayers, without reading in the firmament or musing foolishly over an old deck of cards on a table—that you will have complete success if you pay close attention to what you wish to accomplish. You are at that happy age when everything is possible.

Maîtresse Campan

Caroline appeared beside me, squinting to make out Maîtresse's letter. "What's this about?"

I regarded her with astonishment. She'd publicly embarrassed me at breakfast, stuck out her naked backside at us, and now I was supposed to help her? "It's a letter to us Multis," I said. Coldly.

She grunted. "And what does it say? The writing is too small for me to read."

The truth was that she couldn't read, at least not French. She'd had no schooling until coming to the Institute only eight months before. She was barely at a Blue level, if that. Maîtresse allowed her to wear a multicolored sash because she was sixteen, but she wasn't in classes with the rest of us, at least not for the academic subjects. For those, she had to be privately tutored.

Recalling Maîtresse's expectation that I be helpful, I explained, "The Multis are invited to Maîtresse's apartment for breakfast tomorrow morning."

"Breakfast with the Hook? I think I'm going to be sick."

"Annunziata!" She disrespectfully called Maîtresse "the Hook" because of her nose. "Caroline, I mean. It's because it's our last year at school."

"*Lodate il Signore,*" she said with a smirk.

"*Lodate il Signore*" was Italian for "Praise the Lord," I knew, but when Caroline said it, it didn't sound all that holy.

"We're each to declare two things," I said, "a talent we wish to improve in the coming year and a fault we wish to remedy."

"I'm to come up with a fault?" She looked amused. "The Hook can't be serious."

28 Fructidor, An 6
The Institute, free time
Dear Eugène,
    I know this letter isn't likely to reach you for a long time, but even so, I felt that I had to write to wish you belated birthday greetings. I can't believe that you are seventeen now, so grown. What with

caring for Maman and the journey back to school, I was unable to write sooner.

When I left the mountain spa, Maman was better and walking a bit. She remains determined to sail to join you and the General in Egypt—a thought that unsettles me, I confess. It's bad enough that you are there, so terribly far away.

Ém and Minuse send their love. All Multis have been invited to have breakfast with Maîtresse tomorrow to declare our goals for this coming year. It should be interesting!

Please write. Be sure to send me news of the other aides as well, but especially Major Christophe Duroc, because he's the one who works with you most often—am I right?

Whatever you do, be safe.

Your Chouchoute, who loves you very much, but will nevertheless kill you if you don't write.

Note—Annunziata has changed her name to Caroline. She had to eat at the Repentance Table and was extremely rude.

And another—some of the younger girls are convinced that there is a ghost here at the Institute, but it turned out to be me. Well, not me, but me who supposedly saw this ghost.

And yet another (the last, I promise!)—at the spa Maman was always on about finding me a husband. Could you please write to her and tell her that I am too young to marry?

It was crowded in Maîtresse's drawing room the next morning—there were almost twenty of us squished into chairs and settees, or sitting on cushions on the floor. Some had never seen Maîtresse's private rooms before and were bug-eyed, staring at everything. The air was strong with the sickening smell of nervous anticipation.

Maîtresse's maid Claire summoned us into an adjoining hall. It must have been a guard room in former times, to judge by the fireplaces at each end. The fall weather had turned more temperate, but even so, logs were blazing. Plank tables had been set up and were nicely covered with lengths of multicolored cloth to match our sashes. Clusters of wildflowers graced the center of each table.

In front of each plate was a card set into a wooden holder. On each card, a name had been written in fancy cursive with turquoise ink. (Elegant!) I went from place to place looking for my name and was happy to discover that I had been placed at Maîtresse's table, along with Ém and Mouse. The Fearsome Favorites!

Seated beside my place was an old man. "Allow me to introduce myself," he said, pulling out my chair for me.

He turned out to be Rudé, the generous patron Maîtresse had referred to. "Pleased to meet you, Citoyen," I said. "I understand you donated a piano to the Institute." I'd been so busy, I'd yet to see it, much less play it.

"It gratifies me to help," he said, leaning toward me.

"That is most kind of you," I said. He smelled of sour milk.

"I love to watch little girls," he said, clearing his throat.

His comment made me uncomfortable, so I was relieved when Ém and Mouse arrived, flushed from rushing. I introduced them to Citoyen Rudé.

"Delighted," he said, touching the tablecloth to his dripping nose.

Then—*thankfully*—Maîtresse came in and everyone stood. "Good morning," we all said in unison.

Maîtresse looked over the tables. "Caroline is not here?"

"She was made aware that we were invited," I offered.

"Very well then," she said, taking her seat beside Citoyen Rudé and signaling us to bow our heads for the blessing.

Of course that was when Caroline showed up, making her usual commotion.

Maîtresse made a false smile. "Perhaps a lack of punctuality might be the fault you wish to correct this year, dear girl."

I nearly gave way to a giggle fit over that.

Speaking of which, that was the fault I announced I would to try to overcome that year: *giggle fits*, a weakness Maîtresse attributed to the bourgeois influence of the seamstress I was apprenticed to during the Terror.

As for the talent I wished to improve, I did not tell the truth. I said I would like to excel at playing the pianoforte, which was challenging enough, but my secret aspiration was even more so. Thinking of Maîtresse's words on having the courage to dream big dreams, I decided that the skill I wished to acquire that year was for *creating* musical compositions. I didn't declare it, of course. It seemed too audacious.

As for Mouse, she declared that she'd like to overcome her timidity and to hone her talent for painting. (She was already very accomplished.)

"Charming," Citoyen Rudé said, his eyes moist.

Then Ém declared that she wanted to learn how to speak Italian better, and that the fault she wished to overcome was her fondness for daydreaming, a goal Maîtresse heartily approved.

It took a long time for all of the Multis to admit to a talent and confess to a fault. A number declared that they wished to improve their talent for needlework, or that imperfect needlework was a fault they wished to correct. I could see that this disappointed Maîtresse. Several times she reminded us not to be shy about valuing our intellectual capacities and—especially—our creativity, which made me love her all the more.

When it was Caroline's turn to speak, she declined in her sullen way.

"If you don't suggest a talent you wish to improve, my dear," Maîtresse said, "as well as a fault to correct, I'm afraid that I will have to come up with something for you."

Caroline glared.

"You do have a talent for Italian, of course," Maîtresse said after a moment of reflection, "be it colloquial in nature."

There were a few quiet snickers, for Caroline's Italian consisted mostly of crude curses.

"A study of classical Italian literature would help you improve," Maîtresse suggested. "And it was only in jest that I suggested that you work on not being tardy." She paused before saying, "Although I do have something to recommend, dear girl: that you learn to keep your temper in check."

Caroline clasped her fork and knife in her fists. She was obviously trying to keep her temper in check right *then*.

A SECRET

❖

25 Fructidor, An 6
Plombières-les-Bains
Dear heart,

I am much better, so I am leaving for Paris tomorrow. Director Barras wants me back in time for the Republican New Year. There's to be a civic celebration of Bonaparte's victorious Battle of the Pyramids and his triumphant entry into Cairo. I will write to your excellent Maîtresse Campan and ask her to allow you to leave early from school that day so that we can go to the celebration together. (Our lovely Émilie will be going in later with your grandparents, I know.) All of the Bonapartes in town will be at this festival and I tremble at the thought of facing them alone—especially the General's older brother, "King" Joseph, who is intent on making my life miserable.

On a more cheerful subject, you will be pleased to see how well I am walking. Indeed, I believe I may soon be well enough to sail to join Bonaparte and your brother in Egypt. Director Barras assures me that it is safe to do so, now that the English have been chased from those waters.

I have been giving a great deal of thought to your prospects. I was sixteen when I married your father and you will be sixteen in the spring. You must not be so unrealistically romantic, dear heart. No young man is going to be ideal, but it's wise not to linger—a girl quickly loses her bloom.

You are missed by all here at the spa. Several have mentioned
that we were more like sisters than mother and daughter—but I
would say that we're more like the best of friends, wouldn't you?
I confess to being a bit jealous that I have to share you with the
saintly Maîtresse Campan.

Your ever-loving mother

Note—I am sending along a cleansing salve for the face, to help
against the black points and pimple spots you get on your chin.

I soon got word that Maman was back. Citoyen Isabey, our wonderful drawing instructor, drove me into Paris in his carriage. His young daughter Alexandrine—who was in the Purple level—was bouncing up and down with excitement, but almost immediately fell asleep in his lap as the horses pulled forward.

"How wonderful that your mother has recovered," he said. He was a tiny man with a surprisingly deep voice. "Pixie Isabey" we Fearsomes sometimes called him.

"Yes," I said, keeping an eye out the window as we passed by the quarry where robbers were known to lurk. Isabey's carriage was so shabby no bandits would ever bother with us, I reminded myself.

"You must feel proud of your stepfather," he said, shifting Alexandrine to a more comfortable position.

"Of course," I lied. "Did you know my father?" Isabey had been at Court, along with Maîtresse and her sister, Mouse's mother. He had been one of Queen Marie Antoinette's favorites.

"Your natural father? I regret I never met him."

"He danced with the Queen," I said.

"Did he? That must have been before I was at Court."

"But then he became a Revolutionary," I confessed.

"In life, as in art, there is always a complexity of hues," Isabey said, sensing my confusion. "I owe much of my success, such as it is, to both the Court *and* the Revolutionaries. During the Terror, I was even hired by Citoyen Saint-Just to paint his portrait."

The man who led the movement to behead the King? "Didn't that bother you? Working for a friend of Robespierre?"

Isabey smiled in his lighthearted way. "One must eat, no? The key to survival is flexibility. Now I'm even working for the Directors."

The Directors saved us from the Terror, and were running the country now, but they were known by most everyone to be corrupt. When I was younger, I'd refused to go with Maman to a Directory event—until she pointed out that she owed her *life* to Director Barras and his friends.

I heard the familiar sound of the frogs in the marsh. We were approaching Maman's rutted street on the outskirts of Paris, an area where artists and actors lived. (And kept women, it was whispered.) The dirt road used to be called Rue Chantereine, but its name had been officially changed to Rue des Victoires in honor of the General's victories in Italy the year before. That was a high-and-mighty name for a rutted lane, in my opinion.

"You can let me down at the gate," I suggested. "I walk it all the time."

"Are we here?" Alexandrine asked, sitting up.

"Not yet, peanut," Isabey said, finger-combing his daughter's fine hair. "This is Citoyenne Beauharnais's house."

There was nothing to see but shrubbery. "It's down that long lane," I said, and hefted my schoolbag onto my shoulder.

I waved to Didier, the porter, and raced down the familiar laneway. Maman's house held wonderful memories for me—memories of life before the General. Memories of Maman and me working in the garden together, or of playing chess with Eugène, Maman looking on, tearfully smiling. We had survived the Terror and were precious to one another.

Emerging into the small courtyard, I heard the chickens clucking. Maman's two trunks were still stacked by the steps. Pugdog, snuffling, scurried out to greet me. I picked him up and pressed my face into his furry neck. I had wanted to name him Furry, but Pugdog he remained.

"I'm relieved you're here," Mimi called from the open door. She must have seen me coming.

I let Pugdog down, scratching him behind his ears. "Is something wrong?" Mimi had been with Maman at the spa, and her tone of voice concerned me.

"I'm not sure," she said, taking my cloak. "Your mother met with Director Barras last night."

Of course she would have, I thought, sitting down to unlace my muddy boots. Maman's friend "Papa Barras" was the most powerful of the five Directors and the source of all information, both in France and beyond. If there were letters from Egypt, he would have them. I wondered if there had been any news from Eugène.

"Any news?" I asked, following Mimi into the withdrawing room. The doors to the gardens on each side had been propped open and the light muslin curtains billowed in the breeze.

"She didn't say, but ever since, she's been—" Mimi paused, frowning. "She insists she's fine, yet she's been weeping."

"Actually crying?" Maman was emotional—tender-hearted, people said—but it was rare to see her cry. I suspected that she was somewhat vain that way. It would have ruined her powder.

I heard the stairs creaking. "Maman?" I looked up to see her coming into the room.

"Dear heart," she said, embracing me warmly.

She smelled of jasmine. It was easy to see why people loved her— adored her. (I did get a bit jealous.) She was forever doing favors for people, giving them gifts, flattering them with kind words. She wasn't an intellect, like Maîtresse, yet she remembered the name of every person she met, even the name of a maid she hadn't seen for years, even the names of that maid's children. She *even* knew all the Latin names for the plants in her beloved gardens.

"How was your journey?" I helped her into a chair. I could tell from the way she was moving that she was still in pain.

"We only went into a ditch once," Mimi said.

"You toppled?" I asked, alarmed. Maman had a morbid fear of riding in a carriage, even on good roads.

"Rather, we tipped," Maman said with a smile. "Mimi was my cushion."

"Fortunately I'm well-padded," Mimi said with a laugh.

I heard the carriage pulling up outside. Soon we would be going. "I have something for you, Maman." I rummaged in my canvas schoolbag and pulled out a small watercolor portrait I'd made of Eugène. I'd finally captured my brother's eyes, his open, friendly expression. How I missed him!

"The very likeness," Mimi said, looking over Maman's shoulder. "This is your work, Hortense?"

I nodded, proud. "Citoyen Isabey helped," I admitted. He'd painted in some of the details himself, showing me how to use a fine brush.

With a sob, Maman pressed the image to her heart.

"Maman?" I had meant the portrait to be a comfort.

"Forgive me," Maman said, struggling to rise. "It's lovely," she said, placing the portrait on a side table. "Shall we go, dear heart?" she said with a tight, feigned smile.

THE SCHOOL OF
VENUS

❖

"Hôtel de Ville," Maman instructed her driver, pulling up her long gloves.

Aïe. I hadn't realized that the ceremony was going to be held where the guillotine had stood for most of the Terror. Fortunately, it was not where Father had been executed. There had been so much stink from all the executions at the Hôtel de Ville that the authorities had moved the guillotine to Place du Trône-Renversé on the eastern side of Paris. I'd never been. I didn't have the courage to see where Father had died.

As we got close, the crowds became pressing. Two guards escorted us to an area that had been barricaded off. One of Director Barras's aides showed us to our chairs at the front. The five Directors were standing on the raised platform directly in front of us, looking glum in their red capes embroidered with glittery gold thread. Director Barras waved at us, revealing extravagant lace at his wrist.

I nudged Maman. "There's Ém, with Nana and Grandpapa."

"Tell them I'll be right over," Maman said, seeing her friend Citoyen Charles approaching. "Hippolyte will look after me," she assured me. "Won't you, darling?"

Citoyen Hippolyte Charles was young, only twenty-five, but he acted younger. He swept off his feathered hat and made a tidy pirouette, his long braids twirling. "Always," he said, giving us both a peck on each cheek. He wore a violet scent. "Help you with what?" he added in his marionette voice.

I couldn't help but giggle. Citoyen Charles was so funny.

"There you are," Ém said, wheeling around Grandpapa's invalid chair.

"We were looking and looking for you," Nana said, embracing me. The corset she was wearing was so rigid it was like hugging a marble statue.

"Bon-A-Part-Té!" Grandpapa exclaimed. He was enthusiastic about the General, like most everyone (everyone but me, it seemed).

I stooped to give him a kiss and straightened his powdered wig. "You're a bit crooked, Grandpapa," I said, and he cackled. "Your trip into the city went smoothly?" I slapped my gloved hands together to shake off the starch from Grandpapa's wig. Men rarely wore wigs now, and certainly not powdered ones. The fashion was to look "natural."

"At least we didn't get murdered," Nana said, clucking with disapproval at what I was wearing. "You look like you're wearing a nightdress—and no corset? Your mother lets you out like that?"

My blue gown of light wool was in the new style, without ornament except for a satin ribbon. "This is what ladies wear now, Nana," I protested. Her own ruffled gown was comically out-of-date. She even sported a bustle.

"You should follow the example of *Madame* Lavalette," Nana said, gesturing to Ém, who had wisely covered her "scanty" school gown with a light cloak. "And besides, a married woman may dress as extravagantly as she pleases," she went on (illogically).

Ém made an ever-so-slight roll of her big eyes. I knew how she hated the way Nana made a fuss about giving her the honors a married woman could claim: to be the first to enter a dining room, the first to be seated, and so on and so forth—all those outdated notions having to do with decorum.

"There's Caroline," Ém said, changing the subject. She pointed toward the seats in front of the podium. "And most all of her siblings, it looks like: Pauline, Elisa, Lucien, Joseph. All except Louis and the General, of course."

"And Jérôme, thankfully," I said, craning to see over the crowd. Jérôme was the youngest Bonaparte, only thirteen. He had behaved even worse than Caroline when he was enrolled at the boys' school next to the Institute, and had been put in a military academy so strict he was never allowed out. "But how do *you* know them all?" I asked my cousin.

Ém reddened. "Louis introduced some of them to me."

I crinkled up my nose. The General's brother Louis had introduced them to *her*? When?

"It's a big family," Nana said with a down-turned mouth. "Where are the parents?"

"The father is dead," I said, "and as for their mother, I think maybe she's still in Corsica."

"Here comes Tante Rose," Ém said, pointing out Maman, who was making her way slowly toward us, leaning on Citoyen Charles's arm. I was relieved to see her smiling.

Nana, Grandpapa and Ém hadn't seen Maman for months, of course, so there was much exclaiming and inquiring after her health.

"It's a miracle you didn't die," Nana said, embracing Maman a bit too vigorously, I thought, considering Maman's injuries.

"Bon-A-Part-Té!" Grandpapa exclaimed again, then fell into a doze.

Maman embraced Ém warmly. "Have you met our friend Citoyen Charles?"

He tipped his felt tricorne hat, stylishly trimmed with gold lace. "I am a friend of your cousin Eugène," he told Ém.

Turning to Nana, I explained, "Eugène and Citoyen Charles served on General Bonaparte's staff together in Italy."

Members of a brass band traipsed onto the platform and began to play an out-of-tune rendition of one of Mozart's arias for Queen of the Night.

"But you're no longer with the General's staff?" Ém asked.

"I retired from the military in order to engage in commercial pursuits," Citoyen Charles said.

"*Commercial* pursuits?" Nana said with ill-disguised disapproval

"Yes. Speaking of which," Citoyen Charles said, glancing at Maman, his dark eyebrows raised, "I should have a word with the Minister of the Navy."

"Give Citoyen Bruix my regards," Maman said.

"Bon-A-Part-Té," Grandpapa muttered, shaking himself awake. "Rose!" he exclaimed, addressing Maman by the name we were used to.

"I'm afraid I must be going, my dear," Maman said, kissing his check. "Hortense and I should greet the Bonapartes before the speeches begin."

"You look beautiful," Maman said to Caroline. "How is school?"

"Beastly. I hope to be expelled," she said, fingering an emerald necklace the General had given her. (I wasn't jealous, not one bit.)

"It's useful to have goals," Maman said with sly humor. "Joseph, how are you?" she said, turning to address the eldest of the Bonaparte siblings. "I don't believe you've met my daughter, Citoyenne Hortense Beauharnais."

The General's brother Joseph bowed and smiled (although it looked more like a grimace). I had expected the man Maman sometimes mockingly referred to as "King" Joseph to be formidable. Instead he proved to be a chinless man with a mild manner.

"You remember Julie?" he asked, introducing us to his plump wife.

"Of course I do," Maman said. "How have you been?"

"Busy! We're buying a house in town over on Rue des Errancis," Julie chirped. "They want 75,000 francs for it, but we hope to get it for 68,000 because we're going to have to spend at least half that much on repairs. Plus we're negotiating for a country property."

"Mortefontaine," Joseph said.

I had heard of the Château de Mortefontaine. It was reputed to be one of the largest properties in France.

"Is it not owned by Citoyen Durey, the banker?" Maman asked.

"He was executed," Joseph said, making a lazy slicing motion across his neck. (How could he!)

"So we should be able to get it for an excellent price," Julie said.

"Of course," Maman said, moving on to greet two of the General's sisters: Elisa (severe, but comically hiccupping) and Pauline (the alluring one everyone whispered about, and I could see why). There was also another brother, Lucien, who looked about twenty. He was skinny, with a weirdly small head and half-shut eyes.

I greeted all of them in turn, but they ignored me.

"Are they always so rude?" I asked Maman as we returned to our seats.

She squeezed my arm. I looked up to see Director Barras approaching.

"Well! If it isn't our ever-lovely Rose and her charming daughter."

I curtsied to the Director, who was, as always, gay and charming and complaining of his joints. He bent over my mother's hand and asked in a low voice, "How are you managing?"

It was the type of voice you used when you shared a secret.

"Fine," was Maman's response, but there were tears in her eyes again. "You'll keep me informed?" she asked as he returned to the podium, but he didn't hear her.

Informed about *what*? I wondered.

———

When the speeches were finally over, I helped Maman to her carriage, and, once home, up the steps to her house.

"I will see her to bed," I whispered to Mimi. I wanted time with my mother alone. Why had she responded with such sadness to my portrait of Eugène? Was there a secret between her and Director Barras?

"Maman," I said, sitting down close beside her on her bed. "It's unlike you to be sad."

"I'm not sad," she protested.

"Yet you keep crying." I was worried that something terrible had happened in Egypt, and that it had to do with my brother.

She stroked my hand. "I'm sorry, dear heart, but I can't say."

Ah—so there *was* something.

She wiped her cheeks. "Forgive me. I'm so emotional of late. My doctor at the spa told me I may no longer be a menstruant . . . because I don't get my monthlies anymore."

"The flowers, you mean?"

She smiled at my use of the childish expression.

"But Maman, you're—" I stopped myself in time. She didn't like to be reminded of her age. She was six years older than the General, who was not yet thirty. "Aren't you too young for that?" I associated the condition she was describing with toothless old women, crones with hunched backs and whiskers.

"It's apparently not unusual for women who were imprisoned during the Terror." She managed a sad smile. "My doctor said it's likely why I haven't been able to give Bonaparte a child. *Yet*," she added, with determination in her voice.

I didn't like to think of that possibility.

"Please don't mention this to anyone," she said.

"You know I wouldn't." She knew she could trust me—so why wasn't she telling me what was wrong?

Instead of heading up to my bed under the eaves, I paused in the sitting room outside Maman's bedchamber. I had schoolwork to attend to—an essay on patriotism—but my thoughts were in confusion. I lit a candle from the embers in the fireplace and sat on the chaise longue, pulling Maman's fox-fur wrap around my shoulders against the night chill. Something had happened, something terrible, I feared. Something that had to do with my brother.

I decided to do something drastic. In the corner of the room was Maman's writing desk. Hoping to find a clue, I tugged on the desk top, but it was locked. My heart beating, I found the key. Maman thought it well hidden under a corner of the rug, but I was more clever than that. I unlocked the desk and quickly went through her papers. Under some correspondence regarding money owed, I saw a book.

The School of Venus.

A book about a school? I opened it, only to discover that it was about . . . *it*. Even illustrating different positions! I shut the covers, my cheeks burning.

I put the book back as I had found it, slipped the key back under the carpet and hastened up to my room. The images I saw in that book filled me with disgust. Why would my *mother* have such a thing?

II

LIFE FORCE

1 Vendémiaire – 1 Pluviôse, An 7
(22 September, 1798 – 20 January, 1799)

THE TREE CARD: LIFE FORCE

CALAMITY

✤

On my first day back at the Institute, Caroline caused another ruckus, this time in study hall. We were supposed to be quiet, but as soon as the monitor stepped out she jumped up and crooned, "My brother is the savior of France!" She was flaunting yet another of her jeweled necklaces, puffed up from the celebration in her brother's honor.

Little Eliza turned from where she was sitting at a table with three other Blues. "Erroneous," she said. Her hair, cut short now, flew out in wisps. "Your brother submerged the French fleet."

"That's a lie!" Caroline glared, slumping back into her chair.

"Eliza, what did you say?" I asked quietly, watchful for the monitor's return. Eliza's father was the American ambassador. She might have learned something at home.

"All the French boats"—she did a thumbs-down—"descended."

I glanced at Ém and Mouse, confused.

"Terminated by the British." This last she conveyed in English with an exaggerated British accent.

"Something about our fleet?" Mouse suggested.

"Something about it sinking?" Ém guessed.

I turned back to Eliza. "Are you saying that our fleet of boats in Egypt *sank*?" I asked in a low voice.

"All of it," she said.

All? *Thirteen* ships of war, including the *Orient*, the grandest warship of all time? Over fifty feet wide, it had a printing press on board as well as an extensive library. "That's not possible." Eliza was a child, after all. She must have misunderstood.

"A *ca-la-mi-ty*," Eliza said, slowly sounding out the word. "And all the blunder of the General from Corsica—her brother," she added, pointing at Caroline.

Caroline shot up, ink pots, quills, sand and notebooks crashing to the floor. *"Una maledizione su di voi!"*

I glanced at Ém, who was in my class in Italian. A curse on you? Had Caroline actually said that?

Maîtresse and the monitor rushed into the room. "Big and Little Geniuses," Maîtresse said, quietly threatening, "this room is for study. Have you forgotten the rules? Caroline, dear girl: come with me."

Caroline hurled herself out, her face red as a hot poker.

I was in history class when Maîtresse's maid, Claire, came with a message. "Maîtresse Campan wishes to see you," the instructor informed me.

Puzzled, I scooped up my schoolbag. It was unlike Maîtresse to pull a student out of a lesson.

I was surprised—and not at all pleased—to discover that Caroline was in Maîtresse's study as well.

"Girls, I've had news," Maîtresse began, stroking the feather of a quill. "There has been a reversal, I'm afraid. I thought you two should be the first to know. The British have destroyed our warships in Egypt."

What Eliza had said was true! Was this the secret my mother wouldn't reveal?

"Eugène was unharmed, and Caroline, your brothers—the General and Louis—they are safe as well."

"But they have no boats?" I felt faint.

Maîtresse threw up her hands. "Apparently."

"How can they come home?" Were they stranded now, no better off than if they were on the moon? And what about all their provisions and supplies, which were on those ships?

"It will be difficult, angel," Maîtresse said, rubbing the back of her neck.

"*Angel*," Caroline said in a mocking tone as we left, accidentally-on-purpose bumping me into a wall.

2 *Vendémiaire, An 7*
The Institute
Dear Eugène,

I began feeling a bit ill this morning, so I'm staying in my room. I've decided to write a letter to you in spite of the fact that I will not be able to send it. The British now control the Mediterranean Sea and could capture our mail, so getting news will be difficult too. I've been having bad dreams, and Maîtresse suggests that writing to you will make you seem closer.

If this were a real letter, one I could actually send, I would tell you how Mouse, Ém and I volunteered to decorate the ballroom for the décadi "ball" the day before yesterday. You no doubt remember those occasions when the boys from the school next door come to the Institute to dance. It's worse now because all the older boys are in Egypt. The oldest boy is not yet thirteen and he is shorter than Mouse. Who, pray, are we to dance with?

Speaking of dance, do you remember Father teaching us the minuet? Maîtresse told me he was the best dancer in Paris and that he danced with the Queen. I love that.

All anyone talks of anymore is Egypt, Egypt, Egypt. In geography we make maps of Egypt, in history we study Egypt, and in art class we draw—guess? Egypt. Yesterday I made a drawing of you in front of a pyramid, sitting on a camel. What a strange animal!

There is a new music teacher at our school, a composer of beautiful pieces. Maîtresse is going to introduce me to him soon. She warned me that he's particular about who he teaches, so I'm a little nervous.

The younger students and some girls in the middle levels continue to be convinced that there's a ghost haunting the Institute. Such silly matters seem especially petty in light of what you and the aides must be going through.

I think of you often, and pray for you morning and night, the more so now—you and all the aides, of course.

I'm going to put this letter away in the secret drawer in my trunk and give it to you when you return—which will be soon, I pray.

Your little sister Chouchoute, who loves you very, very much

The next day I was put in the infirmary, sick with a high fever. My bowels were purged—*disgusting*—but fortunately I was not bled. Citoyenne Buchon ("Nurse Witch" to us Fearsomes) reminded me that my body would not heal unless "all poisons are expelled from the body!" This with an operatic flourish of her hand. "The humors must be in balance," she proclaimed. She had terrible breath and I feared I would upheave every time she bent over to check me.

Days passed in a blur. I did nothing but sleep and moan, moan and sleep. One late afternoon the jangle of a ring of keys woke me. I opened my eyes to see Maîtresse standing above me, regarding me with what we Fearsomes called her "Examination Look."

She laid her gloved hand on my shoulder. "How are you doing, angel?" The sun through the window lit up the smile lines around her eyes.

"Better." Better enough to feel bored.

"Wonderful," she said with a smile. "You had me worried—your mother too."

"Maman?"

"You don't remember her visit?"

"A bit," I said, but it was vague, like a dream.

"Nelly got sick as well and we had to send her home."

Nelly had a home? "Isn't she one of the Chosen?"

"A cousin in the south took her in." Maîtresse was silent for a long, *long* moment. "It turns out she has the pox."

I felt heaviness in my chest. People died of the pox, and if they lived, they were often horribly, frightfully, dreadfully scarred. I thought of Nelly's pretty plump cheeks. "Is she going to be all right?" Maman got the pox as a girl, but escaped with only a tiny scar by her left ear, so maybe—

"We don't really know yet."

"But how did she get it?" The pox was contagious. People who got it had to go into isolation, like with the Black Plague. (Which was another thing I fretted about, for it was said that there was plague in Egypt.)

"It's a puzzle." Maîtresse sounded uncharacteristically uncertain. "She never left the school grounds."

I understood Maîtresse's concern. "Were you worried about me because you thought maybe I had it too?"

She nodded. "I'm relieved you're better, angel."

"But I've been"—I rolled up my sleeve to show her a tiny scar— "I think it's called being inoculated." It was something Father had insisted on when I was only three years old, to keep me from getting the pox. "I was one of the first." It had terrified Maman, of course. She had no faith in science.

"I know, and that's an advantage, but it's not a guarantee. We have to be very careful."

AFTERLIFE

❖

Once I was out of the infirmary, I was assigned to look after bossy Fru-fru. "Caroline hasn't been setting a proper example," Citoyenne Hawk informed me, her words muffled because of her ill-fitting teeth.

"But what about Nelly? She'll be coming back, won't she?"

"Don't worry," Hawk said, seeing my look of concern. "Nelly is fine, but she's going to be staying with her cousin."

I was relieved she had recovered, but I would miss her.

I was stunned speechless the next day when I found out that Hawk had *lied* to me. My sweet Nelly wasn't *fine*, not fine at all! The truth was that little Nelly had *died* of the pox.

It was Maîtresse who told me the truth. "Keep this to yourself, angel," she said, handing me a handkerchief to dry my tears.

"Can't I tell Ém or Mouse?" My voice was shaky. My Nelly!

"Yes, of course you can tell them, but make sure it goes no further. People are worried enough about pox as it is."

I left burdened by the secret knowledge of Nelly's death—and angry, too. It was bad enough that she had died, but for nobody to know? Somehow, that made it worse.

I thought of Nelly's clothing label: NC 276. And now she didn't exist? How was that possible?

———

Mouse and I were supposed to have our shift in the kitchen that afternoon. We'd planned to cook a pot of chicken soup and deliver it to an impoverished family in need, but excursions were canceled for fear of contagion.

It was a balmy fall day, so Mouse and I went up to our favorite place on the roof to sketch during free time, in the warm spot between the two chimneys. High up, it afforded a view of the town. From there we could see the big church, the old castle and the river winding through the fields. On some days we could see Paris, but on this afternoon it was overcast.

"My mother died of a fever after going to the aid of a sick family," Mouse said, her voice betraying a hint of a squeak. She got fretful when talking of her mother, who had died only a few days after my father had been executed. It was one of the many bonds we shared. "Now I can't help but wonder if it might have been . . ."

Pox? "I think Maîtresse would have told you if that were the case."

"She doesn't like to tell me anything that might disturb me. She's afraid I'll have one of my faints."

"That's understandable." Sometimes Mouse would drop to the floor. I had seen her do it only twice, but each time it had scared me half to death. She would recover after a bit, and other than bruises she seemed to be all right. It wasn't the falling disease, Maîtresse had assured us, because she didn't shake and she remembered everything—but still.

"Sometimes I get the feeling there is this big secret about my mother's death," she said, "and that nobody will tell me what it is."

"If it were something bad, would you really want to know?" I thought of my father, the horrifying way he had died.

"Covering things up only makes it worse."

Mouse was so very wise. "That could be a Nasty," I suggested.

Nasties were things we Fearsomes found miserable or simply annoying. Most of our Nasties had to do with things like when a buzzing insect got caught in your ear, or putting your foot in a boot that had a beetle in it, but sometimes we ventured into seriously awful Nasties, like one I wrote about being cornered by a pack of dogs in Paris, gone wild after their owners had been executed.

Mouse nodded, writing in the margin of her drawing. "Nasty: When people lie to cover up the truth."

"Like the way we have to pretend about Nelly," I said, my heart aching. I could hear girls playing Prisoner's Base down below. Nelly had loved to watch us play. She would jump up and down whenever I was rescued. It didn't seem right that life just went on and on. "Do you ever wonder if there is an afterlife?"

"I'm sure there is," Mouse said, sniffing a little.

"But then wouldn't it follow that there are also ghosts?" It puzzled me that the younger students continued to think that the Institute was haunted.

"My aunt says there is no such thing." Mouse put down her charcoal and smudged the lines with her index finger to make them soft.

"I know." But what about a person's spirit? Did it disappear, like a candle flame blown out?

"Listen," Mouse said, touching my arm.

Someone had begun to play the pianoforte—or was it the piano?

Which reminded me! "Will you be all right up here alone?" I asked, packing up my supplies. It was unlike me to be late, but since the news of Nelly's death I'd been forgetful.

CITOYEN JADIN

⟡

The theater was cold and smelled faintly of rat. (The school cats had not been doing their job.) All the chairs and benches were covered with cloths—rags, really, gray bed sheets worn thin from use.

A single candle on the piano illuminated the moving form of Citoyen Jadin, his face contorted, his fingers a blur as they raced up and down the keys, the music violently passionate, then lyrical, and yet with the odd occasional dissonance.

Maîtresse and I waited in the shadows. But for the island of light on the stage, it seemed a desolate place.

I could hear birdsong outside, girls shrieking, the sound of the gardener's dogcart on the gravel. This was a mistake, I thought. I had a madcap urge to run.

"Citoyen Jadin," Maîtresse called out, announcing our presence.

His hands slipped lifeless from the keys. "Yes?" he said, without turning to face us. He sounded sad, bereft.

"I have a student to introduce to you," she said, taking my hand and pulling me toward the stage.

He stood, tugging at his sleeves. His patched jacket was small for him.

"That was a beautiful piece." Maîtresse had a firm grip on my hand, as if she knew I might bolt.

"But flawed," he said.

He was slight in figure, about my height. I felt I could knock him over with a touch. I began to feel less afraid.

"I'd like to introduce you to Citoyenne Hortense Beauharnais, stepdaughter of General Bonaparte. Hortense, this is Citoyen Hyacinthe Jadin."

Jadin made a solemn bow and I curtsied in return. He seemed younger than twenty and two, perhaps because of his light hair, which fell in wispy curls. How could someone so young be a teacher? For that matter, how could someone so young have created the piece he'd just played? And how could he *play* like that, with the skill of a master? Was he a genius, like Wolfgang Amadeus Mozart, who had begun composing when he was only five? I'd heard of prodigies, but I'd never actually met one.

"I've mentioned her to you," Maîtresse said. She still had hold of my hand.

Citoyen Jadin looked dazed for a minute, blinking. He might have been a genius, I thought, but he was acting like a dolt.

"She is uncommonly talented musically, but, more importantly, she's . . ." Maîtresse glanced at me appraisingly. "She's driven," she told him, her voice low.

I could feel the heat in my cheeks. "Driven" wasn't the type of thing a girl should be.

"*Ah*," Citoyen Jadin said, as if waking. "Are you good?"

"I'm passable," I admitted.

"She's modest by nature," Maîtresse said. "In truth, she is brilliant."

I liked being praised, but I wasn't being falsely modest. "It depends," I told him. "Some pieces are really hard to get right."

"Such as?"

I could have named quite a few. "Scarlatti's Sonata in G major," I said as the pendulum clock sounded the hour.

"Citoyen Jadin, it's three o'clock. I'm afraid I must go," Maîtresse said, interrupting. "Let me know if you are willing to accept Citoyenne Beauharnais as one of your students."

Citoyen Jadin pulled out the stool for me. The piano looked very much like a pianoforte, only with more keys. "I've never played this instrument," I said.

"That's of little relevance," he said, shuffling through a portfolio. He handed me a score. It was hard to see in the dim light. I moved the candlestick closer. It was Scarlatti's Sonata in G major. How mean of him!

"Begin," he commanded.

Fumbling, I played, wincing at my errors. It was challenging in any case, but the more so because I'd never played a piano before. The feel was different, softer to the touch, yet the effect could be surprisingly loud.

"Enough!"

I sat motionless.

"That was terrible."

"I know," I snapped.

"Play a piece you've mastered, one you can perform without reading a score. Can you do that?"

"Of course I can." Any schoolgirl could. "But what would be the point?" We were off to a terrible start.

"You are not to question me. Do as I say."

So, I played Mozart's Sonata No. 11 in A Major—but played it pounding and loud. I crashed into the finale and sat trembling in the silence, awaiting condemnation.

"You *are* driven," he said with a smile in his voice.

Citoyen Jadin agreed to take me on, and I—at Maîtresse's insistence—consented. Not surprisingly, he proved to be a demanding and difficult teacher, yet in the time after Nelly's death I found solace in the challenge.

I still aspired to compose a piece of my own, so on impulse, after a lesson one crisp fall afternoon, I resolved to speak up. Standing at the door, I cleared my throat.

"Citoyen Jadin?"

He had moved back to the piano stool, his hands on the keys. He looked up, surprised to see me still there. "What?" he demanded, muffled in a gray woolen shawl. I was intruding on his time.

My heart was pounding in my chest. "I want to learn how to compose," I said, hugging my schoolbag.

He frowned, squinting. (I wondered if he might have trouble seeing things at a distance.)

I raised my voice. "I said I want to learn how to compose." I stepped closer. "Original pieces. Of my own." I sounded stupid. "Like you do," I added, only making things worse.

"There are no female composers," he said evenly.

"What about Élisabeth Jacquet de La Guerre? What about Françoise-Charlotte de Senneterre Ménétou?" I'd been doing my homework.

"Correction: there are no women composers of note."

I must have looked discouraged, for he said, "Look, Citoyenne Beauharnais," more kindly now, "composing is a hundred times harder than playing. It would be futile, a waste of your time—and mine, and I don't take that lightly."

I took a breath to strengthen my resolve. "How did *you* learn to compose?" He had five brothers, and they were all said to be excellent musicians. Perhaps he'd had no need to learn. Perhaps it was a talent he and his brothers had been born with. "Did you have a teacher?"

"Yes, of course. He began by having me write out all of Haydn's work."

"Just copy it, you mean?"

"Your tone implies that it was an easy task. How long do you think it took me?"

"A few months, maybe?"

His smile was mocking. "It took well over a year."

He must have sensed that I doubted him. "A full year, Citoyenne, for at least three hours a day, writing the scores out note by note."

"And that taught you how to compose music?"

"It taught me a great deal. Johann Sebastian Bach perfected his craft by copying out the work of a number of composers, including Lully."

I looked away. He was right. I didn't have the patience. It would be futile. "Sorry to bother you," I said, heavyhearted.

I recalled Maîtresse's inspirational message on finding the confidence to dream big dreams and having the courage to fail. I dreamt big dreams, but did I have the courage to fail?

In spite of my doubts, I began. I couldn't resist at least trying. I made a large notebook for copying out musical scores. It took time to draw in the lines, inking them all perfectly. Then I had to decide which score to copy. After going through *Pièces de Clavecin* in Maîtresse's music library, I chose Lully's "Ouverture de Cadmus." It inspired me to think that it may have been one that Johann Sebastian Bach had learned from.

I discovered that copying out a score was arduous work, but I began to understand how one learned from such an exercise. After a time, it was all I wanted to do. Perhaps it was true, I thought. Perhaps I was driven. But was that so very bad?

HAUNTINGS

❦

Poor Ém and Mouse. I woke them that night with my screams, but try as they might they couldn't rouse me from the horror of my dream.

Maîtresse came running in her nightdress and shawl. She held me close, trying to calm me.

"Why?" I wept. Was Father trying to tell me something—something *terrible*? Something about Eugène?

Maîtresse stroked my back. "It's only a dream, angel."

I took a shaky breath. Maman and Mimi believed bad dreams were put in a person's head by demons. It was one of their Creole beliefs—just a superstition, I always thought, although I couldn't help but wonder if there might really be demons in our room.

It didn't help—*at all*—that at that moment someone pounded on our door, which flew open with a crash, making us gasp in fright.

The shadowy form of young Eliza stood before us holding a candle. "I heard a fearful utterance."

"What are you doing up at this hour, Eliza?" Maîtresse demanded, her hands over her heart. "Never knock on a door like that. You will wake the dead." She took the candle from her and set it on the bureau. "And you're dripping wax."

"I am not to strike a door in order to report that I am present?" Eliza asked, pushing up her ruffled nightcap, which had slipped down over one eye. "I must enter directly?"

"No, of course not," Maîtresse said. "Always knock before entering a room—but *softly*, child."

"You scared us, Eliza," Mouse said, her voice tremulous.

"For the reason I smote the door?"

"Because you banged on it," Ém said.

"*That* made you timorous?"

It was impossible to explain. Eliza would never understand the horror of that sound, the pounding on a door in the dead of night. She hadn't been in France during the Terror.

"But why the fearful utterance?" Eliza asked.

Ah—but of course. She thought I screamed because I saw the ghost. "I had a dream," I said, "a bad one." A dream I still couldn't shake.

"Not because of the *spiritus?*"

"*Spiritus!*" Maîtresse frowned.

"She means the ghost the younger girls talk about," I explained. "They're convinced the Institute is haunted."

"There is no such thing as ghosts," Maîtresse told Eliza. "That's folklore nonsense."

"But no! I saw four in a spectacle in the city," Eliza insisted.

"You *saw* ghosts?" I asked. My dream had truly shaken me. I'd begun to think that anything was possible.

"At *Fan-tas-ma-go-ree*." Eliza sounded out the long name slowly.

"*Phantasmagoria*," Maîtresse corrected, ever an instructor, even in the dead of night. "That's Greek, meaning an assembly of phantasms."

"No, Fan-tas-ma-go-*ree*," Eliza persisted.

"She's referring to a popular show they have in Paris, Maîtresse Campan," I said. I'd heard that it terrified people half to death, yet they lined up day after day to go in hopes of seeing spirits and flying skeletons. *Not* that ghosts existed. "It's held in the crypt of a Capuchin monastery near the Place Vendôme."

"In a crypt?" Ém asked.

"How frightful," Mouse said.

Eliza nodded, sensing that she had gained status with this revelation. "It petrified my mother delightfully."

"Were the ghosts real?" Mouse's voice was tremulous.

"Of course they were *not*." Maîtresse stood and smoothed her nightdress. "It's a show, only that," she said, pulling her shawl over her shoulders, "an ingenious use of illusion devised to exploit the needy, a way to play upon the public's gullibility, inducing the naïve to part with coin that would be better spent on food." She opened the door. "Eliza, back to bed. Careful with that candle. Girls, no more talk of spirits. *Sleep*."

"Yes, Maîtresse," we chimed.

The door closed and we were plunged into darkness.

"Mouse?" I whispered after a time. I'd heard her restless tossing.

"I'm awake," she answered softly.

"Me too," Ém chimed in, her voice low and melodious. "I keep thinking of the *Fantasmagorie*. I've heard that there is one in town."

"Here? In Montagne-du-Bon-Air?" I asked.

"Nana's maid Perrine went," Ém said. "I was in the kitchen getting laudanum drops for Nana and she told me about it. She'd gone the night before, though it costs five sous per person. It's held in the abandoned convent."

"That's not far at all."

"Did the maid really see a ghost?" Mouse asked.

"She said everyone was screaming and crying, calling out to their loved ones."

Aïe. "But they saw actual spirits?" I asked, my voice shaky.

"Apparently. She claimed to have seen the ghost of her uncle, killed in one of the riots during the Terror."

Heavens! I snuggled down under my blankets.

"Why didn't you tell us?" Mouse said.

"I feared it might disturb you," Ém said.

Disturb Mouse, she meant.

"I have the shivers just thinking of it," Mouse admitted.

"If you could talk to someone who had died," I said, "someone you loved very much, would you want to?"

"More than *anything*," Mouse said, with obvious longing for her mother.

"I don't know if I'd have the courage," I said. What if Father appeared headless? I would die! But then, too, what if he appeared whole? Would I be able to seek his forgiveness? Would my night-frights end?

FEARS AND TEARS

❖

24 Brumaire, An 7
The Institute
Dear Eugène,

Still no news of you, or anyone. I try not to think of what I've read, of the barbaric tribes in Egypt, of all the awful things that could be happening to you there. Yet the more I try not to think of such things, the more the horrifying thoughts come, so maybe Maîtresse is right, maybe it would help to write down my thoughts and fears.

Your little sister Chouchoute, who loves you very much

"Your playing is stilted today," Citoyen Jadin observed. "What's wrong?" he asked, sitting forward.

I wiped my damp hands on my skirt. There had been rumors. "Our men in Egypt are . . . I heard that they're surrounded." I closed my eyes, but that only made the images in my mind clearer, images of slaughter.

"That's alarming. Are you sure?"

I shook my head, staring down at the keys.

"Being unsure is its own torture, isn't it?" he said kindly.

My eyes stung.

"Play what you're feeling, Citoyenne."

"I . . . I can't. I'm sorry." Music could be so emotional, it frightened me.

"Trust me."

And so I did, hesitatingly at first, but then I put my heart into it, my fears and my tears. In the silence after—that heavy, poignant silence that hovers after a piece has been played—I saw that he was weeping.

In Paris, at Maman's house for our usual *décadi* together, I confessed to her how frightened I was, how my thoughts ran away with me, imagining Eugène injured, or *worse*. "I can't sleep," I said, breaking down. I was having trouble concentrating on my schoolwork.

"Your prayers keep your brother safe."

"But he's *not* safe," I said, telling her what I'd heard, that our soldiers were losing, that they were surrounded.

"Dear heart, those rumors are false."

"How do you know?"

"I am the wife of the General," she said, crossing her arms. "I would have been informed."

I must have looked doubtful, for she said, "Hortense, people will be watching us. Hold your head high. *Always.* Show by your expression that you know that Bonaparte is victorious."

I stared down at the floor. It was all just an act.

30 Brumaire, An 7
La Chantereine
Dear Eugène,

How does one know what's true and what's false? These letters, for instance. Since it's unlikely that you will ever get to read them, I can confess my midnight thoughts, my midnight fears that you are dead.

My music instructor says that music is like prayer. If that's the case,

67

I am holy indeed. I hope that my music can reach you from afar.
Somehow. Can you not hear me? Surely you can.
Your sister Chouchoute, who misses you terribly

In drawing class Citoyen Isabey said it was important to draw at least five sketches a day. He added that all prominent artists did this, and that even musicians "sketched" out their compositions. "Important work does not come from one sudden flash of genius," he said. "It comes from persistent daily effort."

I started a section in my music composition notebook for such sketches: one a day. It would help keep my mind off Egypt, I thought. In time, I had nine—most of them quite bad, but a beginning.

The news of Egypt—what little managed to get through—continued to be alarming. A placard was pushed through the school gates claiming that the General and *fifty thousand* of his men had died.

"Lies!" Maîtresse said, tearing it to shreds.

With Maîtresse's permission, I began to play the piano in the hour before the evening meal. I closed all the doors and played quietly, so that nobody could hear. I would begin by practicing one or two of the pieces I had been taught, followed by one I was copying, analyzing how it was constructed. And then I would play a piece of my own from my composition notebook. They were pathetic imitations, but every now and then there would be a phrase that pleased me.

There was one melody in particular that haunted me. I could imagine it, but I couldn't play it. Almost, but not quite.

The rumors continued to be dire, but the worst was yet to come. Early one wintry morning, Eliza burst into our room, breathless from climbing the stairs. "The General is demised!"

Ém, Mouse and I all turned from making our beds.

Eliza, her cheeks rosy, was wearing a heavy coat, boots, mitts and even a knit cap. She'd just been dropped off after visiting her family in Paris. "I thought to tell you first," she lisped. She'd recently lost two front teeth.

I picked up my sack of clean clothes from the laundry and sat down on my bed. "Demised?" What did that mean? I wondered, folding my clothes, beginning with the biggest pieces, my dress, smock, nightgown and petticoats.

"Deceased, maybe?" Eliza said, clutching her raggedy cat.

"You can't mean that," Ém said.

"Surely not," Mouse said.

"That's impossible," I agreed. Even so, my hands shook a bit, pairing my stockings. "These stories are lies spread by our enemies," I said evenly, putting my folded clothes into my trunk and lowering the lid. "If something like that had happened, my mother would have been the first to know. She would have sent word."

"My father was enlightened of this intelligence this morning," Eliza said.

This gave me pause. Eliza's father was privy to news from abroad. It was possible that he knew things before Director Barras. "Did your father tell you this?"

"No, I spied," she said proudly.

One of Maîtresse's maids appeared in the door. "Citoyenne Hortense, Maîtresse Campan wishes to see you."

"Oh no," Mouse said.

Caroline was standing in the foyer outside Maîtresse's study. "Do you know what this is about?" she demanded, chewing on her thumbnail, tearing a sliver off and swallowing it.

"No," I said, although I had a fearful hunch.

The door swung open. "Good, you're both here," Maîtresse said. "Come in." Her expression was grave. "Have a seat." She gestured to the two wooden chairs, and settled into the armchair behind her cluttered table. "I've had"—she paused to swallow, her hand on her chest—"news," she said, picking up a sheet of paper.

I gathered my shawl around me. I trembled, but not from the cold.

"This *news* out of Egypt came by a circuitous route—overland, I've been told."

Caroline was swinging her feet, still gnawing on her thumb.

"General Bonaparte has been—" Maîtresse paused to clear her throat. "I very much regret to have to tell you that the General has been wounded," she said, her voice quavering. "Fatally."

The word hung in the silence.

"I'm so sorry," she said.

Caroline sat still as a statue beside me.

"So very, very sorry," Maîtresse repeated, her voice tearful. "It appears to have been an assassination," she said, offering Caroline the document. She paused before adding, "Your brother Louis wasn't hurt, and Eugène was untouched as well, angel. It was only the General who was—" But she didn't finish. "I know what a shock this must be," she said, dabbing her eyes with a handkerchief.

Caroline stared at the sheet of paper. She couldn't read well at all, and usually pretended. She passed the paper to me.

The stationery was thick, of fine quality, embossed with a seal that looked official. It was signed by Director Barras's secretary.

"Read it out loud," Maîtresse suggested.

I cleared my throat. "*It has been confirmed,*" I read, my voice unsteady, "*that an Arab fatally shot General Bonaparte with a pistol at close range.*"

"It's a lie!" Caroline blurted out.

"I wish to God that it were, dear girl," Maîtresse said. "Your families have sent for—"

Caroline hit the table with her fist. "A blasted lie." She stomped out, slamming the door behind her with a shuddering thwack.

Maîtresse opened a notebook, took up a quill, dipped it in ink and made a careful note. I sat on the edge of my chair, waiting to be dismissed. The General, my stepfather, was *dead*? I felt numb. It couldn't be true.

"This is tragic," Maîtresse said, putting down the quill. She stood to embrace me. "We are all of us going to have to be strong, angel—your mother especially."

LOVE LETTERS

❖

Maman was in a pitiful state, too overcome to get out of bed. Her room looked as if a storm had swept through. Papers were scattered all over the floor—letters, they looked like. Usually Maman was annoyingly tidy.

"In time all will be well." I couldn't think what else to say.

"I'm frightened, dear heart," Maman said.

I put my arms around her. "Don't cry." It pained me to see her so broken.

Mimi handed Maman a small glass. Laudanum, I guessed, by the medicinal scent. Wincing at the bitter taste, she gulped it down.

"Sleep now, Yeyette," Mimi said, smoothing the pillows, calling Maman by her childhood name.

"I can't," Maman moaned, but soon she quieted.

I followed Mimi into Maman's dressing room.

"She's been like this since the news came," Mimi told me, pulling black mourning gowns and veils out of a trunk to air.

"She must be worried about Eugène." I certainly was.

"Hortense!" Mimi turned to face me, her hands on her hips. "Your mother is grieving the death of her *husband.*"

"I'm sorry. I don't mean to sound uncaring." In truth, I didn't know what I felt.

I folded the papers I'd picked up. Because of the messy handwriting and misspellings, I guessed that they were letters from the

General. Letters from a man now dead; like footsteps in sand—easily erased.

That night, as I was putting my notebooks into my schoolbag for the return to the Institute in the morning, I looked at the letters. They were, as I had guessed, from the General, letters he'd written to Maman shortly after they'd married.

I was revulsed! Horrified. For they were letters of scandalizing passion.

A thousand kisses as fiery as my soul . . .

I love you to distraction . . .

I embrace you a million times . . .

My adored Josephine . . .

I worship you more every day . . .

A kiss on your heart, and one much lower down, much lower!

I will never forget the little black forest.

Little black forest? Just thinking that made me *sick*.

"You must feel devastated," Citoyen Jadin said as soon as I arrived for my afternoon lesson at the Institute.

"Yes, of course," I said with a shrug.

"What's the matter?" he asked, taken aback, no doubt, by my indifferent expression.

I confessed my confusion. I would never wish anyone dead, I told him, but I hadn't felt sad on learning that my stepfather had been assassinated. Rather, I felt numb.

"It has been a shock to us all," he said.

"But I never understood why my mother married him. He was nothing like my father."

"Were you close to him?"

"My father? I *loved* him." Idolized him.

"But were you close to him?"

"I'm not sure what you mean," I said, positioning myself on the stool.

"Did you do things together, the two of you?"

"My father had important things to do, and he was often away, so no, not really."

"Did he write to you?"

"You mean letters?" Of course Citoyen Jadin meant letters, but I was perplexed. The only time I'd seen my father's small, neat handwriting was in the margins of his books. "I wrote letters to him, but I didn't send them."

"Why not?"

"I was only a child, and a girl, at that. He had high standards." Then, unaccountably, I burst into tears.

Citoyen Jadin pulled a handkerchief from within his jacket and handed it to me. "Was it something I said?"

I took a shuddering breath. No. No. "It's just that the last time I saw my father, he was in prison, with my mother."

"Which prison?"

"The Carmes."

"Oh," he said heavily. The Carmes was known as one of the worst.

"A woman took us to a house that overlooked the prison. The shutters on a prison window opened, and there they were."

"Your mother and father?"

I nodded, drying my cheeks. "It must have been arranged," I said, taking a breath. And then another.

"How old were you?"

"I'd turned eleven a few months before."

"So young. That must have been hard."

"It *was*. I cried out for my father. I couldn't help it. The prison guards heard and came to take him away." I took another shaky breath. *Oh, Father.* "And then they sent him to the guillotine."

Sobs came over me, my breath coming in gasps.

"It wasn't because of you," Jadin said, his voice full of feeling.

But it was.

"Told you!" Caroline crowed, jabbing me in the ribs with her finger and then bolting off.

Mouse glanced at me, puzzled. "What was that about?"

Ém, sitting on a courtyard bench, glanced up from the book she was reading, a romance (disguised as a book on science). "Did something happen?"

"I think so," I said.

I glimpsed Eliza running toward us, weaving in and out of the other students as if in a race, her breath streaming out in clouds. "Agreeable news! The General is *not* demised!" she called out, twirling Henry by his tail.

Mouse looked at me with astonishment. "The General is *alive?*"

"Indubitably," Eliza exclaimed, tossing Henry into the air and catching him neatly.

Mon Dieu.

20 Nivôse, An 7, décadi
La Chantereine
Dear Eugène,

I am home with Maman in Paris. She is euphoric. We'd been told that the General had been assassinated, and I feared for her health. Of course that news was false. Now she has faith that you and the General will return. She is even having the General's study on the ground floor refurnished for him. I have come to my room in an attempt to escape the noise and commotion below.

*Her joy is infectious. My heart gladdens imagining your return—
and that of all the other aides, of course.*

Stay safe. Come home.

Your little sister Chouchoute, who loves you very much

*Note—I think of you always, but when I dream, it's Christophe
Duroc who appears. I hardly know him, yet I get faint whenever I
think of him. Does that mean I love him? How can one tell? My
music teacher says that the human heart is a mystery, and I believe
he is right.*

*Speaking of mysteries, some of the girls at the Institute continue to
be convinced that there is a ghost there. Strange!*

THE MORNING
CHRONICLE

✦

"I have something to demonstrate to you," Eliza said, taking a newspaper out of her schoolbag. "Is the name of your brother Eugène? It displays a communication from him."

"In a journal?" I'd become skeptical of news. The General had been killed; the General was alive. What could be trusted anymore?

"Here. Read it!"

It was an issue of the London *Morning Chronicle,* published almost two months before.

My dear mother, I have so many things to say that I don't know where to begin.

My heart jumped. It *was* a letter from Eugène, printed in both French and English. I devoured my brother's words, and then I didn't know what to think. I read it again. In his letter, he warned Maman that the General was unhappy because he'd been told she was having an *amourette*—

An affair of the heart?

—that she was having an *amourette* with *Hippolyte Charles.*

Stunned, I leaned against a pillar. Silly Citoyen Charles with the long braids and marionette voice?

Eliza, hugging Henry, looked concerned.

"Did you read this?" I asked, my voice weak.

"Of course. It is English. But what's an *amourette*?"

"It's a French word meaning friendship," I lied. "A close friendship."

"Like you and me?"

I nodded, letting out a deep breath. "May I keep this, Eliza?"

Once in my room, I built up the fire and threw the newspaper on it, watching until it was only ashes. I didn't want anyone to see it. I recalled the disturbing images in the book in my mother's desk. To think of Citoyen Charles and my mother as . . .

Impossible! It couldn't possibly be true. Hippolyte Charles was only twenty-five years old, if that. He was my brother's friend. I thought of Maman's delight at his antics, her smiles—and my own delight as well. We were all fond of him. He was a family friend.

Yet *might* it be true? I thought of how Maman had cheered in his company at the civic celebration, leaning on his arm. I recalled seeing her touch his hand.

Nasty: Reading a passage in a book over and over without understanding its meaning.

I spent the following *décadi*—a bitterly cold day—at Maman's house in Paris. She was uncharacteristically gloomy, which of course made me wonder. Had *she* seen that newspaper? Did she know what had been printed?

"Has Maman said anything about the English press?" I asked Mimi.

"No. Why would she?"

"Oh, no reason."

I resolved, several times, to ask Maman about it—but each time I failed. Finally, I blurted it out. "Maman, did you see the London *Morning Chronicle*?"

"What do you mean, dear heart?" she asked, picking up a nightcap she was embroidering for me.

It was a question, but not really. "I mean the issue with a letter from Eugène printed in it," I said, darning one of my woolen stockings. "It was published months ago."

"I don't know anything about it," she said, but *coloring*.

"His letter was written to you. Someone at school showed it to me."

"Showed you the actual newspaper?"

I nodded. "Eugène said in his letter that the General was unhappy, because he believed that . . . that you were—"

"Was it Caroline who showed it to you?" Maman asked, squinting her eyes with suspicion.

"Someone else." I didn't want to tell her that it had been the daughter of the American ambassador.

"You know, of course, that the letter can't possibly be authentic," she said.

So, she *did* know of it.

"As an aide-de-camp, Eugène would have been told to be very careful about what he wrote because correspondence might be intercepted—and exploited—by the British. He would never have written to me about such a thing."

About such a thing.

"Of course," I said, heavyhearted. She hadn't denied it.

Nasty: When you fear your mother might be having an affair of the heart.

My first day back at the Institute, I had a lesson with Citoyen Jadin. I had been looking forward to it, yet I fumbled terribly.

"What's wrong?" He had the most penetrating eyes. (Were all geniuses like that? I wondered.)

"I'm worried," I said.

"About your brother in Egypt?"

"Yes." Although that wasn't what was really bothering me. At least not just then.

"I gather that you are close."

"Very. During the . . . the Terror, we only had each other." I thought of the letters I wrote Eugène, letters I would never send.

"I'm close to my brothers as well, and I have five. They call me Confessor because they come to me with their problems."

"They must trust you." Who could I trust? Maîtresse knew Maman well. Too well. I couldn't even talk to Mouse or Ém about certain things. "May I confide in you?"

"The confessional is open," he said with a smile.

Did I have the courage? "Promise never to tell?"

"I will take your confidence to my grave."

"It has to do with my—" But I could not say, *dared* not. "It has to do with someone I love. Someone I've always thought of as pure virtue and goodness." My voice gave way.

"That's rather a lot to expect of someone," he said.

"I expect it of myself."

"I'm not surprised." He smiled.

I must have looked forlorn, for he added, gently, "Citoyenne Beauharnais . . ." He paused. "One never knows what personal wars a person might be fighting."

"I don't understand."

"I mean, if you're tempted to think ill of someone, remind yourself that he—or she?—may have reason for what they are doing. One must learn to trust, and to forgive."

I wished I could trust Maman. I wished she had given me reason not to believe what Eugène had written in that letter. (If it really was his letter.) "I don't know if I can, Citoyen Jadin," I admitted.

"I understand how hard it can be." He gestured to the keyboard. "It might help to play."

And so I did, played confused and sad and angry and disappointed, played all those things. In the end there was only one thing left, and that was love.

Was I in love with Hyacinthe Jadin? I did not know. I was not attracted to him, not *in that way*. He had a sweet face, without a doubt, and the nicest eyes, if somewhat pale (and sometimes scary). And certainly I was in awe of his talent, his genius.

But most of all I liked talking with him, confiding in him. He was patient, and he listened. He didn't tell me I was silly (like Eugène sometimes used to do), and he didn't lecture (like Maîtresse would sometimes)—unless it had to do with music, of course.

What I liked more than anything was his faith in me. Maîtresse had faith in me, but then, she had faith in most every girl in the school. (Maybe even Caroline.) Maman loved me, but that was different, and I didn't think she had faith in me, in truth. She thought I should study harp, be prettier, more pleasing to the young men she insisted I meet. I suspected I was a disappointment to her, which made me sad. And Ém? Well, we were like sisters, and as for Mouse, dear Mouse, she would do anything for me, but there were things I couldn't talk to her about because she might get agitated and have one of her spells.

And so . . . ?

And so Citoyen Jadin and I talked often, and as I continued my lessons, I found myself telling him more and more—although never revealing to him my heartsick doubts about Maman and Citoyen Charles.

III

DECEIT

24 Ventôse – 9 Thermidor, An 7
(14 March – 27 July, 1799)

THE SNAKE CARD: DECEIT

AN UNEXPECTED
VISITOR

❧

Late one spring afternoon at school, a courtyard monitor handed
me a note written in Maîtresse's elegant hand: *Come to my office
immediately.* I ran up the winding stairs two at a time, but then took
the steps more slowly.

Maîtresse met me at the landing. "I have a surprise for you." She
took my elbow and guided me into her study.

I yelped when I saw someone standing by the shelves. He was
wearing a dark-blue cut-away jacket with red facing and gold epau-
lettes. The tricolor armband on his upper left arm indicated that
he was an aide to the General. He had big, sad eyes, a long nose
and pouting lips.

Wasn't it *Louis*, the General's younger brother, who was supposed to be in *Egypt* with my brother?

Mon Dieu. It *was* him.

"Louis," I burst out, "what are you doing here? Where's Eugène?"
I feared I would weep and giggle at the same time. "He must be
with you. Why isn't he with you?" My mind was racing from one
thought to another. "How did you get here? Where are the others?"

I felt Maîtresse's grip on my shoulder. "Sit, angel. *Breathe.*"

"But Maîtresse, how is it possible for *him* to be here?" Our fleet
had been destroyed, and the long journey overland was treacherous.

"Louis left Egypt some time ago, released from his duties for
reasons of health," she explained, gesturing him to the chair beside

me. "He left before the disaster," she explained, sitting down behind her cluttered table.

Ah. So: he'd been able to sail without risk of capture.

"He sailed to Corsica, where he has been with his mother, regaining his health."

Louis shifted in his seat beside me, crossing his legs. "I have a rare form of rheumatism," he said.

"But what are you doing *here*?" I demanded, leaning away from him.

"Hortense, please, refrain from interrogating this young man. The Captain and his mother arrived in Paris only yesterday, and he has been kind enough to come directly out to the Institute to give you something."

Something for me? That was curious.

"I have a letter for you, from your brother," he said.

"*Eugène?*" My heart did somersaults.

He withdrew a folded paper from his stained leather satchel. "It got wet on the ship," he said. "Some of the ink smeared. The crossing was dreadful, with ferocious ocean swells."

I snatched the parchment out of his hand. I had no time for Louis's poetic details!

I teared up seeing the pattern of tight lines and swirls Eugène always put under his name. His "mark," he called it, as a boy, drawing it with care on the list of the laundry we took to our parents in prison.

My dear Chouchoute, little sister . . .

I scanned the letter quickly: how he was, what he ate. Something about horrid camels. No mention of Citoyen Charles—I was relieved on that account—but nothing about Christophe Duroc, either. There was no date on the letter, but it must have been written over six months ago, before the destruction of our fleet.

"I don't suppose you know how he is?" I asked Louis. "Now?"

"I don't even know how my brother is," he said. His brother, the General.

"Luigi!" Caroline burst into the room like a torrent and threw herself into her brother's arms, very nearly knocking him over, sending his satchel flying. "*Il mio tronco è imballato. Sono pronto per andare,*" she exclaimed, ignoring Maîtresse and me. (I knew a little Italian, and I guessed she was saying that her trunk was packed and she was ready to go.)

With a look of annoyance, Louis reached for his bag. A small book had slipped out of it. I picked it up and handed it to him. A slim volume of poetry, it looked like.

"Annunziata must return to Paris with me," he informed Maîtresse, "to see our mother."

"I'm *Caroline* now, Luigi. Not Annunziata."

"And I've been *Louis* for some time," he said curtly. "Not Luigi."

Glad that's settled, I thought. *Bonapartes!*

A triangle sounded: it was time for the older students' afternoon reading. Maîtresse suggested that Louis put off their departure for a half hour. Caroline began to object. "We are all of us thirsting for news," Maîtresse insisted. "We would be grateful to hear at least a short presentation on that far-away land."

Everyone chirped with excitement when Louis entered the salon. We'd never before invited a male to join us for the readings.

Mouse was up at the front, helping her aunt. I slipped into a chair near the back beside Ém.

"Can that be *Louis*?" she said. He spotted her in the crowd and stared, holding her gaze. "He looks so very well," she said, grinning.

I thought he looked poorly, frankly. "Ém . . ." I could see the emotion in her eyes. "You must not—"

"Not *what*?" she challenged.

I wanted to remind her that she was a married woman now, and that a girl's reputation must be safeguarded, for it didn't take much to sully it. We'd been taught that once one's reputation was ruined, there was no getting it back, and life after would be one long, downward spiral. But instead I said, "He had to return for health reasons." It occurred to me that I could lie and say that he had a contagious disease, maybe gonorrhea, something sinful like that.

As I was thinking such disgusting thoughts, Louis approached. He stooped down beside us—beside Ém. (Was he wearing thigh pads under his breeches to make his legs look muscular?)

"I have something to return to you," I heard him tell her, withdrawing the book that had fallen out of his pack.

Ém had *given* him that book?

"I want to thank you for it," he said.

"You are most welcome, Louis," she said softly.

They were whispering, looking into each other's eyes. It was as if they were in their own world, as if no one else existed.

"I thought you might like the poems," Ém went on. "The ones on death especially."

"As well as those on love," he said, speaking so quietly that it was hard for me to hear. "They saved my life, over there." Then he took her hand and *kissed* it.

I glanced up to see Maîtresse watching, watching and *frowning*.

Louis stood and walked away. Ém pressed the book to her heart and slipped it into her schoolbag.

Maîtresse rang her bell. "General Bonaparte's brother, Captain Louis Bonaparte, can't be with us long today," she announced, "but I'm sure we all have questions about Egypt. Captain, I must first ask after the General's aide-de-camp, Captain Antoine Lavalette, our Émilie's husband. We've heard accounts of his bravery."

Ém stared down at her boots, her cheeks an angry red.

A DINNER PARTY

❖

The following *décadi*, I broke the news to Maman.

"Louis and his mother are in Paris?" she said.

"Yes. He came out to the school. He gave me this." I handed her Eugène's letter.

Maman touched it with reverence, as if it were a holy object.

"The ink was smeared by seawater," I explained. "It's from before the loss of our fleet. Louis left Egypt before that happened because of weak health. He's been staying with his mother in Corsica."

"But he's here now? With Signora Letizia?"

Maman had met the General's mother in Italy. She described her as an attractive woman with a steely heart.

"I think they're staying with Joseph," I said.

"On Rue de Rocher? How long have they been here?"

"I'm not sure," I lied. I knew Maman would be rankled to learn that her mother-in-law had been in Paris for days. "Likely not long." I realized I had to tell the truth. She would find out, in any case. "Five days, I think."

"*Five* days! Why have they not called on me? Or at least sent word. This is ludicrous. I'm Bonaparte's wife!"

A faithless wife, they perhaps believed.

"Maybe if you invited them here?" I suggested.

———

Maman and I went into a flurry of activity, planning a fête in Signora Letizia's honor.

First, the guest list. Of the Bonapartes, we had:

1. Signora Letizia
2. Louis
3. Caroline
4. the General's older sister Elisa (the severe one who hiccupped)
5. wanton Pauline (whose husband was not in Paris)
6. "King" Joseph (whose wife was staying at Mortefontaine, their country estate far from Paris)

And, of course, Maman and me. That made eight in all—perfect.

The Bonapartes preferred country cuisine made to look sophisticated, so we decided to begin with only one soup—a turnip puree—followed by rabbit fillets, quail with bay leaves, roast chicken and pheasant pie. Two additional dishes sufficed: eggs with gravy and cocks' crests (*delicious*). Last, for desserts, cream puffs and madeleines, of course. A small but tasty feast, and not too expensive, either, because we had cream and butter from our cow, eggs from our chickens, turnips from last summer in the cold cellar and chickens running free.

Once the invitations were sent out, Maman and I turned our attention to our attire, spreading gowns, ribbons and shawls all over her dressing room.

Nasty: When you invite people to a fête and nobody comes.

Maman and I sat in silence in the front parlor, which we'd decorated with a profusion of daffodils from her garden. Heavenly scents of pheasant pie and roast chicken wafted up from the cellar kitchen.

"Why couldn't *any* of them come?" Maman said, shifting in her cushioned chair by the fire. She'd been working hard preparing; her hip was bothering her again.

Wouldn't come, I thought, chagrined. I feared they had heard stories of Maman's *indiscretions*.

At that moment Mimi announced that the musician Maman had hired had arrived.

"We should send him home," she said sadly.

"We already paid him," Mimi said.

"Then he might as well stay and play for us," I suggested.

Mimi went back to the foyer and returned, followed by a young man.

"Citoyen Jadin!" I exclaimed.

He smiled, making an elegant bow. He looked handsome in the old-fashioned black velvet tailcoat he was wearing.

"You know each other?" Maman asked after Mimi had left to show Jadin to the pianoforte.

"He's my music teacher."

"At the Institute? But he's so young."

"And he's a composer, too," I said, with pride. I listened for a moment. "That's one of his compositions he's playing now." His Sonata in C minor was one of my favorites. It sounded better on the school piano, but it was beautiful on our pianoforte, nonetheless.

Someone was at the door again. "Maybe it's the Bonapartes," Maman said with a hopeful shine in her eyes.

Mimi reappeared, followed this time by a big woman with a gold tooth. It was Citoyenne Lenormand, the famous fortune-teller. Predicting the future had become a fashionable salon diversion, so Maman had invited her to our fête. She knew Lenormand from prison, where she'd foretold Robespierre's death.

"Such a wind!" Citoyenne Lenormand exclaimed, her face red. One of her eyes was strange—a "wandering" eye, it looked off to one side.

"My dear Citoyenne, there seems to have been a change of plans. There isn't to be a dinner party." Maman's voice was tearful now.

"But Maman," I said, inspired again. "Perhaps there is, but just for us?"

"Yes, of course, please, do join us," Maman said, instructing Mimi to extend the dinner invitation to Citoyen Jadin, as well (which he declined).

And so it was that Maman, Citoyenne Lenormand, Mimi and I dined sumptuously while listening to heavenly music.

A PREDICTION

❧

After dining, Maman insisted that Citoyen Jadin share cordials and sweetmeats with us.

"Bravo!" We applauded when he appeared.

He slipped into the chair Maman indicated at the head of the table (the chair Signora Letizia was to have occupied). It seemed strange seeing him outside the Institute, in my family home. With my mother.

As we indulged ourselves with cream puffs, sugar-dusted almond madeleines and Maman's black cherry brandy, Citoyenne Lenormand showed us a German card game called *Das Spiel der Hofnung*—the Game of Hope. "But it can be used as an oracle, as well," she said. She was not a pretty woman, and her roving eye was unsettling. "Who would like to know their future? Citoyenne Bonaparte?"

"Oh no, thank you, not *me*," Maman said, "but perhaps Citoyen Jadin?"

"*No*," he said firmly.

"Why not?" Maman gently persisted. "I foresee nothing but fame for you. My daughter tells me that the compositions you played for us tonight were of your own creation. I dare say you are our very own Mozart."

"My future has already been revealed to me," he said with puzzling sadness.

"I'm sure it will be glorious," Maman said. "How about you, dear heart?" she suggested with a be-polite-and-don't-quarrel look.

I glanced at Citoyen Jadin. He inclined his head quizzically. We had talked together of many things—personal things, things I couldn't share with anyone.

"Dear heart?" Maman nudged.

"Very well," I said, sitting forward. I had many (many) questions about my future, but what might be revealed?

"There are a number of ways these cards may be used to foretell," Citoyenne Lenormand began, shuffling the deck. "You could simply draw one card and reflect on its meaning, or, if you have a specific question in mind, draw out one, two or three. But since this is your first reading, Citoyenne Beauharnais, I recommend that I cast a *grand jeu* for you, a full spread." She handed me the deck. "Hold them while considering your question, and then cut."

Of course I wanted to know about Eugène, but also about Christophe. Were they safe? When would they return? *Would* they return?

Lenormand laid the cards out in four rows of eight, and then a fifth row of the remaining four at the bottom. Each card had an image on it: a snake, a ship, a heart and so forth. "This is you," she said, pointing to the third card in the second row. "The Lady card. The two cards to the left of it show your past."

One showed clouds, and the other a mouse. "What do they mean?"

Lenormand gave me an apologetic look. "The Cloud card combined with the Mice card signifies anxiety, doubts and confusion."

Aïe. Might this have to do with my doubts and confusion about my mother's relationship with Citoyen Charles? I wasn't sure I wanted to go on.

"The cards to the right of the Lady—the Star and the Garden cards—point toward your future. They indicate some sort of public event. A celebration, perhaps," she said, "a grand ball?"

That could be anything, I thought.

"Whatever it is, it will be significant for you in some way. And the four cards at the bottom are the conclusion." These cards showed a heart, a stork, a bird and a tower. "The verdict," she pronounced.

"Which is?" I asked, holding my breath.

She tapped each card thoughtfully. "They reveal that in matters of the heart, you await developments."

Citoyen Jadin raised his eyebrows.

"Dear heart, you've turned bright red," Maman said in a teasing tone.

"So, Citoyenne Beauharnais," Jadin said, as he was leaving, "what developments do you await in matters of the heart?"

"It's only a game," I protested. I could hear Mimi and the scullery maid clearing the dining table. Maman was in the salon with Lenormand, sharing stories of their prison days.

"I'm sure," Jadin said with a doubtful smile. He smelled strongly of the black cherry brandy we'd all been sipping. "You and your mother are gracious hosts. Are you learning to forgive?"

"Pardon?" I handed him his threadbare cloak.

"I'm referring to that person you regard as all virtue and goodness."

Maman. "There's a fiacre stand near the end of the laneway. I'll walk you out to the road," I offered, reaching for my shawl. I didn't want anyone overhearing.

The stars were bright and the moon nearly full. We didn't need a lantern. "This was supposed to be a bigger party tonight," I said, pulling down my hat. The night air smelled of smoke drifting from the chimneys.

"So I gathered."

"A number of those invited didn't come," I said. Our footsteps made crunching sounds on the gravel. "Most of them, in fact. All members of the General's family."

"That's curious. Nothing . . . grave, I hope?"

"Grave in its way," I admitted. "I suspect it's because they think that Maman is—" I paused, shame coming over me.

He bent his head toward me. "Yes?"

"That Mother has a—" But I couldn't bring myself to say it.

"That she has a lover," Citoyen Jadin said, his voice low.

"You've heard?"

He nodded. "A little."

I felt ashamed.

"Rumors can be vicious, Citoyenne, particularly about women— and most particularly about women in the public eye. Is there any truth to it, do you think?"

"I'm . . . I'm not sure." I told him what I knew.

"*Hippolyte* Charles, did you say?" he asked, stopping at the road. "An amusing young man, quite dapper?"

"You know him?"

He chuckled. "I believe it safe to say that people are mistaken with respect to this so-called affair of the heart."

But more than that he would not reveal, in spite of my entreaties. Soon a fiacre happened by and then he was gone. I walked back down the laneway, puzzling over this curious revelation.

The next day, back at school, Caroline sidled up to me outside the dining hall. "Enjoy your dinner?" she asked in a sweet voice, false as a fox.

I looked over my shoulder. "*Why* didn't anyone come?"

"We have our reasons," she smirked.

We: the Clan. I grabbed her arm. "You owe my mother an apology."

"We don't owe her anything." She yanked her arm free.

"My mother is your brother's *wife*." Like it or not.

She rubbed her arm. "Not for long."

That stopped me. I waited for three girls to go by. "I beg your pardon?"

"He loves *another woman*," she hissed. "My brother Joseph got an overland message telling him all about it. The soldiers call her his Cleopatra."

The General kept a mistress in Egypt? "Some whore, no doubt." That's what soldiers did, I'd heard.

"Hardly. If she gives him a child, he intends to divorce your faithless mother and marry *her*," she countered.

"Good!" I exclaimed, but burst into tears.

OF AN AGE TO
MARRY

❦

Not long after, Ém and Mouse surprised me by showering me with spring flowers on rising one morning. "You're sixteen," they sang.

It was my *birthday*? How could I have forgotten? Since my "discussion" with Caroline, I'd been walking about as if under a dark cloud.

They presented me with a deck of Game of Hope cards, which they'd arranged to acquire from Citoyenne Lenormand.

"We got instructions, too," Mouse said, holding up a pamphlet, "both for the game, and"—she lowered her voice, dramatically mysterious—"fortune-telling."

"Why don't you pick a card now?" Ém suggested.

With my thoughts on my day, I drew the Moon.

"Aha!" Mouse said, turning the pages and finding the explanation. "The Moon card signifies success in acquiring something long desired."

Ém nudged me with a wink. "What might that be?"

I thought of Lenormand's prediction.

Now that I was sixteen, I was allowed to put up my hair. Ém coiled and pinned my braids for me. "This signals that you're old enough to receive a man's advances," she said, teasing out wisps of curls around my face.

"What if I don't want to receive a man's advances?" At least not until A Certain Someone returned from Egypt.

"You are so unromantic, cousin," she said, flashing her eyes at me.

I shrugged with a mysterious smile. Little did she know.

Primidi, 21 Germinal, An 7
Montagne-du-Bon-Air
Dearest Granddaughter,

Now that you are sixteen, it is my duty to caution you with respect to the challenges a girl faces going out into the world. Your mother is of a relaxed disposition and isn't likely to warn you, I know. To that end, I am enclosing a gift, a little book titled The Rules of Courtship, *which I'm sure you will find enlightening. It contains advice on the proper way to conduct yourself with young men.*

Your grandmother,
Nana

I glanced through *The Rules of Courtship* and put it away. There weren't any young men in my life, so what was the point?

After our midday meal, Maîtresse invited me into her study. "For a chat," she said. "You and me."

"Oh?" I wondered if she had heard talk of the General's "other woman." It humiliated me to think she might know about it.

But then Maîtresse had sweet red wine served. "Don't tell the others," she said with a sly smile. "Now that you are sixteen, you will be served unwatered wine. It will be prudent for you to learn to imbibe moderately. To your health," she said, raising her glass.

I made a show of taking a careful sip. (Maman had been allowing me to imbibe unwatered wine, and sometimes even rum, since I was seven.)

"You have developed into a lovely young woman," Maîtresse said.

"Thank you." I smiled, but wondered: Was I finished growing? My breasts were still small.

"And now that you are of age, your mother must find a husband for you."

The old pendulum clock ticked and tocked. The time it showed was hours off.

"But what if I don't wish to marry? *Yet*," I added.

"It's not wise to wait, frankly. A girl of sixteen is like a peony bloom at the peak of perfection. Likewise, as with the peony, her attractions quickly fade."

Once I turned seventeen, in other words, I would begin to coarsen.

"This is your year, angel." She raised her glass again. "Make the most of it."

As I accepted her toast, I couldn't help thinking of Christophe, so very far away. Would I be wilted by the time he returned? (If he *ever* returned.)

Soon after, Maman arrived with a carriage full of trinkets. She glowed, handing out little gifts and sweetmeats to everyone. "And this is for you, dear heart," she said in a private moment, presenting me with a parcel wrapped in striped silk. "For those certain special occasions."

I gasped. It was an exquisite gown of beige crepe. I held it up to my shoulders. It had a high waistline and short puffball sleeves— but a rather low neckline, almost to my niplets.

"Th-thank you, Maman," I stuttered. Did she *want* me to be wanton?

21 Germinal, An 7

The Institute

Dear Eugène,

If you were here, you would wish me a happy birthday. You might even have a silly gift for me, nothing extravagant, but something to make me laugh. But this year is different for all of us. Someday soon, I pray, we may all be together again.

I've been lectured a lot today on marriage, and it has caused me to wonder. Is it foolish of me to value fidelity? I know of the rumors about Maman and Citoyen Charles. Most times I think it impossible, but then, at other times, I'm not so sure. I've been told—by Caroline, of course—about the General and "Cleopatra." Caroline told me that the General intends to divorce Maman and marry Cleopatra if she can give him a child.

Does marriage mean so little? Are my dreams of marriage to a man I love and a man who loves me—a man who will be true—are these naïve fantasies? I think of Ém, her unhappy marriage to a man she doesn't love (to say the least). I think of Maman, her loyalty to the General and his humiliating betrayal. I bristle at how she is being slandered, yet wonder, too, if there is any truth to the rumors.

I often dream of Major Christophe Duroc, but aren't such wishful imaginings as unrealistic as the romantic novels Ém likes to read?

Be safe, my dear brother. If only you could come home and advise me.

Your sister Chouchoute, who loves you very much

Note—Two days ago would have been Easter Sunday by the old calendar. Five years ago, on that night, Maman was taken away. I remember being awoken by the sound of pounding on the door. I sat up trembling. Government inspectors! I could hear Maman weeping, men's boots, their gruff voices. I had just turned eleven, but I was so paralyzed with fear I made water in my bed. It shames me to think of it, even now.

BAD HOUSE

Maman stopped by school after the midday meal. The spring weather being fine, I was outside playing Prisoner's Base with some other girls during free time. I was, at first, alarmed to see her, thinking, of course, that it might be news of Eugène—*bad* news. But then I noticed the happy way she came walking toward me, swinging her arms and smiling. She was wearing a chain of spring daisies on her head, as if she were a young woman.

I conceded my base to Mouse and ran to greet her. "News?" But just then Maîtresse and Citoyen Isabey came out to greet her.

"And?" Citoyen Isabey asked mysteriously.

"And?" Maîtresse said.

Maman threw her arms up in victory and they embraced her with cheers.

"I believe this calls for a celebratory libation," Maîtresse said, inviting us up to her rooms.

"Come," Maman said, taking my hand. "I'll explain."

And news it was. Maman had *bought* a country property. I couldn't believe it!

Maîtresse and Citoyen Isabey already knew about it. They were both of them pleased.

"Bonaparte wanted to buy it before he left for Egypt," Maman told me, "but he thought it too expensive. The owners dropped the price this year, so . . ."

It turned out she'd been negotiating for over four months. "And you didn't tell me?" How much more did I not know?

"I didn't want you to get your hopes up, dear heart. Malmaison is an old estate, not far from here. You pass it on the way to Paris, just after the road turns in from the river."

"We do?" I tried to remember.

"How many acres?" Maîtresse asked.

"Only three hundred, so it's not very big, yet it brings in twelve thousand a year."

"Excellent," Maîtresse said. (I imagined she looked forward to being paid for my tuition.)

"In fact, it's quite productive. There are five farmers living on the property and they all pay rent. The grapevines produce over a hundred barrels of wine—"

"We shall enjoy helping you with that," Isabey said, and we laughed.

"Dear heart, you will like this. There are seven horses."

At last!

"Farm horses, for the most part," she qualified, before I got too excited. "Although there's one rather old bay mare and an ill-tempered pony we can ride."

As well as a donkey, over a hundred sheep, plus pigs, chickens, twelve cows . . .

A real farm, I thought, a bit giddy.

"There's a farmhouse, as well as the manor itself, of course," Citoyen Isabey added, but Maman rather laughed at this.

I gathered it wasn't grand. "Is this . . . *manor* habitable?" I asked. Maman had a weakness for ruins, which she found poignantly romantic.

She glanced at Isabey. "What would you say?"

"Fairly," he said, tilting his head. "Well, most of it."

"I would describe it as *rustic*," Maman told me with a smile. "But the grounds are beautiful, and it's a pleasant walk to the village."

"Will we move there?" I couldn't imagine Maman giving up her little house on the outskirts of Paris.

"We'll spend time there now and then, especially when the weather is pleasant in the summer."

"But it's called *Mal*maison?" I made a face. *Bad* house?

I loved Malmaison the instant I saw it. It was rundown, and not very big, to be sure, but full of promise. The grounds would be lovely once tamed.

"Where did the money come from for all this?" I dared to ask Maman as she gave me a tour of the tower, dovecote, mill and other outbuildings.

She looked uncomfortable. "Citoyen Charles and I . . ."

My heart sank.

"We have a company, I suppose you'd call it," she said. "We provision the army, just as several of Bonaparte's brothers and sisters do. We've made a bit of a profit recently, so I used some of that for Malmaison."

Nasty: When Citoyen Charles *shows up and Maman is all smiles.*

3 Floréal, An 7
Malmaison,
Dear Eugène,
    Did you know about a property called Malmaison that the General wanted to buy before leaving for Egypt? Maman just bought it! I'm here right now. It's lovely, although rather in disrepair. Maman fancies it "bucolic." (Alas, the only musical instruments are an

out-of-tune pianoforte and an ancient harp missing three strings.) I think you will love it, especially for the riding trails.

It's raining—five leaks in the roof!—so it will be a good day to attend to my studies. Tomorrow I return to school, which is really close, only a half hour by carriage, if that, so I will be going back and forth quite a lot.

Au revoir. I pray that you are safe and out of danger, you and all the other aides. Ém and Mouse pray for you, too.

Your Chouchoute

Note—If one dreams and thinks of someone constantly, does that mean one is in love? How can one know? Maman thinks I'm going to end up an old maid if I don't marry immediately. It's making me lunatic!

Uh-oh! Speaking of Maman, Citoyen Charles has just arrived to talk to her about their "business dealings"—dealings that helped finance the purchase of this property. I'm heartsick over it, to tell you the truth. I don't know what to think.

AN UNWELCOME
GUEST

The next time I visited Malmaison I was kept awake by yapping dogs, which of course got Pugdog going.

"Where did all those dogs come from?" I asked Mimi at breakfast, yawning.

"Citoyen Charles is staying in the farmhouse," she said.

"He's staying *here*?" I made a face. "At Malmaison?"

She grimaced. "And with all his dogs."

At that moment, Maman came into the room. "It won't be for long, dear heart," she rushed to explain. "Hippolyte needs a place to stay for a spell. He has helped us so much, I could hardly refuse."

My heart sank.

Citoyen Charles called at the manor shortly after the midday meal, a bouquet of wilting wildflowers in his hand. Maman was all gracious smiles. Even Pugdog greeted him eagerly. (The traitor.)

"Good day, Citoyenne Beauharnais," he said in his marionette voice, something I had always found amusing—*before*.

"Good day, Citoyen Charles," I said civilly, without so much as a smile. Quickly, I turned away, lest he kiss my cheek.

All that afternoon—pretending to attend to my studies—I watched Maman and Citoyen Charles going over their "business accounts." They covered the billiard table with papers and frowned over them together. Then he would say something silly, and Maman would laugh and laugh.

I began to beg off going to Malmaison, using my music lessons and the heavy rain that summer as excuses, but on one stormy hot day Maman sent a note to Maîtresse. I was to come to Malmaison immediately.

"Is something wrong?" I asked Mimi, putting down my wet book bag and shaking off my hat. I picked up Pugdog and gave him a cuddle.

"She's not feeling well. She said for you to go on up."

I put Pugdog down. I didn't like that he smelled of violets—Citoyen Charles's scent. "Now?" I asked, unlacing my dirty boots. Maman was strict about her afternoon rest—her "beauty sleep," she called it.

"She insisted," Mimi said.

Maman was in her dressing room, stretched out on the chaise longue, her eyes closed. She looked aged, asleep like that, without face paint. I started to tiptoe back out—I didn't want to disturb her—but the creak of a floorboard gave me away.

"Hortense?" she said, sitting up.

"Is something wrong, Maman?" Her eyes were rimmed red.

"Come here." She shifted over so that I could sit beside her.

Aïe. This must be serious, I thought.

"Dear heart." She put her hand on mine. "Eugène has been wounded."

Badly. A bomb exploded close to where the General had been talking with his aides-de-camp. Eugène was hit, knocked unconscious and buried by rubble.

"And this is *true?*" We heard false reports so often.

"Director Barras confirmed it," Maman said, her voice tremulous. "For a time it was thought he had been . . . that he had been killed."

The thought made me sick. "But he's not?"

Maman wrapped her arms around me. "Only injured."

That could mean so many things. "Where?"

She grimaced. "His head."

Oh *no.* I'd seen the wounded soldiers, the village idiots. "Will he heal?" I knew what a head wound might mean.

"We can only pray."

Maman, Mimi and I made an altar to Eugène in the withdrawing room, setting candles and flowers under the portrait I'd made of my brother long ago, the one that had made Maman weep. And now she had reason to. I imagined Eugène returned to us in a crippled state, with that vacant, unseeing stare. I imagined him thus and wept.

I was awoken the following morning by the pounding of a horse's hooves. I scrambled to my window and pushed open the shutters. I recognized Director Barras's courier. By the time I was dressed and down the stairs, Maman had reached him and was opening a missive.

"News?" I called out.

"Nothing about Bonaparte or Eugène, dear heart," she said, examining the document. "But one of Bonaparte's aides has died from his wounds."

My heart stopped. "Which one?"

"Captain Croisier," Maman said, thanking the courier and giving him a coin. "I don't remember him. Do you?"

"No." *Grâce à Dieu.*

———

Maman and I walked to the church in town to light candles. After returning, I played the old pianoforte, working on a melody I'd begun last fall, a melody I'd never been able to get right—until that moment. It infused my soul like a heavenly presence.

Music is pure emotion.

Music is prayer.

Music is forever.

Citoyen Jadin's words. I played my composition again and again, imagining the notes flying to my brother. Imagining them giving him life.

27 Messidor, An 7
Malmaison
Dear Eugène,

You have been injured—badly. You may be dying and we would have no way of knowing. I can't sleep for worrying about you. I love you so much. Please get well. Maman insists that I go back to school tomorrow, in preparation for the annual Exercice. *I can't stand the thought of all that gaiety.*

Maman and I learned that an aide—Croisier by name—died of his wounds. If only news would come of all the other aides, especially your friend Major Duroc.

Your Chouchoute, who loves you very, very much

Note—I've composed a piece of music for you, my first—at least it's the first I've considered "finished."

If only I could send this.

If only you could read it.

If only . . .

PAGE FORTY-THREE

❧

Maîtresse sent for me as soon as I arrived back at the Institute.

"Angel, I've been thinking about you," she said, putting down her quill. "I understand how worried you must be about your brother, but it will be beneficial for you to be back at school."

"That's what Maman said," I said glumly.

"You are going to love the *Exercice*. It's going to be even better than the one last year."

I shrugged. "I'm sure." I'd heard how wonderful the last *Exercice* had been, the one I'd had to miss.

Maîtresse wiggled her fingers. "We are all *trembling* with excitement."

Exactly what I feared. "I don't know, Maîtresse Campan—I don't think . . ." It didn't help that my courses had come on so strong I feared I would flood. "I *can't*. I don't have the heart." And then the stupid tears.

She led me over to the divan by the fireplace. On the low table there was a platter of sweetmeats: sugar puffs, figs and two chocolate madeleines.

"I'm so afraid for Eugène," I burst out, wiping my cheeks with my sleeve. I cautiously sat down. The wad of rags between my legs felt soggy. I perched on the edge of the divan. "I can't sleep."

"You must have faith," Maîtresse said, stroking my back.

My faith, such as it was, could not save my brother.

"Coffee and cakes, angel? I know you fancy chocolate madeleines, but these sugar puffs are especially tasty."

"No, thank you." I wasn't hungry. "I'm sorry." I stood, feeling impossibly awkward. "I must go. I have a lesson with Citoyen Jadin."

"So soon? His lessons don't usually start until the afternoon."

"I need to organize my notebook before I see him," I said, which was almost true.

The doors to the theater had been propped open because of the heat. Citoyen Jadin was sitting on the piano stool, but slumped over the keys, his head in his arms.

"Citoyen Jadin?" I approached, pressing my composition notebook to my chest.

He lifted his head, blinking.

"It's me, Citoyenne Beauharnais."

He stood, ceding the piano stool to me with a wave of his arm. "I must have fallen asleep."

He looked thin. His clothes hung from him. How could the composer of such powerful music look so frail?

"I heard about your brother being wounded," he said, lowering himself onto an armchair. "That's terrible. Have you learned anything?"

"No," I said, my voice tremulous. It was hard not knowing—not knowing if Eugène had recovered, not knowing if he was dead or alive, or if he was damaged in some awful way.

"I can imagine. Well, actually, I can't. I love all my brothers— *most* of the time," he added with a wan smile, "but I think I would die of grief if something were to happen to any one of them."

To *die* of grief. I'd always thought it was only an expression, but now I thought it possible. "Do you ever think about that? About death, I mean?"

"All the time," he said. "It's one reason music is so important to me."

Music is forever. I thought of the score I had with me, the one I had written for Eugène. "Sometimes I think it's how I pray," I said, "by playing music. Does that sound lunatic?"

"Not at all. God listens. Or, rather"—he rolled his eyes—"the Supreme Being."

"I have something to show you," I said, handing him my composition notebook. "Page forty-three."

"What are these?" he asked, leafing through.

"Compositions I copied. Lully's, mostly."

He looked at me, his eyes questioning. "This is a considerable amount of work."

"You said it's how you learned to compose."

"And you want to—?"

"Yes. I want to learn. To compose." There. I had said it.

"And these are your own compositions?" he asked, opening to a section of some of my earliest attempts.

"Oh! Don't look at those." If only he would skip forward to page forty-three. "I wrote them when I was just beginning."

He turned the thick pages slowly, pausing at each. "Tell me, Citoyenne Beauharnais, what sort of music do you most love playing?"

This took me aback. "Sonatas, like the ones you write, that type of thing."

"Of course, but when you're tired, or sad and in need of solace, or even when you're especially happy—what do you play then, just for yourself?"

It seemed a strange question. "Well, I do enjoy romantic melodies, melodies that . . ." That made me cry. That made my heart feel full.

"The type of music one hears on the street?"

I flushed. Yes.

"Then that's what you should be composing."

"But they're so simple." And yet the composition I had created for Eugène was of this type—simple, yet heartfelt.

"Not in the least. Not the exceptional ones. But my point is, you can only create from love, from what *you* love. Page forty-three, you said?"

I nodded, choking up. "The page with the folded-down corner." I couldn't bear to watch. "At the end."

At last, he came to it. He read it through and sat back. He exhaled, and then read the score through one more time.

"Play it," he said, holding the notebook out to me.

"I don't need the score," I said. I knew it by heart.

Never had silence seemed so weighty. "Again," Citoyen Jadin said.

And that was it. I played my piece, he listened, but said *nothing*. We finished the lesson with my usual drills, and then I left.

"Citoyenne Beauharnais," he called out as I reached the door.

I turned, expectantly. "Yes?" Was he going to say something about my composition?

"Your notebook. You forgot it."

Was that all? He wasn't going to say anything more? "I don't need it," I said.

I went to my room, crushed. I felt so ashamed. Over a year before, I had made a secret vow to learn how to compose—or, rather, to "become a composer," a vow that embarrassed me. So lofty, so *naïve*. So foolish.

I thought of Maîtresse's words, about dreaming big dreams and having the courage to fail. But what if one did fail? What then?

THE *EXERCICE*

❖

The next few days were given over to frantic preparation for the *Exercice*. That was just as well. It helped keep me from worrying constantly about my brother's injury and fretting over Citoyen Jadin's rejection. I might have been miserable, sick with fear whenever I thought of my brother's injury, but at least I was busy.

On the afternoon of the *Exercice*, over thirty carriages were parked along the road. I was surprised that it had become such a big event. People had come from all over.

Inside the theater, pots of flowers had been set along the edge of the stage. (The piano, draped with a cloth, had been moved to the back to make room.) We girls, all in white muslin gowns and white boots, our hair in ringlets, stood off to one side of the stage. In the front, facing us, were the two judges, stern-looking members of the National Institute wearing dark coats embroidered with green laurel leaves.

Teachers and the invited guests started filing in, and Caroline showed them to their seats. She had been given the "honor" of greeting them (and thus spared the humiliation of being publicly shamed on stage during the *Exercice* itself). She wore an official sash, which gave her the appearance of being in charge. Clearly, she was enjoying the role.

Soon most all of the seats were taken, even in the galleries above—but no sign of Maman. I spotted Nana and Grandpapa and nudged Ém. "At least our grandparents are here."

Some of the privileged few—old Citoyen Rudé among them—sat on the stage in a boxed-off section to one side.

"Isn't that the man who sat with us at the Meeting of the Vows?" Ém whispered. "The school patron?"

"Yes. The man who wiped his nose on the tablecloth," I said. It made me uneasy the way he was gawking at us.

"Ew," Mouse gasped, but then quieted: Maîtresse had gone to the front of the stage.

After Maîtresse's welcome, the little girls in Green, Purple and Orange came out. They curtsied, said their names and ran out giggling. I blinked to keep from tearing. Nelly should have been among them.

Then came the Blues and the Reds, who were required to read out loud from a text and perform some elementary mathematics. Eliza, clutching Henry, did surprisingly well at her numbers, which pleased me.

Then a round table was carried onto the stage, and twenty-two of us older students took seats around it. The first exam was dictation, which the judges were to examine for handwriting, spelling and punctuation. Then we each read a sentence from *Émilie* by Jean-Jacques Rousseau, declaring the part of speech of each word. (This took a long time: I heard someone in the audience snoring.)

After that came geography and history, which were more interesting, with the judges asking questions. They always responded "Marvelous!" to whatever answer was given, so I felt more at ease.

We finished by reciting the poems we'd learned by heart. My recitation of "The Dove and the Ant" was very well received.

Then came the part everyone loved best: the prizes. All the students won for something (even Caroline won for Italian), with some winning more than once. Ém won for handwriting and grammar, and Mouse for spelling and figure drawing. I won for landscape drawing, dancing and *piano*—which astonished me.

"Well done," Maîtresse said, giving me the award in Citoyen Jadin's absence.

I was shocked speechless. (Could this mean he liked my composition?)

And then came the award for the Rose of Virtue. One by one, Maîtresse announced the winner at each level, finally getting to the Multis. I was surprised to get it again. It was my third, so I was presented with a porcelain vase as well, embossed with my name. I could hear Grandpapa exclaiming "*Brava*," which made me love him all the more.

4 Thermidor, An 7
Montagne-du-Bon-Air
Dearest Granddaughter,

I am as proud as a duchess over your many awards, but worry, I confess, to see you rather too pale. Watch that you don't acquire a greenish tinge, for this would indicate Green Sickness, a disease of the nervous system that is tragically fatal to many young women. Do you have depraved tastes, such as for pencil dust or clay? This is a warning sign you should be aware of.

    Your grandmother,
    Nana

4 Thermidor, An 7
La Chantereine
Dear heart,

I'm sorry to have missed the Exercice, *but I had urgent matters to attend to in town. I am comforted knowing that Nana and Grandpapa were able to be there, at least, to add to the applause. I heard that it was a big success. I'm proud that you won awards in literature and music (for harp?). I hear that you won the Rose of Virtue, as well. Isn't it your second one? I am so proud of you.*

No further news about your brother, alas, but I did learn that Major Duroc, a friend of his, was injured in the same attack. Do you remember him? He was tall, and handsome in his way, although rather solemn. Bonaparte thinks highly of him, I know.

Your ever-loving mother

Christophe! Injured? Oh no!

"What's wrong?" Ém asked, seeing my distress.

"An aide was injured." I feigned to read the letter over more closely. "But not your husband, Antoine," I assured her.

"Too bad," she said, indifferently.

"Ém!" How could she be so cruel?

5 Thermidor, An 7
The Institute
Dear Eugène,

I try not to think of how you and others might be suffering, try not to think of how badly you might be hurt—or worse.

Is it true that your friend Christophe Duroc was injured at the same time as you? How awful! If only we knew more.

I won my third Rose of Virtue, which I now display in a porcelain vase with my name embossed on it in gold. I also won a prize for piano. I was surprised. Shortly before, I'd played my teacher the composition I'd written for you, and he appeared not to like it. Now I don't know what to think.

I feel silly writing these letters to you, knowing that I will never send them. Perhaps, somehow, thoughts travel the world. In that case, you know how much I love you.

Your Chouchoute

Note—Do you remember the annual tradition Mouse, Ém and I started, of wearing a black ribbon on our sleeve at this time of year?

Mouse's is to honor the memory of her mother, and Ém wears hers in memory of her missing father. Mine, of course, is to honor Father's.

Strangely, there is little I remember of the day Father died. All I can recall is that there was a violent thunderstorm that morning. For some reason, I was alone—and terrified. Where were you?

ILLUSIONS

❖

"So this is the latest in fashion?" Caroline said, sneering at the black ribbon on my sleeve.

It was the last day of school before the summer break. "I wear this every year at this time," I said—coolly, for I didn't trust her. I stepped aside for a group of Purples. "Ém, Mouse and I all wear one." I guess that made it sound like we were a club or something, a club she would never be part of. "It's in honor of our family members who died during the Terror." And for Ém's father too, although that was hard to explain.

"Ohhhhh, the dreaded Terror."

"You don't understand."

"You're right," she said with a smug expression. "I don't. Why would Mouse want to honor her mother's suicide?"

What a horrible thing to say! "What?"

"You heard me." Jutting out her chin.

"You are mistaken," I said evenly. "Mouse's mother died of a fever, after helping a family of sick unfortunates."

"So the story goes," she said. "The fact is, she threw herself out a window for fear of—" She made a slicing motion across her neck.

"That's not true!"

"Are you calling me a liar?"

"I'm calling you a lying bully!"

"Don't believe me? Ask the little American, why don't you?" she said, spraying spittle.

Eliza?

"She knows everything. She ferrets out the most hidden secrets."

Why would Eliza know anything about Mouse's mother?

"But what I really can't understand," Caroline went on, gloating, "is why *you* honor a man who wasn't your father."

"Excuse me!" I glanced around. Our "conversation" was attracting notice.

"Has nobody told you?" She leaned in as if to tell me a secret, but I stepped back. "Your so-called father didn't think he was your father," she said. "In fact, *he publicly denied it.*"

"That's a *lie!*"

She grabbed hold of my arm, hard. "Turd in your teeth. Ask your whore of a mother," she said with a mocking grin.

And that's when I hit her.

Of course Caroline screamed bloody murder.

"Angel, you, more than anyone, know that there is *never* a reason for violence," Maîtresse said, lecturing me as if I were a child.

I hung my head. "I know, Maîtresse Campan." Yet I wasn't repentant. I was *angry.* "But she—"

Maîtresse held up her index finger. "*No* excuse. You're to stay in your room for the rest of the day."

A humiliation!

On the way up, I encountered Eliza. "Did you say anything to Caroline?"

"Around?" she asked, twirling Henry by his tail.

"*About* Mouse's mother."

"Yes, *about* her slaying herself through leaping from a high window."

"Hush!" I said, standing back to let four girls in Red pass. "That's not *true*. Who told you that?"

"Everyone knows it, my mother said."

"Your mother?"

She nodded, biting her cheek, realizing the gravity of what she was claiming.

So —Eliza had told Caroline that Mouse's mother killed herself. How awful! And then I remembered what Caroline had said about my father.

"Did you say anything to Caroline about my father?"

"The illustrious General Bonaparte?"

No. "General Beauharnais, my natural father."

She scrunched up her nose. "*Was* he your father?"

"Of course!"

"But my mother said—"

I went to my room and collapsed onto my bed, trying not to cry. I took Father's miniature portrait out from under my pillow and stared at it. Was he my father? If not him, who? For a lunatic moment I even wondered about Citoyen Charles. (Of course that made *no* sense; he wouldn't have been ten years old.)

I heard the door creak open. I pushed the miniature under my pillow and sat up, wiping my cheeks.

Mouse sat down beside me on my bed, handing me an apple. "Are you hungry?"

"No, thanks," I said glumly. "I'm being punished."

"I heard," she said, placing the apple on the table beside my bed.

"I have to stay here until school lets out." Of all days, the day when everyone exchanged friendly notes before parting for the summer. I was missing all that.

"What happened?"

She didn't know? "I hit Caroline."

Mouse covered her mouth with her hands. "You must have had reason," she said, ever loyal.

Her sweet expression only made me feel worse. "I don't want sympathy."

She made a puzzled frown. "Are you angry at me?"

"No! I'm—I don't know. I just found out that my father probably wasn't my father."

"But that can't be true." She pushed her spectacles up onto the bridge of her nose.

"Things are not what we think, Mouse. It's all an *illusion*." My father wasn't really my father. My mother was a faithless sinner. "We think one thing, and it turns out to be another."

"Like what?" she asked, in all innocence.

I took a shaky breath. "Like that your mother didn't die of a fever."

She looked at me with an expression of naïve bewilderment, her eyes huge through her thick lenses. "What does my mother have to do with this?"

"Because how she died is an *illusion*. It's a story, a made-up tale. You're always saying that you want the truth." I gulped. "Well, the truth is she didn't die of a fever."

Mouse fingered her black armband. "Then how did she die?" She seemed to sincerely want to know.

In the moment that followed, I could have held back, but I didn't. I felt reckless, angry and confused. "She threw herself out a high window." Five years ago today.

"She would never have done that!" Mouse said, her voice a squeak.

"But it's the *truth*."

Abruptly, she stood, staring at me with a look of pity. And then she ran out the door, slamming it shut behind her.

———

In the silence that followed, I packed my trunk. Maman would soon be arriving to pick up Ém and me, take us to Malmaison. I put the miniature of my father away in the secret drawer in my trunk, along with all the letters I'd written my brother. I stood motionless for a moment, pressing my hand over the black band on my arm, as if soothing an injury. My heart ached thinking of what I had told Mouse, remembering the pain in her eyes. It made me ill to look at my vase with the silk rose in it, my award for being a good person. A good person I certainly was *not*.

CONFESSION

Maîtresse glanced up from her long table, covered with books and papers. "Aren't you supposed to be in your room?"

"I have to talk to you," I said, my breath still shuddering.

"You understand, of course, that I had to punish you."

"Which is why I can't accept this." I placed my vase with the Rose of Virtue in it on top of a stacked six-volume set of *Plutarch's Lives*.

"Hortense, everyone voted—the staff, all the students. You misbehaved *once*. You deserve the Rose, and certainly the vase."

"No, I don't," I said, my lower lip quivering.

She led me over to the divan. "You've been through quite a lot of late, what with worry about your brother and all. It's understandable that you're not your usual self."

"It's not because of what happened with Caroline."

She regarded me with a question in her eyes.

And so I told her the awful thing I had done to her niece, Mouse, my dearest friend.

Maîtresse covered her heart with her hands, her eyes filling.

"Is it *true?*" Part of me prayed that it was a fabrication, a cruel rumor.

"I'm afraid so."

"How awful!"

"I've kept it a secret because I didn't think Mouse could bear it."

She frowned. "But how did you find out?"

"Caroline told me."

Maîtresse sat back. "How could she . . . ?"

"Eliza told her." I twirled my fingers. "Her mother knew. She goes to all the salons, and, I guess, there is, you know, *talk*."

Maîtresse smoothed the ribbons of her linen cap, her fingers trembling. "It was inevitable that people would find out one way or another. Where is Mouse now?"

"I don't know."

Maîtresse reached for a service bell. "Find my niece," she instructed Claire, the maid who appeared. "Tell her she's to come see me immediately. And Émilie, as well."

Ém too? I cringed.

"Don't worry, angel," she said. "I've learned that it is best for everyone to speak openly. Our health, our energy, our essential vitality is oppressed when we carry a burden. Keeping a secret, even with the best of intentions, is only that: a burden."

Was she forgiving me for revealing to Mouse how her mother died? I'd crushed the soul of my dearest friend. How could that ever be right?

I heard footsteps on the stairs, the raised wooden heels of boots, a tap on the door.

"I could only find one of the girls," Claire reported.

Indeed, only Ém followed her in. "We looked everywhere," Ém said, pulling up her black armband, which had fallen down to her elbow. "Even in the infirmary."

A thought—more like a flash of an image—came to me. With a jolt of fear I jumped to my feet. "I'll be right back."

I took the steps two, three at a time. Gasping, I emerged onto the narrow terrace that rimmed the peaked roofs. It was a cloudless day—I could see Paris in the distance.

And then I saw her, standing near the edge. "Mouse!"

She turned to look at me—quizzically, as if I were a creature from another world.

"Mouse." *Don't jump.* "I'm so sorry." I moved closer and linked my arm through hers. "Maîtresse wants to see us. She's waiting in her study."

"Oh," was all she said, but I could feel her trembling.

I pulled her back, toward the door.

Safe now.

Maîtresse had set out coffee and chocolate madeleines, as if for a social occasion. Ém looked up to see us, but did not smile. It seemed we'd all aged.

"Good afternoon, little one," Maîtresse said, standing to embrace her niece, kissing each cheek. She took Mouse in with her eyes, assessing. "You had me worried."

Mouse nodded, staring at the floor.

Maîtresse looked over at me with a question in her eyes.

"She was up on the roof," I said, tearful now.

"I see."

Something in the way Maîtresse said that made me think that she *did* see.

She took Mouse's hand. "We need to talk." Her sad eyes addressed Ém and me. "All of us."

There followed moments of activity and fuss: china clattering, serviettes being passed.

Would you care for . . . ?

Sugar?

How many?

The social rituals put me on edge with their meaninglessness, knowing what was coming.

"Hortense," Maîtresse announced, stirring her coffee with a tiny wooden spoon, "perhaps you could begin."

The portrait of Mouse's mother hung on the wall in front of me, wreathed with flowers. How awful to be having this conversation on the anniversary of her tragic death.

"Explain what you told me," Maîtresse prodded.

I cleared my throat. I didn't want to have to do this. "May I first explain what happened before?"

"If it is relevant," Maîtresse said.

My cup shook in my hand. I set it down carefully. "Caroline told me something disturbing this morning, something to do with my father. My real father," I said to clarify, but then bit my lip. *Was* he my father? "It helped explain why he had no love for me." My voice trembled saying that. I'd always made excuses for him, I realized, telling myself that he was too busy to make time for me.

Ém put her hand on my shoulder. "Hortense—"

"Whether or not it was true is beside the point," I persisted, glancing over at Mouse. She had pulled off her armband and was clutching it, twisting it. "I felt it to be true, and that's when Mouse had the misfortune to try to comfort me." I touched my serviette to my eyes.

"Go on, angel," Maîtresse said.

My heart was pounding. "I told Mouse something else Caroline had told me, about how her mother died."

"Mouse's mother?" Ém asked.

"*Is* it true?" Mouse asked her aunt.

"Little one," Maîtresse said, putting her arm around Mouse's shoulders, pulling her close, "I wanted to protect you. You feel things so intensely. I intended to tell you when I felt you were strong enough."

"But is it *true*?" Mouse was insistent.

"I'm afraid so," Maîtresse said with tears in her voice.

Mouse looked at Ém and me accusingly, over her spectacles. "Did you know all along?"

"I learned it this morning," I said.

"I don't know what this is all about," Ém said.

"My mother didn't die of a fever," Mouse told her angrily. "She threw herself out a window. Right?" Mouse glared at her aunt. "She *killed* herself."

Maîtresse nodded, blinking back tears.

Outside, I heard girls laughing. But not in here. We were none of us laughing, none of us joyous.

"What else have I not been told?" The tip of Mouse's nose was bright red.

"I'm not sure," Maîtresse said, glancing over at me. "Angel, did you tell her *why* her mother . . . ?"

"I don't know why." How could Mouse's mother—any mother—have done that? Mouse was so young, only ten.

"Little one," Maîtresse began, "your mother, my much beloved sister, learned she was to be arrested. She knew she would be tried, convicted and . . ."

Beheaded.

Maîtresse held up her hands. "But that wasn't the reason. Your mother didn't fear death. Of all the Queen's attendants, she was the bravest. The Queen"—Maîtresse crossed herself—"the Queen called her a lioness."

We knew the story well. Mouse's mother, the Queen's *lioness*. Her beautiful, brave, lioness mother.

"What your wonderful and *very* loving mother knew was that if she was convicted, as she surely would have been, the officials would confiscate all your family property."

That was the law then, I knew. My father had lost his life, and all his property was taken.

"Château Grignon, everything." Maîtresse put out her hands, as if a supplicant. "She couldn't bear to leave you impoverished, and so . . ."

I stared down at my hands, clenched in my lap. Was it all about property, then? That didn't seem right.

"But for what?" Mouse lashed out, her face white. I feared she might have one of her faints. "Robespierre was arrested the very next day." She threw her black band on the carpet. "My mother died in vain. She would have been . . ."

Safe.

"I know, my pet, I know," Maîtresse said, weeping now too. "She had no way of knowing."

How capricious it all seemed. Mouse's mother had given up one day too soon.

"Truth hurts, but secrets can be damaging as well," Maîtresse said, addressing us all. She put one hand over her heart. "Let's vow to be open with one another."

"I so vow," we repeated listlessly, hands over our hearts.

The pendulum clock chimed.

"Maîtresse Campan, my mother will be here soon." I hated to leave at such a moment.

Maîtresse stood and opened her arms. We formed one big embrace as we had so many times before. I felt Mouse pressed beside me, her slender form, her thin, bony shoulders. Would she ever forgive me? (Would I ever forgive myself?)

"*Safe now,*" Maîtresse whispered, and we repeated it after her.

I squeezed Mouse's shoulder, but she didn't squeeze back.

IV

TRANSFORMATION

9 Thermidor, An 7 – 24 Vendémiaire, An 8
(27 July – 16 October, 1799)

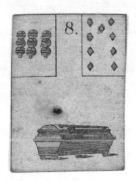

THE COFFIN CARD: TRANSFORMATION

MALMAISON

❧

The school courtyard was jammed with carriages collecting children for the summer break, everyone bidding adieu. I felt like a sleepwalker, emerging into another world.

"Mouse will be all right," Ém said. "She's stronger than we think."

But would she ever forgive me? Had I lost my dearest friend?

I saw Caroline climbing into Citoyen Isabey's shambles of a carriage for the return to Paris. It seemed like forever since I'd lashed out at her, yet it had only been that morning. She glanced my way and made a rude gesture.

Citoyen Isabey, who was helping the driver load Caroline's trunks, called out, "Where were you? You missed my class on two-point perspective."

I was relieved he hadn't heard I'd been punished, confined to my room for hitting Caroline. I winced to think of the story she would no doubt tell him.

"Do you need a ride in?" he offered.

"Maman should be here any minute."

"Going to Malmaison?"

I nodded.

"I've never been," Ém offered.

"You'll find it enchanting," Isabey said, pulling on the ropes that were holding the trunks, making sure they were secure. "I think that's your mother now," he said, slapping his gloved hands clean.

I turned to see a big coach pulled by six gray horses come to a noisy stop outside the gates.

"Have a wonderful summer, girls," Isabey said, climbing onto the step of his carriage. "But remember, Hortense—" He wagged a finger at me before pulling the door closed. "*Five* sketches a day."

It *was* Maman. She rarely used the fancy coach that had been reclaimed from my father's property, thanks to Director Barras. The six gray horses had been a gift to the General after he'd negotiated the peace treaty of Campo Formio. (People thought us wealthy with such a rig, but they didn't know that Maman rented out the coach and horses.)

"I needed room for your trunks," Maman explained, climbing down. She was wearing a simple country gown of brown muslin and looked for all the world like a virtuous woman. I thought of what Caroline had told me, that my father wasn't really my father. I thought of Citoyen Charles. I hoped he wouldn't be at Malmaison.

"As well as room for these." Maman held the coach door open to reveal crates of seedlings and plants. "But *most* importantly," she said, stacking the crates to make room for us, "I have excellent—" She stopped short, taking in our attire. "Why the black armbands?" She looked concerned. "Has someone died?"

"We do this every year, Tante Rose," Ém said, climbing in ahead of me.

I realized that this was the first time Maman had seen us during our ritual days of mourning. There was so much she didn't know about me. She had been absent from my life for years. "It's to honor the memory of Mouse's mother," I explained, wondering if Maman knew the truth about her death.

"And my father," Ém said.

"And mine," I added, my voice weak. *Was* he my father?

"Oh," Maman said, taken aback.

Ém scooted over to make more room for me. "You were saying, Tante Rose, about something important?"

"Yes!" Maman squeezed in and pulled the door shut. "I have wonderful news."

I needed good news.

"I was going to write, but I thought it best to tell you in person. Eugène has recovered from his injuries!"

Eugène!

"*And* he's been promoted to lieutenant."

Lieutenant Beauharnais. Imagine! "He's going to be . . . ?"

Maman nodded, beaming. "He's going to be fine, dear heart. Our prayers have been answered."

I couldn't believe it. "*Really?*"

"Really."

I wept with joy, Ém too.

The manor was as rundown as before, but Maman's passion for gardening had brought some improvements: trees, bushes and flowers had been planted. The place looked cared for. Loved.

I looked to see if Citoyen Charles's carriage was anywhere in evidence. It wasn't, which was a relief.

"Smells wonderful," Ém said, coming in the door.

Maman untied her bonnet. "I asked our cook to make mille-feuilles, cherry confits, apple flan and—especially for you, dear heart—madeleines, to celebrate you winning the Rose of Virtue again."

I didn't want to tell Maman that I'd returned it, that and the vase. "Ém won awards too," I said.

"Of course!" Maman said, heading for the cellar kitchens.

"This is lovely," Ém said, in the way someone says something only to be polite.

I raised my brows. "It needs work." Expensive work. "Maman thinks of it as *rustic*."

"There's a billiards table?" Ém glanced into the dark room to the right of the vestibule.

"The felt top is moth-eaten, but we can still play." I wondered where Pugdog was. Usually he was at my ankles, looking up at me with bulging eyes, every bit of him wiggling with happiness, knowing I would give him a cuddle. "Just don't play against Maman," I said, leading the way upstairs to show Ém to her room.

"Why?"

"She always wins."

"Where's Pugdog?" I asked Maman later. I was going to show Ém around the "estate," and he always loved an adventure outside.

"Citoyen Charles has taken him, dear heart," she said, counting out the tableware.

Taken him? "Taken him where?"

"To the city," she said, glancing up with an apologetic shrug. "Hippolyte found accommodation."

So, Citoyen Charles would no longer be a guest at Malmaison? I was happy about that. "But why would he take Pugdog?" I asked tearfully. He was our dog. *My* dog.

Ém joined us. She'd found her wide-brimmed hat.

"It's hard to explain," Maman said, swallowing. "And Pugdog is—Well, he's happy with all those dogs." Not mentioning Citoyen Charles's name.

He really must have been a gift to Maman from Citoyen Charles, I realized, a gift she wanted to hide.

Ém looked puzzled. "Pugdog's not here?"

"No," I said, turning away before I burst into tears. *My* little Puggy.

TRUTHS

❖

Maman went to bed early that evening and Mimi retired as well. A pleasant summer breeze had come up, so Ém and I helped ourselves to more Malmaison wine and sat outside.

"I'll tell you a secret if you tell me one," I suggested. I thought it time we spoke honestly of *certain things*. "I'll begin," I offered. "It was cruel of me to tell Mouse what I did, even if it was the truth. My only explanation is that I was profoundly distressed because of what I'd learned about my father—"

"From Caroline? And that's why you slapped her?" There was a hint of admiration in her voice.

"That, and some other things she said." It was hard for me to believe, thinking back. I'd hit her hard. "She told me my father didn't think he was my father."

Ém nodded. "He thought that at first, but then he realized his error," she said.

I was shocked. "How would you know?"

"My *nounou* told me, long ago."

Her *nounou*? I remembered well the severe woman who had looked after Ém when she was little.

Ém swirled her wine in her glass. "This was before the Terror, before my father fled, when we still had our big house and my mother hadn't yet been arrested and gone to jail."

Back when life was good. Back when her mother was sane.

Ém pushed her hair back off her forehead. The moonlight touched her cheeks, giving her skin a glow.

"She told me that you were born early."

I knew this. Maman claimed it was the reason my health was sometimes delicate.

"And because of that, your father was suspicious." She took a sip of her wine. "He didn't believe it possible for a baby to be born early."

"What?" Not *possible*?

"It was a common belief at the time, and since he hadn't been in Paris when . . . Well, you know, nine months before you were born, he became suspicious. He knew Eugène was his child, but he had doubts about you because of your early birth."

I closed my eyes, as if to shut out the truth.

"Are you sure you want to know all this?" Ém asked.

I did. Sort of.

"So he and his . . . his lover—"

"*His* lover?"

Ém nodded with an "I'm sorry" look. "They were in Martinique together, your father and his—his *lady friend*, let's call her. They went looking for evidence that your mother was by nature lascivious."

Maman? I groaned. I thought of *that book*.

"And that she'd behaved immorally before sailing to France to marry him. So they paid your grandparents' workers—"

"Their slaves, you mean?" Maman grew up in the New World, where people could buy and sell people—*own* them—which wasn't allowed here. Mimi had been a slave before coming to France; now she was free.

"Of course," Ém said. "Your father offered your family's slaves lots of money to tell stories about your mother. Only *one* came up with an account, to get the reward, of course. He was a child, merely ten. Based on his fabricated story, your father claimed that your mother was a sinner by nature and that he was not your father. And then he ordered your mother into a convent."

"I have no memory of this."

"Of course not. You were a baby with a wet-nurse in the country at the time. I was only four or so, but I remember Tante Rose crying. She had to move into a convent with Eugène, who was still little. She was in there for almost two years. When I was older, my *nounou* explained everything. Your mother took your father to court for telling lies about her, for harming her reputation. She *won*, so then she could leave the convent and live where she pleased."

A gentle, warm breeze brought with it the intoxicating scent of a gardenia shrub in bloom. A wife suing her husband? And *winning*? I was amazed.

"It was brave of her. Nana and Grandpapa were all for it. They loved your father, but they didn't approve of what he'd done. My father didn't like it either, even though Alexandre was his little brother. My *nounou* said that nobody in the family would speak to your father."

I felt unsteady. The things I didn't know! I thought of Mouse, and the shock *she* must be feeling. I wished I could reach out to her, comfort her. I wished I could take away the truth.

"My *nounou* said it was all this lady friend's doing. She wanted to turn your father against your mother so that she could marry him herself."

"So what happened to her, this . . . this *friend*?"

Ém laughed. "She left your father for a richer man and your father came to his senses." She reached out to touch my shoulder. "He and your mother remained separated, but at least he realized that he really was your father. He admitted as much in court." She smiled. "You look just like him, you know."

I wiped my cheeks dry. My father was my father—but did I want him as a father now? After what he'd done to Maman? I had always blamed her for driving him away, but now I understood how cruel he'd been to her.

I heard an owl hoot off in the distance. With a trembling hand, I poured us both more of the Malmaison wine, which tasted better now, not quite so bitter.

"Thank you," I said. "Now it's your turn."

"But I have no secrets, Hortense," Ém said.

I looked at my cousin's lovely face. How could she lie and yet look so innocent?

"Well, maybe one," she admitted, pulling her shawl close around her.

"Tell me," I said, smiling so that she would feel comfortable about confessing. She needed to know that I would love her *no matter what.*

"I like to read romances."

"That doesn't count." And it was hardly a secret.

She looked offended.

"Look," I said, "we've made a vow to be honest, right? I think it's time that you confessed to the nature of your"—I was in it now, there was no stopping—"your *relationship* with Louis."

She stared at me. "You don't understand," she said, in a tone that was almost condescending. "Louis has the soul of a poet. You don't know what it means to love, to really, really love someone."

(I longed to tell her how wrong she was.)

"But you're married, Ém." Like it or not.

"Louis and I have done nothing wrong."

"But what you *feel* for him is wrong. Exchanging books and notes with him is—it's not right, and you know it."

The moonlight made Ém's eyes gleam. "You're always so sure, aren't you," she said.

That took me aback. It wasn't a question. "I don't know what you're talking about," I said.

"You think you always know the right thing to do."

"That's not true!" I protested, though wincing.

"You pride yourself on it. You were cruel to Mouse, all in the name of honesty."

"That wasn't—!"

She stood so abruptly her chair fell over, her glass of wine breaking on the flagstones. "You're *blind*, Hortense, blind to your own faults."

"Ém?"

She turned from the door. "Sometimes I *hate* you," she said—but calmly, which made it even worse.

And with that, she was gone, and I was alone, picking up shards of glass.

A VOW

❦

10 Thermidor, An 7
Malmaison
Dear Eugène,

　Today is the fifth anniversary of Robespierre's death. I'm not sure of the hour, but it's very early. The fireworks haven't started going off yet in the village and nobody is awake, not even the servants.

　I was hugely relieved to learn that you have recovered from your injury. I needed some good news, because yesterday I had fights with Caroline, Mouse and even Ém.

　It all started because I had reason to think that Father was not really my father. Now I believe he was—but then I learned things about him that disturb me.

　Do you remember the day when Maman was freed from prison? You and I were living with our Aunt Fanny because Father had been executed and Maman was still in the Carmes. Or so we thought. I was playing Aunt Fanny's out-of-tune pianoforte when I looked up to see a frightful creature standing in the door. You were in the room as well, and maybe Ém? (I'll have to ask her—not that she's talking to me.) The "creature," of course, was Maman. She'd just been released. She was incredibly thin and her gown was filthy. She stank! It was days before I let her near me.

　Poor Maman—I must have hurt her terribly. I can't seem to do anything right.

Please, please, please stay safe. I don't know what I'd do without you.
Your Chouchoute
Note—Pugdog has gone to live with Citoyen Charles. I'm heartbroken.
Plus, it makes me suspicious of Maman again, and I don't like that.

At breakfast, Mimi and the kitchen maid set out food on a table in the sunny room with lots of windows. Down the center they put platters of madeleines, cold mutton, dried sausages and slices of warm milk bread with pots of freshly churned butter.

"Hortense, could you go get Ém?" Maman asked, adding warm milk to her chocolate.

"She's latched her door shut," I told her. "I knocked, but she didn't answer." It filled me with remorse—and anger, I confess. I'd called out *I'm sorry*, but she hadn't even answered. "Maybe you could try."

Maman looked at me, puzzled, the cup of chocolate in her hands. She had wound her head in a scarlet scarf, Creole-style. It was chilly for a summer morning.

"We had a disagreement last night," I explained, my eyes stinging. I hadn't told Maman about my trouble with Caroline the day before at school, much less about all that had happened with Mouse. Ém had accused me of thinking I always knew the right thing to do, of priding myself on it. Was I blind to my faults?

"Ah, my sweet," Maman said, putting her chocolate down and taking me into her arms. "These things happen. You and Ém are like sisters." She put up two fingers, intertwined. "And sisters do have squabbles. Have something to eat. I'll go talk to her."

Ém came back down with Maman and took a seat at the table, not meeting my eyes. She looked pale, yet her cheeks were blotched. She conversed with Maman, but spoke not a word to me.

Then, as soup was being served, she swooned, slumping over into Maman's arms.

Maman and Mimi helped her back to bed and then Mimi went into the village for a doctor.

A doctor? Why not an apothecary? I wondered. A doctor was sent for only when it was serious.

It was almost six o'clock by the time the doctor arrived on horseback.

"It's only a fever," Maman told me after, making the sal prunella elixir the doctor had prescribed.

I was relieved! I helped myself to a third madeleine.

"Émilie has broken out in spots," Maman told me after dinner. "Promise you won't go in her room."

"But you go in," I said.

"I had the pox as a child." She pointed to the scar by her ear.

Ém had the *pox*? How awful! I thought of Nelly, dead from that horrible disease.

"And one can only get the pox once," Maman went on.

"But I'm protected too," I said, my voice shaky. I pushed up my sleeve to show her my scar.

"I know, dear heart, but we dare not risk it," Maman said. "*Promise* me."

Dear God, I prayed, *please do not take Ém. I can't bear to lose her. I would die.*

If God spared her, I promised Him, I would give up madeleines. *Forever.*

Every morning, I set a chair outside Ém's room and read to her from *Paul and Virginia*. She did not make a sound. She might have been sleeping, for all I knew, but I liked to think she was lying there, quietly listening.

The story was a romance, which I rather liked, much to my surprise. It was about a boy and girl who were friends as children, and then fell in love, but it was also about life on their island, where everything was perfect and natural and uncorrupted by artificial sentimentality or the modern world.

I skipped over the love poem about bleeding bosoms.

After days sitting outside Ém's door, I heard her speak, but it was fever-talk. It made no sense. I heard her call out for her father, as if her very life depended on it. The emotion in her voice made me weep.

There was a nauseating odor coming from her room, sweet and pungent, like that of rotting flesh. The doctor, Maman and Mimi donned masks, smocks and gloves before going in. After, Mimi took Ém's soiled linens out to a woodpile and burned them.

Late that night, I woke from a night-fright. This time, it was not my usual dream. This one felt different, and it wasn't about Father. In the dream Maman came to me, and said, "We may lose her." She didn't speak in the dream, but somehow I knew that's what she said. I also knew she meant Ém, and I said to her, "Do you mean she might die?"

I sat up, my back against the down pillows. What was going to happen to Ém? By the light of the night candle, I saw my Game of Hope cards scattered on top of my trunk. I gathered them up and returned to bed. I stacked them, cut them and shuffled them four times. Then, thinking of Ém, I withdrew two cards at random, getting the Moon card followed by the Ship, which (according to Lenormand's booklet) signified disagreement leading to misfortune.

Aïe. I withdrew one more card: the Coffin.

I quickly hid the cards away. They were scaring me. I lay back on my bed, pulling my blankets over my head. I knew that the Coffin card meant transformation, but it also could mean death.

The doctor told Maman we should prepare, which made her sob.

I was sick with dread. Ém's last words to me were *I hate you.*

I kept seeing Mouse at the edge of that roof. She could have died—because of *me*, because of the awful thing I told her.

I felt chilled in spite of the heat. Maman put her hand to my forehead. "I'm fine," I told her angrily, ducking away. *Stay away from me. I'm evil!*

10 Fructidor, An 7
Château Grignon
Dear Hortense,

Thank you for your letter. I was horrified to learn that Ém has the pox and I'm relieved that she's recovering. I wanted to come visit, but Maîtresse forbade it. There is quite a bit of uneasiness here at the Institute, especially after little Nelly. How is it possible that Ém caught the pox and we're all fine? We did everything together.

But that isn't the only reason I'm writing. I want you to know that I have been thinking more about what happened, about what you told me about my mother. I had to learn the truth about her death at some point. I do wish I might not have been told in that way, but I understand that you did not mean to hurt me. None of us are perfect creatures, as much as we'd like to be.

I also want you to know that I didn't intend to jump. I went up to the roof to be alone, and to be closer to the sky, and to feel my mother in the heavens. Please believe that this is the truth.

I embrace you, my friend. We have all lost so much. We must treasure what we have, treasure each other.

I miss you.

Always,

Your Mouse

Note—I have been painting with watercolors, using the wash techniques Citoyen Isabey taught us. I am in love with cobalt blue. I have made some brushes from squirrel hair—one of these is for you. Also, I have ten lumps of bread drying. The bread our cook makes is of a perfect density for erasers.

Along with Mouse's letter was a package, wrapped with a pretty blue and white striped satin ribbon. It was the porcelain vase with my name on it. Inside was the rose I'd won, and a simple note from Maîtresse: *This is yours, my angel, and always will be.*

AN APOLOGY

❖

The doctor finally pronounced Ém free to come out of her room. She had been sick for a month. She had survived, but what would she look like?

A veil covered her face. Maman led her by the hand into the sitting room, as if she were blind. I thought for a moment—with alarm—that she *was* blind. One often saw blind beggars with pox-scarred faces.

"My darling girl," Maman said, for she loved Ém truly. (I admit I was sometimes jealous.) "Raise your veil. We want to see your eyes. You will always be beautiful to us."

"That's true," I said, although I had doubts.

"Come." My mother's voice was low and caressing. "We're your family."

Reluctantly, Ém raised her veil. I was prepared to smile no matter what, but my eyes flooded. My cousin, the most beautiful girl in school, looked . . . well, frightening. The skin on her cheeks was that of a pitted creature, like a lizard's skin. I felt I might upsick, but I dared not look away, lest she notice.

"Oh, Émilie, it's not too bad," Maman lied. "And with time it will get better."

Grâce à Dieu, we'd taken the precaution of removing the looking glasses, I thought. "We're so grateful for your *life*," I said, my voice unsteady. That was true.

"My life is over," she said.

It broke my heart to hear those words.

Maman and I strolled with Ém in the garden the next morning, but soon she begged to return, fatigued. We walked her back to the house, as if she were a child. "No need to see me in," she told Maman.

I kissed her cheeks—her skin was rough—and Maman and I returned to our stroll, disheartened.

"Fortunately, she's already married," Maman said, putting her arm around my shoulders.

But to a man she didn't *like*. Ém didn't care that he was lost to the sands of Egypt. Worse, she was glad of it.

I told Maman I'd overheard Ém calling out for her father. "If only there was a way to find out if he's alive, and maybe even bring him back."

Maman made a clucking sound of doubt.

"That would be such a comfort to her," I persisted.

"It's not possible, dear heart. He's an émigré, considered an enemy. His name is on the List."

The List: the names of the thousands of men and women who had fled France during the Revolution, men and women forbidden ever to return.

"There's something I must tell you," I told Ém one lovely summer morning.

We were in the withdrawing room, where she could rest on the settee while I worked on my embroidery and mending. She had her veil off, so I could see her eyes, which were still strikingly beautiful, although dull, without spark. Her battle against death had hardened her.

"I want you to know that I'm sorry."

She looked at me, puzzled.

"I'm sorry for what I said," I went on, "before you got sick. It was wrong of me to judge you."

"What did you say?"

She didn't remember? I was relieved, but also perplexed. How was I to apologize?

"Oh, something about . . ." I didn't think it wise to mention Louis. I cleared my throat. I was making a mess of things. "I was being judgmental, and you got mad."

"At *you*?"

"It had to do with your husband, Antoine." That wasn't entirely true—but it wasn't entirely false, either. "I said that you should write to him," I lied. Although I *did* think that.

"No wonder I got angry," she said bitterly.

"I want you to know that I'm sorry." Truly, truly, truly.

In spite of Ém's recovery, Maman was despondent, and soon I discovered why. Looking in her desk for paper to write Mouse a letter, I—of course—glanced through her correspondence, happening upon a note to her from Director Barras.

16 Fructidor, An 7
Petit Luxembourg
Chère Citoyenne Bonaparte,

Very well. I'll see what I can do about getting François de Beauharnais's name erased from the List. I wouldn't be too hopeful, however. There is a murderous mood in Council these days.

Speaking of which, you should be aware that opposition to your husband is growing. What news we receive is worrisome, and now it's being claimed that thousands of his men have died of thirst because the desert wells were filled with sand by his enemies. It's also said that he has lost the confidence of his troops, who are on the point of rioting.

Much of this is slander, of course, but I advise you to give up your life of retirement. I can't fight this battle alone.

Barras

I couldn't sleep, much less eat. My mouth was dry and I had a twitch in my right eye. Maman fussed over me. "I'm not sick," I protested—yet I was. Sick with worry. *Thousands* of our soldiers had died of thirst?

On Eugène's birthday, Maman organized a celebration for him, putting aside gifts "for when he returns."

If he *ever* returned. I tried not to give in to despair, but it was hard, thinking of the letter Director Barras had written Maman.

"What's wrong, dear heart?" Maman kept asking.

"Nothing," I insisted, for I dared not say I'd been snooping.

Four days later, Maman announced to Ém and me that she planned to move back to Paris after we returned to school.

"I must plead for a rescue," she said, "plead for the Directors to authorize sending a fleet to bring Bonaparte and Eugène home, *all* our men. It's the only way."

I advise you to give up your life of retirement, Director Barras had written. *I can't fight this battle alone.*

"School?" Ém said with dread in her voice.

I understood. We'd been away the entire summer because of her illness. She would be returning scarred.

FIRST DAY

The fall air was brisk. Girls were skipping about in the school courtyard, jumping rope, running hoops or chasing each other. Caroline was standing in the shadows (plotting revenge against me, no doubt). We'd not spoken since "the incident." It seemed a minor matter to me, in truth. Ém's brush with death from pox had put everything in a different light.

I looked for Mouse but didn't see her. Even though we'd been writing, we hadn't seen each other since that terrible day. Would things be different between us?

Eliza ran up to us, her bonnet ribbons hanging loose. "Why do you wear a curtain of inscrutability?" she demanded of my cousin, referring to the veil Ém was wearing.

I threw Ém a sympathetic glance. The first day back was going to be especially hard.

"Ém got the pox this summer," I told Eliza.

Eliza clutched Henry to her heart and stepped away, as if Ém's pox were catching.

"She's fine now," I assured her. "Aren't you, Ém?"

She managed only a nod, looking out at the world from behind her white veil.

On entering our room, I was disappointed (and a bit relieved) that Mouse wasn't there. Her bed was as tidy as ever and her sketchpad and sticks of charcoal were lined up on the study table we shared. I noticed a drawing of Ém and me tacked to the wall and my heart warmed.

I also noticed the hand mirror on the little table we used for our toilette. Unfortunately, Ém noticed it too.

"Give it to me," she said, raising her veil.

"You're still healing," I pleaded.

"I have a right to see my own face."

Reluctantly, I handed her the mirror. "The scars will get better with time."

But Ém wasn't listening. She was staring at her reflection, her big eyes glistening. "I look like a monster," she said, putting the mirror back on the table.

"That's not true!" In spite of her scars, she still had a lovely grace.

I turned at the sound of someone outside our door. Ém quickly let down her veil.

Mouse burst into the room and jumped to embrace Ém. "My prayers were answered—you *lived*. I was so frightened. Take off that veil. I'm your dearest friend! And yours, too," she said, embracing me shyly.

Dear Mouse!

Ém lifted off her veiled bonnet. There was silence as Mouse took in Ém's transformation, her once-perfect face now poxed.

"I frightened myself just now," Ém said, sniffing.

"It's getting better every day," I said. A *bit* better.

"You'll always be our lovely Ém," Mouse said with all her heart.

Ém and Mouse left for Maîtresse's opening address, but I hung back to change my gown, which I'd somehow stained. As I was arranging my Multi sash, Ém burst into our room. She threw off her bonnet and veil, and fell down on her bed. "I want to die," she sobbed, pressing the bed sheet to her eyes.

"What happened!" Had a student humiliated her? Had she been shunned? I imagined the worst.

"Louis is down there," she said, her breath coming in gasps.

What was *he* doing at school?

"He wouldn't look at me," she said. "He got *Caroline* to bring me a book I had given him."

Ém had given Louis *another* book—which he'd asked his sister to return? "That's awful," I said, although of course I was thinking that a quarrel between Ém and Louis was not such a bad thing. "I know how much it must hurt," I said truthfully.

I heard the triangle clang: the assembly would soon begin. "We should go down," I said.

"I can't," Ém said, weeping still.

"Maîtresse will understand," I said, embracing her.

Cutting through the garden to the theater, I chanced upon Louis sitting on a moss-covered bench. He was picking apart a rose and throwing the petals one by one into the fountain. Or trying to. Mostly he was missing.

"How could you do that to her?" I was furious at him for causing Ém such pain. After all she'd been through!

"You don't understand," he said feebly.

"I don't. You dishonor a married woman without any care to her reputation, and then you won't speak to her because she's poxed?"

"That's not the reason."

Was he blinking back tears? "Then what is?"

"It's my fault, what happened to her," he said, his voice raspy.

What?

"Our love for each other was sinful—"

It certainly was!

"—and God has chosen to punish us by taking away her beauty," he said, trumpeting into a lace-edged handkerchief. "You are right to detest me, Citoyenne Beauharnais. I see her scars; I have my own."

I sat through the assembly without listening as Maîtresse introduced five new students and a geography instructor, followed by a review of the rules, an introduction to the staff and the usual rousing speech about our intellectual and creative capacities. All I could think of was how angry I was at Louis. He was a weakling, feigning to justify his cruel behavior with a burden of guilt. I despised him!

THE RACE

❧

A month after returning to school I got sick. It was not the pox, *Dieu merci*, but the infirmary was full, so Maîtresse sent me to Maman's in Paris to recover. I was happy to escape Nurse Witch's vigorous care, but even so, it was tiresome. I ached from head to toe, too ill to draw or play the pianoforte.

Nasty: Wishing to know the hour, but having a fit of coughing as the clock begins to chime and losing count of the bells.

Nasty: The grating, scraping sound of a maid shoveling cinders when you are trying to sleep.

Maman came home one afternoon agitated after meeting with Director Barras. "He said that the other Directors don't care that Bonaparte's stranded," she said, her manner despairing. "They have no intention of instructing the Minister of War or the Council of Ancients to send a fleet to bring them back. They could—they have that power—yet they refuse!"

"But how are they going to return?" Would I *ever* see my brother again? And what of Christophe?

Maman sank onto a chair. "I just don't know."

———

Late the next night, a carriage pulled down our laneway. Half-asleep, I heard Maman's voice, curiously excited. It sounded as though she was talking to old Gontier, her man-of-all-work.

I put on my fur-lined slippers, grabbed a shawl and hurried down the stairs, the flame from my night candle threatening to flicker out.

"Maman?" She'd been to dine at the Petit Luxembourg with Director Gohier and his wife, hoping to persuade him to support rescuing the General and his men.

"Dear heart," she called. "They're *back*."

"General Bonaparte is back!" old Gontier yelled out from behind her, his arms full of wood for the fire.

"And your brother is with him," Maman said, stepping aside for him.

"Who?" I put my candle down on a side table. Back where?

"Bonaparte and Eugène."

I thought, *This must be a dream. A good one, for once.* "Eugène?"

"Yes! He was the one who sent word to the Directors, from a port in the south."

I followed her into the salon, where a fire was now roaring. I moved the wooden rocker close.

"I'm going to meet them on the road," Maman said, standing, rubbing her arms. "Agathe will help me pack linens, provisions, blankets." She started to pace. "Director Gohier's loaning me his sleeping coach." She clasped her hands to her heart. "Dear heart! Our prayers have been answered. They managed to get past the English ships."

It *wasn't* a dream. "Are you sure?" I wondered if Christophe was with them. "And you're going?" That made *no sense*. People were robbed by highway bandits—murdered sometimes. "It's dangerous, Maman." Even the drive to and from school was risky. "Why not wait for them here? They'll arrive in time."

"Darling." She sat down across from me, methodically taking off her gloves, pulling at each finger in turn. She smoothed them out on her lap, laying one neatly over the other. She looked at me. I'd never before realized how strangely big her eyes were, especially by candlelight. "They'll turn him against me. They've already tried."

They: the Bonaparte clan, she meant. I could feel the heat in my cheeks. They would tell the General about Hippolyte Charles, tell him that Maman had been unfaithful to him, that she was wanton.

"I must see him, *before* they poison his mind."

"Then I'll have to go with you," I said.

"But you're sick, dear heart. You have a miserable cold. I'll not be stopping, not even to eat. I'll be sleeping in the coach to save time."

"I'm fine," I said with a sneeze.

"You'll wear your fur bonnet?"

"Anything," I grunted. Even my ugly fur bonnet.

Maman and I left at dawn, rolling over rough roads, the coach lanterns clanking against the window frames. The coachman stopped at post houses only long enough to change the lathered horses for fresh ones.

As the coach rocked side to side, we ate hard-cooked eggs from a basket Agathe had prepared, finishing with comfits and bonbons—and brandy to keep us warm. As night fell, Maman raised a panel in the back, revealing a lumpy feather bed. Covered by musty-smelling furs, we stretched out and tried to sleep, in spite of the ceaseless jolts.

We read the newspapers at every stop. The General had planned to disembark at Toulon, we learned, but the English had driven them back. Another journal claimed that his flotilla of two frigates and a transport vessel had been sailing for forty-seven days before landing at Fréjus, a port not far from Toulon.

Forty-seven days! I skimmed the articles, wondering if Christophe was with them.

One lengthy account in the *Moniteur* was rapturous. I read it out loud to Maman:

"General Bonaparte arrived at Fréjus accompanied by Generals Berthier, Lannes, Marmont, Murat and Andreossy, and citizens Monge and Berthollet."

"No mention of Eugène?" Maman asked.

Nor of Christophe. Perhaps aides didn't count.

"Not yet," I said, and continued reading. *"He was received by an immense crowd of people crying 'Long live the Republic.' He left the army of Egypt in the most satisfactory position."*

"Excellent," Maman said.

"Tumultuous and repeated applause has been heard from all sides," I went on. *"Everyone was drunk."*

"Drunk?" Maman frowned.

"That's what it says," I said with a shrug, and we laughed.

On the second day, we had to take a break at a post house in Auxerre while one of the coach wheels got fixed. We took a room to refresh ourselves, covering the bed with our shawls before stretching out, for fear of fleas and lice. My cold was better, but it didn't help—at *all*—that my courses had started. In the tavern below, I could hear men toasting, *To our greatest general! Returned to save France!*

And then off we went again, careening south. In every little village, it seemed, people had erected triumphal arches bedecked with wilted flowers and grasses. The farther south we went, the more well-wishers we encountered at each stop. At one, a man yelled to us, "Is it true? Is the Savior coming?"

It's my brother *I'm rushing to meet*, I wanted to cry out. *Not the General.*

Nasty: Snail cream for breakfast, with chalky, musty, bitter bread.

Nasty: Coming away from a soiled necessary with a wet bottom.

As soon as Maman and I walked into the tavern at the Chalon-sur-Saône posting station, a traveler accosted Maman.

"Citoyenne Bonaparte." He bowed deeply.

She nodded politely and moved past him.

The man turned to Jacques, our coachman, speaking earnestly in an undertone.

"He has news of General Bonaparte, Citoyenne," Jacques informed us, shifting from foot to foot. He was a wiry man with buck teeth.

"If he has news, bring him here," Maman said.

I helped her to a wooden bench. Her hip was inflamed again from the constant jolting of the coach.

The young man approached, cloth hat in hand, bobbing his head reverentially with each step. He was shaven, not much older than me—and handsome enough that I regretted my ugly fur hat.

"You have news of the General, Citoyen?" Maman asked.

"I saw him two days ago," he said, addressing Jacques, too shy to look at Maman directly.

"You *saw* him?" Maman's voice was gentle.

"I did. In the theater in Lyons."

"Two days ago?" I interjected. Lyons wasn't far—a day's journey at the most, we'd been told. "Then they should be this way soon, Maman."

"No, not here," he said.

Maman sat forward. "Please explain what you mean, Citoyen. Is the General in Lyons?"

"No. He and his party left at sunrise yesterday."

"Yesterday?" Maman glanced at me with a puzzled frown. "Then they must have passed us."

"They took another route, Citoyenne," he said, flushing bright, "the Bourbonnais road through Nevers."

"But the road through Nevers is dangerous," Maman objected. "It's barely passable."

"Aye," the man said, and our coachman concurred.

"So we've missed them?" I asked, incredulous myself. We'd been racing pell-mell. Had it all been for naught?

The young man shrugged, hands palms up, as if it was his fault and he was sorry. "General Bonaparte was being stopped at every village for celebrations and speeches and the like. The other way, through Nevers, there aren't many villages of account, and few "

"We have to turn back." Maman told Jacques, her voice listless. Back to Paris. We'd be too late, then. The clan would get there first.

V

HAPPY TIMES

27 Vendémiaire – 2 Brumaire, An 8
(19 October – 24 October, 1799)

THE BOUQUET CARD: HAPPY TIMES

LOCKED OUT

Coming into Paris, Maman tried to nudge me awake. I groaned, snuggling into the musty furs. I hadn't slept very much at all, kept awake by Maman's tossing. We'd been traveling recklessly for what seemed like forever.

"Dear heart, sit up. We're home," she persisted.

Home? Our coach had come to a stop. I pulled back the leather window covering. I could make out sleeping forms at our hedge. Beggars? A man sat up and called out, slurring, "*Vive la République.*" Quickly, I closed the curtain, alarmed. What were these people doing here?

"What time is it?"

"It's after midnight," Maman said, arranging her tangled hair. Or trying to.

I heard Jacques pounding on our porter's door. Some of the sleeping forms had risen. Draped in blankets, they looked like ghouls. Jacques warned them to step back.

"What's happening?" I asked.

"I'm not sure," Maman said. She let down a window. "Jacques?"

Holding a torch, the coachman approached. "Citoyenne Bonaparte, the porter is under orders not to allow anyone in." His breath made mist in the freezing air.

"Yes, but anyone but us," Maman said, pulling on her gloves.

"Everyone, Citoyenne—including you and your daughter." His face was pale in the frosty light.

"Is the General not here?" Maman asked.

And Eugène! I thought. (And possibly *Christophe?*) I slipped off my ugly fur hat and found my felt one, pushing my hair into the crown as best I could.

"These are the General's orders," Jacques told Maman. "The porter says—" He stopped, swallowing. "He says your belongings are in trunks in the guardhouse."

"*Your* things?" I asked Maman, fastening the top button of my cape. I was still groggy.

"I don't understand," Maman told Jacques.

"The General, he—" Jacques looked away. "He's moved you out."

Maman shoved open the coach door.

"We're walking? From here?" I clambered down after her.

"Keep back!" Jacques made a threatening gesture at one of the shadowy forms. There were three of them standing now—standing, and watching.

"Open the gate, Didier," Maman commanded her porter.

"It's against orders," he mumbled.

"I'm giving you an order now."

Didier crossed his arms, unmovable.

"I can climb that gate," I told him. He'd seen me do it, too.

Maman cast me a warning glance. "Open the gate, Citoyen. No one will punish you if you do."

After a long moment, he opened the gate and stepped aside.

"I'll accompany you," Jacques said, unhooking one of the lanterns from the coach.

"We'll be fine," I said, taking the lantern from him.

———

The lane was icy, so we made our way slowly, Maman leaning on my arm.

"How are you doing?" I asked, squeezing her hand.

"I'm nervous," she admitted. "And furious," she added, which made me smile.

Two windows were faintly illuminated. I could smell the smoke of a wood fire. I was near giddy with joy: Eugène! Safe back home.

In the dark verandah, I yanked the bell rope, my heart pounding. "I hear someone coming." I peeked through the tiny window in the door. "It's Mimi. Oh! I see Eugène!" A giggle fit came over me. "He's dark, Maman. He looks like an Arab." I was happy and relieved and uneasy all at once.

"There you are," Mimi said, opening the door wide for us, and then closing it quickly behind us to keep out the cold. "Finally."

I peered behind her. I couldn't see Eugène. Had I imagined it?

She pulled out an enormous handkerchief and blew her nose. She was still sick with my miserable cold. "They made me trunk up your things," she told Maman.

"Who made you do it?" I demanded, anger rising. I put the lantern down on the side table. Swords, hats and boots were heaped in a pile in one shady corner. Three big trunks were stacked to one side. Everything smelled of the sea.

"The General's mother," Mimi said, picking up a man's boot and putting it with its mate against the wall. "Signora something."

"Letizia," Maman said, slipping off her hat and cloak. "Signora Letizia."

"What an offensive woman," Mimi said, raising her eyes to Heaven.

I heard the coach and horses pulling up outside. Maman's porter must have come to his senses and let them through.

"At first I refused," Mimi paused to cough, "but she started throwing your things into a trunk, not caring if anything got torn or broken, so I took over. I sneezed right onto her face. I hope she gets my cold."

"*My* cold," I said, stepping back to make way for Jacques, hefting one of our trunks.

"Bring it in here," Mimi said, leading the way into the parlor. "It's your mother and sister!" I heard her say.

EUGÈNE, AT LAST

❧

Standing in front of the fireplace was a thin young man, wrapped in a gray wool blanket. He grinned, his teeth flashing white against his sun-bronzed skin.

I covered my cheeks with my hands in wonder. Lieutenant Beauharnais, wearing the tattered armband of an aide-de-camp. My big brother, truly grown. He looked whole, in one piece. *Grâce à Dieu*, he looked *himself*. He even had that silly tuft of hair standing up.

He threw open his arms. "Chouchoute," he said tenderly, calling me by my baby name.

"We thought you had died," I said, embracing him, my voice quavering. He smelled of tobacco.

"Baby," I heard Maman whisper behind me.

He pulled us all together, Maman and I both weeping. I thought my heart would burst. I had feared I would never see him again, or that he would return terribly altered. "How are you?"

"Yes, how are you?" Maman exclaimed.

We laughed at the fervor of our interrogation.

"We were told you were wounded," I said. *Badly.*

He pulled back his hair and showed us a raw scar behind his left ear. Maman and I both gasped. "It has healed well," he said. "The General went to great lengths to find the best surgeon."

The same General who had turned our mother out of her own house.

"Where is he?" Maman asked.

"Upstairs." Eugène grimaced. "I think he's locked himself in."

"Locked *in?*" I scoffed.

"Well, rather, locked everyone out," Eugène said.

"Locked *me* out," Maman said, taking up a candle and heading for the stairs.

"Maman, you can't just . . ." Eugène protested, almost stuttering in his alarm. "You know, he thinks—"

"I know," she said over her shoulder, and disappeared up the stairs.

Eugène and I looked at each other. There was so much to say.

"I must look a fright," I said, kicking my travel boots free and taking off my gloves, my cloak and hat. "We've been in a coach for *five days.* We took the route to Lyons by way of Dijon." It was all a blur now.

"Ah, so we missed you. We took the wretched Bourbon route back."

"Isn't it unsafe?"

"We got robbed. But at least we didn't overturn."

"Maman was disconcerted to have missed you." There were so many things I wanted to know. "How did it go? With the family?" With the *Clan.*

Eugène blew air out in exasperation, stooping to pick up the blanket. "Only Signora Letizia and Caroline were here when we arrived."

Caroline? I hated to think of the stories she would tell at school. *Hortense's mother is a whore. My brother kicked her out.*

"But then they all descended, like a pack of wild dogs: Joseph, Louis, Pauline and Elisa, and the other brother . . . Lucien? Even Jérôme was allowed out of school for the occasion."

"That can't have been pleasant," I said.

"Facing an enemy army might have been easier. Speaking of dogs, where's Pugdog? Mimi said he's gone to another home, that he's being looked after by someone else."

I sighed. Anything I said would only raise questions, questions I didn't feel comfortable answering. "It's hard to explain," I said instead. "Did you know Maman's porter wasn't going to let her through the gate?"

He threw up his hands. "There was nothing I could do." He looked chagrined. "Would you like this?" he asked, offering his blanket.

"No, *merci*. It's hot in here." The fire was blazing.

"But never hot enough," he said, throwing more wood on the fire. "We got used to the desert heat." He sat down, huddled in the blanket, visibly shivering.

"Are you sure you're not sick?"

"I'm *fine*. If it's the plague you're worried about—"

"Were you in contact with plague victims?" I hadn't considered the Black Plague.

"A number of our men were stricken."

"How awful!" With the plague, one day you were fine, and only days later you were dead, your body covered in painful sores, your swollen tongue black. In ages past, one person in three had died of it. There hadn't been a plague outbreak in France for some time— the quarantine laws were strict. All boats coming from the east had to be held offshore for thirty days.

All boats. Eugène's ship had come from the east.

"It's a frightful disease, Chouchoute, but don't worry. We were on that boat for forty-seven days without any outbreaks."

Of course. I was relieved. "Who returned with you?" I asked, thinking of Christophe.

He named Generals Berthier, Lannes and Murat. "And Marmont and Bessières. The General's secretary, Fauvelet Bourrienne," he added.

I'd heard those names before. "And Captain Lavalette?" I asked. Ém's husband.

"Antoine? He stopped to visit his family on the way back, but he won't be long. He's eager to see his wife."

"Is he aware that she got the pox this summer?"

"Ém? Poxed?" He looked stricken.

Aïe. I'd been writing confessional letters to Eugène for so long, I'd half-expected him to know. "Yes. I'm sorry."

"Is she . . . ?"

I grimaced. "Her face, it's—"

He groaned, but I pushed on, desperate to know. "What about your friend, Major Duroc?"

"Christophe? He's Colonel Duroc now. He'll be here tomorrow." Tomorrow! I clasped my hands together nervously.

"It's late, you must be hungry," he said. "I'll find something for us both."

"Don't go," I said. "Agathe can do that."

"She's abed with Mimi's cold."

Her too? "*My* cold," I said with a yawn. I was exhausted.

I turned at the sound of footsteps on the stairs. Maman? But it was a dark-skinned boy about my age, wearing a turban and bright, baggy clothing. A jewel-encrusted scimitar dangled from a thick cord at his side. He looked like a character out of a fairy tale.

"It's Roustam," Eugène said, and rattled off words I could not understand. (Arabic? I was impressed.) The boy bowed. "He'll find something for us to eat," Eugène said. "And perhaps some brandy?"

"And coffee, too, if there is some," I said, and the boy slipped away.

"He's a Mameluke," Eugène said. "The General made him his

bodyguard, although he is really sweet-natured. He's fifteen, sixteen maybe? He was kidnapped at thirteen and sold as a slave to the Governor of Cairo, who gave him to the General as a gift."

"He's the General's slave?" I crinkled up my nose.

"No, of course not. He's free to do as he pleases, but he's devoted to the General. He sleeps in front of his door. He must have startled Maman," he said with a chuckle.

All was silent upstairs. I wondered how she was doing. Had the General opened his door, let her in?

Eugène got up and rummaged in a soiled haversack, withdrawing a dark-green shawl, which he handed to me.

"For me?" I caressed the silky, lush cashmere. "But you're the one shivering," I said, handing the shawl back to him.

"Now all I need is a bonnet," he said, layering it on over his blanket. I laughed. He looked like an old lady. "Speaking of bonnets." He reached for the haversack again. "This will amuse you." He withdrew a long length of striped cloth, folded it lengthwise and, holding one end in his teeth, wrapped it around his head. "Not exactly a bonnet—"

"A turban?" How bizarre!

"It's warm. We got to like them," he said. "And it kept the bugs out."

My brother the French soldier, draped in a blanket and a cashmere shawl with a multicolored turban on his head. I tried not to giggle.

Roustam came in carrying an enormous platter loaded with figs, walnuts, slices of ham and wedges of cheese, next to a teetering coffeepot, a crystal brandy decanter and demitasse cups and tiny glasses.

"Thank you, Roustam," I said, accepting a glass of brandy and a tiny cup of strong coffee, as well.

"You are very welcome," he said.

"You speak our language," I said.

"You are very welcome," he repeated.

"He understands a *bit*." Eugène fired off another volley of incomprehensible words. Roustam flashed white teeth and exited the room backwards, bowing as if we were royalty. "They are a fastidiously clean people. Unlike *us*," he said, raising his brows. "And they're just about as brave."

"I have so many questions." I froze at the sound of Maman's voice upstairs.

"*Please!*" I heard her cry out. "*I love you.*" Followed by sobs.

"Uh-oh," Eugène said under his breath.

A DIFFICULT
REQUEST

❖

Eugène and I found Maman leaning against the wall on the landing. "He won't open the door," she said, drying her cheeks with her shawl.

A shard of anger went through me. The General was putting us through so much grief. He'd locked Maman out of *her own house*—had her belongings packed up and moved out—and now he wouldn't speak to her?

Keep that door locked forever, for all I care, I thought, digging out a handkerchief I had tucked into my sleeve and handing it to Maman. We would be better off without him—*all* of them, the whole Bonaparte Clan with their bullying, rude and arrogant ways.

"This is futile. We should all go to bed," I said with a sneeze.

"You go, dear heart," Maman said. "You're still not well."

"Yes—go," Eugène said.

I ached from the grueling days and nights in the jolting coach. The thought of snuggling into a bed—a real bed, *my* bed—was inviting.

"We will fetch you if we need you," Maman said.

"Promise?"

In the morning, everything would look brighter.

I must have fallen into a deep sleep and was dreaming of my father again—a disturbing but not scary dream this time. We were in a sort of dressing room and his hair was being powdered by a servant in livery. There was a mirror in front of him: he could see himself, but not me. I was invisible to him.

"Hortense?" The voice was soft, and the touch as well. "Heartling?"

"Maman?" The dream was still with me. "Careful, you'll get powder everywhere," I said.

"You're having a dream," she said, hanging a lantern from the ceiling hook.

"What time is it?" I said, blinking from the light. It was cold; I hugged my blankets around me.

"I'm not sure. Maybe two?"

"What's the matter?"

"Bonaparte refuses to speak to either Eugène or me," she said, her voice breaking. Her breath made mist in the air.

"You must be cold," I said, opening my covers. Shivering, she slipped in beside me.

"Ah, you're warm," she said, snuggling in.

I inhaled her lovely scent of jasmine. When I tried the same tincture, it didn't smell nearly so nice.

"But he might listen to you," Maman suggested.

"Me?"

I felt her nod. "Eugène has tried, I've tried." She sighed. "Mimi suggested you talk to him."

Plead at his door? That was asking a lot. "I wouldn't know what to say, Maman." But most of all, I *wanted* the General out of my life—out of our lives.

There was a long and uncomfortable silence. "I'm sorry," I said, "but I don't think I would be of any help."

"Hortense, Bonaparte is so fond of you—"

"He hardly knows me."

"I know you have little affection for him."

I was surprised by her blunt statement, surprised she knew. I'd always been careful to hide my feelings for my stepfather, at least around Maman.

"And too, I understand how intensely loyal you are to Alexandre's memory," she went on, her voice soft.

Alexandre: my *father*.

"But listen to me, dear heart. I loved your father, but he didn't love me in return. And now—now I have married a man who cares for Eugène and wants him to succeed, and who wants to be a good father to you."

I made a sputtering sound. I couldn't help it.

"But most of all, Bonaparte loves me."

Or *did*. If the General truly loved her, why wouldn't he open the door? How could he bear to hear her weep?

"And I've come to love him," she added, her voice soft.

I heard a night owl screech. I thought of the General's messy, passionate letters. It was easy enough to see that he had once loved her, that he'd been moonsick over her, but how could she love *him*? He was rude and uncouth. Even his accent was grating.

Maman propped herself up on an elbow. "But, more practically, consider what would happen if Bonaparte's family turned him against me, convinced him to forsake us? What would that be like, do you think?"

Life without the Bonapartes? I would have loved that.

"You would be unhappy," I offered sullenly. It was a stupid question with an obvious answer.

"Profoundly."

She said this so quietly I hardly heard. She said it with such feeling, it tugged at my heart.

"But I also want you to consider the more mundane aspects. How do you see this happening, this coming apart?"

"You would be legally separated?" I offered. She and my father got a legal separation. Nana got a legal separation from a man she had married young, and even Maîtresse, long ago, had got a legal separation from her husband because he was gambling away her dowry.

"I'm afraid not. Bonaparte would want to remarry, so he would insist on a divorce, which could ruin Eugène's career."

Eugène loved being an officer. I thought of how miserable he would be in any other employment.

"And as for you, dear heart, you know what happened to our dear Émilie."

"She married?" I guessed, confused.

"Yes, but perhaps you're not aware of the men Bonaparte and I approached who wouldn't consider marrying her."

Other men had been offered Ém's hand? I was surprised by this revelation. Did Ém know?

"Why?"

"Mainly because her father was an émigré, but also because her parents were divorced."

An awful thought occurred to me: What if Christophe wanted to marry me, but Maman and the General were divorced? Would he go against his commanding general? *Never*.

Maman shifted under the covers. "Hortense?"

"Yes?"

"Well . . . could you?"

I closed my eyes, exhaling noisily. "What do you want me to do, Maman?"

She gave me a squeeze. "Just *see* if you can get Bonaparte to open the door. That's all. Beg if you have to."

"I can't do *that*, Maman."

"Consider it a part you have in a performance," she said. "Maîtresse Campan told me that you have a talent for acting."

I was flattered, I admit.

"Do it for your brother, for me," she persisted.

I sat up. "Very well—but on one condition." Did I have the courage? "I have to know the truth about Citoyen Charles, Maman."

SAD VICTORY

❖

I heard Maman catch her breath. "I've told you," she said. "Hippolyte and I are friends—and business partners. That's the truth."

"But *all* the truth?" That was kinder than accusing her of lying.

She put her right hand over her heart, like a schoolgirl. "Ask me a question, and I will answer it truthfully."

"Did you—did you ever sleep with him?" I felt shame for asking such a thing of my mother. "I don't mean 'sleep,' of course. I mean, did you . . . ?" But I could not say it.

"Almost," she admitted.

I was shocked. I thought of the illustrations in that book. The thought of my mother doing *all that* with Hippolyte Charles made me feel sick. But what did "almost" mean?

"Did you tongue-kiss?" My cheeks were burning.

"How do you know what that is?" Maman asked with a playful smile in her voice, snuggling back under the blankets.

"I've . . . I've read about it," I said, putting on a show of bravery. "But you didn't answer my question."

"Once," she said.

Once! That was more truth than I could bear.

"I thought Bonaparte was dead and that I was a widow again. I was bereft, and Hippolyte tried to console me. But, well, we realized how foolish it was. I don't know how to explain this exactly, but do you know . . . ? Are you aware that some men prefer other men rather than women?"

"Yes," I admitted. It was whispered that Director Barras was one such. (And sometimes I wondered about Citoyen Jadin, in truth.)

"May I tell you something in confidence?"

"Of course."

"You won't tell Émilie or Mouse?"

"I promise."

"This must be between you and me: our dear Hippolyte is of this inclination."

I didn't respond at first, taking this in. "Oh?" I thought of the times Citoyen Charles had dressed as a girl—for fun, he always said. And then I remembered Citoyen Jadin saying that he knew Citoyen Charles (or that he knew *of* him), and that there was no truth to the rumors that my mother and Citoyen Charles were lovers. Was this why?

"Does this shock you?"

"No," I offered. It didn't, somehow.

"He keeps it hidden, so you must not betray my confidence."

"I won't, I promise."

"He has been kind to me, helpful when I needed it most. He gave me Pugdog, but it wasn't meant to be a romantic gift. He knew how sad I was after Fortuné was killed."

Maman's first little dog, Fortuné, had been tragically killed by a mastiff in Italy.

"But people insist on interpreting such things otherwise. There doesn't seem to be a place in our world for a friendship between a man and a woman. So I had to give Pugdog back to him."

"I miss Puggy."

"Me too—but we'll get another. I'll have Bonaparte pick him out. I will have to insist that he choose a small creature. He likes everything big."

It was nice to hear the smile in her voice.

"That is," she added, "if he ever speaks to me again."

"I'll go, Maman," I said. Beg if I have to. I would do it for her, and for Eugène. I would do it for my family.

Eugène was sitting on the landing, a candle melting down beside him.

"Chouchoute," he said sleepily. "I'm not having much luck." He took the length of cloth that was hanging over one eye and tucked it back up behind his ear. "Where's Maman?"

"She's in my bed upstairs," I said, my lantern raised.

"No—I'm here," a voice behind me said. I turned to see Maman, wrapped in a blanket. She handed me another. "Don't get cold," she said, and I pulled it around me.

I wondered what time it was, and, as if the world could hear my thoughts, the pendulum clock downstairs chimed three. "Is the General awake?" I asked.

"I don't think so," Eugène said, yawning.

"Well, then, let's raise a racket," I said, reckless with fatigue. "You could fire off a gun."

"Why not start more reasonably?" Maman said, her voice reflecting alarm. "Let's all call out."

And so we did, together and by turns. "Open the door. Please!"

Finally, we heard movement within.

"Bonaparte, don't believe the slander. I have *not* betrayed you," Maman called out. "I love you." And with this she began to weep. She was speaking from her deepest heart. My eyes stung to hear.

She slid down beside Eugène. He put his arm around her, kissed her forehead. "Hortense?" she gestured weakly.

I'd said that I would, and now it was time. The General was fond of me, Maman had said, but would he listen?

"General Bonaparte, this is Hortense," I began.

And then I was stuck. I didn't know what to say, so I imagined that my father—my real father—was on the other side of that door.

"Your daughter," I said, my voice husky with emotion. "Please, won't you open the door? I long to see you."

I found myself weeping in earnest. I did long to see my father: my real father, not the fantasy father I'd imagined. I longed to see the father I'd never really known, not truly.

"Every day I have been thinking of you, and praying for you, and now that you are here you refuse to speak? I am sixteen, a girl about to go out into the world. Am I to do it without a father's protection?"

I heard Maman moan. The door was never going to open. My heart aching, I cried out, "Do you not love me? Please! Open the door."

And with that the door opened and the General stood before us, his cheeks wet. He looked surprisingly frail, his head wrapped in flannel. Maman staggered toward him, dropping the blanket behind her. He opened his arms and she fell into his embrace.

I glanced at Eugène, who mouthed, with a grin, "Well done."

We slipped away, but my victory shamed me. I went to bed, and sobbed into my pillow. I had wanted my father to be there—my *real* father.

A CERTAIN
SOMEONE

❖

I woke to the sound of horses in the courtyard. And then I heard Eugène say, "Christophe, tie your horse by the door. The General will be going out soon."

Christophe?

Oh, *mon Dieu*, my heart about stopped. I jumped out of bed and rang for a maid to come help me dress.

Mimi appeared, panting from the climb. "This house will soon be swarming with soldiers," she said with a cough. "It's been frantic in the kitchen getting ready to feed them all." She still sounded sick, but insisted that she was fine.

"How is Maman?" I asked, the awful events of the night before coming back to me.

"She's all smiles." Mimi chuckled. "Even the General."

The General too? I couldn't imagine *him* smiling.

"You should have seen the miserable look on the face of the General's brother when he discovered them cozy in bed together."

I didn't much care for that picture myself. "Which brother?" I asked, struggling out of my nightdress.

"The one who puts on la-di-da airs."

They all did.

"The rumpled old one in spectacles," she said. "The one who looks like a spider."

Ah, Lucien. "Old? He's only twenty-four." If that.

"He *is?*"

I scoffed. "He fancies it fashionable to look old and rumpled. Anyone else?" Other than my brother. Other than *Christophe*.

"Of the Clan? Only the spider one—and he left in a huff."

I cursed as a button went flying.

"Easy, child. Why the hurry?"

"I want to see Eugène! Fetch the gown Maman gave me for my birthday."

"But it's not yet midday," Mimi said with a frown.

"Maman wants me to wear it when we have visitors," I argued. Well, visitors on special occasions. On special evening occasions. On the occasion of introducing me to a potential husband (in her eyes). But might not Christophe be a potential husband? "But a nice partlet to go with it," I yelled after her. It was indeed not yet noon. I must not be indecent. That would not make a good impression. "And my best bonnet."

My slippers? They would have to do. I glanced at my face in the hand mirror and pinched my cheeks. If only I were pretty. I rubbed dried mint leaves on my teeth to freshen my breath and reminded myself to keep my mouth closed to hide my crooked teeth. (The curse of my family.) Fortunately, it was considered refined not to show teeth.

Mimi came back with my gown. "I brought you an apron to wear over it," she said.

"I'll look like a schoolgirl in that."

"You are a schoolgirl—remember? And I won't have you staining your best gown." She turned me so that she could fasten me up the back.

There wasn't time to pin up my hair, so I bundled my braids up under my bonnet.

"Why all the fuss?" she asked slyly. "It wouldn't have anything to do with the soldiers downstairs, would it?"

"Mimi!"

"Don't break your neck," she called out as I ran headlong down the stairs. I slowed to a ladylike pace at the bottom, catching my breath. I could hear men talking: Eugène and someone else.

And then I heard my brother say his name.

Christophe.

I stood with my back against the wall, out of sight. What if Christophe didn't like me? Worse, what if he treated me like a child?

And what if I'd been wrong about *him*? I'd built up a romance in my heart. I'd come to believe it was real, true love, but *now*—What if I didn't like him?

"Dear heart, you're up." My mother surprised me coming in from the garden, wrapped in a cloak. She was carrying a bouquet of winter greens. "There's food and coffee on the sideboard in the dining room. Eat however you can manage. The table has been taken over by Bonaparte's secretary, Citoyen Fauvelet Bourrienne," she added. "You remember him?"

"Chouchoute, is that you?" Eugène called out.

"Go. He's been wanting me to wake you," Maman said with a kiss.

Eugène *and Christophe* were sitting on the bench outside the General's study, sharpening sabers.

I became aware of my foolishness, my impossible dream. Christophe—Colonel Duroc—was a *man*, not a boy, and a supremely fine-looking man, at that. I guessed him to be twenty-five years old, perhaps more. Why would he be at all interested in me?

"Christophe, have you met my sister?" Eugène asked, laying down the saber and standing to greet me with a kiss on each cheek. (I resisted the urge to brush a loose hair off the shoulder of his jacket.)

Christophe had difficulty rising. It appeared that his left leg had been wounded—and had yet to heal, I gathered, from his slight wince of pain.

"Hortense, this is my friend, fellow aide-de-camp Colonel Christophe Duroc. First aide-de-camp now, that is."

First aide-de-camp? *And* a colonel. I was impressed. I curtsied, my eyes lowered. "I don't believe I've had the pleasure." (I'd rehearsed this moment many times.) I glanced up and just about died. Surely, he was the handsomest young man alive—slim, with broad shoulders, curly black hair and round black eyes.

"The pleasure," he said, touching his hand to his heart, "is mine."

He had an elegant, respectful demeanor, which I found extremely pleasing. I reached for the back of a chair to keep from falling over in a faint.

"Christophe keeps me out of trouble," Eugène said teasingly, oblivious to my distress.

"Someone has to," Christophe answered with affection.

And then—alas!—the General barked out for them and they went rushing into the study.

I lingered for a moment in a reverie, recalling the tender way Christophe had held his hand to his heart, recalling the sweet sound of his voice as he'd said, *The pleasure is mine.*

I turned to go into the dining room to eat, but Christophe reappeared in the door to the General's study. "Citoyenne Beauharnais?"

My heart did a flip-flop. "Yes?"

"The General wishes to speak to you."

"Oh?" Apprehensively.

He stepped back to bow me through (very elegantly). He smelled wonderfully of citrus.

The small office room was stuffy, sweltering hot from a blazing fire. Eugène looked up from a table where he was seated with Fauvelet Bourrienne, the General's secretary. Books, maps and papers covered every surface. The General, wearing a curious red felt round hat, was sitting at his desk, absorbed in reading correspondence.

"Hortense!" He came around his desk to greet me. "You look well," he said, his hands behind his back. He was wearing an olive-green greatcoat, in spite of the heat.

It had been almost a year and a half since I'd last seen him. I hadn't realized how short he was, at least compared to his older brother, "King" Joseph. Frankly, he looked somewhat ugly. He had a round knob of a chin, and his mouth was small.

"You've grown," he said.

I made a curtsy, thankful that he hadn't reached out to pinch my ear, as had been his habit. "Thank you." I flushed, aware that Christophe was behind me.

"General, I'll be at my desk," Fauvelet Bourrienne said, pushing past with his arms full of journals. (His desk? Our dining room table, he likely meant.)

"Ready, Christophe?" my brother said, standing.

"I'll be out front," Christophe said, reaching for his hat.

Then they were all of them gone and I was alone. With the General.

"Have a seat." Pacing, he knocked over a jeweled scimitar, which clattered noisily to the floor. He picked it up and leaned it against his desk, but it fell over again. "*Basta*," he said, and left it.

"Thank you," I said, lowering myself onto a plain wooden chair.

"This chair is more comfortable," he suggested, gesturing to one of the strange chairs Maman had had specially made in an Egyptian design.

"Thank you, but no, I'm fine." I sat up straight, my hands clasped in my lap. I wondered how I was going to get out of there.

"You are doing well at the Institute," he said, leaning on the fireplace mantel. He had a certain charm when he smiled—which happened rarely.

Was it a question, or a statement? I wasn't sure. "I try," I said.

"How is my sister doing?" he asked, cracking his knuckles.

Caroline? *Aïe*. "You'd have to ask Maîtresse Campan," I suggested, trying to be diplomatic.

He cleared his throat. "Perhaps you could influence her," he said, taking a pinch of snuff out of a battered tin.

"Influence?" His accent was heavy. It was hard to understand him sometimes.

"Yes. My sister."

Influence Caroline? Impossible! "We study different subjects," I said, squirming.

"She's a thoughtless idiot," he said, kicking the logs, causing sparks to fly. "Not a brain in her head."

I thought of how Caroline boasted about her big brother Napoleon. She was proud of him. Clearly, the feeling wasn't mutual.

"She'd make an accomplished politician, frankly," he added, "were it not for her sex. In politics stupidity is not a handicap."

"She's smarter than she lets on," I said, actually coming to Caroline's defense.

And then—thankfully—Fauvelet Bourrienne rushed in about some urgent matter and I was reprieved. *Grâce à Dieu.*

THE RULES OF
COURTSHIP

❖

28 Vendémiaire, An 8
The Institute
My dearest friend,

I am so happy for you. I can imagine your joy having your brother safe back home.

What is it like in Paris? There is much excitement here about General Bonaparte's return. I'm not surprised that you have so much correspondence to answer! Just remember: Fearsomes come first.

I've started a portrait of you. You are sitting on a rock with a sketch-book. In the background, in the trees, there are spirits hovering. Perhaps left behind by Fantasmagorie? *Which is no longer here in Montagne-du-Bon-Air, by the way. During one of their events a girl fainted and could not be revived for some time. It was feared her heart had stopped.*

I am running out of room on this scrap of paper. Write to me as soon as you can. Tell me all about the soldiers. Are you in love yet?

Ém promises to write. She is relieved to have her cousin Eugène back home safe, but she dreads the prospect of her husband's return.

We miss you so very much.

Your Mouse

Note—You forgot to take The Rules of Courtship *home with you. I'm sending it along with this letter. I think you may need it now!*

And another—I still haven't gotten my monthlies.

Nasty: When a clump of tooth-brush bristles gets stuck in your teeth.

I spent a little time reading through *The Rules of Courtship*, the book Nana gave me on the occasion of my sixteenth birthday. Here are some rules suggested for a young lady:

1. Display modest reserve.
2. Avoid the public eye.
3. Appear disconcerted if a man looks upon you with admiration.
4. Never encourage a man's advances.
5. Do not confess your feelings until you are absolutely sure of a man's intentions. Only after a gentleman has made an offer of marriage may you reveal your feelings.
6. Don't look at a man unless he has made an advance.

I can't imagine not looking at Christophe

30 Vendémiaire, An 8
The Institute
My angel,

Your absence is too much for the heart of your friend. I want to be near you, take every opportunity to develop the reason that nature has given you, which, without the benefit of experience, still needs a loving guide. Even so, I have bowed to your lovely mother's request to allow you to stay with her in Paris for fifteen more days. I was obliged, in fairness, to grant Caroline the same leave with her family, although she needs every minute of schooling she can get.

People write to you from everywhere to congratulate you on your happiness. Be sure to answer all letters with care. Remember that what you write is a testament to your education, but it can also be used against you by your enemies. One never knows where a letter will end up. It is childish, unforgivably childish, to write to someone: "This letter is messy, please don't show it to anyone."

The person you are writing cannot promise anything. A letter might be forgotten on the fireplace mantel, fall to the ground, be picked up, read and judged. The custom now of not wearing pockets means that there is more of a chance that this might happen.

Kiss your mother tenderly for me. Tell her how much I share in her joy.

Once more, adieu, my dear Hortense. You know how much I love you.

Maîtresse Campan

30 Vendémiaire, An 8
The Institute
My dearest friend,

Surprise! Another letter from your Mouse!

Maîtresse tells us that both you and Caroline have been given an additional fifteen days to be with your families. That's an eternity. You've already been gone for twelve! Unbearable!

What a dull life you must have now, surrounded by handsome soldiers. (Ha.)

Nasty: Writing with ink so thick it leaves blobs.

I can't imagine your brother in a turban. I'm making a portrait of the General in a round Turkish hat and carrying a scimitar under his green overcoat. Of course I have yet to see this apparition, but I've read accounts.

Nasty: Having to sit and wait for ink to dry before starting a new page because there's no blotting paper, sand or a fire in the chimney to dry it by.

My apologies for writing such a messy letter. Please don't show it to anyone.

I miss you.

Your Mouse

Note—Eliza's mother learns all the Paris gossip and then Eliza snoops and finds out, as you know. She told me that there's a lot of talk now about your stepfather (of course)—most of it agreeable—but that there's also talk about his family—most of it terrible. For example, that the General's sister Pauline entertains three lovers whenever her husband is away, and that his older brother Joseph is getting mercury treatment for syphilis. Did you know that? I gather that it's not the first time.

And also (I told you this would be a long letter), the mother of the whole lot of them lived openly in sin with the governor of Corsica for years while her husband was working in Italy, and he's Lucien's real father. And possibly the General's?

No wonder Caroline is the way she is. I almost feel sorry for her.

(On second thought, burn this letter.)

30 Vendémiaire, An 8
The Institute, free time
Dear cousin,

Mouse is writing to you, and insists I do, as well.

I take comfort in Eugène's return, and I imagine that you do too. Does he know I got the pox this summer? I dread the thought of him seeing me. I am using a new face cream Maîtresse had the cook make up, but it stinks and it's not doing my scars any good.

Nana and Grandpapa always ask when "my husband" will be back from Egypt, and I tell them that all I know is that he landed with the General, but stopped en route to visit his parents in the south—where I hope he'll stay.

Forlorn,
Your cousin Ém
Nasty: Being married to a man I don't like.
Nasty: Being the ugliest girl in the school.

MOONSICK

❖

Maman's house was full to bursting. Eugène's bed had been squeezed in under the eaves in the tiny room on the west side of the attic. His new valet, Constant, had to manage on a camp bed in the passageway. The scullery girl slept on a pallet in the cellar kitchen, and the housemaid slept by the fire in the parlor. Others made do in the rooms over the coach house or in the stable or guardhouse.

During the day, it got busier as aides and officials came and went. The General's secretary, Fauvelet Bourrienne, had completely taken over the dining room. Mimi, Maman and I had to make sure that the side table was always laden with food because the men were hungry *all* the time. Beginning at dawn, they drank coffee, beer, wine and spirits (although watered—the General was strict about that).

Caroline came to visit regularly with her family. I made an effort to be polite, but she ignored me. She was clearly only interested in the soldiers. She laughed and exclaimed loudly every time General Murat demonstrated how a bullet went in through one of his cheeks and exited out the other. (It was a story he told rather often.)

Meanwhile, I furtively watched Christophe. He was manly, yet gentle in his demeanor—and so very handsome I could hardly stand it. I noticed that he liked pork crepeinettes and forcemeat quenelles, so I made sure that these platters were always full. He ate very politely, never making a mess or talking with his mouth full. (Unlike the General.)

I took to putting *a bit* of powder on my nose before going down-stairs. Fortunately, Maman didn't notice.

From *The Rules of Courtship:*

Five times touching is permitted—

1. He puts a shawl around your shoulders.
2. He helps you onto a horse.
3. He helps you into a carriage.
4. He helps you climb stairs.
5. He takes your arm through his, to support you out walking.

If only Christophe would *look* at me.

One morning, as I was putting out a platter of food, I glanced over at Christophe. I smiled and he smiled *back*. I could hardly breathe.

I began to write my own Rules of Courtship.

Five signs that you are truly in love—

1. You can't stop thinking of him, not even for a moment.
2. You feel faint in his presence.
3. You can't bear to meet his eyes, the feeling is so strong.
4. You are drawn to wherever he is, as if by enchantment.
5. You feel it is *the end of the world* when he doesn't notice you.

Nasty: Desperately loving someone who hardly knows you exist.

Three signs that you are meant for each other—

1. You end up with "He loves me" when you tear all the petals off a daisy.
2. You get the Heart card in the Game of Hope.
3. His last name sounds perfect with your first name.

———

Four signs that he doesn't love you—

1. He eats the last two cream puffs, not leaving one for you.
2. When you come into a room, he doesn't look your way.
3. When he sees you, he says, simply, *"Hello,"* and begins talking to someone else.
4. He pays more attention to your mother than to you.

"Hello." It was a man's deep voice.

"Yes?" I said, absorbed in my task of clearing the empty dishes on the dining room side table. I glanced up. *Mon Dieu.* It was Christophe. Was there a more comely young man in the world?

I didn't know what to do, much less say. I'm usually, if anything, *too* chatty, so this was strange for me. I put the plates down. "Hello," I said.

"Hello," he said.

I opened my mouth to say something—*anything*—but no words came out. "I'm shy," I blurted. Stupidly!

"Me too," Christophe said with a smile. "Sometimes." As if it were a secret he was sharing.

That was *so sweet* of him to say. "No, you aren't." And immediately I regretted it. Why was I being combative, of all things? "I—I'm sorry," I stammered.

"Why?" He seemed genuinely curious.

"I've studied the art of conversation." Another mistake. Making conversation was supposed to appear to come naturally.

"That's interesting." He put his thumb over the adorable cleft in his chin.

"And I'm not doing a very good job of it," I said with a laugh. (*Fortunately* not a giggle, although—alarm!—I could feel the beginning of a fit coming over me. I took a deep breath.)

"The *art* of conversation?" He paused, stroking his chin. (He was clean-shaven, which was nice, I thought.) "That's actually something I'd like to learn."

"Why?" Another failure. One of the rules of the art of conversation was to ask questions, but *not* one-word questions. "I mean: Why do you wish to improve your conversational art? For what purpose?" I swallowed—with difficulty. "You seem, to me, to have mastered the art quite well." I was on the right track. Or, at least, a better one.

"I get tongue-tied in polite society," he said, "or when conversing with a member of the fair sex." He inclined his head toward me. "Such as now." He grinned. "You're a student?"

I nodded. I hoped that didn't make me seem hopelessly young to him.

"At an actual school?"

"Yes." Most girls learned from their mothers, at home. "At the Institute." We were having an actual conversation! "It's a school for girls in Montagne-du-Bon-Air."

"Didn't that used to be Saint-Germain-en-Laye?"

"Yes," I said, but at least refrained from stupidly nodding like a puppet. "I believe so. Before the Revolution." He was so much older than I was. He *remembered* life before.

"What kind of subjects are you taught there?"

"Oh, music, singing, drawing," I said, listing off the "pleasing" accomplishments that were considered important for girls to learn. "And dance, of course. That type of thing." Not mentioning Latin, Greek, history, philosophy, literature, mathematics and science, for fear of scaring him off.

"I noticed that you're reading Brumoy's book on Greek theater."

Aïe. That gave me away. "You've read it?"

"The General had a small library in Egypt—the few books that were still with us after the ships went down—and there were times when there wasn't much to do, so . . ." He shrugged. "I love reading, learning new things. Do you?"

"To tell you the absolute truth," I said, lowering my voice, "I'm really not proficient at academics." And I wasn't saying that just to impress him, either. "I'm reading Brumoy because I love theater." *And* because I was writing an essay on Greek theater for school, but that sounded too academic.

"Ah, me too."

"Oh?" All soldiers loved theater, of course. Loved *actresses*. I wondered if Christophe was like that. But of course he would be. Most men were, maybe even my brother. "In f-f-fact," I stammered, "I love all the arts: theater, music, painting."

"You play the pianoforte exceptionally well."

When had he heard me play? "I have a excellent teacher at the Institute, Citoyen Jadin. *Had* an excellent teacher, that is." My last lesson with Hyacinthe had been months before, when I'd made the mistake of showing him my composition. I hadn't had a lesson with him since.

"I admire Jadin's work—his compositions especially."

"You know him? Well, I mean, you know his music?" I was flailing. I cleared my throat. "Have you heard his sonatas?" *Aïe!* It was a question that could be answered by a simple yes or no. "I mean, what do you think of his sonatas?" That was better.

"They're *amazing*."

"I agree! They are so—I can't explain. So *passionate*." I flushed at the word. "Without music, I think I might die," I foolishly went on. "I believe God speaks to us through music. It's as though one becomes possessed by a spirit."

I stopped, my cheeks burning. What had I done? "I tend to get carried away. I must sound—" *Moonsick*, crazy. "I have to leave now!" I said, rushing up the stairs to my room.

CLEOPATRA

❖

One subject that was never talked about was *that woman*: the General's mistress in Egypt, his so-called Cleopatra. I got up the nerve to ask Eugène about her while he was working on a scrapbook in his room.

"May I ask you something personal?" I asked, sitting on a upholstered stool.

"That depends," he said, stirring the thick paste. The scrapbook appeared to be about the General.

"It's just that, I heard that the General had a . . . a mistress over there. In Egypt."

He sighed uncomfortably. He didn't think his "innocent" sister should know about such things. I assured him I already knew about "such things" (which mortified him), but even then he was reticent.

"I know this type of thing can happen," I assured him, "particularly when—" I cleared my throat. "I know what the General was told, about Maman. Because of your letter, the one that was printed in an English news journal."

"What letter?" he asked, trimming a news clipping.

How much he didn't know! "The letter you wrote to Maman, about Citoyen Charles."

"About Hippolyte?" He threw back his head, letting out a long breath. "It was printed?"

"Yes, in the London *Morning Chronicle*."

"*Mon Dieu.*"

"But it's not true," I told him, "about Maman and Citoyen Charles."

He tilted his head, looking skeptical.

"I'm serious. I talked to her about it."

He let out a long, low whistle.

"And I believe her. They're only friends, and Citoyen Charles is—" I stopped myself in time. I had promised not to say. "But what about Cleopatra?" I asked, swerving back to my original question.

"It's true," he admitted, telling me how awful it had been having to go out in public with her and the General, so bad that he'd looked into having his post changed. "But when the General found out, he stopped asking me to be present when she was with him," he said, brushing on paste and positioning the clipping. The scrapbook was already thick with clippings. "He didn't want to embarrass me, but even so I . . . I knew he was seeing her."

Seeing her. That was a polite way of putting it.

"I hated it," he said, smoothing the clipping. "If she had given him a child, he would have divorced Maman and married her."

That was what Caroline had told me. I thought of Maman's fear, that she couldn't have any more children.

"I was relieved when the General left her behind." He smirked. "I think he was finding her tiresome."

"Ém told me something similar about Father," I confessed.

"Our father?" He looked startled by the swerve in the conversation.

"That he . . . *you know*. That he had mistresses."

Now it was Eugène's turn to flush.

"Ém told me that there was one in particular. This was before Father ordered Maman to move into the convent. Do you know anything about it? About what he did? To Maman?"

Eugène grimaced. "Why does it matter, Chouchoute? All that's in the past."

Why *did* it matter? Did I want to know who to blame? Or was it more about finding out the truth?

"Do you remember when we last saw him? Do you remember how I cried out, before the guards came running?"

"All I remember is the guards." He put the cork in the jar of paste and wiped his hands on a rag.

"I wrote about it. In a letter to you." One of the many I'd written.

"Really? I never got it."

I threw up my hands in a helpless gesture. "Because I never sent it. It was too risky. I wrote quite a few, actually. I was so frightened that something would happen to you, and I have trouble with . . . trouble sleeping sometimes, and Maîtresse suggested that writing to you might help, even if I couldn't send them. And so I did. And it did help—a bit. I just wish I could remember the day Father died. I don't remember anything."

"Ah, Chouchoute." He got up to sit beside me. "I remember that you cried. You wanted to go with Aunt Fanny and me."

"*You* went?" To the guillotine? *Aïe.*

He bit his lip. "He was brave."

"You watched?"

"I closed my eyes at the last moment," he admitted.

"Yet you were there." He would have heard the awful sound of the blade, the cheer of the crowd.

Yes, he nodded, clearing his throat.

"There is so much I don't know," I said, my throat tight.

"Have you seen this?" he asked, pulling a scrapbook from under his bed.

"I didn't know that you made one about Father," I said.

"It has lots about him in it."

"May I?" I asked, holding it close.

The weather was unexpectedly mild, so I went outside with Eugène's scrapbook. I sat on the wide bench under the apple tree, turning the pages slowly. There were copies of the speeches Father had given when he was President of the National Assembly, as well as accounts of his battle victories in the north. There was also a copy of a letter proposing that he be made Minister of War, and another of his declination.

I was absorbed in reading an account of the battle he had lost which led to his arrest—it was thought he had *intentionally* aided the enemy—when a shadow fell across the page. I glanced up: it was the *General*.

"Schoolwork?" he inquired, sitting down beside me on the bench. He offered me a cinnamon drop, which I declined.

"No," I said, flustered, closing the scrapbook.

"Ah, this looks like one of your brother's projects," he said. "The scrapbook he made about your father?"

I flushed. It was easy enough to tell from the portrait of Father on the cover.

"No need to be embarrassed. You and your brother are fortunate. You have a father you can be proud of."

"Yes," I said uncertainly. There were some things about Father I was not proud of. "Doesn't everyone?"

The General's eyes were big, a curious shade of gray. It made him look transparent. "Not really," he said, with a hint of sadness. "My father was a spendthrift, a ladies' man, a dandy."

I'd heard whispers, but it surprised me to hear the General say it.

"And, in truth, I'm not really convinced that he was my father," he confessed.

He said it so matter-of-factly. I remembered how terrible it had been when I'd not been sure if my father was my father. "That must be hard, General," I offered, in sympathy.

"We are who we are," he said, standing abruptly. "We create ourselves." And with that, he returned to the house, plucking a purple aster on the way in, an offering to Maman, no doubt.

PLACE DU TRÔNE-
RENVERSÉ

I went back to my room and rummaged in my trunk, pushing aside my bag of small linens and sliding open the secret drawer. The letters to my brother were all there. I glanced through them, putting aside several that were clearly about Christophe. As I was putting the offending letters back in the drawer, I felt an object. It was Father's portrait, the brass-edged miniature.

I looked at it as if I'd never seen it before. He looked severe. Had I ever really known him? He'd done remarkable things—Eugène's scrapbook was a clear testament to that—but he'd been weak and fallible, too. And I'd been quick to judge him, quick to condemn. I'd expected him to be a god, an idol, but he was, instead, simply a human being. Like me. Like Eugène. Like Maman. And even like the General?

I slipped Father's miniature back under my pillow, where it had always been, where it belonged.

The next morning I returned Eugène's scrapbook. "Thank you," I told him, feeling uncomfortable.

"You can keep it longer if you like," Eugène said, buttoning his jacket. His valet, Constant, was picking hairs off the shoulders.

"Thank you, but no, I read it all." I put it on his bed, my hand lingering on the cover: *Father*. My free hand clutched the letters I'd written Eugène. I'd made up my mind to give them to him, but now I wasn't sure. "May I show you something—in private?" I gestured toward the hall.

"I'll be right back," he told his valet, and we stepped out of the room.

"These are some of the letters I wrote to you while you were in Egypt. I promised myself I would give them to you when you returned."

"Oh?" He weighed the stack in his hands. There *were* quite a few.

"You don't have to read them, at least not right now. Any time," I hastened to add.

"No. No—I have time. I'll read them now."

"Now?"

I waited in my room, my stomach in knots. Finally, he appeared.

"Let's go for a walk in the gardens," he suggested.

I jumped up. The public park behind the Luxembourg Palace was lovely.

Outside, the air was crisp, the world golden. The trees and shrubs had begun to turn. We meandered silently for a time, avoiding the shady paths, where whores practiced their trade (and men relieved themselves).

"Would you like to see my new horse?" Eugène asked. "The riding school isn't far."

"You have a new horse?"

"The General got him for me. He's a beauty."

"I'd *love* to see him."

Pegasus was indeed a beauty. A thoroughbred, over sixteen hands, with perfect conformation. I stroked his chest, pressed my face into his neck to inhale his horsey scent. "I've envied you your horses, you know," I confessed. Horsemanship was considered an important part of a boy's education, but our father felt that it was a waste of money to buy a girl a horse.

"You can ride Pegasus if you like," Eugène said, pulling a burr out of the horse's mane. "So long as you promise not to race," he added with a grin.

I made a sad clown face.

"Chouchoute," he began, "your letters, they . . ."

I held my breath. I thought of some of the things I'd written that I'd never thought he'd read.

"They made me cry," he said.

I swallowed. "I'm *sorry*."

He smiled his big-hearted grin. "I was touched. Truly." He leaned over to peck me on the cheek. "Thank you for being such a wonderful sister."

We walked back through the gardens, talking and sharing memories. He suggested that we go to Place du Trône-Renversé that afternoon, to see where Father died. "It might be easier for the two of us to go together," he said.

Eugène choked up as we dodged horses and carriages, crossing the busy Place du Trône-Renversé to place a bouquet of flowers in the center.

"These won't last long here," he said, pulling me back from a cantering rider.

We dashed back to safety, and stood for a moment as he explained where he and Aunt Fanny had stood. "There was a fearsome thunderstorm that day."

"I remember that," I said.

"We got soaked, but then it cleared."

He explained what direction the trundle had come carrying Father and the other prisoners, their hands tied behind their backs.

"He was one of the last," Eugène said, swallowing. "*Dieu merci*, it went quickly."

"You said he was brave," I said.

He nodded, blinking, not trusting himself to speak.

"Thank you for bringing me here," I said, taking his arm as we turned to head back. "I know it can't have been easy."

"It's important not to forget," he said

"And to forgive," I said.

He squeezed my hand. *Yes*. "You know, Father used to brag about you."

"Whatever for?"

"He was amazed by the way you could dance, for one thing. You could do intricate steps at a very young age. And he was charmed by your quickness, too. He thought you were exceptionally bright."

I stared up at the sky, the clear blue sky. "You're not just saying that?" Skeptically.

He scoffed. "Trustworthy, honest me?"

I loved my big brother so much.

VI

CHANGE

3 Brumaire – 20 Brumaire, An 8
(25 October – 11 November, 1799)

THE RIDER CARD: NEWS OF CHANGE

REUNION

❖

"Your mother and brother wish to see you," Mimi informed me the next day, breathless from climbing the stairs. "Your cousin's husband is here, Captain Lavalette."

"Antoine Lavalette? He's back in Paris?"

I grabbed a shawl and rushed downstairs. Antoine was sitting with Maman and Eugène by the fire.

"How good to see you, Captain Lavalette." It was true, as Ém claimed, that he was a rather ugly little man, quite round.

"I am anxious to have news of my wife," he said, clutching his worn felt hat.

Maman glanced over at Eugène, who had curiously decided that it was the perfect time to polish his riding boots. (And he never polishes his boots.) "Eugène, did you say anything to Captain Lavalette?" she asked.

"About?"

"About Ém."

Aïe. Ém's husband hadn't been told?

"Is there a problem?" Antoine asked.

Maman inclined her head in my direction.

Why did I have to be the one?

She gave me dagger-eyes.

"Captain Lavalette," I began, "last summer—" I swallowed.

"This last summer, Émilie had the misfortune to come down with . . ." There was nothing to do but to *say* it. "The pox."

Antoine's cheeks turned scarlet. Eugène reached over to give his friend a companionable pat on the shoulder.

"Fortunately, she recovered fully," Maman rushed to explain.

"*Grâce à Dieu*," Antoine exclaimed.

"Although she does have some scarring," Maman warned, touching a finger to each of her cheeks. "On her face." She made a gentle, but regretful grimace. "Also, you should know that she has become . . ." Maman paused, biting her lip.

I knew what she was trying to say. "Ém's become melancholic," I offered. That was a kind way of putting it.

"It will be my goal in life to make her happy," Antoine said, his eyes gleaming.

"We are planning to go to our country place tomorrow," Maman said, visibly touched, "but we could stop by the Institute. Perhaps you would like to come with us?"

Antoine's face flushed with gratitude.

We set out early for Montagne-du-Bon-Air, the General, Antoine, Maman and I in the carriage, Eugène riding beside us on Pegasus. Antoine was wearing a jacket he'd borrowed from my brother, regrettably too big on him. He was clutching a parcel—a gift for Ém, I guessed.

It had rained in the night and the roads were rutted, so it was noon by the time we arrived at the Institute, much jostled. Maîtresse met us in the foyer, wearing her black cape.

"General Bonaparte!" She made a deep curtsy.

Claire, hovering behind her with an empty basket, followed her example, looking terrified.

"We weren't expecting you," Maîtresse said, giving Claire her cloak and whispering instructions. "Come in, come in!"

"Forgive us for stopping by unexpectedly," Maman said, "but we're going to Malmaison"—she glanced at the General, who was examining the notices on the board—"and thought we'd stop by for a quick visit."

"Always a pleasure," Maîtresse assured her.

"Eugène is here too," I said, warmly embracing Maîtresse. "He's seeing to his horse."

I had been away from the Institute for seventeen days—seventeen and three-quarters—but it seemed like forever. In that time, Eugène and the General had returned from Egypt, Maman and I had raced south to try to meet them (and failed), the General had tried to throw Maman out of her house and then peace had been restored (if you could call living in a house with soldiers coming and going at all hours peaceful).

"You remember Captain Lavalette?" Maman said, gesturing Antoine forward.

"Of course," Maîtresse said. "Émilie has been awaiting your return." (This made me wince.) "Come, make yourselves comfortable in the reception room," she said. "I'll go fetch her."

"I'll get her, Maîtresse Campan," I quickly offered. Ém would need a warning.

It felt strange going up the stairs to my room, greeting teachers and friends at every turn. On the landing, I nearly bumped into Citoyen Jadin, who was startled to see me.

"You're here," he said, bundled in his gray, moth-eaten shawl.

"Just briefly," I said, taken aback. The pendulum clock struck the hour. Girls began streaming out of rooms, chattering two by two. "I never got a chance to thank you, Citoyen Jadin."

"Whatever for?"

"My award?" Did he not remember? "For piano, at the annual *Exercice*."

"Oh." He seemed distracted. "Yes."

"Citoyen Jadin?" someone called out from below—Nurse Witch, it sounded like. "I can see you now."

"Coming," he answered with a cough.

I watched as he left, a slight figure making his way down the spiral stairs, one hand on the railing.

I turned and headed on up to the Fearsome room. Ém looked up from her desk. "Hortense!" She stood to embrace me. "Mouse just left for her drawing lesson. Are you staying?"

I made a sad face. "We're going to Malmaison. Maman, the General and—and Captain Lavalette."

Ém sat down on her narrow bed in the corner.

"Ém, he loves you."

"He's ugly," she burst out, the scars on her face inflamed.

"At least give him a chance."

"I will *not* see him."

I heard a light rap on the door. "Aren't you and Émilie coming down?" Maman asked.

"She refuses," I said in a low voice.

"She won't come?"

"I don't think so," I said, standing aside.

Maman sat down at the foot of Ém's bed. "Are you afraid?" she asked softly.

"No!"

"What is it then?"

"I don't want to be married to him. I wish he were dead."

I glanced at Maman in chagrin.

"Émilie Louise Beauharnais," Maman said slowly, "you owe it to your husband to at least speak to him."

"Eugène is here too," I said, to tempt her.

Antoine was sitting by a window sipping coffee. A china plate of chocolate madeleines had been set out on the low table before him. My mouth watered seeing the delicious madeleines, and I looked away. I'd made a vow to forsake them forever if God spared Ém.

Antoine glanced up at us hopefully, spots of cream on his mustache. His eyes filled to see his wife's scarred face. She'd entered without letting down her veil, as if intentionally to repulse.

"So, it's true, you've been poxed," the General said.

Ém stared at the toes of her boots. "Yes, General Bonaparte, sir." She glanced over at Eugène. She hadn't seen him since he'd left for Egypt, a year and a half before.

My brother managed to hide his dismay. "Your husband saved my life," he said, embracing her. "Several times." (Which alarmed me anew. How many times had Eugène's life been at risk?)

"Saved his hide," the General said, tapping his foot.

"Captain Lavalette?" Maman glanced at the parcel he was clutching. "You have something for our niece?"

"Oh. Yes!" Antoine pulled up the coat sleeves and approached Ém. I feared he was going to attempt to kiss her hand, but wisely he refrained. Shifting from foot to foot, he told her how grateful he was that her life had been spared.

"Thank you," she said, but not meeting his gaze.

Awkwardly, he presented her with a gilt-edged book bound in leather—a novel, *The Sorrows of Young Werther,* by the German writer Goethe, translated into French.

"A good pick," the General said.

"I told Antoine how much you love to read," Eugène said.

I squirmed, knowing that the novel was about a man who loved a woman who loved another man.

A triangle sounded. "I must go," Ém said, lowering her veil.

"Sometimes it is best to give a bride time, Captain Lavalette," Maîtresse said, breaking the awkward silence. "I know you have been married for well over a year—"

"Soon it will be a year and a half," Antoine said, his hand over his heart.

Maîtresse bowed her head. "But you and Émilie have only known each other for a few days, in truth."

Maman sat forward. "And now, with the misfortune of her altered visage, she is rather overwhelmed." She glanced at the General, who was pacing, anxious to go. She pulled on her gloves. "It is not uncommon in such cases, particularly for a girl."

"Time will, as it is said, heal," Maîtresse said in an effort to be encouraging.

I doubted that it would be so easily solved. In truth, I was angry at my cousin, her cold, cruel heart.

"May I?" I asked Maîtresse, reaching for the plate of chocolate madeleines. I offered the plate to Eugène, and then took one for myself, breaking my vow.

CHOICES

"Would it be possible for Hortense to stay longer?" Maîtresse asked Maman as everyone prepared to depart.

Yes! I had yet to even see Mouse.

"My driver could deliver her to Malmaison before the evening meal," Maîtresse suggested.

"That would be lovely," Maman said with a smile my way. "Hortense has been missing her friends."

As soon as everyone had left, Maîtresse invited me up to her study. "Just for a little chat," she said.

I welcomed the opportunity, in truth, for there was much on my mind.

"I'm afraid time will not heal Ém," I confided, once settled cozily on her divan. "She wants nothing to do with Captain Lavalette."

"Does she love another?" Maîtresse asked, pouring us both a coffee.

I sat back, astonished by her blunt question.

"Actually, angel, it's not hard to guess that she harbors a passion for the General's brother Louis."

I glanced away.

"I *see*," she said with a sly smile, noting my response. "Now I must ask you something delicate." She stirred in several spoonfuls of sugar.

I flushed, suspecting what that question was going to be—and I was right, for she asked, "Was Émilie's marriage ever consummated?"

I shook my head no, my cheeks burning. I was surprised Maîtresse didn't know.

"Ah—in that case, it's possible she could get an annulment and remarry."

Marry Louis? Even if he wanted to marry Ém—which it was clear he did not—the Clan would never allow it. "I don't think so, Maîtresse Campan. After she got the pox, Louis wouldn't speak to her."

Maîtresse put a hand over her heart. "Oh, the poor girl."

"And who would marry her? Maman told me that the General offered her hand to a number of men, but they all refused because her father was an émigré." *And* because Ém's parents were divorced. *And* because she was penniless, without any dowry whatsoever.

"I know. Your mother consulted with me at the time. We were both pleased with Captain Lavalette. Has Émilie discussed any of this with you?"

"Not really." Only her contempt for her husband.

"Well, it's time." Maîtresse rang for her maid. "Summon Émilie Beauharnais," she told Claire. "Angel, I'm going to have to speak bluntly," she said softly, her hand touching mine. "We all love Émilie—she has rare and wonderful qualities—but she is not the sort of girl who could manage to live independently."

Ém appeared, looking lifeless. As angry as I was, my heart went out to her.

Maîtresse gestured for her to sit on the wooden stool. "Émilie, you disappoint me," she began. (I cringed.) "You have been cruel to a worthy man. Have I not taught you the importance of basic civilities?"

Ém stared down at her clasped hands. "I cannot remain married to a man I do not love, Maîtresse Campan."

"That's romantic nonsense. How do you intend to feed yourself?

You can't expect your aunt and the General—much less your grandparents—to provide for you forever. Without any means of support, what are your choices?"

Ém remained silent, her head bent. It wasn't that she didn't know the answer. We all knew that a girl had two respectable choices in life: to become a wife or a governess. Before the Revolution, a girl might have chosen to become a nun, but the nunneries had all been closed down, so that was no longer a possibility. Most unmarried girls lived with their families forever, but Émilie did not have a family to go to. Her mother and stepfather wanted nothing to do with her, which was why my mother had had to provide for her.

"Allow me to clarify," Maîtresse said, offering Ém a cup of lukewarm coffee, which she sullenly declined. "If you aren't married, your reasonable choice would be to become a governess. You would live in some isolated château, condemned to eat alone, for you'd be considered too lowly to join the family and too educated to join the kitchen staff. You would converse only with your charges, who would do everything to thwart you. Too, I would be remiss if I did not caution you that as a governess, you would likely be forced—quite literally, I'm afraid—to allow the intimate attentions of the various men of the household."

Ém looked up, shaken—as I was. Stories of girls being forced were whispered, but rarely openly acknowledged. I had assumed such accounts were fabrications.

"There is, of course, one other vocation an unmarried woman may choose, but I don't think I need to spell it out."

I grimaced. No—she did not.

"I've made sure that all my girls are taught logic, and I'm sure you can deduce the conclusion. You are old enough now to use reason to consider what you will do: make amends with a husband who cares for you very much, become a governess—or a whore."

And with that, we were dismissed.

Mouse jumped up from her desk as Ém and I came into our room. "Hortense! Are you coming back to school?"

"I'm sorry, *no*," I said, embracing her. "And I'm afraid I can't stay long."

Ém pushed by me and threw herself down on her bed.

Mouse looked at me. "What happened?"

I closed the door and leaned against it. As stubborn and unreasonable as my cousin was being, she just wanted to be happy. Was that a crime?

"Captain Lavalette was here, and—"

"Your husband, Ém?" Mouse said.

Ém buried her face in her pillow.

"And she got a talk about her choices," I told Mouse.

"From my aunt?"

I nodded. "A talk about *no* choices."

Mouse and I did our best to comfort Ém. I felt sad for her, but for Mouse and me, too, all girls. I felt such excitement about life sometimes, about all the things I wanted to do—be a composer, a painter, an actress! Maîtresse believed girls should get a good education, but what was the point, in truth? Did it really always come down to only two possibilities, to marry or be a governess, and nothing more? Some women tried to support themselves in other ways, true—by painting portraits, for example (as Citoyenne Godefroid, one of the instructors at the Institute, did)—but they were publicly ridiculed, considered an embarrassment to their families. Our true options seemed narrow indeed.

At last, with our affection and jokes, Ém managed a smile. I was going to suggest the Game of Hope, but refrained. What if a dire prediction emerged—or a card suggested something about Louis? It was too risky.

DECEIT

The first day back in Paris, I was summoned into the General's office. He shut the door behind him with a thwack. I felt as if I had been invited into a lion's lair—a very messy lion's lair, for there were maps, newspapers and journals everywhere, the waste bins overflowing. I hung back by the door.

"Sir, Hortense, I'm not going to attack you," the General said, as if he could read my thoughts. (*Could* he read thoughts? I wondered.) "However, I am far from pleased." He scratched at a boil on his neck. "I saw Caroline at Joseph's this morning. She doesn't want to return to the Institute." His nostrils flared. He looked like an angry bull. "*Ever*. And all because you are cruel to her. She says you make her life there a living Hell."

All I could manage to say was, "*Caroline* said that?" How could she!

"You disappoint me," he said, cracking his knuckles. "I thought you'd be able to help her."

"But I do," I said in my defense. This in a pathetic, squeaky voice.

"Yet you belittle her efforts and mock her in front of others?"

"That's not true!"

"*Basta!*" He held up his hand to silence me. "You stand warned."

Shortly after, Caroline arrived with her brothers for their *décadi* visit.

"Well, if it isn't *angel*," she said with a mocking tone, joining me in the upstairs salon.

I grunted, taking up my work basket. *Courage.* "You told the General I'm cruel to you at school." She had an extraordinary command of her emotions, for she betrayed not a blush. (I envied her that.) "*Why?*" I heard men laughing downstairs. I lowered my voice. "I try to help you."

"Like when you *hit* me?"

"You called my mother a whore!"

"I'm not the only one."

"That's not the point!" I tried to rein in my anger over the falsehoods people spread. "I helped correct your perspective in drawing class. I read things to you. So why did you lie to the General?"

She smiled. (*Smiled.*) "I have my reasons."

"Perhaps you would do me the kindness of sharing," I said.

"I don't want to go to school, that's why."

"So? Tell the General." Most girls didn't go to school at all. They stayed at home to help their mothers.

"I have! Many times. But he always insists I stay because he thinks *you're* so great."

This last with such mocking scorn I almost laughed.

"He says I must study and work hard so I can be like *you.*"

Well. That was a surprise. "That would be hurtful," I admitted. My own father had always praised Eugène, who was a terrible student.

"I don't care about that so much. I just never want to go back."

"But then what would you do?" I couldn't understand why anyone would want to leave the Institute.

"Easy! I'll get married."

"You're betrothed?" She would have needed her family's approval. How could I not have known?

"Almost," she said, reddening.

What did that mean, *almost?* "And so who is the lucky man?"

She didn't notice my mocking tone, for in a rush of candor, she declared that she had been moonsick in love with General Murat for some time.

Baby-faced Joachim Murat, with his thick lips and greasy ringlets? He was manly in a coarse, swaggering fashion, a giant of a man with a penchant for dressing flamboyantly—and for seducing women, it was whispered. Then I remembered how loudly Caroline laughed at his rather stupid jests, and how she marveled anew *every* time he displayed the scars on his face from the bullet that had gone in one cheek and out the other.

"And *he* loves *me*," she said, clasping her hands under her chin.

I was skeptical. General Murat was rumored to "love" a number of women, mostly actresses. "I hope you haven't been foolish." It was in Caroline's very nature to be foolish.

"Nothing below here," she boasted, her hands at her waist.

That was rather far down!

I heard Mimi and a maid chattering on the landing. "You must not give your favors so easily," I whispered. To keep a boy's attention, a girl had to hint at reward—but never more.

"That's why I told him we must be married to swive."

"Caroline!"

"Joachim likes it when I talk like that." She grinned. "He likes it a lot."

"You must be careful!" Once a girl lost her virtue, she was lost to the world. Nurse Witch had cautioned us against this many a time.

"But I want to be his wife so bad!" She pressed her hands over her heart.

"Well, he must first propose," I said, bewildered by the turn of events. Suddenly I had become Caroline's confidante; I was no longer her enemy. "Go down on one knee and all that."

"I've hinted and hinted and hinted." She threw up her hands in frustration. "He's dumb as an ox."

I had to agree.

"Someone has to put the idea in his head," she said. "He's often here. You could say something to him."

Me? "Usually a girl's parents approach a man's parents," I suggested. "Or the other way around."

"But his parents live far away, God knows where. My father is dead and my mother doesn't speak French. It would be easy for you to say something to him, put the idea in his thick head. All you'd have to do is mention it."

I paused to consider. Maman had taught me the all-essential skill of give-and-take. If I did a favor for Caroline, what might she do for me in return?

"I'll say something to General Murat," I suggested slowly, tapping my nails, "if you tell the General that you told him a lie about me."

She winced. "He'll kill me."

Caroline came out of the General's office looking as though she'd been crying.

"I did it," she said. "I admitted my lie. You owe me."

"Did he punish you?" I almost felt sorry for her.

She shook her head no. "I worked up some tears and told him how hard it was being at a school with so many smart girls, but that the truth was that you were different from all the others, understanding and always trying to be kind, and—"

"Thank you."

"—and that sometimes you helped me cheat on tests."

"Caroline!"

"He said to tell you that he wants to talk to you."

The General? Oh no.

———

"General Bonaparte has asked to see me," I informed the General's secretary.

"You are not on the list," Citoyen Bourrienne said in his silly high voice, examining a ledger.

Then who should come out of the General's study but *Christophe*. "Ah, Citoyenne Beauharnais," he said, standing to one side. "The General is expecting you."

Heart pounding, I curtsied to The Most Handsome Man on Earth and glided by, close enough to catch a hint of his citrus scent.

The General stood to greet me. He was wearing the leather breeches Maman had borrowed for him from her actor friend Talma. (She found it challenging getting the General to dress properly.) "Hortense, I owe you an apology," he said, reaching out to pinch my ear.

"Thank you, General Bonaparte," I said, gasping. His pinches *hurt*.

"I should have suspected Caroline was up to her usual mischief."

"We have made amends, General," I told him. Sort of.

"Good, because she's moving in with us."

6 Brumaire, An 8
The Institute
My dearest friend,
Maîtresse told me that Caroline is to stay with you *in Paris. Won't it be awkward? Are you speaking to each other?*
My sympathies. Must run—more later!
Your Mouse

Caroline's two big trunks arrived well before she did. Mimi had them placed in the walkway between my room and Eugène's, next to his valet's cot. "She's going to have to sleep in your room," Maman told me.

"But where will she fit?" My bed was tiny. There was hardly room for me.

"Bonaparte has a folding camp bed she can use."

Eugène brought the camp bed up and assembled it in moments. "I've had practice," he said, but even so, I was impressed, because it was complex. The frame was metal and supported a mattress and drapes. Once hung with the green damask curtains, the bed looked like a little tent.

I stretched out on it after Agathe made it up. I was surprised how comfortable it was. I decided to kindly offer Caroline my bed.

"But I want the camp bed," Caroline said, contrary as usual. And thus began our first conflict.

I took refuge in the sitting room outside Maman's bedchamber as Caroline settled in, covering my bed with her petticoats and gowns and stringing her stockings from the rafters in the passageway. How was this ever going to work?

I woke screaming that first night. Eugène and his valet came running, their dark forms and the unfamiliar dark shape of the camp bed frightening me even more. It took me a few moments to recover my wits.

"I'm sorry. It was a bad dream." About our father.

Luckily, Caroline was a sound sleeper—she didn't stir.

I was up early the next morning to help Maman and Mimi. Caroline didn't show up until nine, arriving for breakfast in her nightdress and with her hair down, yet her cheeks and lips pinked.

"Where are the men?" she asked, glancing about. Where was Joachim Murat, she meant.

"They went early to the riding school." As always. Eugène, Joachim, Christophe and some of the other aides went most every morning.

Just then Maman came in from the garden. "Caroline, there you are. You were comfortable last night?"

"Josephine?" It was the General, calling out from his study. (I still couldn't get used to him calling Maman *Josephine*.)

"Darling?" Maman called back. (They were disgustingly affectionate, even in public.)

"What time is my meeting with Barras?"

"This afternoon at two. There is roast chicken here for you."

He came charging into the dining room, but stopped abruptly on seeing Caroline.

"Good morning, dear brother," she said, all innocence.

"Go back upstairs and dress properly," he barked.

Caroline swiped two sweet rolls off a platter and sauntered off.

"Since when is she allowed to wear face paint?" he demanded, and Mother just sighed.

PREPARATIONS
FOR A BALL

❧

9 Brumaire, An 8
The Institute
My dearest friend,
    It's said that Citoyenne Recamier is giving a big ball in eight days.
That's perfect for you and Caroline because you're not due to come back
to school until the following day. You probably know all about it, but
in case you don't, it's to be held at her Château de Bagatelle in the Bois
de Boulogne. I gather that most everyone is going—everyone but Ém
and me, that is. I'm not of age yet, and Ém fears her husband might be
there and then she would have to dance with him. The poor man
comes out to the school every décadi, *but she still hardly nods to him,*
in spite of my aunt's scolding.
    How are you and Caroline getting on? Should we be jealous?
    Your very own Mouse

Caroline and I were thrilled to find out that there was going to be a
big ball, Caroline especially so after Eugène told us that Joachim
would be going. *And* Christophe, he said, but I pretended that that
was of no concern to me. Of course I couldn't help but think of the
fortune Citoyenne Lenormand had predicted, that something like a
ball would be significant for me in matters of the heart.

    Caroline and I immediately set to making shoe roses and hair
ornaments to match our gowns. It was good for us to have an

activity to do together. Maman, who loved to see us agreeable, gave us each a pair of cast-off scented gloves.

Caroline even asked me to teach her how to dance. I found a perfect piece by Bach that had a sarabande followed by the bourrée and then a gigue. It was an excellent way for her to learn all the forms. She liked the gigue because it was "bouncy." (And because it showed off her big breasts.)

After our second session, she persuaded me to sneak into Maman's dressing room where we experimented with her rouges and powders. "You look much better that way," she told me. "Not so washed out." I was careful to scrub it all off before Maman returned.

Other than schooling his horse Pegasus at the riding school, Eugène had little to do most days but await the General's orders, opening the door for whomever the General's secretary officiously cleared through. He was bored with this unexciting life, so I often sat with him. One morning he told me he'd been teaching Joachim and Christophe the bourrée in preparation for the ball.

"How are they doing?" I asked (thinking of Christophe, of course).

"Well, Joachim is . . . expressive, let's say." Eugène never had a mean thing to say about anyone, but he did kind of snicker.

"And Christophe?"

He paused to consider. "He already knows most of the steps—"

Well, of course he would, I thought with a smile.

"—although his injured leg proves a bit of a problem."

"Is it healing?" I asked, seeing an opportunity to find out more without it looking suspicious.

"Fairly well, he says."

"Did it happen at the same time you were injured?"

"It was earlier that same day," he said.

"Not a good day," I said.

"*Not* a good day," he said with a wry smile. "My injury looked fatal, yet I recovered rather quickly. Christophe's looked relatively minor, but it is taking much longer to heal. He will likely always walk with a limp."

"War injuries are something to be proud of," I said.

I would have been happy to sit chatting about Christophe all afternoon, but the General's study door opened and Eugène leapt to his feet.

As Caroline and I prepared for the ball, I began to notice how the adults kept going off into corners whispering. Men came and went at all hours and disappeared with the General into his study.

"Is something going on?" I asked Eugène.

"I'm organizing a breakfast party for my officer friends," he said.

I was quite sure that all this activity had nothing to do with a breakfast party.

"It was the General's suggestion," he said.

That struck me as truly suspicious. The General disliked parties.

"Which is why I want it to be perfect. I've invited a comic actor from the Comédie Française to entertain. Milk-bread, black bread or rye bread—which do you think?"

"Offer all of them. Can Caroline and I join you?" Both Christophe and Joachim would no doubt be there.

He patted me on the head as if I were a little girl. "It's only us men," he said.

Unfair!

11 Brumaire, An 8
The Institute
My dear angel,
This is a brief note to let you know that I am delighted that you and Caroline are getting along so well. I like your suggestion very

much. *I will see to it, and rest assured that I will honor your request to keep it secret. Family is so very important.*

Maîtresse

Five days before the ball, the seamstress arrived with our gowns, which she'd made out of Maman's castoffs. Caroline's was purple, festooned with sequins and ribbons, and mine a deep blue, fashionably simple, of a very light wool, as suited the season. It was beautiful—and just a bit *daring.*

Caroline showed me how to make my breasts look bigger by tucking stockings under them. Maman took one look at me and told me to remove them immediately. I was mortified, and Caroline's muffled giggles only made it worse.

12 Brumaire, An 8
The Institute
My dearest friend,

Another bed has been installed in our room! My aunt won't say who it's for—she only smiles mysteriously. Ém and I are not happy about this, as you can imagine. How can we share secrets if a stranger is in here with us?

Your Mouse

Note—Guess what has come back to town? The Fantasmagorie! *It turned out that the girl who was thought to have fainted from fright of spirits had imbibed rather too much in the way of liquid spirits. Ha!*

After reading Mouse's letter, I couldn't help but wonder again about the spirit show, the *Fantasmagorie.* Intellectually, I didn't believe spirits existed, but if they did, would I want to see one? Would I want to see Father? Wasn't it bad enough that he appeared to me in dreams the way he did?

MYSTERIES

❧

I was in bed when I heard someone cantering into the courtyard. Quietly, without waking Caroline, I peeked out the window to see if it might be Christophe. Alas, it was the General. Then I heard a loud bang downstairs, and what sounded like something breaking. *Aïe!*

I slipped down the stairs and crouched on the bottom step in my nightclothes.

"Are you eavesdropping?" Eugène asked, coming down the stairs behind me.

"I heard a bang."

"I heard it too," he said.

"What's going on?"

"I'm not sure," he admitted.

The mystery was soon solved. Mimi told us that the General, angry about something Director Barras had said, had punched the wall with his fist and toppled a china vase. The next morning he was glowering, his hand bandaged.

The days before the ball were torture, especially for Caroline. She spent hours plotting.

"I'll pretend to love Christophe, and then, when Joachim is on the verge of challenging Christophe to a duel—"

"Why would he do that?" I asked.

She regarded me with disdain. "Because he's a man."

"Not all men are so foolish." Although Joachim well might be.

"Listen! At that point you're to casually mention that when a man proposes marriage, that solves everything."

"Solves what?"

"Solves who I belong to."

Did marriage mean that a girl belonged to a man? Did Maman belong to the General? I didn't think so.

"Caroline, I can't be part of such a scheme."

"You owe me!"

Late that night, long after candles had been blown out, I heard arguing. The voices were coming from Maman's bedchamber below. Maman and the General? That surprised me because they never so much as spoke a cross word to each other.

The only thing I could make out was the General saying something about *surviving*, and then something about *perishing*.

What was going on? (*Safe now?*)

Then all became silent, but even so, I couldn't sleep.

The following evening, while Caroline was visiting her sister Pauline, I joined everyone in the salon: Maman, the General, Eugène, Christophe, Director Gohier and Citoyen Fouché, the Minister of Police. Maman was sitting on the divan between Director Gohier and Fouché. I took the cushioned stool close to the hearth and arranged my skirts, aware of Christophe standing with my brother near the door.

Picking out my best embroidery to work on, I heard Director Gohier ask Fouché if there was anything new happening.

"Oh, just the usual nonsense," Fouché said, picking his teeth.

I cast a shy glance at Christophe and he gave me a little wink. A wink! I pretended to concentrate on my needlework, smiling in spite of myself.

"What about?" Director Gohier asked. He was sitting rather close to Maman.

The Minister of Police shrugged. "Oh, just something regarding a conspiracy."

Maman gasped. "*Conspiracy?*"

Of course then everyone in the room went silent, even Eugène, who had been telling Christophe about his breakfast party. All the while the General was leaning against the mantel, grinning and saying nothing. He hardly ever smiled, so that struck me as curious.

"What conspiracy?" Director Gohier demanded.

Fouché took out a battered tin snuffbox and tapped it with his yellow, pointed thumbnail. "*The* conspiracy," he said.

That was when Maman "suggested" I go to my room.

I lingered at the foot of the stairs, furious to have been treated like a child—especially in front of Christophe.

"But you can rely on me," I heard Fouché say. "I know what's going on. If there were a conspiracy to overthrow the government, heads would be rolling by now."

Then a man arrived. "We're waiting," I overheard him tell Maman.

Waiting for *what?*

The day before the ball, Caroline and I had our coffee and rolls in my room. I felt I was going to die from both dread and anticipation. What if Christophe asked me to dance? But then again, what if he *didn't?*

We'd been drawing a card from the Game of Hope every morning, to see what our day might bring. I went first because Caroline had gone first the day before. I got the Whip card, which meant conflict. "I don't know what to make of that," I said, slipping the card into middle of the deck and then shuffling.

Caroline cut the deck, hovered over the possibilities and picked a card. She frowned. She'd got the Whip card as well.

"How strange," I said. "Double conflict?"

And *that* was when Maman came into my room.

"Girls, I'm afraid that you're going to have to go back to school."

I looked at her, puzzled. So? We were scheduled to return to the Institute the day after next, after the ball.

"The carriage is being hitched for you now."

"But the ball is tomorrow," I said.

"This is important, I'm afraid."

"We're going to that ball. You can't send us away!" Caroline exploded. (I cringed.)

"This is Bonaparte's order."

Caroline headed for the door. "I'll have a word with him."

Maman caught her arm. "He's left for the morning."

Caroline yanked away. "I refuse to leave."

"You have no choice, my dear," Maman said, trying to be gentle, I could tell, but not too successfully.

"We'll stay at my brother Joseph's then."

"Bonaparte doesn't want either of you anywhere near Paris right now."

I glanced at Caroline and then back at my mother. There was more to this than was being said.

"Pack up your trunks," Maman said. "Mimi has put aside some sweetmeats and figs for you."

"You'll be safe, Maman?" I asked fearfully.

"Of course," she said, but with a tremor in her voice.

WEST TEN

❖

Some of the younger students were playing in the school courtyard, in spite of the bitter cold.

"Hortense!" one cried out, and then they all rushed to embrace me.

"Caroline too," I whispered, and they did as they were told, although with somewhat less enthusiasm.

Caroline pinched their ears, a habit she had picked up from the General. "Ow!" they shrieked.

"Citoyennes?" the school porter asked, hefting Caroline's trunk onto his shoulder. "Where does this one go?"

"East Seven," Caroline told him.

"No," I informed him. "West Ten."

"That's my trunk," Caroline protested.

I grinned. "I know, but now you're with *us*."

"What do you mean?"

"What I said: you're with us now, in West Ten, with me, Ém and Mouse."

Caroline flushed, but with anger or pleasure, I couldn't tell.

"That is, if you want to," I added, unsure. "Don't you?" Had I made a mistake?

"What if—?" She waited for a group of students to pass by before leaning in close to say, "What if they don't want me?"

"Don't worry," I said, taking her hand and practically dragging her up the stairs.

———

Mouse and Ém regarded Caroline with surprise.

"I'd like to introduce you to our new roommate." I smiled at Caroline, who looked terrified.

"So that's who the extra bed is for," Ém said.

"We've been wondering," Mouse said.

"Caroline and I are sort of sisters—and now we're even friends."

"Then welcome!" Mouse said, the first to embrace our new member.

Did I see tears in Caroline's eyes?

We stayed up far too late talking about a million things, but mostly about Caroline's "secret" love of General Joachim Murat and her grief over not being able to go to the ball the next day.

"After all your hopes and dreams," I said sympathetically. And *mine*.

"Why did you get sent back early?" Mouse wanted to know.

"We don't know why," I said.

"Her mother wouldn't say," Caroline said with annoyance.

"Tante Rose made you leave?" Ém asked.

I nodded. "She said that the General wanted us out of Paris."

"That's strange," Mouse said.

Yes, I thought. *Quite.*

Before we put out the candles, Ém warned Caroline that I sometimes woke up screaming.

"*Really* loud," Mouse said.

"It won't wake Caroline," I said.

"How do you know?" Caroline said.

"It happened once at my mother's house."

"In Paris? You screamed?" she asked.

I nodded.

"When I was there?"

"The first night. It's because of a scary dream I keep having."

"It's like she is haunted," Mouse said.

"Ghastly," Caroline said, but grinning. (She *liked* scary stories.)

"Speaking of haunted, guess what's back in town," Ém said.

"I wrote to you about it, Hortense," Mouse said.

"The *Fantasmagorie*?"

"The spirit show in Paris that everyone is talking about?" Caroline asked. "There's one here?"

"And it's not far at all," Mouse said. Her voice squeaked with excitement.

"I want to go!" Caroline said.

"I don't think my aunt would ever let me go to that type of thing," Mouse said.

"Or any of us," I said, torn between curiosity and dread.

The next day, the day of the Recamier ball, Caroline was determined to figure out a way to go to it. First, she tried to talk Citoyen Isabey into driving us back to Paris, but he wasn't going into the city that day. Then she tried to talk the stable hand into saddling two riding horses for us—"Just for an afternoon exercise," she lied. As if we could ride all the way to Paris! Fortunately, one of the riding horses had pulled up lame and an instructor needed the other one. I was relieved. We would have been seated at the Repentance Table for life.

"Let's think about how to get into the spirit show instead," I suggested, to distract her.

"I've got it," Caroline announced. The four of us—the Fearsome Foursome we were now calling ourselves—were huddled in our room during free time. Plotting. "We'll leave shortly after six. It's almost dark by then now. We won't go as a group, but two and two, and we'll wear hooded cloaks."

"Won't we be recognized?" Mouse asked.

"We'll be masked."

"But it's illegal to wear a mask at night," I said. It was one of a number of laws aimed at cutting down on all the crime. A person's face had to always be fully in view.

"We'll just say we're going to a ball in the old château," Caroline said.

"But it's abandoned," Ém said.

"Vagrants live there," she protested. "They must have parties too."

"But how would we leave school?" I asked. That was the hard part. The doors and gates were locked and guarded. Even the ground-floor windows had bars on them (to keep boys out, Maîtress claimed).

"We could go bundled in the laundry," Caroline said.

"But wouldn't we suffocate?" Mouse looked worried.

"I hadn't thought of that," Caroline admitted.

I shuffled the Game of Hope cards, asking: "What should we do?" I drew the Key card, which meant unlocking opportunity.

"Appeal to Maîtresse?" Ém looked doubtful.

"Maybe I should try," I suggested. "We can't go anywhere without her permission."

"Especially at night," Mouse said, shivering.

"I'm really getting along well with Caroline now," I told Maîtresse the following afternoon. We were seated on the divan in her familiar study.

"That shows maturity on your part," Maîtresse said, smiling her approval.

"I think of her as a sister," I said, knowing she would like that. "She badly wants to go to the spirit show in town," I added, bringing the conversation around to the purpose of my visit. "I promised her I'd talk to you about it. We were very much looking forward to going to Citoyenne Recamier's ball—"

"Is that not soon?"

"It was last night! Caroline has been miserable about missing it. If we could go to the *Fantasmagorie*, it would cheer her. And if Ém and Mouse came too, all the better. We're all of us getting to be friends."

Maîtresse looked at me thoughtfully, a china cup in her hand. "Do you think my niece is strong enough for something like that?"

"Oh yes," I assured her. If that was Maîtresse's concern, we were close to getting approval. "Mouse never faints anymore." That much was true. I took a sip of sugary coffee. "The *Fantasmagorie* is just a show, after all. I've been told that there's an exhibit of scientific curiosities, educational things. My mother wouldn't mind, I'm sure." This was likely true.

"How is your dear mother?" Maîtresse asked.

"She's preoccupied," I said truthfully. "There are meetings all the time, having to do with the General."

"What sort of meetings?" Maîtresse's tone was suspicious.

"Oh, just meetings with some of the Directors, Barras and Sieyès, mostly. And Director Gohier. And that other man—the Minister of Police?—Citoyen Fouché. I didn't pay much attention because I was busy with my studies." A lie!

"Curious that you would be sent back early, and so abruptly," Maîtresse observed with a frown.

"The General insisted on it. He wanted us out of Paris."

Maîtresse set down her cup with a clatter. "Angel, tell me, are your mother and the General well guarded?"

"Oh, yes." I nodded, smiling. (Thinking of one guard in particular.)

"Have there been any incidents? Anything to cause concern?"

"They had to come home from the theater the other night, before the performance had started," I offered.

"Why?" She sounded alarmed.

"Because everyone wouldn't stop cheering the General."

"Ah, the fervor of the populace," she said with a sigh.

The pendulum clock struck the hour.

"So?" I said with what I hoped was a winsome smile. "You don't object? You'll write us a note? For the show?" I reminded her (not mentioning spirits). "We wouldn't be gone long, and we'd all be together, so we'd be perfectly safe."

"You'll have to have a chaperone," she said with a distracted air.

"Ém will be with us," I offered. A married woman was considered a proper chaperone (although Ém hardly counted, I knew).

Maîtresse was staring at the portrait of the Queen. Had she heard me?

"Maîtresse?"

"Oh, yes," she said faintly, her hands over her heart. "Of course." She looked at me with tears in her eyes. "It does me good to see you girls getting along so well," she said, going to her work table and reaching for a quill. "Nothing is more important. My father used to say—"

I knew the story well, she told it all the time. "I know," I said, trying not to sound impatient. "Brittle sticks are strong when held together."

"Like a family," she said, handing me the note.

FANTASMAGORIE

❧

"We can go!" I announced, bursting into our room waving Maîtresse's letter of permission. We would need to show it to Citoyenne Hawk at the door and the caretaker at the gate.

Caroline, Ém and Mouse looked at me in disbelief. I had to laugh. They looked like ghosts, their faces covered in white paste.

"The spirit show?" Caroline asked without moving her lips.

"What about a chaperone?" Mouse mumbled.

"Ém will be with us."

"I'm to be your chaperone?"

"Ah, the married woman," Caroline said. "Handy."

"You smiled," Ém said.

"We're not supposed to," Mouse explained without moving her lips. "Or move our lips," she added.

"Fartleberry," Caroline cursed, feeling her left cheek. "It cracked."

"Fartleberry?" What did *that* mean?

"You know—the poop that hangs from the hairs around a man's butt-hole," Caroline said.

"Men have hair *there*?" Mouse's eyes went big in horror.

And then, of course, they laughed uncontrollably, cracking their masks.

There was a long lineup of people waiting to get into the *Fantasmagorie*, in spite of the threat of rain. The bells would soon ring seven, but it was already dark and unusually cold. Wisely, we had bundled in layers.

The line moved forward. "Here we go," Caroline exclaimed.

I stood close with my friends, starting to feel anxious. "Are you going to be all right?" I whispered to Mouse.

"Don't worry. I brought this," she said, showing me the vial of smelling salts she wore hanging from a ribbon around her neck.

"And I brought *this*," I said, showing her my rosary. "For protection," I said, tucking it back out of sight.

"Protection from what?" Ém asked, turning from the ticket window.

"Protection against the spirits of evil," Caroline said in her spooky ghost-story voice.

The ticket vendor laughed, but not merrily.

We stepped into a gallery displaying paintings and various exhibits. "Is *this* it?" Caroline demanded, crinkling up her nose. She hadn't expected it to be instructive.

I looked into an eyepiece that made things look big. I could see insects crawling around in soggy flour. Another one offered a close-up view of fleas.

"But where are the spirits?" Caroline asked impatiently.

"In there?" I pointed to a sign above a plank door: *Fantasmagorie*.

We shuffled in, holding on to each other, for it was black as pitch inside. An usher with a candle appeared and led us to a bench. We felt along it and sat huddled together.

"I'm terrified," Ém admitted.

"I'm fine," Mouse said, but with a tremor in her voice.

"Are you sure?" It was so dark. "We don't have to stay."

A voice boomed out of nowhere. "Citoyens and citoyennes, the spirits are gathering. The *Fantasmagorie* is about to begin." A man's white face appeared, illuminated by torchlight. "They are with us," he said solemnly.

I leaned across Ém. "Caroline?"

"She's not next to you?" Ém asked.

Had we lost her?

With grave ceremony, the man called forth the spirits of Virgil and Voltaire. *Aïe!* They looked so *real.*

"And now, for something more current," he said, throwing documents onto a burner. "These are reports pertaining to the massacres five years ago." His face looked ghoulish in the flickering light. "And these are denunciations . . ."

I felt a sudden chill. Had Father been denounced?

More flames! "And this is a list of suspects . . ."

Had Father been suspected?

The dark chamber filled with the scent of burning paper. Then three apparitions came into view, moving slowly toward us. One was aristocratic in dress. He was wearing white gloves.

Father? My heart jumped. *Could it be?*

And then everything went black.

The acrid smell of ammonia brought me to my senses.

"Hortense?" I heard Mouse hiss.

"Hortense?" It was Ém's soft voice.

I was stretched out on a bench. I struggled to rise, but I was too weak. Ém helped me sit up. Was it possible I'd seen my father? Seen him *whole*?

"You fainted," Mouse said.

"*I* fainted?"

"I had to use my salts." Mouse sounded pleased.

An usher stood over me with a lantern. "Citoyenne?"

"I'm fine," I assured him. I didn't want to get us in trouble.

"We can look after her," Ém said, holding my arm.

The door to the gallery opened, letting in light. With Ém's help I stood, a bit unsteadily. We walked toward the door, arms linked.

Once out of the musty, dank vault and through the two galleries, we stood outside, shivering in the cold.

"Where's Caroline?" Mouse said, pushing up her glasses.

"Good question," I asked. How could she have disappeared like that?

"What foolery," she said, appearing behind us.

Caroline!

"Where did you go?" I said.

"I was in back, behind the curtains. Did you see the man operating a box-like thing?"

"A box?" Ém said.

"You didn't see him?" Caroline asked.

"No. I fainted," I said.

Caroline frowned. "I thought Mouse was the one who fainted."

"It's a good thing I had salts," Mouse said.

"What do you mean, a box-like thing?" I asked Caroline.

"It was like a big lantern, but on wheels. A man put panes of glass into it with images painted on them, and then the images appeared on the gauze."

"You mean the ghosts?" Ém asked.

"They weren't ghosts. It was a trick."

"Caroline, we *saw* them," I said.

"What gauze?" Mouse asked.

"That curtain of gauze right in front of you. You couldn't see it through all the smoke? Which another man was busy *making*, by the way."

"It didn't smell like smoke," Ém said.

"Whatever it was, it was misty," Caroline said. "So clever!"

The crowd dispersing, we headed back toward school, stepping cautiously over the icy cobbles, watchful of the shadows.

Had it all been a hoax? I hadn't seen my father after all. The thought was crushing. I'd been foolish. Worse, I'd been naïve.

TERROR

❦

At the gates to the Institute, I showed Maîtresse's letter of permission to the night caretaker. Then a sleepy Citoyenne Hawk let us in the big door and her maid showed us up to our room, leading the way with her lantern.

Quickly, we changed into our nightshifts and caps and jumped shivering into our beds. I snuggled under my comforters, feeling for the bed-warmer with my toes, seeking comfort. I'd been elated, thinking I'd seen my father—seen him *whole*. I'd been played for a fool.

"Hortense?" It was Mouse. "Are you crying?" she whispered.

I wiped my cheeks on my bed linen. "A bit."

"Me too," she said.

"Me too," I heard Ém say.

"All right," I said with a quiet chuckle, "Into my bed, you two."

"Is there room for me?" Caroline asked from across the room.

"Of course!"

"We'll huddle," Mouse said.

"Let Caroline be in the middle," Ém said. "She's never been in a huddle."

"You've done this before?" Caroline asked, climbing in.

"In emergencies," I said.

"And *this* is an emergency?" she asked with an incredulous tone.

"We're sad." I pulled the blankets up over us all.

"Because of that show?"

"Sort of," I said.

From somewhere below a girl began screaming.

"Uh-oh," Ém said.

"Not again," Caroline said with a moan.

"Maybe the ghost is back." I meant it as a joke.

Caroline giggled. "I don't think so."

She sounded so sure, so pleased. "Why?" I asked.

"Because *I'm* the ghost," she said.

"What do you mean?" The girl below had stopped, to my relief.

"The ghost with a beard?" Ém asked.

Caroline sniggered. "That was just *me*."

"You!" Mouse squeaked.

"Caroline! You terrified the little girls," I said.

"That was the point!" She laughed.

"But you shouldn't have—the kids here, the teachers, Maîtresse, we've all been through so much, and . . . well, something like that, it—"

"You mean because of the Terror?"

Yes, because of the Terror. Because of the deaths that haunted us. Because even an ocean of tears would never bring a loved one back.

"I sometimes wonder what it was like for all of you." Caroline sounded almost sad.

I'd never considered how strange it must have been for her, an outsider. Ém, Mouse and I had all been through that terrible time. We'd seen what beasts humans could become. But Caroline was from another world. Her father was dead, true, but he'd had the grace to die naturally in his bed. He'd not been sent to the guillotine, reviled with spittle and jeers.

"Most everyone in this school saw awful things," Caroline went on, "yet it's as if it's a big secret. Why doesn't anyone ever talk about it?"

"It's because we're ashamed," Mouse said in the silence that followed.

Shame. The word surprised me with its truth. We had not cared whose head rolled, so long as it wasn't ours, or that of someone we loved.

"Why should *you* be ashamed?" Caroline demanded. "You didn't do anything wrong."

"We survived," Ém said.

I tried to put it into words, that awful feeling that was so often with me. "And maybe because we know how terrible people can be."

"Nights were the worst," Mouse said, her voice hushed.

"Because that's when they would come for you," I said. It chilled me to think of that sound, the pounding on the door in the dead of night.

"Oh, *scary,*" Caroline said.

"They came for my mother in the dark," Ém said.

"Mine, too," I said.

"Why didn't people just hide?" Caroline asked.

"You couldn't," Ém said. "They would stab knives through the bed covers to see if anyone was hiding under them."

"Marcelline in White has a scar from that," Mouse said. "From being stabbed in her bed."

"I didn't know that," Ém said.

"But the executions happened during the day," I said. To immense fanfare, the cheers of a crowd, a drum roll. "Which was worse, in a way."

"Did you ever see one?" Caroline asked.

"I was kept away." But it was impossible to keep out the smells. Deep gutters had to be dug around the square because of all the blood. "Eugène and I were staying with our aunt when our father was . . . when he was sent to the—"

"Your father was *beheaded*?" Caroline asked, awed.

How could she not have known? "Yes," I said. "Eugène and my aunt went—"

"Eugène *saw*?" Ém said. "How terrible."

"—but they didn't take me. They told me that they were going to the prison with provisions."

"Prisons were the worst," Ém said with feeling. She herself had gone to the prison her mother was in to try to save her.

"Maman once told me how awful it was in the Carmes," I said, "knowing that every day might be your last. The women kept one good dress for the day they would be taken away. They cut off their hair so that the blade would cut through their neck more easily. Men too."

We prayed for a clean cut, a fast cut, Maman had told me in a moment of despair. Botched executions were a horror. Eugène told me Father's had gone quickly. That was a comfort, of sorts.

"I thought short hair was the new fashion," Caroline said.

"It is now," I said.

We must have all fallen asleep, for the next thing I knew I was sitting upright, terrified by the sound of pounding on the school doors.

I cried out and Ém gasped. Mouse bolted upright in fright. It was so loud!

I could hear screaming from below. Little kids—a chorus of them.

I heard men's voices, the sound of horses in the courtyard. I sat up, trembling. Government officials had come to take us all away, throw us in prison, *execute* us.

"What the devil?" Caroline protested sleepily.

Maîtresse appeared at our door. She was shaking, her lantern light jumping around. Her maid, Claire, was behind her, carrying a firearm nearly as tall as she was.

"Don't worry, girls. I'll see to it," Maîtresse said, her voice atremble, and they hurried down the stairs.

Caroline crawled out of bed and threw on her fur-lined robe. Holding the night candle, she pried open the wooden shutters.

I crept out of bed and looked over her shoulder. It had rained—there were puddles everywhere, glistening in the moonlight. I could make out four men holding torches, their horses standing by. Hussars, they looked like, judging by their white breeches and tall plumed hats, their long swords.

"What's going on?" Caroline called down to the men in the courtyard below.

They looked up, surprised. "Citoyenne Bonaparte?" one of them called out. Caroline's Corsican accent identified her easily.

"Yes?" she answered, but guardedly.

"We're General Murat's men. He sent us to inform you of the most glorious news: your brother, General Bonaparte, is victorious!"

Caroline turned back to us in the room. "Joachim sent them to tell me!"

"Sent them to tell you what?" Mouse asked, still huddled in my bed with Ém.

"Something about Napoleon's victory."

"But a victory over *what*?" I demanded. What had the General done?

A CURIOUS GIFT

❖

A tight cluster of students stood shivering in their night robes at the foot of the spiraling stairs. I noticed Eliza among them. She offered Henry to a weeping younger student, who clutched him fearfully.

"Tell your commander he's never to do that again!" Maîtresse said, berating the four hussars who stood in the foyer. She was pale as a corpse in the lantern light.

Their commander: Joachim Murat. I glanced at Caroline. She looked more elated than alarmed.

Nurse Witch helped Maîtresse to a wooden bench and draped a wool blanket over her shoulders. The big doors had been shut, but it was still freezing in the foyer. Maîtresse pressed her hands to her heart. I thought of running up to our room for Mouse's vial of salts, but it was dark. Berthe, our head cook, appeared with a bottle of vinegar, which Maîtresse inhaled to keep from fainting.

"What's this all about?" Citoyenne Hawk demanded of the men, her words hard to understand without her teeth in.

The tallest of the four hussars stepped forward, his tasseled boots tracking mud. "There's been a coup, citoyennes," he said, the plume on his tall hat bobbing.

What did that mean, a *coup*? I glanced at Ém, Mouse and Caroline. Wasn't that like a battle?

"The Directory no longer exists," he clarified. His three companions hovered by the door, in the shadows.

Maîtresse moaned.

The Directory, *gone*? Did that mean that the Directors were dead? I thought of Maman's "dear" Director Barras and her friend Madeline's husband, Director Gohier. I remembered her looks of worried concern. No wonder Caroline and I had been sent away!

"But bloodless," he assured Maîtresse.

"*Grâce à Dieu*," she said, pushing the vinegar aside.

"Everyone is safe?" I dared to ask. "What of my brother, Lieutenant Beauharnais? What of the aides? What of Colonel Duroc?" (I *spoke* his name!) "And Captain Lavalette?" I added (to cover up).

"Nobody was hurt," he said.

"Yet the Directory no longer exists?" Maîtresse pressed, standing now, but with her right hand on Nurse Witch's shoulder.

"Now there is a Consulate headed by three men," he said. "General Bonaparte is one of them."

"Who are the other two?" Caroline demanded. (I knew what she was thinking, that Joachim Murat might also be one.)

"Former Directors Sieyès and Ducos," another of the men said.

Caroline made a look of disgust.

The night monitors began ushering the younger students back to their rooms. Eliza, shepherding the younger girl who clutched Henry, glanced up. I smiled encouragement, pleased to see her being so caring.

"We will have a lot to talk about in the morning," Maîtresse told the older students as Citoyenne Hawk saw the men out the door, "but I will allow you to sleep until eight, just this once."

If I can sleep, I thought.

I was awoken late the next morning by Caroline, who was shaking my shoulder. "Wake up! We have to leave."

"Leave what?" I asked, bleary from little sleep. I'd been dreaming of the spirit show, but in the dream Maîtresse was with me, trying to pull me out. Trying to save me.

"The Institute!"

Caroline was dressed, but where were Ém and Mouse? I sat up, rubbing my eyes. The fire was blazing. Had I missed the wake-up triangles?

"But we just got here." What time was it? I remembered that we'd gone to the *Fantasmagorie* the evening before, remembered *fainting*.

"Get dressed! The Hook wants to see you."

Ém and Mouse ran in all aflutter.

"Is it true, Hortense, you're going back to Paris?" Mouse asked.

"I am?" This was all too much to take in. I felt half-asleep, still in a dream. Was this how people felt after fainting? I wondered. Then I recalled, vaguely, four scary hussars in the night. And something about a coup? Had *that* been a dream?

"I'm going too," Caroline said, opening up her trunk and taking out stained silk stockings, small linens and a musty feather boa.

"You are?" Mouse said.

"You are?" I said.

"We get so bored without you," Ém objected.

"Without you both," Mouse said.

"Hortense, *get up!*" Caroline grabbed hold of one of my hands and tried to pull me out of bed. "She said to tell you to come to her study. Sorry, I ate all the sugar puffs."

Caroline had talked with Maîtresse? Had she told her that I'd fainted?

I approached Maîtresse's office with foreboding. She'd been right— the *Fantasmagorie* was a fraud. How could I have doubted her? She'd been like a mother to me in so many ways, a wise and loving mother. She'd been the one to explain the changes a girl went through, the one to help me through all the embarrassing moments. What would I have done without her?

"Caroline told me we're being withdrawn from school," I said the instant I saw her. "I'm sorry! We went to the spirit show, and you were right, it was—"

"Breathe, angel," she said, leading me over to her cozy nook. "Everything will be fine. You'll be safe at home."

Safe? From spirits? And then I realized that what she was trying to tell me had nothing to do with the spirit show. Rather, it had to do with the hussars pounding on the door in the middle of the night. They had not been a dream.

"Because of . . . because of the coup?"

"Yes. Your schooling will continue, but in a different way," she said, arranging the down pillows on the divan. "I will write you often."

This gave me pause. It sounded as though I was going to be away for more than a day or two.

"You will have tutors," she went on, offering me a plate, mostly crumbs now.

I took the one remaining fig, annoyed at Caroline for eating all the sugar puffs. My newest Fearsome Friend was something of a glutton.

"But I have tutors *here*." The way Maîtresse was talking made me think I might be leaving the Institute forever.

"Citoyens Jadin and Isabey will continue to teach you," she said, "but privately, in Paris."

"I'm . . . I'm not coming back?"

"Caroline will have to return, no doubt—she needs more schooling—and you, too, but from time to time, to visit."

Was I really leaving the Institute, my home for the last five years? "But I've not finished." What about the play I was going to be in with Ém and Mouse? What about the report I was writing on Greek art? What about the next *Exercice*, my last one?

"The General has sent a carriage for the two of you," she said, taking a shaky breath. "I would have preferred to have you near, angel, always and forever, but . . ." She touched a handkerchief to the corner of her eye.

Now I was afraid *she* was going to cry.

"I knew this moment would come," she said, "but I couldn't have predicted that it would come so soon, much less so suddenly. Nor could I have ever predicted that it would be precipitated by such an enormous change for us all. However, the essential thing is for you to be safe."

"I'm safe *here*," I said. The pendulum clock sounded. Nine o'clock already?

"You have to understand: the General is wildly admired, but he also has enemies. You will likely have to be guarded."

Tears flooded my eyes.

She stood, withdrew something from a cabinet and handed it to me with a curious sense of ceremony. "I want to give you this before you go."

It was a tiny bottle, stoppered with a bit of cork.

"I carried it with me while in service to the Queen." I could see her trembling. She paused to collect herself. "If you ever have reason to think you've been poisoned—"

Poisoned!

"—drink it down."

"But Maîtresse . . ." I was only going home.

She put her hand on my shoulder. "Promise me, angel. Promise me that you will keep this with you *always*."

"Of course," I said meekly.

She embraced me so tightly I could hardly breathe.

VII

NEW POSSIBILITIES

20 Brumaire – 1 Ventôse, An 8
(11 November, 1799 – 20 February, 1800)

THE CROSSROADS CARD: NEW POSSIBILITIES

PROMISE

✦

The courtyard of Maman's house was half-covered in horse dung. Many of her plants had been trodden. Caroline and I raised our skirts as we picked our way through the muck.

"What happened?" I asked old Gontier, Maman's man-of-all-work.

"You should have seen it yesterday morning," he said, leaning on a barn shovel.

"It looks like a cavalry regiment came through here," Caroline said, cursing at the muck on her white boots.

He chortled. "Close. Most all the General's officers gathered here on horseback before setting out."

Before setting out to oust the Directors and take over the government? How was such a thing done?

Maman met us in the salon, looking exhausted. Her face paint failed to hide the dark circles under her eyes. "Bonaparte didn't come home until three this morning."

"We were woken in the middle of the night by four hussars," I told her. "At the Institute."

"That must have alarmed Maîtresse Campan," Maman said, her hands at her throat.

"They were General Murat's men." Caroline beamed. "He sent them with a message just for *me*."

"Why the crates?" I asked. There were three big wooden boxes stacked in one corner, and an open one on the floor.

"We're moving into the Luxembourg," Maman said, with an eye on Agathe, who was wrapping an enameled glass decanter.

We were moving? La Chantereine had been our first family home. Our *only* family home.

"To the Luxembourg *Palace*?" Caroline made wide eyes.

"Where the government meets?" I asked. And where Father had once been imprisoned.

"The *Petit* Luxembourg," Maman said. "Right next to the palace."

"But that's where the Directors live," I said.

"No longer," she said with a sigh.

Aïe. "Because of the coup?"

"Yes. Now we have a Consulate instead of a Directory. Bonaparte is one of the three Consuls in charge. It's confusing, but don't worry, dear heart," she said, embracing me and then Caroline. "We're safe now."

I thought of Maîtresse's unsettling gift. "Where's Eugène?" I asked, unexpectedly anxious.

We found Eugène in his bedchamber, helping his valet pack.

"Where is Joachim?" Caroline demanded.

Or Christophe, for that matter.

"Likely with his men," Eugène said, gulping down the dregs of a coffee.

"We're moving into the Luxembourg Palace," Caroline said.

"The *Petit* Luxembourg," he said, yawning. "The General is there now with Fauvelet, drafting a proclamation."

"You should see the crowd at the road," Caroline said.

"We're told that nobody was hurt," I said. "Is that really true?" I'd seen a poster saying that the General had narrowly escaped death at the hands of twenty assassins.

"Yes! Amazing."

"Was it scary?" Caroline asked.

"It was!" he said, slipping on his jacket.

"It was?" I asked, alarmed.

"I had to address the Council of Ancients!"

I laughed. Eugène always trembled on a stage.

The General returned that evening, insisting we move to the Petit Luxembourg immediately, but Maman persuaded him that she needed a few days because there were so many things that had to be arranged. Who would look after the cow and the chickens? Who would look after the two geese?

The next day, I was startled to encounter Christophe at the foot of the stairs.

"Citoyenne Beauharnais! May I help you with that?" he asked, indicating the box of school notebooks I was carrying.

"No, thank you," I said, fool that I was. Why didn't I accept his offer? "You already have your arms full," I added, gesturing at the bulky package he had under one arm.

"It's the proclamation announcing the new Consular government, to be distributed throughout the city. I'll put a copy out for you to read," he offered.

"Thank you," I said. "I'd like that." Although there was nothing more tedious than a government proclamation.

"In the salon?" he asked.

Did he want to meet me in the salon?

"Shall I put it in the salon?" he clarified.

"Ah. The proclamation. Of course. Yes. In the salon. That would be perfect. Put it there."

"I will," he said with a grin.

I put my box of notebooks by the door and raced back up to my room, overcome.

I was outside helping Mimi gather eggs the next morning when I heard horses galloping down the laneway. Only the General rode at such a reckless speed. Soon I heard voices: it was the General—and *Christophe*.

"We have enough eggs for now," Mimi said, putting her basket down to wipe her hands on her apron. "The cook will be needing them, now that the General is back."

"Would you mind taking mine in?" I dunked my mesh basket into the washtub we used for cleaning the eggs. I had it in mind to linger in the garden for a spell, out of sight. I felt mortified about how awkward I'd been around Christophe the day before. (Plus, another pimple spot had appeared on my chin overnight.) "They're not heavy," I pointed out.

"Good, then *you* take both baskets in, child," she said, handing me hers. "I have laundry yet to get down off the line."

Groan!

The way down to the kitchen, unfortunately, was through the house. I decided to go in through the front entrance. From there I'd be able to cut across the dining room and over to the stairs down to the cellar kitchen. The men, no doubt, would be in the General's office, at the back of the house.

I was edging around the dining room table (which was *covered* with maps, books and news journals), making my way carefully, for the two mesh baskets *were* rather full, when a hand grabbed my boot. I screamed and dropped one of the baskets.

"Christ!" a voice cursed.

It was Fauvelet, the General's secretary, emerging from under the table.

"Careful!" There were broken eggs all over the carpet.

"*Merde*," he said, standing.

"Why did you grab my foot?" And what was the General's secretary doing under the table?

"I thought you were the maid."

"Agathe?"

He looked sheepish. "She makes the funniest yelp."

"Well, Citoyen, she's going to get a true fright seeing the mess she's going to have to clean up."

Just then, who should come in but *Christophe*. "Wha—?" he exclaimed.

There I was, with a puddle of broken egg yolks and whites at my feet, standing next to the General's secretary who was *covered* in slime. "I—I d-d-dropped a b-b-basket," I stuttered, covering my chin with my hand. "Of eggs."

"I guess I startled her," Fauvelet said.

He *guessed*? He'd been under the table. He'd grabbed my boot!

"Citoyenne Beauharnais, let me help you," Christophe offered, chuckling. He took my basket and rang the kitchen bell.

Agathe cursed like a sailor when she saw the mess and rushed back downstairs for a mop and bucket.

"What's going on?"

We all froze. It was the General, scowling.

Fauvelet held out his arms with a helpless expression.

"He's made an omelet?" Christophe offered, with a sly smile at me.

I did my best not to break into a giggle fit.

To everyone's relief, the General laughed.

That evening the men sat around the fire—the General, Fauvelet, Eugène, Joachim and Christophe—telling stories of the coup while Maman, Caroline and I took up our needlework. (Or, rather, Maman and I did, for Caroline didn't take her eyes off Joachim even once.)

Christophe explained how Eugène's breakfast party had served as part of the plan. Other aides had been asked to host similar gatherings, each with high-ranking officers. The morning of the coup, Christophe had ridden to each group, told the officers what was happening and sent them to join the General.

"That way," Christophe went on, "when the General rode out, he was surrounded by his best men."

"The Breakfast Party Plot," Eugène said with a grin, proud to have been part of it. "Trouble was, we didn't have time to *eat*. Would anyone care for some leftover duck with oysters?"

We moved to the Petit Luxembourg two days later: me, Caroline, Eugène, Maman, the General and his secretary, Fauvelet, crowding into our old carriage. The timing of the move had been kept quiet, so we weren't bothered by the usual crowds.

"Will we get a bigger carriage?" Maman asked, for we were tightly crowded.

"One that doesn't break down all the time?" I suggested, watching out the window for Christophe, who was riding alongside with the dragoons escorting us. He saw me looking and smiled. I glanced away, my heart jumping.

The General drummed his fingers. "The carriages at the palace have disappeared."

"We'll have our own riding arena," Eugène said. "Won't we?"

Caroline poked me with her elbow. "Aren't you excited? It's like we're going to be princesses now."

"Is there a piano?" I asked. "Or maybe a pianoforte?"

"I'm afraid all we've acquired are debts," the General said, drumming his fingers.

A PRINCESS LIFE

❖

The rooms previously occupied by Director Gohier's family were grand, though decrepit, with moldy wall coverings and high ceilings covered in flaking gold leaf. Worse: Caroline and I had to share the bed of the Gohiers' sixteen-year-old son. I tried not to think of the sinful habits he likely indulged there. Mimi took away his dirty linens, but his sour smell was everywhere.

Our windows overlooked the Luxembourg Palace, now to be called "Palace of the Consuls." Another name change. As if erasing memories could be so easy. It had been used as a prison during the Terror, and I remembered visiting Father when he was incarcerated there. He pretended—or perhaps he even believed—that it was simply a temporary measure. *Soon I will be free,* he told us.

Almost directly in front of us was the Rue de Tournon, where my great-aunt Fanny had lived. Eugène, Ém and I had had to stay with her for a time when Maman, Father and Ém's mother were all in prison. Not far, in the other direction, a short walk up the Rue de Vaugirard, was the Carmes, where Maman and Father had been imprisoned, the last place I'd seen my father alive.

I also remembered Director Barras (*former* Director Barras) hosting an elegant dinner at the Palace, celebrating the anniversary of the King's execution. I hadn't wanted to go—I didn't want to celebrate our King's death—but Maman insisted. I was seated beside her, and on my left was an ill-dressed man who kept talking feverishly to her. I had to sit back, away from my plate, in order to avoid blasts of his cinnamon breath. That was my first encounter with the General, and I was not impressed.

Unpacking, I came upon Maîtresse's curious little gift. I took the cork out and sniffed it. It had an almond scent. I dipped a finger in and tasted it. It was a little bitter.

Safe now?

30 Brumaire, An 8
The Institute
My dearest friend,

It's dreary here at school without you. And to think that you are living the life of a princess. Perhaps, when we do see you, we'll have to kiss your feet? For sure I'll want to kiss your cheek.

Your Mouse
Nasty: Writing with a split quill. (I must make some more.)

16 Frimaire, An 8
The Institute
My angel,

Yesterday and the day before yesterday all your friends came to my room at mail-delivery time with the most touching eagerness to see if there was anything from their dear Hortense—and yet not one word from you. I tenderly scold you, my dear girl. Ask your mother to provide you with a writing desk that is well stocked with everything necessary.

But enough: I scold, I forgive, and if I were near you, I would embrace you.

Maîtresse Campan
Note—I suggested to Citoyens Isabey and Jadin that they arrange to give you lessons at the Luxembourg.

———

The life of a princess proved to be woefully dull. Caroline and I couldn't go anywhere without guards. There was nowhere to go, in any case, much less anything to *do*. Any visitors we wished to invite had to be officially approved, but—worse—the rooms the General had taken for his office were below us, on the ground floor. Eugène, Christophe and the other aides spent all their time down there. It wasn't at all like at Maman's little house, where it had always been rather easy to *accidentally-on-purpose* happen by. In our first five days, Caroline saw Joachim barely once and I didn't see Christophe at all.

In spite of the monotony, Caroline complained loudly and at length about having to return to school. I badly wanted to go back to the Institute with her, but Maman insisted she needed my help. "It's time for you to learn how to behave in society," she said, examining my chin for black points and pimple spots. "Be introduced to prominent families."

I scowled. Meet a potential husband, she meant.

"Eugène, would it be possible for you to talk to Maman?" I bit my thumbnail, unsure how to put it. "About potential suitors? For me?"

"Who do you have in mind?"

"Nobody! But she seems to be focusing on the sons of politicians." I made a face. "They've never served in the army. They're . . ." Pathetic.

"You'd prefer a fighting man?" He picked up his riding crop and made a playful dueling lunge at me. "Like *who*?"

I caught the tip of the crop and, with a surprise twist, deftly pulled it out of his hand. "Seriously."

"Seriously?"

"Yes." I wagged his crop at him. "This is serious. You'll see, when your turn comes." Boys weren't considered marriageable until they were well into their twenties. It was different for girls.

"Very well," he conceded. "I'll consider the possibilities and suggest them to Maman."

"Perhaps you might be kind enough to consult with me first?" I suggested, tapping him playfully with his crop before giving it back to him.

"I talked to Maman," Eugène said, later that day.

"That was quick!"

"I needed to know her criteria before I went shopping, so to speak."

I focused on my embroidery. I was beginning to regret having recruited my brother as a go-between.

"She requires that the ideal suitor be of a good family, and that he preferably be titled."

I scrunched my nose. "Why? No one has titles now."

He shrugged his shoulders in a "who knows?" gesture.

"What about . . ." *Did I dare?* "What about Colonel Duroc? His family is of the nobility." Sort of. In a minor way. Maybe.

"You fancy Christophe?" He raised his eyebrows.

"Simply a possibility." But my blush gave me away.

"Problem solved," Eugène reported back, looking pleased with himself.

"What problem?" I said, looking up from drawing a horse. I couldn't get the neck right. I had had a lesson with Citoyen Isabey that morning, and soon Citoyen Jadin would arrive.

"Your husband problem."

Aïe! "And?" Could he possibly have suggested Christophe?

"At least solved for now," he qualified.

"What does that mean?"

"I talked to the General."

Oh no!

"And he talked to Maman, and persuaded her to stop trying to find you a husband right now."

"Really?"

"Yes, *really*—because of your immaturity."

"I'm not immature!"

Citoyen Jadin was pale. I wondered if it was because of the dim light, which filtered in through the tall windows. Had he always been so gaunt? Perhaps I'd not noticed before.

"Welcome," I said, shifting uncomfortably. "Welcome to our palace." I rolled my eyes. The tattered yet ostentatious grandeur embarrassed me.

He looked around the room as if lost in a foreign realm, pulling his coat cuffs down over his wrists. "It's cold," he said.

"I know." It was the beginning of winter, and not all that cold outside, yet it was freezing in our rooms. "How have you been?" It seemed strange talking to him so formally. My last lesson with him had been over four months before, in the heat of summer, and since then so much had happened.

"A bit ill, but I'm better now." Leaning on a side table, he lowered himself onto a chair by the fire.

"Are you sure, Citoyen Jadin? You seem . . ." Frail. "We could postpone for another day."

"We've lost too much time as it is," he said, gesturing for me to take the stool in front of the old pianoforte we'd had moved from La Chantereine.

"I know! My mother has had me on a busy social schedule. She's intent on finding a husband for me."

"Is that what you want?" he asked absently, going through his sheaf of scores. "Marriage?"

"Someday, certainly." There had been a time when I could talk to him about almost anything, but now he seemed aloof. "Fortunately, Maman has given up, at least for now." I glanced at the score he handed me. Bach's Prelude No. 1 in C major. I loved it—who didn't?—but it was suitable for a beginner. "Citoyen Jadin, do you think I'm immature?" I said without thinking.

"Why do you ask?"

"The General and my mother think I am." I was still indignant about it.

"You're playful," he said, his chin in the palm of one hand, "but that's not the same thing. You have a sense of humor, yet take things seriously. You're energetic." He glanced at me. "Why do you frown?"

"My grandmother thinks I'm too energetic. She's forever telling me to settle down."

"Imagine what she would say about all my brothers."

I laughed to imagine. I'd forgotten how charming he could be when he smiled.

"Have you continued composing?" he asked.

No. Because the one composition I had played for him hadn't been worthy of so much as a word! "I've been busy." An excuse.

"You must make time for the things that matter."

It was true, I knew, but sometimes . . .

"I want you to work on composing every day. Start a notebook. Even if you just glance at it," he said, meeting my eyes. "Promise me?"

"I promise," I said, but halfheartedly.

He began to say something more, but stopped, his hand on his chest. "Play the Prelude," he said, once he could speak.

"Citoyen Jadin, respectfully, I learned this piece when I was eleven."

"Don't be fooled by simplicity. I want to hear your creative energy when you play." He paused to cough, then said, "Play as if your very life depended on it."

A NEW CENTURY

Shortly after, I learned that Christophe had been promoted to colonel and sent to Austria to negotiate peace. I was proud of him—it was an honor to have been chosen for such a big responsibility—but I was miserable that he was gone.

Twelve days after Christophe had departed, I overheard an interesting conversation at dinner. It was a special affair because the General had been named *First* of the three Consuls, and was now officially in charge of the country. After numerous toasts and discussions about matters political, the Minister of Foreign Affairs (Citoyen Talleyrand, but nicknamed the Lame Devil because of his clubfoot) mentioned that Colonel Duroc—Christophe!—had made a strong impression in Austria and that the King was pleased with him.

I wanted to hear more, but then Talleyrand and the General launched into a discussion of the proposed new Constitution, which was soon to be voted on by the public. I hid a small yawn behind my serviette.

"A constitution should be short and obscure," the General said. "Now that the cork is drawn, we must drink the wine."

Whatever that meant!

Every evening the General's younger brother Lucien joined us for dinner, reporting on the tally of the votes on the Constitution so far that day. "Over 12,000 ayes—12,440, to be exact," he said, helping himself to all the venison. "Plus 12,000 more from the garrison."

"How many voted no?" the General asked.

Lucien looked down at his notes. "Ten?" He smiled. "I think it's safe to assume that it's going to be ratified."

"Exactly. In five days we'll proclaim it," the General said, tearing off a chunk of bread and cleaning his plate with it.

"That would be Christmas Eve," Maman noted.

"All the better," the General said.

"Proclaim it before the vote is concluded next month?" Eugène asked.

"We can't sit around waiting," the General said, reaching over to pinch Eugène's ear. "Let's get to work."

"Yes, sir!" Eugène took a few more bites of chicken and stood to put on his gold-embroidered jacket with red cuffs. He looked smart in his new uniform.

"It's a good fit," Maman said. She was proud of him. We both were. At only eighteen, he'd been made Captain of the Mounted Guards, commanding over one hundred men, all of them older, veterans of the Italian and Egyptian campaigns.

Eugène grinned, trying to appear dignified, but his dimples gave him away. That and the swinging way he walked, following Lucien and the General out the door.

"Will we celebrate Christmas?" I asked Maman after the men had left.

"Yes, and *Easter*," she said, handing her plate to Mimi. "And— who knows?—there might be a masquerade ball at Mardi Gras."

"Ooh la la," Mimi said. "That would be something."

"There hasn't been one for years," Maman said.

"Not since before the Revolution," Mimi said, leaving with a tray stacked with dishes.

"What about the Revolutionary festivals?" I asked, helping myself to two more chicken thighs. Dining with the General was always abrupt. It was challenging to get enough to eat.

"No more," Maman said, pushing back her chair.

No more Festivals of Virtue, Reason and Labor? No more Festival of Recompense? A relief!

On Christmas Eve the new Constitution took effect. Outside our gates, the street was thronged, everyone yelling, "*Vive* Bonaparte! The Revolution is over!" I felt trapped by their fervor.

The next day, Christmas Day, the General asked me to fill in for his secretary, who was ill. "You are well-schooled, Hortense," he said, "and your penmanship is certainly better than mine."

(Was that a compliment? I wasn't sure. His writing was terrible, impossible to read.)

My fingers trembled a little when I realized I'd be writing out letters to the King of England and the Holy Roman Emperor! More and more I was beginning to comprehend the enormous changes in our lives.

Resting my hand while the General was out for a moment—he expected me to keep up with his dictation and he spoke very quickly—I noticed a letter from the French ambassador in Austria. Squinting a bit, I made out a sentence or two about how the King was impressed with *Colonel Duroc*.

I was all puffed up with pride, but at the same time miserable. If only he would return!

Nivôse 9, An 8

The Institute

My dearest friend,

   It's hard to believe that soon it will be 1800 (by the old calendar, of course), a new century. It seems strange to be celebrating a new year in winter, and not in the fall, as we usually do. Plus, I can't get used to some people addressing me as Mademoiselle. Can you? Doesn't it sound strange to you? I'm going to stick with Citoyen and Citoyenne.

   I imagine that you will be doing something exciting to celebrate the new century. Not us, alas. Maîtresse is going to have us all awakened—as if we'd be asleep!—and everyone (except for the Little Geniuses, of course) is to stand together in the ballroom holding candles and thinking Improving Thoughts. I love my aunt dearly, but she can be frightfully serious.

   She also had everyone make what she called "resolutions" for the coming year. This sounds rather like what we did at that Meeting of the Vows a long time ago, remember?

   Ém took over your role of the wicked old woman in our play, and was actually fairly good at it.

   Your Mouse

   Note—Caroline had to eat at the Repentance Table again. It didn't seem to bother her, strangely enough. Ém asked her, half jesting, if she was trying to get expelled, and she said yes, she was! Might this have something do to with wanting to get to Paris to see her beloved General Murat?

On January 1, 1800, the first day of the new year—and new *century*—I resolved to:

   Attend to my studies every morning.

Improve my handwriting.

Write more often to Mouse, Ém and Caroline. And Maîtresse. And even Nana and Grandpapa.

Sketch every day.

Play the pianoforte for an hour a day.

Make a new composition notebook and at least *glance* at it once a day, as I had promised Ciroyen Jadin I would.

ARRIVALS AND
DEPARTURES

On the second day of the "new year"—it was still just 12 Nivôse to
me—Maman informed me that our stay in the Petit Luxembourg
was temporary. My heart leapt thinking that we would be moving
back into La Chantereine and that everything would return to
normal, only to have my hopes cruelly dashed with her next words.

"We're to move into the Tuileries Palace," she said.

Aïe. The thought of living where the King and Queen had lived
gave me gooseflesh. "Why can't we just go home?" I missed Maman's
little house.

"Our lives have changed, dear heart," she said sadly.

The next day we toured the Tuileries, which we were to call the
Palace of the Government (yet another name change). Surrounded
by miserable shanties sunk into mud, the stink was so strong it
made me ill, despite a bitter wind off the river. I hated to imagine
how it would smell in the heat of summer.

Inside, it was worse. The royal apartments had been empty for
over six years and everything looked a wreck. I saw bloodstains on
the wall. I wondered if these were from when a mob broke in.

"It's only red paint," Eugène told me, but I didn't believe him.

"It's so dark," Maman said. The windows were high up and
caked with grime. Many were boarded over.

"And gloomy," I said.

"Gloomy like all grandeur," the General said, leading the way. It would be easy to get lost in those halls. "We'll be lodged by the river. Moving in won't be difficult. The hard part will be staying." He paused at the door of what must have been the King's chambers. "Louis XVI sat here."

"*That's* the throne room?" I asked. Like everything else, it was in shambles.

"A throne is nothing more than a bench covered in velvet," he said.

"And the Queen?" Maman asked, shivering.

"Her rooms were below," the General said. We followed as he led the way down to a lower level, which was colder.

Then, as we stepped into the suite where the Queen had once lived, Maman fainted! Fortunately, Mimi caught her.

"I saw a ghost," Maman told me later, once we'd returned to the Petit Luxembourg.

"Maman, that's—" *Uneducated*, I started to say. I thought of how we'd been foolishly deceived by the *Fantasmagorie*.

"It was a woman wearing a simple white gown. Her hair was entirely white," she said, her voice tremulous. "It was the spirit of our poor *Queen*."

The next evening, I headed for the reception salon in the Petit Luxembourg, dressed for dinner in my usual white gown and gloves. I was expected to be there at six every evening to help Maman entertain. I had taken care with my hair, braiding it and securing it with a lovely tortoiseshell barrette I'd bought that afternoon in a shop in the Palais Égalité.

I heard my brother's voice, and that of several other men and women. Mother wouldn't appear for another half hour, and the General would arrive a moment before dinner was served. I paused at the door as Maman had taught me, composing myself before entering, standing straight and quietly reciting *p*-words like *prune*, words that were supposed to give my mouth a more attractive appearance. My efforts at composure were all for naught, however, for on entering I gasped—for who should be sitting by the fire with my brother but *Christophe*.

They both jumped to their feet.

Christophe was as devastatingly handsome as ever. I took a calming breath. People were watching us.

"How was your journey, Colonel?"

"It went well, thank you, Citoyenne Beauharnais," he said, offering me his chair.

I lowered myself onto it, feeling its warmth—*his* warmth. I flushed violently and turned toward the fire, hoping that its heat would be assumed to be the cause.

Eugène, Christophe and I talked quietly for a time of Christophe's experiences, his challenges and obvious successes. He inquired how the vote on the new Constitution was going.

"It looks encouraging," Eugène said, "although we won't know definitively for about forty more days."

"Ah," Christophe said. "Too bad. I won't be here."

"But you've just returned," I said.

"I'm afraid I must return. Peace treaties take time," he said, sitting forward.

"So I gather," I said, pleased to show that I knew something of diplomacy. "The General has me occasionally writing letters and other documents for him. I have found it enlightening." (Boasting a bit.)

Mimi glanced in to summon me to help with the table.

"You'll stay to dine with us, Colonel Duroc?" I asked, proffering my hand and making a slight curtsy.

"Thank you, but I'm afraid I have another engagement," he said, "with Citoyen Talleyrand."

"Our Foreign Minister hosts an elegant table, I'm told," I said. "Another time, perhaps?"

"Yes," he said, lightly kissing my gloved hand, "another time."

I left the room with the appearance of composure, but my legs trembling.

THE ART OF GIVE
AND TAKE

❖

21 Nivôse, An 8
The Institute
My dearest friend,

Thank you so much for the horsehair paintbrush you made me for
my birthday. I love it.

How delightful that we are now both sixteen. I haven't yet started
to You Know What, so I'm not getting talks about finding a husband—
at least not yet. Thank goodness for that.

Do you know that Caroline succeeded in getting expelled? Or,
rather, was "allowed to go" is how my aunt tactfully put it. I take it
she's going back to live with you? At least now you will have one
Fearsome with you. She's been desperate to get back to Paris, and I
know you can guess why.

I'm a little worried about Ém. She continues to suffer from low
spirits. At least Caroline was a distraction.

Your Mouse

"I *finally* managed to get out of there," Caroline said, pulling off her
gloves by biting the fingertips, one by one. "Where are the men?"

Where was Joachim Murat, she meant. I told her that he was
either with his hussars or with the aides downstairs, where we were
forbidden to go.

"That's cruel!" she said.

I had to agree, now that Christophe was back. "We rarely see the aides anymore."

"That's unacceptable!" she said.

It didn't take Caroline long to change the situation, for six days later she announced, "I'm going to *die*."

She didn't look like she was dying. In fact, she was aglow.

"Of happiness!" she exclaimed. "Joachim asked for my hand."

I screeched.

Mimi looked in. "Girls?"

I covered my mouth, a giggle fit bubbling up.

"Quiet down," Mimi said, giving us a "look."

"When? What did he say?" I demanded, once the danger of a fit had passed.

"Just now, as I was coming out of the closet downstairs. The one where the men keep their cloaks and swords."

She'd been down in the General's offices? And hiding in the *closet*? How bizarre. "What were you doing down there?"

"Eavesdropping. I overheard Joachim exchanging stories with Christophe, your brother and two other aides." She laughed. "They sure were surprised when I emerged from the closet. That's when Joachim said, *That one over there would make a jolly wife*. Pointing at me."

That was most irregular!

"And so I said: *I dare you to find out*. Standing like this." She took a saucy stance, hands on her hips. "And he said, *What do you dare?* And I didn't say anything, just ran my tongue over my lips like this"—she demonstrated—"and the men all hooted."

"Even Eugène?"

"No, of course not your saintly brother," she said, rolling her eyes. "And so then I said, batting my eyelashes, *My brother the General is taking his morning coffee. He's free to discuss such a matter right now,* and they all poked Joachim in the ribs and shoved his shoulder, and—all red in the face like you wouldn't believe—he went in to talk to Napoleon."

I muffled a squeal. "And?"

"And they're still talking!"

Poor Caroline.

"My idiot brother won't consent," she wept.

I stared at her, dumbfounded. Joachim had asked the General for Caroline's hand in marriage, but his offer had been declined? "Why?"

"Because he's an innkeeper's son! He says Joachim's a vain rooster. He wants to marry me to someone grander."

"Maybe he'd prefer you to marry a prince." The General would think something crazy like that.

She made a blubbering sound of disgust. "That I could understand, but he intends for me to marry Christophe!"

My heart just about stopped. For a moment my breath stuck in my throat. I couldn't move, much less think. No doubt she meant someone else. "Colonel Christophe Duroc?" I asked, to be sure. "Joachim's friend?"

"Of course. Stupid Christophe—none other."

"Christophe is not stupid," I protested, revealing more than was wise. I'd succeeded in keeping my feelings for Christophe secret— *so far.*

"He's as dumb as a donkey!"

I was incensed. If anyone was stupid, it was her darling Joachim. Wisely, I kept my feelings to myself. (Self-control!) "Can your brother make you marry whomever he wants? Even if you don't agree?" Maybe this was how it was done in Corsica. In France, marriages might be arranged by the parents, but both the boy and girl had to agree.

"My mother would have to approve, but Napoleon can get her to go along with most anything. As for the rest, when they put up a fight, he just bribes them or something."

"Has the General already settled this with Christophe?" I asked fearfully.

"He's leaving it all up to your mother."

"*My* mother?"

"Yes, *your* mother. Excuse me while I go throw myself in the river."

"Hold on," I said, heading for the door.

Maman was having her hair dressed while discussing the next day's menu with the cook.

"I'm sorry for interrupting," I said, "but I need to talk to you about something crucial."

"What is it, dear heart?" she asked in her caressing way.

"It's a private matter," I said under my breath, glancing at the maid and the cook.

Maman paused Agathe's hand. "May I have a moment with my daughter? We won't be long, will we?" she added, looking over at me.

I waited for the servants to close the door.

"General Murat has asked for Caroline's hand in marriage," I said, sitting down beside her. In the bright morning light, it was easy to see all her wrinkles. She'd resorted, of late, to using an anti-baldness cream and slimming pills in an effort to look young.

Maman didn't exactly look surprised. "And what did Bonaparte say?"

"He told Caroline that it's up to you." Well, exaggerating a bit. And not mentioning the part about Christophe.

"That I very much doubt," she said with a smile.

"But he listens to you, Maman, and—"

"Tell me: Did Bonaparte outright refuse Joachim's offer?"

Yes! I nodded. "And they're so much in love."

"They've made that quite clear in public," she said with a disapproving tone.

"But, well, it's more than just dancing," I said, thinking of their trysts in hidden passages.

"Oh?" (I knew immediately what she was thinking.) "And how far has this *sentiment* gone?" she inquired, as delicately as the subject permitted.

"Caroline remains chaste," I assured her. Sort of. More or less. "But it would be wise for them to marry." *Soon.*

"I see," my mother said, furrowing her brow.

"Could you persuade the General? Please? They love each other so much."

"There are other things to be considered, dear heart. Joachim is of lowly birth."

Were we not all equals now? "He's brave in battle," I protested. "The General often says so." Foolishly brave. Brainlessly brave.

"Without a doubt, but consider his background. Before becoming a soldier he was clerk to a haberdasher in a small country town."

"But the General promoted him." I was losing ground.

"Hortense, you have a good heart, and it pleases me that you care so much about Caroline's happiness, but there is another concern as well. General Murat has a reputation for trysts with actresses."

I didn't want to let on that I knew about Joachim's mistresses. Caroline knew, too. She would reform him once they married. "But—"

"Dear heart," Maman said firmly, "Bonaparte really does know best."

"There are other considerations," I suggested, an idea coming to me. Maman had been the one to teach me about the art of give-and-take, after all. "Caroline is moonsick in love with Joachim. If you were to persuade the General to change his mind and allow them to marry, she would be eternally grateful—to *you*." I didn't have to point out that the Bonapartes were my mother's sworn enemies. It might help to have at least one member of the Clan on her side.

Maman said nothing, but I could see her thinking. "I will see what I can do," she said at last.

"Bonaparte's not happy about it," Maman reported back.

My heart sank.

"He claims impassioned couples only consult their volcanic feelings."

Volcanic indeed! "But?"

"He agreed."

I cheered.

"After I sat on his lap," she added with a sly smile.

MORTEFONTAINE

❧

Caroline came into our room doing a bouncy jig. "We're to be married day after tomorrow!"

That was *fast*. "Where? Here?"

"At Joseph's château in the country."

Aïe. Mortefontaine was a long way away and Christophe was only going to be in Paris for thirteen more days. I didn't want to miss any opportunity to see him.

"Napoleon and your mother won't be able to come, but Eugène will, and Christophe—"

Christophe was coming too! I tried not to show my elation.

"—and some of the other aides as well." She took my hands, dancing spritely, hopping steps. "I. Am. So. Happy. How will I ever thank you?"

"I do have one request," I began. The rule of give-and-take. *Did I dare?* "Who is Joachim's best friend?" I began, hesitantly. I had a fluttery feeling in my stomach. "Other than you, of course."

"Christophe." She signed herself. "Jesus, Mary and Joseph, *grâce à Dieu* I don't have to marry *him*."

"You have to admit he's handsome." And loyal, and kind, and brave.

"Has this to do with your wish?" she asked, squinting with suspicion.

My cheeks burned hot as embers. "Don't tell Ém or Mouse." It wasn't fair that Caroline knew, and not them. "Or anyone. Promise?"

She stopped to consider. "Actually, that's perfect. Joachim and me, Christophe and you."

"There's one big problem, however," I said. "He hardly knows I'm alive."

"I'll fix that," she said.

Which of course was exactly what I had in mind.

28 Nivôse, An 8
The Institute,
My dearest friend,

Really? *Caroline is getting* married *to General Murat? Just like that? We are amazed. Be sure to write us all the details.*

Your Mouse

Nasty: Doing needlework with a thimble with a hole in it, and not knowing until the needle runs under your nail.

Caroline quickly settled on a gown for her wedding, a white muslin with lace trim and an abundance of pink ribbons. She gave it to her maid to freshen, and asked her to set it aside along with a pink hat, scented pink gloves and embroidered pink boots. So pretty! She also intended to wear the pearls the General had given her as a wedding present.

"You're going to look beautiful," I told her, but she burst into tears.

"I don't know what to do!"

"About what?" Everything had been taken care of.

"I can't talk to my mother about such a thing, and even my sister Pauline is hopeless. She knows all about flirting, but as for the Act, all she says is to lie there and make noises, but I know there's more to it than that."

I had an idea. Maman and Mimi were in the kitchens, occupied with staff. "I'll be back in a moment," I told her.

The key to Maman's desk was not in its usual place. I pulled at the desktop and it lifted. Maman hadn't locked it! I found the secret compartment and withdrew the slender volume.

"This is *your* book?" Caroline asked when I showed her *The School of Venus.*

"Not exactly." I wasn't going to let on that it was Maman's.

"Ooh la la," she exclaimed, glancing at the illustrations. "It looks like a hog's pudding," she said, examining a drawing of a naked man.

"Pudding?"

"You know—a male's *parts.*"

She said the craziest things!

"Read it to me?"

We settled into the divan under a window that let in sunlight.

"How about this chapter? *A remark on the age fittest for Parents to marry their Daughters.*"

"Tiresome."

"Or maybe: *The first appearances of young Men's love to Maids.*"

"Isn't there anything about playing hot cockles?"

"Hot *what?*"

"You know. Poop-noddy."

I couldn't believe her language. Maybe it was a Corsican thing.

"*Copulation,*" she explained with a roll of her eyes. Didn't I know anything?

Flushing, I glanced over the chapter titles. "*How a young Man puts his—*" I paused for shame. "*His* you-know-what *into a Wench's . . .*"

She brightened.

The roads to Mortefontaine were either icy or clogged with snow. Fortunately our carriage didn't topple, and fortunately we weren't robbed. *Un*fortunately, I looked a fright by the time we arrived, and Christophe was already there. Fortunately (well, not *really*) he hardly noticed, talking about horses with my brother.

By ten o'clock most all the family and friends were there, as well as a few aides, generals and other officials. (Well, everyone that is except my mother and the General, who weren't able to come—and didn't really want to, I suspected.) In spite of all the excitement, Joseph's wife Julie made Caroline and me retire early. "*Tomorrow* is the big day," she insisted. Protesting, we headed off, but stayed up for hours, nonetheless.

In the morning, Eugène, Caroline and I toured the property, riding the grounds in Joseph's elegant calèche pulled by a handsome pair of bays. I had no idea that the Mortefontaine grounds were so huge, fifteen hundred hectares. (I thought Malmaison was big, but it was only sixty hectares.) There were four lakes, a kennel, orchid greenhouses, several stables and a large English-style garden, which I had to admit was lovely. The château itself had twenty-two rooms plus a grand ballroom.

On our return, Caroline immediately disappeared with Joachim. I found them in a pantry closet. They were to be married in the village that afternoon, but keeping them apart until then was not going to be easy.

Much to my chagrin, Christophe happened by as I was trying to lock Caroline into her room.

"What are you doing?" he asked, smiling in his adorable way.

"Caroline keeps trying to sneak off with Joachim," I blurted.

"Why would she want to do that?" Teasing.

"Oh, I don't know!" I said, turning red as a *beet*.

All that time Caroline was banging on the door!

"I only wanted to show you something!" she insisted, emerging in her wedding ensemble.

She looked lovely all in white and pink, but reeking of almonds. She'd discovered the little jar Maîtresse had given me and used it as perfume, used it *all*.

"I'm going to be a married woman. I can wear scent if I want," she said.

"But—!" I didn't know what to say. "It was a gift to me from Maîtresse." In case I was ever poisoned. Of course I didn't say that.

Caroline made wide eyes of astonishment. "The Hook approves of girls using scent?"

I breathed a sigh of relief when Caroline and Joachim were finally married. Joachim was soberly dressed (for once) in a dress coat and top hat. They shamelessly tongue-kissed in front of everyone as soon as the papers were signed. We walked the icy lane back to the château following an old fiddler, villagers gathered on all sides to watch our merry procession.

Back at the château, the newlyweds drank from a two-handled cup and immediately disappeared into Caroline's room. They emerged in time for the wedding supper, Caroline pressing herself against her husband at every chance. A wife was not supposed to show affection for her husband in public—and this was more than mere "affection."

"I can hardly walk," Caroline whispered to me, pleased with her showy ring and exalted status.

"Citoyen General and Citoyenne Murat," we toasted, getting giddy on Joseph's expensive Champagne.

"I finished first," Caroline crowed, displaying her empty glass.

Joachim and the men all groaned and the ladies laughed, for that meant Caroline would rule their family. Of that I had no doubt.

The cook made pyramids of tiny wheat cakes, which we delighted in breaking over Caroline's head, much to her annoyance. Christophe caught one of the cakes I had hurled across the table at her, and the two of us laughed. It was a wonderfully merry evening, and I wanted it never to end.

I rose early the next morning, shortly after dawn. I had put a piece of wheat cake under my pillow the night before, but I hadn't dreamt of any man—much less my future husband. I didn't feel at my best, no doubt because of all the Champagne I'd enjoyed. I was surprised and a little embarrassed to encounter Christophe getting a coffee and rolls, fully dressed in uniform and riding boots.

"You're up early, Colonel Duroc," I said. "Going for a ride?"

"I've a long day ahead," he said. "Best to take advantage of the sun."

I must have looked quizzical, for he added, "I'm going to Austria."

Now? "I didn't think you were leaving for another ten days." And then I winced, for I'd made it rather clear that I'd been counting the days.

"That was my plan," he said, "but Mortefontaine is so far north of Paris it made more sense to leave from here."

"Of course," I said, crestfallen. "That makes more sense," I added, repeating his words.

"Would you care for a madeleine?" he asked, proffering the platter.

"No. No, thank you," I said, returning to my room before I burst into tears.

I set out for Paris later that morning, sharing Maman's carriage with Eugène and another officer, their horses tied behind. Caroline and Joachim had decided to stay at Mortefontaine for a time. When they returned, they would be setting up house in Paris. Marriage was such a big change for a girl, I wondered if Caroline and I would still be friends.

And what of Christophe? Would I *ever* see him again?

THE LIST

❖

The miserably cold and lonely days that followed were taken up with politics. All anyone ever talked about was the vote on the new Constitution.

"Over three million people voted in favor," Maman said when the final tally was in. "And fewer than two thousand voted against."

I nodded, sitting by the chimney studying a pile of bed curtain fabric samples. We were scheduled to move into the Palace of Kings—Palace of the Government, that is—in only ten days. *Another* move.

"As First Consul now, Bonaparte has even more to do, so he has put me in charge of the List," Mother added with a weary sigh.

I looked up. "*The* List?" The list of aristocrats who fled France during the Revolution, and who would never be allowed to return. "*You're* in charge of it?"

She nodded. "So of course, the first person I removed from the List was François," she said with a smile.

My Uncle François, Ém's *father*. "He's alive?" Ém had never been sure.

"Yes! And living near the Black Forest."

"And now he's off the List?"

"Free to come home." She beamed.

"Has Ém been told?"

"Not yet. I promised I wouldn't—"

"This will make her so happy!" Mouse had been worried about Ém's lack of spirit.

"All of us," Maman said. "Antoine left this morning to find him, escort him back. He specifically requested that Ém not be informed. He thinks she will be heartbroken if he fails. He loves her so much," she said with a sad smile, "yet she'll likely not notice he's gone."

Worse, she'll be glad of it, I thought.

18 Pluviôse, An 8
The Institute
My angel,

Come this décadi, *if your mother allows. We will be giving a concert. I have sent an invitation to our darling Citoyenne Caroline Murat and her husband as well.*

I regret that I won't be able to see the big procession celebrating the First Consul's move into the Palace, but I look forward to calling once you are settled. It's a palace I know rather well.

Farewell, my angel. I'm yours for life.

Maîtresse Campan

Maman and I spent a full day in Montagne-du-Bon-Air that *décadi*. First we went to see Grandpapa, who had turned eighty-six. (Eighty-six!) "I will die an unhappy man," he said, looking at the portraits of his sons: my father and my uncle François. My mother and I exchanged a hopeful smile.

After, we went to the Institute, which I had been missing so very much. Mouse was delirious to see me. Even Ém seemed happy, in her muted way. She told me that she was relieved that Antoine was no longer in Paris, no longer coming out to the school to visit. (If only she knew, I thought.)

And then Caroline—Citoyenne Murat—arrived. The Fearsome Foursome!

The concert, however, was a disaster. I was expected to perform!

"I can't do that," I told Maîtresse. I was fearless in theatrical performances, yet just the thought of performing *music* in public made me so anxious I got ill.

"I've already announced it," she said, looking over the crowd. "We're counting on you." She gave my hand a squeeze. "*I'm* counting on you."

I made several mistakes, of course. I was thankful Citoyen Jadin wasn't there.

As soon as the concert was over, I sported on the green with my dear Fearsomes, which made me feel better. We snuck off to a private spot in the shrubbery. I'd decided to bravely reveal to Ém and Mouse my hopeless affection for Christophe. It wasn't right that only Caroline knew.

"I have a confession to make," I began.

That immediately got their attention.

"This is absolute foolishness on my part." I shrugged up my shoulders. "But I can't help it. I . . ." *Love*? I was too shy to say it. "I am infatuated with . . ." I swallowed. "Colonel Duroc."

Mouse exchanged a knowing glance with Ém.

They knew? "Caroline! You told?"

"I didn't!" Caroline protested.

Ém laughed. "You talk in your sleep."

Before I could respond, Caroline began scolding Ém for her stubborn chastity. "You owe it to God to swive your husband," she said.

I hid my face in my hands. "Citoyenne Murat, please!"

"It's in the Bible!"

And then we heard a giggle in the shrubbery: *Aïe*, Eliza?

She was gone before we could catch her.

A SURPRISE

On the day of our move into the Tuileries, Maman, Caroline, Ém and I sat in the window of one of the pavilions to watch the enormous procession celebrating the General's—rather, the *First Consul's*—move into the former royal palace. We tried to be composed and dignified, but soon we were waving and cheering like everyone else.

The carriage of the General and the two other Consuls was drawn by six white horses and escorted by Eugène at the head of his mounted guards. He looked splendid on lively Pegasus. Caroline threw a rose to her husband as his regiment went by. He kissed it and pressed it to his heart. (*So* romantic.)

After the Council of State, the senators and the cavalry had gone by, Caroline, Ém and I excused ourselves to go to the room for ladies.

"One moment, dear heart," Maman said, holding me back.

"I have to *go*," I whispered.

A military band had stopped below us. Maman put her gloved hand over mine. "Bonaparte wanted you to hear this," she said.

That puzzled me. "Why?"

An orderly ran out with a stool for the conductor. This was curious behavior for a marching band.

"I don't know, but he insisted," Maman said.

The conductor stepped onto the stool, raised his baton, and the band began to play.

"Can't we go now?" Caroline asked impatiently.

I raised my finger: *wait a moment.* The tune was familiar. I knew it well, yet couldn't place it.

And then it came to me: it was the composition *I* had written, the one I had composed when I was so worried about Eugène in far-away Egypt.

"Dear heart, isn't that something I've heard you play?" Maman asked.

It *was* mine. I couldn't believe it. "That's my composition."

"What do you mean, *your* composition?"

"I wrote it, Maman."

She frowned, puzzled.

"What was that all about?" Caroline asked when I joined her and Ém.

"The band played something I composed." I wondered how they had come by the score.

"You mean that melody we just heard?" Caroline asked.

"*You* wrote it?" Ém asked.

"Yes," I admitted.

"I didn't know girls could do that," Caroline said.

After the festivities were over, and Caroline and Ém had left, Maman and I awaited the General in the Palace. We sat in the yellow drawing room, huddled by a smoking chimney, watched over by guards we didn't know. I kept thinking back to that moment of hearing *my* musical composition. It had sounded splendid, but who had given the band my score? The General? But how did he know about it? For that matter, who had arranged it so that it could be played by all the instruments in a band? My mother, obviously, knew nothing.

Maman suggested we move to her dressing room, which was warmer. We weren't there long before the General burst in.

"How did it go?" he demanded of Maman in his usual abrupt fashion. I was sitting off to one side. "What did your daughter think?"

Maman turned to smile at me. That's when the General realized I was there. "Oh!" he said.

I stood, my cheeks burning. "I was honored," I said.

"Were you surprised?"

I nodded.

"You're a good composer, Hortense," he said, tugging my ear (gently for once).

I wanted to ask how the band had got hold of my score, but lost courage. Overcome, I excused myself.

I am a composer, *he said.*

I woke the next morning in the Palace of Kings. The Palace of *Kings* was now my home. It took me a moment to make sense of it.

My room was enormous, and so very cold I could see my breath. I climbed down off the high bed and found my fur slippers and wrap. A fire was burning—a maid must have quietly come and gone—but the big wooden shutters hadn't been opened. I unlatched one and folded it back, surprised how bright it was, mid-morning. My room overlooked the wintry public gardens.

I sat down at a little writing table, inlaid with an intricate pattern in mother-of-pearl. Had it belonged to Queen Marie Antoinette? The desk was the only real piece of furniture in my room, other than a bed so high I needed bedsteps to get on and off it. I didn't like to think of those who might have slept in that bed. I didn't like to think of their fates.

I intended to spend that first day organizing my belongings. I had a small room off my bedchamber for drawing and painting. A piano—an actual *piano*—had been installed in another small chamber I decided to call my music room.

I sat down on the piano stool and ran my fingers over the keys. I'd only shown my score to Citoyen Jadin, so how could my composition have been played in public like that? Had he shown it to the General?

After finishing coffee and a roll, I found the General in the courtyard with a horse and groom. Roustam and an aide, both on horseback, waited by the open gates.

"Your music teacher showed it to me," the General said when I asked him.

As I'd suspected.

"He thought it might be a good piece for a public event," he added, mounting his fidgety white stallion and taking up the reins.

Jadin had said that?

"And perhaps an anthem, although I'm not so sure about that." He took a riding crop from the groom, spurred his horse and cantered off, followed by Roustam and the aide.

"Hortense, there you are," Mimi called down from an open window. "Citoyen Jadin is here to give you a lesson. He's waiting for you in the music room."

Jadin was sitting in a chair by a roaring fire. "Good day, Citoyen Jadin," I said, taking the piano stool.

"Good day." He looked weary, older than his years.

"I beg your forgiveness for being tardy." I was being purposefully formal and aloof. The more I thought about it, the more I didn't like that something I had created, something private and precious to me, had been taken out of my hands, displayed to the world without me knowing. "I was unaware I had a lesson scheduled."

"I know, but time is pressing," he said, going through his sheaf of scores. "How was the procession?"

"Good." With a cheerless voice. "Although I was rather *surprised,* let's say, when the military band played my composition."

"They *played* it?" He pulled out his gray handkerchief and coughed into it, a sickening rattle.

"You showed my composition to the General," I burst out.

"I should think you would have been pleased," he said evenly.

Of course I was pleased, but annoyed, as well. "You should have asked me first." Or, at least, told me.

"You would have said no."

True, but—

"It's time you stopped hiding your talent, Citoyenne Beauharnais," he said with a scolding tone.

"I don't have *talent*," I countered peevishly.

He smiled wanly. "Have you been composing, as you promised?"

"*No*." Not looking at him. I was acting like a child, I knew.

"Citoyenne, you are one of my most promising students."

I looked at him. He was being serious.

"You play beautifully, expressively and with energy, and apparently you can also compose." He paused, pressing his hands to his chest. "So yes, you do have talent, but you *must* apply yourself. I won't always be here to encourage you. You must find that resolve from within yourself. You do have it, you know you do. Continue what you were doing, copying out the compositions you love, creating compositions of your own." He wrapped his wool scarf around his neck. "But more significantly, you must have confidence in your work, and, most of all, confidence in yourself. It's not right to hide your creations from the world."

"I'm only sixteen, Citoyen Jadin."

"I was nine when my first composition was published."

"It's different for a girl."

Never call attention to yourself.

Display modest reserve.

Avoid the public eye.

"You're a creative *person*, Citoyenne, and creativity is by its nature generous." He coughed again, more violently.

"Are you all right?" I asked, alarmed.

"I'm fine," he said, once he could speak. "*Play*." He handed me a score, which trembled in his hand. "We don't have much time."

VIII

ROMANTIC FANTASIES

2 Ventôse – 6 Ventôse, An 8
(21 February – 25 February, 1800)

THE MOON CARD: ROMANTIC FANTASIES

A MYSTERY

❖

Maman was uneasy in the Palace, because of its cold grandeur, its lack of a private garden, its history—but also because of its "ghost." She kept hearing a woman singing, and she insisted that the sound came from her dressing room, not from the public gardens, where women of ill repute plied their trade. One morning Mimi found the cupboard doors in the dressing room open, which was troubling because she always kept them closed. And *then*, on the floor one morning, she found an embroidered headscarf with the Queen's initials on it.

"Her calling card," Mimi said, refusing to touch it. She burned sage leaves in Maman's bedchamber and dressing room, "to drive her away."

Her: the ghost of the dead Queen.

I resolved to look for clues, to figure out who could be playing this cruel trick on us. I would have suspected Caroline, but she was never around, too busy playing "poop-noddy" with her husband.

"There's my angel," Maîtresse said, sitting with Maman in the yellow reception room in front of the roaring fire. She'd come to help advise Maman on Palace protocol and staffing.

"What do you make of our new home? It's rather grand." *Too* grand.

"I'm having a hard time getting used to it," Maman admitted, making room for me beside her on the settee. "I hate to think of all that happened in these rooms."

"Indeed! I was very nearly murdered on those stairs," Maîtresse said, gesturing to the gallery that led to the winding marble staircase. "During the September Massacres of 1792."

"Goodness," Maman said, crossing herself, something she'd taken to doing of late.

"The King and Queen and their children had been taken away, but then the hordes broke in and hacked down all the guards in the most brutal way. Hundreds of them! I had to climb over the dead and the dying to escape. I was on the stairs when a man seized me. I fell to my knees, knowing how painful his blow was going to be, but someone yelled from below saying not to kill women, and the brute threw me down with a curse. Less than five months later, the King was beheaded. The poor Queen. How she suffered! Her children taken from her, she knew her time was coming."

"I keep thinking I see her," Maman said.

"The *Queen*?"

"I've never had to live with a ghost before, and I don't really care for it," Maman added with a grimace.

Maîtresse laughed, as if Maman were joking.

"Do you recognize this?" Maman asked, showing Maîtresse the embroidered headscarf. "Mimi found it on the floor of my dressing room."

"It's the Queen's," Maîtresse said, examining the embroidery. "It smells of *Parfum de Trianon*, a scent that was created for her."

"And all the closet doors had been left open," Maman said.

"No sign of a robbery?" Maîtresse asked.

"No! And Maman keeps hearing a woman singing," I offered.

"The public gardens can be noisy," Maîtresse said.

"I wondered about that too," I said, "but we keep the windows and shutters closed because of the cold. And why would the dressing room doors be open like that? And why the headscarf?"

"There is always a rational explanation," Maîtresse said. "A clever prankster, no doubt?"

"No doubt," I echoed doubtfully.

"Do you remember Citoyenne Lenormand?" Maman asked me after Maîtresse had left.

"The fortune-teller? She came to your dinner party." Her failed dinner party, the one in honor of the General's mother, the one the Clan refused to attend. "She showed us the Game of Hope." Her prediction for me had not come true.

"I'd like to consult her about this haunting business, but I dare not invite her here."

Indeed. Visitors had to be approved, and the General was strict. I could imagine what he'd say about the eccentric fortune-teller.

"Mimi would go with me, but she's busy with new staff. I know you have a lesson with Jadin scheduled, but could you—?"

"He cancelled." With no explanation. Was he angry at me? The last time I saw him I had lashed out at him for showing my score to the General.

"Perfect. I thought I would drop by Lenormand's place. We'll go in one of the plain carriages so people won't think it's Bonaparte."

That was wise, I thought. Every time we went out in an official carriage, crowds of people gathered, gawking.

Citoyenne Lenormand's house was on the other side of the river on Rue de Tournon, not far from the Petit Luxembourg and where my great-aunt Fanny used to live. Her salon was not at all what I expected. It was more like a bookshop, with stacks of books everywhere—stacks of books with strange titles:

The Sibyl at the tomb of Louis XVI
Oracles and prophetic memories

The ghost of Henry IV at the palace of Orléans

All by Citoyenne Lenormand, I noticed.

A maid ushered Maman and me into another chamber, this one rather like a waiting room, with chairs set around the perimeter and journals and books stacked on low tables. A table to one side was cluttered with writing implements: an inkstand, sandbox, papers and quills. Two cats were stretched out in a patch of sun. Their smell was strong, as was that of a printing press I glimpsed in the room beyond.

A tiny man in a pompous old-fashioned wig emerged from a concealed door, startling us. "Is Citoyenne Lenormand expecting you?" His teeth were black from chewing tobacco.

"Is she in?" Maman asked.

"Jean, who is it?" Citoyenne Lenormand called out as she entered, dressed in a lacy morning gown. "Goodness." She put her hand on her cap, from which her curly black hair escaped in wisps. "Citoyenne *Bonaparte!*" Her right eye looked off in a different direction from her left. I'd forgotten what a frightening creature she was.

"Good day, Citoyenne Lenormand," Maman said. "Please forgive me for calling on you unexpectedly like this. You remember my daughter, Hortense Beauharnais?"

"I do indeed." Lenormand had a sweet smile, which softened her frightening appearance. All her teeth were intact. "Jean, fetch the girl. She's out back feeding the chickens. You'll have refreshments?"

"No, no thank you." Maman pulled off her gloves and folded them neatly. "I'd like to talk to you—"

"A card reading is one livre, but free for the wife of the First Consul," she added with a fawning reverence. "It will be sure to reveal a glorious future."

"I was hoping for something more like a consultation," Maman said. "We've moved, as you may know."

"Into the Tuileries Palace!" Lenormand's knees creaked as she made a deeper reverence.

"Palace of the Government," Maman corrected. "But I keep seeing a . . . what I think might be—" She glanced at me, unsure how to put it.

"A ghost?" I offered.

"Really." Lenormand's good eye glowed.

Maman dipped her head. "And I'd like to find out how to make her . . . *it* . . . go away."

"This is not something I usually do," Lenormand said, swaying on her feet.

"Perhaps if you could just try, Citoyenne?" Maman asked, pressing a small cloth purse into her hand.

Lenormand tossed it lightly, feeling its weight. "Very well," she said, turning a knob in the wall, which opened a hidden passageway. "We shall see."

COMMUNING WITH
THE DEAD

❧

Citoyenne Lenormand led us into a dark sitting room. It was surprisingly pleasant, comfortably furnished and smelling of wax. Pleasant, that is, until my eyes adjusted to the gloom and I made out the décor. Bats had been nailed by their wings to the ceiling. Two stuffed owls graced the top of a bookcase. A human skeleton was perched on a chair in one corner.

Maman cast an anxious look at me. She had noticed it too.

"Please, Citoyenne Bonaparte," Lenormand said, setting down her lantern. She gestured toward a chair set in front of a round table covered with a fringed green cloth. She pulled out a second chair for me and sat down across from us.

On top of the table were several packs of large cards. One of the cards had the image of a man riding a horse on it. I recognized the Rider card from the Game of Hope.

"First, Citoyenne Bonaparte, I must ask you some questions," Lenormand said, gathering the stacks of cards, squaring them up and slipping them into a drawer. "It's a formality of sorts."

"I don't mind," Maman said.

Lenormand shrugged apologetically and asked, in a whisper, as if there might be someone close enough to overhear, "How old are you?"

"Thirty-six."

I was surprised. Maman told everyone she was thirty-four.

"What's your favorite color?"

"Yellow—Indian Yellow," Maman added, to be specific.

I was also partial to Indian Yellow, a rich hue made from the urine of mango-fed cows or buffalo.

"Your favorite animal?"

"Dogs. Well, pug dogs."

"The first letter of your name?"

"My last name?" Maman asked.

I wondered what all this had to do with spirits.

"Your Christian name."

"Rose, so R. Although I now go by Josephine. So J?"

Lenormand turned down the oil lamp. "And the first letter of the place you were born?"

"T," Maman answered, for Trois-Îlets, the town in Martinique where she grew up.

"And last, the number you are most partial to."

"Three?"

"Thank you," Lenormand said after a moment of silence. "One last question: Have you any idea who this spirit might be?"

Wouldn't she know? I wondered. Wasn't she a seer, a soothsayer, the "Sibyl of the Salons"?

"The . . ." Maman paused. "The *Queen*," she said.

Citoyenne Lenormand sat back. "*The* Queen?"

"The late Queen," I said, to clarify. "Queen Marie Antoinette."

"It sounds outrageous, I know," Maman said, "but yes. I'm fairly certain it's Her Majesty."

Lenormand took a deep breath. "*Mon Dieu.*" She closed her eyes, her hands flat on the table. "And the Queen's full name is . . . ?"

"Maria Antonia Josepha Johanna von Habsburg-Lothringen," I said.

Maman looked at me, surprised.

"Maîtresse Campan taught us that," I explained.

"I brought a headscarf I'm told belonged to her," Maman offered.

Lenormand put up her hand. "There is *someone* here," she said slowly.

I looked around. No doubt this was a hoax, as the *Fantasmagorie* had been.

"But it is not the Queen," Lenormand said. "It's a girl. She's wearing a green . . . a green sash? She wants you to know that—" She tilted her head to one side. "Rather, she wants your daughter to know."

Me?

"It's something to do with letters? Does that mean anything to you, Citoyenne Beauharnais?" she asked, looking at me with her good eye.

"No," I said.

"She's spelling something out. Something to do with the letter M, and the letter N?" Her wild eye stared off into a corner.

"N-Nelly?" Was it possible?

"Nelly?" Maman said. "Who is that?"

Could it be that Lenormand was in contact with my Nelly? How else would she have known about the green sash, the test for M and N?

"She's a happy little soul." Lenormand chuckled. "She loves flying around."

"Dear heart, who is Nelly?" Maman asked.

"A little girl from school," I said, sniffing. "She died of pox."

"Goodness."

"Ah! There she goes," Lenormand said with a smile, waving her hand through the air.

I felt like weeping. My little Nelly!

"Citoyenne Lenormand," Maman said, "about the Queen—"

Lenormand held up her hand: *silence*. "I have someone else here now. He's tall, well-dressed." She paused. "Fashionable," she pronounced. "He's wearing white gloves, and a feathered hat." She chuckled. "A woman's hat?"

"Is the hat mauve with long feathers?" Maman asked, sitting forward.

I glanced at her. Now I was the one who was confused.

"Long peacock feathers, *yes*." Lenormand chuckled again. "He seems to be . . . *dancing*?"

"Citoyenne Lenormand, is it—?" Maman clasped her hands together. "Is it possible that it might be my first husband?" She put her hand on my arm. "Your father once wore one of Nana's feathered hats to a ball. It was meant to be amusing."

"I believe it is he," Lenormand said gravely.

I looked back over my shoulder, into the dark corners. "Citoyenne Lenormand," I said, my voice quavering, "if it is my father . . ." My fingers were tingling. "I have a question I need to ask him."

Lenormand closed her eyes, the palms of her hands on the table. "Go ahead."

I took a deep breath. "Ask him if I was . . ." My hands began trembling like those of an old woman with palsy. "Ask him if I was the cause of his death."

"Dear heart!" Maman exclaimed.

"*Please*," I implored. "Just ask."

Lenormand held up a finger. "He's saying . . ." She closed her eyes, as if to hear better. "He's saying: *I . . . am . . . the victim*." She opened her eyes. "But that's it." She exhaled, her breath rancid. "Now he's gone."

VICTIM

❖

Maman and I emerged into the dusty front parlor, blinking against the light. The cats scurried into hiding, as if we were predators.

I began to feel faint. Citoyenne Lenormand settled me on an over-stuffed chaise longue and excused herself to get me something to drink.

Maman sat down beside me and handed me a handkerchief.

"You never talked to your ghost," I told her, still numb from it all.

"I think we've had enough ghosts for today," she said, putting her arm around me. "Dear heart, you know your father, he—"

Citoyenne Lenormand reappeared. The cats rushed over to her, meowing and looking up expectantly. "Shoo!" They scattered. "My apologies, Citoyennes. We only have brandy, so perhaps—"

"Thank you, Citoyenne, but we're leaving," Maman said, helping me to stand. "Careful," she whispered as I stumbled toward the door. "Can you do it?"

Yes, I nodded, although I wasn't sure.

"We need to talk," Maman said, once we were settled in the carriage and headed back to the Palace. "Why do you think—?"

"It's hard to explain." I felt shaken. *I am the victim,* he'd said.

"Is it because of your dreams?"

She *knew*? But of course she would. Mimi or Maîtresse would have told her. Screaming in the night was no way to keep a secret.

"No." I pressed her handkerchief against my eyes. It smelled of jasmine.

"Then *why*?" Maman asked, gently stroking my back.

I didn't want to tell her.

"I wish you could confide in me, dear heart," she said, imploring.

"I don't like to distress you, Maman."

"I *promise* I won't be troubled," she said.

We were on the bridge, crossing the river, and almost to the other side. It began to rain, an angry pelting.

"I *promise*," she repeated softly. "Tell me."

I blinked back tears. She had so often been *away*. "It's because of when . . . when Eugène and I saw you and Father in the window of the prison," I began, taking a deep breath.

"I remember," she said. There was so much sadness in her voice.

Our carriage came to a standstill, stuck in the muddy congestion around the Palace. My throat felt thick. I coughed to try to clear it. "I cried out," I said, "and then the guards came." *I am the victim*, he'd said.

"And . . . you thought—you think—that that was why he was . . . ?"

I nodded. Why Father was executed. Why he was dead.

Maman softly moaned.

I bit my tongue, an actor trick, and tried to swallow. "We can walk from here," I suggested, my voice feeble. It was still raining, but lightly, and we were close.

Mimi met us in the foyer. "The General wants to see you," she told Maman anxiously. "He's unhappy about his costume."

"His *costume*?" Maman asked, pulling off her boots.

"For the masquerade ball," Mimi said, taking Maman's hat, shaking it off.

I glanced at my face in the hall mirror. My eyes were red and puffy.

"Is something wrong, baby?" Mimi asked, taking my hat.

I shrugged off my cloak. "It's nothing," I said, but not meeting her eyes.

"Mimi, tell Bonaparte I won't be long. Dear heart, come with me," she said, taking my hand.

Maman led me to a space hidden behind her dressing room, a closet within a closet. "I have something to show you," she said, holding up a candle. The shelves were lined with boxes, each one neatly labeled in her hand. She found the one she was looking for, pulled it out and rummaged through the papers within, withdrawing a document.

The paper was thin, cheap, with blurred text printed on it, like something to pass out to crowds.

"What is this?" Like a sleepwalker, I followed her into her bed-chamber, where there was light.

The document was dated the fourth of Thermidor, in the second year of the Republic—the day before Father was executed.

I turned it over, puzzled. At the bottom, I read:

Farewell.

For the last time in this life, I press you and my children to my heart.

—Alexandre Beauharnais

I lowered myself onto the chair by the fireplace.

"It's his final letter," Maman said, sitting down across from me. "He asked that it be printed after his death. He wanted to clear his name."

Father had written this? These were his words? I turned it over.

The trial I have been subjected to today reveals that I am the victim of a treacherous calumny of a few aristocrats.

I read it again, and these words leapt out at me:

I am the victim.

"I don't understand," I said, sniffing back tears.

"Your father and a number of other prisoners were falsely accused of planning an escape." She leaned forward, reaching out to touch my arm. "*That's* why he was executed, dear heart. It had *nothing* to do with you."

I sat for a moment, holding the paper in my hands. I glanced again at the printed words, some smeared, some faint, some blotched. I turned the document over.

I press you and my children to my heart.

"Excuse me." It was Mimi again, at the door. "Yeyette, the General, he—"

"Tell him I'll be a moment," Maman said, standing. She leaned over and tipped up my chin. "Are you going to be all right, dear heart?"

"I'm fine."

"You're sure?"

I nodded, smiling through my tears. "I'm sure," I said, my voice husky. "Go." I squeezed her hand. "Thank you," I whispered. *Maman.*

She embraced me warmly and was gone.

I sat for some time in the stillness.

HOPE

❖

I was working on a charcoal sketch of Roustam in my new art room next to my bedchamber when Maman came in. "I have marvelous news!" she exclaimed. "Captain Lavalette has arrived back, *with* your Uncle François."

I gasped. "Really?"

"*Really*. They are with your grandparents in Montagne-du-Bon-Air. I've called for a carriage."

"We're going? Now?" We had planned to go out to Malmaison later in the day.

"Immediately! I haven't seen François in *ten* years."

I jumped up and took off my art-smock. "Does Ém know?" She should be one of the first to greet her father.

"I'm sure Antoine has seen to that," Maman said with a smile.

A mud-spattered carriage was stopped in front of Nana and Grandpapa's house, the horses asleep in their harness. Weathered leather trunks were stacked on the front porch.

Nana threw open the door. "Oh, my heart!" she exclaimed, her hands pressed to her chest.

"Is something wrong?" Maman asked, alarmed.

"I can't bear so much elation!" Nana said.

"Where is Ém?" I saw her cloak, thrown over the back of a chair in the foyer.

"Upstairs," Nana gestured. "Come!"

Grandpapa greeted us at the door of his bedchamber, spritely in his chair on wheels. "My firstborn son has returned!" he announced. "Now I can die," he added jubilantly.

"Don't be doing that just quite yet," Nana scolded him. "I've got your favorite roast on the spit."

I spotted Ém sitting by a window, her husband Antoine hovering close by. She was in tears—happy tears. I assumed that the tall man standing next to her was her father—and *my* uncle. I'd been barely six when I last saw him.

"Rose!" he exclaimed, embracing Maman. "You look as lovely as ever."

Maman started to say something, but she was too choked up to speak. "François, this is Hortense," she said finally, beckoning me forward.

"Your little girl?"

I curtsied. My uncle was a dignified older man. I wondered how much he resembled my father.

"Yes, my baby," Maman said, blinking back tears.

"All grown now," Nana said, dabbing her eyes as well. "Just like your Émilie."

"Indeed," Uncle François said, reaching for Ém's hand.

"My son Eugène would have come, too," Maman said, "but he's working for my husband, the First Consul."

"Bon-A-Part-Té!" Grandpapa exclaimed.

My uncle shook his head in amazement. "Such changes we've seen."

Sniffing and teary, we made ourselves comfortable as Ém's father related an account of their harrowing journey. "My dearest Émilie, my beloved daughter," he said, "it pleases me to see you well-married. Were it not for this gentleman, Captain Lavalette, I would not be here today."

Ém's head was bowed, but I saw a hint of a smile.

After a celebratory meal, Maman and I left for Malmaison. The General, Flauvelet and Eugène were still working, so Maman and I played billiards (she won, as always) before retiring for the night. I fell asleep thinking of the miracle of my uncle's return. It made me happy, especially for Ém, but also a little sad. My father's absence was irrevocable. Nothing would ever bring him back. I thought of Citoyenne Lenormand "contacting" my father's spirit. Had that really happened? Lenormand may have known what father had written on that handbill, but she couldn't possibly have known about Nelly's test for M and N, or the color of her sash. I was beginning to believe it possible that spirits were with us, that *Father* was with us—and that gave me comfort.

I woke the next morning to an empty house. Eugène was out fishing and Maman and the General had gone early into the village. As I was finishing my second coffee and a dish of pudding with stewed prunes, Eugène came back with an enormous carp he'd caught.

"Perfect," Mimi said, summoning the cook. "We'll roast it for our guests this afternoon."

Maman and the General returned shortly after—with *four* pug dogs, identical tan puppies with black faces, all squealing, chewing, yapping and snuffling. They were *adorable*.

"Bonaparte insisted we take the entire litter," Maman said, laughing. She was happy at Malmaison. Even the General didn't glower quite so much when there.

"But how will we tell them apart?" I asked, picking one up and holding her to my cheek. She licked the tip of my nose.

"With different-colored trimmings," Maman said, showing me a basket of ribbons. "We'll make collars for them this evening."

"Why not now?"

Maman glanced over at the General, who was absorbed in a book on Italian geography. "Bonaparte has something he wants to show you. Bonaparte?"

He looked up, distracted.

"You have something for Hortense?"

"Oh! Yes." He jumped up.

"Eugène, you go too," Maman suggested.

Eugène and I followed the General out to the ramshackle stable. "What's this about?" I asked Eugène in a hushed voice.

"You'll see," he said mysteriously.

Coming out the stable door was a boy with a mare, a beautiful gray with black socks and a white blaze.

"She's for you, Hortense," the General said, taking the rope lead and handing it to me.

"For our ride?" We'd been planning a tour of the property.

"Not exactly," he said.

Then? I was confused.

"I mean, it's *your* horse," he said. "To keep."

I glanced at Eugène, who nodded.

"Don't you like her?" the General asked, for I was speechless.

"No," I said brightly, "I don't." I felt my cheeks flush. "I *love* her," I said, stroking the mare's neck. She had big, intelligent eyes.

Eugène grinned. "We thought you might. Christophe and I helped pick her out."

Christophe? "But Colonel Duroc's in the north."

"We chose her before he left," Eugène said. "She needed a bit more schooling. She's spirited, but she has a smooth gait and she listens well."

A *horse*, a horse of my own! "Thank you," I told the General, overcome.

"No racing," he said, teasing. (*He* was the one who loved to race.)

"She goes nicely astride or sidesaddle, whichever you wish," Eugène said.

"Hortense would ride too fast astride," the General said.

"Then astride it will be," I said, teasing back. "And bareback," I added, for good measure. "What's her name?"

Eugène made a face. "Clockwork, but—"

"*Clockwork?*" How bizarre.

"You could change it," he suggested.

"Very well. From now on, she'll be Game of Hope." It just popped into my head.

They looked at me like I was lunatic.

"But Hope for short," I said with a grin, stroking her neck, her soft muzzle. *Hope*, indeed.

Hope was *fast*. I outdistanced Eugène on Pegasus!

Nasty: Swallowing a flying insect.

Caroline and her husband arrived early, shortly before one. She was lavishly dressed, flaunting her married status. I felt shabby by comparision. I was still wearing the patched riding habit Maman had passed onto me.

Despite Caroline's finery, she was eclipsed by her husband, who wore a gold-embroidered harlequin coat, purple pantaloons and bright-yellow boots. Three ostrich plumes and an expensive heron plume graced his hat. (The General called him "Franconi" after the famous circus clown.)

Up in the room we'd assigned to "the Murats," Caroline showed me the oriental dancer costume she was going to wear to the masquerade ball.

"Your husband will let you be seen like that in public?" The top was scanty, to say the least.

"*He* suggested it."

"I'm going as a nun," I said, half-jesting.

"That's no fun," Caroline said.

"I know." After all, Christophe wouldn't be there.

I was about to change into a presentable gown when more guests arrived: Maîtresse, Mouse and even Isabey with his daughter, little Alexandrine. We were settled out back when Ém, Antoine and my Uncle François surprised us with a visit. We greeted them with exclamations of joy.

"I'm so happy for you, Ém!" Mouse exclaimed, embracing my cousin heartedly.

"How delightful that you were able to come by today after all," Maman said, sending Mimi for more chairs.

"Grandpapa was napping, and what with this lovely warm spring weather, we thought we'd go for a short drive," Ém said.

"Perfect," Maman said. "We're just about to eat. Please join us." A table had been set up close by and Mimi and a scullery maid were setting out china.

"Yes, please do," said Eugène, juggling two of the puppies in his arms.

"We're having a carp Eugène caught this morning," I said.

"An *enormous* carp," he said, handing the puppies to me and stretching his arms out wide.

"It's huge," I assured everyone, cuddling the pups.

"And it's being baked now," Maman said.

My mouth watered to think of it. Carp stuffed with bread, almond paste, currants and herbs was delicious.

"I'm sure your grandmother would understand if we stayed," Antoine told Ém.

"I'd like that," Ém said, smiling up at him.

Maman caught my eye. *At last.*

"Will you be going to the masquerade ball?" Eugène asked.

"Yes," Ém said, her big eyes shining. "Even Nana and Grandpapa."

"In costume?" I asked, surprised.

"Of course. And my father, as well," Ém added.

"Don't tell! I want to surprise them," Uncle François said, laughing.

"The fact that you're back here in France is all the surprise we need," Eugène said, patting his uncle's shoulder.

"We have almost all our costumes figured out," Maman said. "Everyone but—"

"Everyone but me." I made a sad face. "I can't decide," I said, letting the squirming puppies down onto the grass to frolic with the others.

"But it's tomorrow evening," Ém said.

"I know," I said with a disheartened shrug.

We heard the sound of a cantering horse out front. "Now who can that be?" Maman said, and headed back into the house to see.

"Hortense," I heard someone hiss.

CHECKMATE

❖

I descended the stairs slowly in a fresh white muslin gown with a wide sash of shimmering yellow silk. I'd decided on my rustic straw hat because it was adorned with yellow cloth daisies and a hat band to match. I heard men's voices in the room the General was using as a study. I paused for a moment, listening. It was the General and *Christophe*.

"Dear heart!" Maman's voice startled me. "Come, we're ready to eat," she said. "You look lovely."

I hoped she wouldn't notice that I had pinked my lips.

"Where's your apron?" she asked.

"I must have left it upstairs," I said. Intentionally. "What about the General?" What about *Christophe*?

"He'll join us in a moment," she said, leading the way outside. "He's with Colonel Duroc, who just arrived. What a surprise!"

Most everyone was already seated at the long table, which looked wonderfully festive. Set along the length were platters heaped with food, interspersed with bottles of Malmaison wine, pitchers of mint water and clusters of golden primroses.

"Hortense, this is for you," Mouse said, patting the seat beside her. Across from us were Ém, her husband and father, with Caroline and Joachim on our right.

"The General is with his secretary and Colonel Duroc," Maman announced, taking the chair between Maîtresse and Isabey at the

I glanced up. It was Caroline, leaning out her bedchamber window.

It's Colonel Duroc, she mouthed.

I frowned. Christophe? That wasn't possible!

She nodded vigorously.

Aïe! "I'd better see if Mother needs my help," I said, excusing myself. Once in the house, I ran up the back staircase to my room to change.

far end of the table. "They will join us shortly. Bonaparte insisted that we begin," she said.

"Colonel Duroc came all the way from *Austria*," I whispered to Mouse as we helped ourselves to the carp, pigeon pie and duck stew. It all smelled so good!

"Caroline told us!" Mouse said, her eyes wide.

We'd had more of the Malmaison wine and several helpings of the delicious food by the time the General, Christophe and Flauvelet appeared. "Bravo!" we all cried out, and then laughed at our merriment.

Christophe looked wonderfully distinguished in a pale waistcoat and doeskin breeches, a pristine white cravat at his neck. Maman placed him at the far end of the table between Eugène and the General. We toasted his diplomatic successes in the north, again and again.

"Thank you," he said graciously, "but the negotiations are far from over." He'd come back to consult with the General and had to return immediately, he explained.

(I was not happy about this—not in the *least*—but dared not show it.)

"But surely you could stay for a few days more, Colonel?" my mother suggested, offering him the carp. "There's to be a masquerade ball tomorrow night in Paris. Even the First Counsel will be going."

"Colonel Duroc has crucial things to attend to," the General said, helping himself to the roast chicken.

"Negotiating a peace treaty is imperative, indeed," Maîtresse said with approval, and we toasted yet again to Christophe's success.

I was awed—and so very, very proud—but disheartened, none-theless. If *only* Christophe could stay for the ball!

After pistachio custard, four macarons and a madeleine (just *one*— I'm trying to honor my vow, at least a bit), I had a chance to tell

Christophe how pleased I was with my horse. "I've decided to call her Hope," I told him. If he only knew what it was I hoped for!

I was about to tell him how fast Hope was when Caroline stood up. "Attention everyone!" she called out.

"Quiet!" Joachim joined in.

"Citoyenne Bonaparte has a suggestion," Caroline said.

A hush settled and Maman stood. "I was thinking . . . The weather is so lovely, perfect for a game of Prisoner's Base."

We cheered! Well, most of us, for Maman caught the General's arm as he was attempting to escape. "Just one game?" she asked with a caressing smile.

"I'm already a prisoner," he joked affectionately, sitting back down and pulling Maman onto his lap.

"Of love," Joachim said with a guffaw, and Caroline tapped him playfully with her fan.

We decided to play boys against girls. On the boys' team there was Christophe, Eugène, Flauvelet, Roustam, the General, Isabey, Joachim, Antoine and my uncle François. On the girls' team there was Maman, Mimi, Mouse, Ém, Caroline, Eliza, Alexandrine, me and even Maîtresse. It was a boisterous game with lots of shouting—and the girls *won*!

"I *love* that game," I said breathlessly. My straw hat had blown off and my hair was wild, but I didn't care.

"Hortense's team always picks her to be the prisoner because nobody can catch her," Eugène said, panting.

"We'll have to see about that," Christophe said with a smile, retrieving my hat and putting it gently on my head.

I looked up at him with a smile, my eyebrows raised. "And what might you mean by that, Colonel?" I dared to say, but before he could answer the General called out and he and Eugène went sprinting back to the château.

At the entrance, Christophe glanced back and tipped his hat at me. The door closed behind him and I swooned down onto the grass, gazing up at the blue, blue sky, my heart full to bursting.

Later, after many of our guests had left, Caroline poked her head into my bedchamber. "Writing your secrets?" she asked, trying to peek over my shoulder. I closed my composition notebook. A melody had come to me, and I wanted to put it down.

"Well, I have one," she said with a little pout.

Of course I was thinking that perhaps she was in an *interesting condition*. But that wasn't it.

"Christophe told Joachim that he *will* be able to go to the masquerade ball after all," she said.

I squealed, pressing my hands to my heart. "But I thought he had return to the north immediately."

"The morning *after* the ball, it turns out. But that isn't my secret." She beamed. "Christophe also told Joachim that he thinks you are . . ."

And then she wouldn't say! She was provoking me on purpose.

"Clever," she finally said.

I made a face. Boys didn't like girls to be clever.

"And . . ." She took my hand and danced a gigue around me. (She still didn't have the steps right.) "*And* that he likes you!"

Christophe!
Christophe!
Christophe!
Christophe!
Christophe!
Christophe!

———

That evening, in the salon, the General invited me to play chess. "I'm told you are hard to beat," he said, offering me the seat for playing white.

"Did Maman tell you that?" I asked, arranging my skirts, keenly aware that Christophe was watching.

"No, I did," Eugène said with a grin. "It's true, though, isn't it?"

He and Christophe pulled up chairs close beside us.

"I've lost a *few* games," I said, placing my rooks, knights and bishops before lining up my pawns. At the last, I placed my king and queen, pausing before putting them down.

"Uh-oh," Eugène joked. "She's putting a spell on them."

"Cheating already?" the General said.

"Never!" I said, glancing at Christophe. Would he not like it if I won against the General?

"Don't distract her," Christophe said, sitting forward with his elbows on his knees.

"Whose side are you on?" the General asked, reaching out to pinch Christophe's ear.

We played in silence for some time, the General frowning down at the board. His attention diverted, he would glance at the books on a side table, or, more often, stare off into space. Each time I took one of his pieces he exclaimed as if I'd killed him, making everyone in the room laugh.

I thought my king was safely put away by castling when the General took one of my pawns with his queen.

"Papa!" I cried out in protest.

Suddenly the room fell silent. Maman looked over, smiling. The General had a little grin too, and even Eugène. I glanced away, embarrassed.

"Checkmate," the General cried out, scooping up my king with his queen, and we all groaned, me especially.

MASQUERADE

❖

We returned to Paris the next day for the masquerade ball. I was looking forward to it now that Christophe would be going, but I didn't
have a costume. The fabric shops were out of silk because so many
people were having exotic costumes made. Mimi found a blue velvet
corset I could wear over a simple muslin gown and suggested I go as
a milkmaid. The corset was well-fitted and showed me off rather
nicely (*she* said). I hooked my skirts up with ribbons, revealing a
lovely rose underskirt. A black velvet mask covered my eyes. *Perfect.*
I wondered if Christophe would recognize me.

The ball was held at the Théâtre des Arts, which took up an
entire city block. We stepped into a spacious vestibule with a
high, richly ornamented ceiling. A liveried footman in a mask
handed all of us cards engraved with dances on one side and lines
for our partners' names on the other. A tiny pencil dangled from
a narrow red silk ribbon.

Twenty-one dances! We would be dancing until dawn. Citoyenne
Lenormand had predicted that a public event would be significant
for me. Was *this* to be the night?

"Your teacher Citoyen Jadin will be playing during the refreshment break," Maman noted, squinting to read the small print at
the bottom.

"Wonderful," I said, although my feelings were mixed. He'd

canceled another lesson. I feared he might still be angry—or, worse, disappointed in me.

Maman, Mimi and I headed into the women's cloak chamber, a large room lit by candles and crowded with gray-clad servants helping ladies with their cloaks and hoods. They bundled and labeled ours by name. "Citoyenne *Bonaparte*?" one exclaimed to Maman, and that caused a bit of a flurry. As the wife of the First Consul, Maman was becoming a celebrity.

We retreated to a private alcove with a stuffed armchair and a comfortable chaise longue for reclining. Under a gilt-framed mirror, a low table displayed a supply of hairpins, combs and a box filled with sewing notions, in case a repair was needed. Mimi opened a small tin. "Salts," she said, crinkling her nose.

Eugène and the General were waiting for us in the long gallery, with Roustam hovering behind.

"Ready?" the General demanded, yanking on his toga. He hated being in costume.

"Don't worry," Maman said with a smile, securing his full-face mask and adjusting the tilt of his laurel crown. "Nobody will guess that it's you."

"Are you excited?" Eugène asked, offering me his arm. He was well disguised in a mask and an Egyptian robe of an ancient design.

From the roar of voices inside, it sounded as if all of Paris had come. I wondered if Christophe was there.

Much to the General's chagrin, he was instantly recognized. Everyone stepped back as he approached. Some people even bowed.

A man dressed as Death appeared before us, but his rank smell gave him away: it was Citoyen Fouché, Minister of Police. He whispered in Maman's ear. I glanced behind to make sure Roustam was close. (*Safe now?*)

We followed an attendant to the box Maman had rented in the first tier. From there we could see everything. Countless candles gave the vast space a heavenly glow. On the stage, at the front, musicians were setting up. Off to one side was a piano on a platform—for Citoyen Jadin, I guessed. My heart ached to think I'd offended him, and I promised myself that I would make amends. I would practice more often and faithfully continue to compose, as he'd told me I should. I missed his beautiful music, our frank talks, our *friendship*.

I looked out over the crowd, seeking familiar faces. The women were masked, many in dominos. A few men were in full dress and without masks, but most were in costume. I spotted Ém in a medieval gown, the lovely rose shawl Antoine had long ago given her draped over her shoulders. He was beside her, dressed as a knight. Her father, a Revolutionary in a *bonnet rouge*, stood behind them.

"Can that be Nana?" Eugène asked.

Dressed as a gypsy! "With Grandpapa." He was sitting in his chair on wheels, looking about brightly in his ancient Commander of the Navy hat. "See Joachim and Caroline? They're to the left, between the two columns."

"Ooh la la," Eugène said, raising his eyebrows at Caroline's costume.

I waved, but they didn't notice, mooning into each other's eyes.

Maman pointed out the General's brothers Joseph and Lucien, costumed as pirates. (How appropriate, I thought.) Louis, who was not in costume, was standing with them, looking glum.

"Where is Colonel Duroc?" I asked Eugène.

"Getting ready for his trip north. He's to leave at dawn tomorrow, but his horse started bobbing its head."

Aïe. Christophe rode a stunning black stallion. "Is it lame?"

"Likely, so he has to find another mount. He didn't think he was going to be able to make it tonight after all."

My heart sank.

After dancing the opening march with Eugène, I found Ém. "I didn't recognize you," she said, admiring my costume.

I adjusted my mask and sat down beside her, disheartened about Christophe not coming.

"Who is on your card?" she asked.

I shrugged. "A few more dances with Eugène, of course."

As well as one with Louis, I didn't want to mention. He had pressed himself upon me rather forcefully. "And Citoyen *Rudé*." I wrinkled my nose in disgust.

"The man who wiped his nose on the tablecloth at the Meeting of the Vows?"

"Yes, the old lecher who drools staring at us." If I had refused him, I would have had to refuse all other partners for the rest of the evening.

A tall young man in a yellow hussar costume approached us. He was walking with a slight limp, I noticed. Could it be? Yes! It was all I could do not to exclaim in surprise—and *elation.*

"How are you, Citoyennes Beauharnais?" Christophe said, addressing both Ém and me. He saluted Antoine, who was standing close by with Ém's father.

"You are mistaken, Citoyen," I said, disguising my voice. I was near faint with happiness to see him. "I am Aurelie Challamel."

"I beg to differ," he said with a sly expression. "Citoyenne Hortense Beauharnais has an unmistakable grace."

"It's rather hard to be graceful just sitting," I countered in my fake voice.

"I watched you in the opening march with your brother," he said with smiling eyes.

"Moving with an unmistakable grace, no doubt," Ém said, poking me in the ribs.

"Are you two in league?" I protested, taking off my mask.

"You found a mount, Colonel?" Ém's husband Antoine asked, joining us.

"I did, Sergeant. Thank you for your help."

"Is your stallion going to be all right?" I asked. "Eugène said . . ."

"Thankfully, yes. He needs time to heal, is all," he said. The musicians took up their instruments. Christophe inclined his head toward me. "Citoyenne, may I have the honor of this dance?"

Ém raised her eyebrows at me, her big eyes twinkly.

I took Christophe's arm and we proceeded to the dance floor. I felt giddy, light as a feather. "Does your injury bother you?" I asked, then immediately regretted it. Had I offended him?

"I'm learning to live with it," he said.

"A war injury is a badge of bravery," I said.

"Except that I got mine sitting."

"On horseback, no doubt." There were seven other couples on the dance floor, not many, but enough.

"I was in a ditch," he said with a laugh.

I wanted to tell Christophe that I admired his honesty— usually, soldiers falsely embellished their war stories—but then the music started, a delightful minuet by Lully. Christophe made a formal bow to me, and I curtsied (with an unmistakable grace, I hoped). More couples had come onto the dance floor, but I hardly noticed, utterly absorbed in the touch of our gloved hands, the measured pace and complex hops of the minuet. The slow, intricate dance was no longer favored. Few knew how to dance it, so I was astonished that Christophe performed every step fault-lessly, especially the one-and-a-fleuret, in which the half-coupé was followed by the bourrée. (This was my favorite sequence. We were perfect for each other!)

"The minuet is no longer admired," I noted, making the sink that prepared me for a fleuret.

"Regrettably," he said.

Slip behind, half-coupé forward to the right, left hand presents. "Yes," I responded. Yes, yes, *yes!*

LOVE...
AND GRIEF

❧

"You really *are* in love," Ém said teasingly, after Christophe had escorted me back to the seat beside her.

"Why do you say that?" I asked, fanning myself rigorously. I wondered if it was possible to expire from bliss.

"It's obvious," she said, grinning.

"Fearsome!" we heard someone call out. I turned to see a girl costumed as a mouse wearing spectacles. Mouse!

"Maîtresse let you come?" I exclaimed.

"She *made* me come with her," she said with a glare. "Now that I have begun my You Know What—"

"You have?" both Ém and I exclaimed.

"—she is intent on finding me a husband." Mouse made a face of wretchedness, crinkling her painted-on whiskers.

"Dressed like that?" I laughed. "Maîtresse is here too?"

"We watched you dancing with that *very* handsome man," Mouse said, smiling slyly.

And then—the *worst* thing possible—Citoyen Rudé presented himself for "the honor of our quadrille." I'd forgotten that he was next on my dance card.

"I'll see you after," I told Ém and Mouse, rolling my eyes in chagrin.

Citoyen Rudé, costumed as a medieval knight, danced in a ridiculously archaic style, making ostentatious gestures with his arms. But that was not the worst of it. As we awaited our second turn to go up the form, he had the impertinence to grab hold of my hand and announce, *in a booming voice*, "Citoyenne, you would do me the supreme honor of embellishing my meager existence by bequeathing me your hand."

It took me a moment to understand that he had proposed marriage! I pulled my hand out of his grasp, muttered something about an urgency, and fled from the ballroom in confusion.

Mimi found me on the chaise longue in the women's cloak chamber. "What happened?"

"A man proposed," I said, wiping away tears. A revolting man!

"That's not usually something to cry about," she said with a smile. "I'll find your mother."

Maman appeared shortly after. "Dear heart, you offended the Marquis de Rudé!"

He was now a marquis? How pompous was that? "He proposed to me!"

"So I'm told. You publicly insulted him by your rude response and he's left in a huff."

I was happy about that.

"I will have to write him an apology," she said, "and you will have to as well."

"But Maman, you'll let him know that I . . . that I won't . . . ?"

A beggar woman approached and raised her mask.

"Maîtresse Campan!"

"Angel, I understand that the Marquis de Rudé made you a proposal of marriage."

Did *everyone* know? Did Christophe?

"Which she rejected," Maman said. "And none too gracefully."

"Now, unfortunately, everyone is whispering about it," Maîtresse told her.

I didn't like the way they were talking about me as if I weren't there.

I found Mouse, Ém and Caroline standing at the entrance to the ballroom.

"What would these people have me do!" I asked them indignantly, relating all that had happened.

"Marrying is the goal of every girl," Caroline said, flashing her wedding ring.

"Marrying a good man," Ém qualified. "You were right to refuse, Hortense."

Mouse concurred. "Citoyen Rudé is menacing."

"I think so too!" It wasn't just me. "But Maîtresse isn't happy about it. He's an important donor to the Institute."

"I hope she doesn't want *me* to marry him now," Mouse said.

"She would never do that," I assured her.

The musicians began to play a military song and the crowd started cheering: *Vive Bonaparte! Peace with Bonaparte!*

"We saw you dancing with Christophe Duroc," Caroline said, teasing.

"Speaking of whom!" Mouse squeaked.

I turned to see Christophe making his way toward us through the crowd.

"We need to refresh," Ém said, dragging Mouse and Caroline away.

"Citoyenne Beauharnais." Christophe made a courtly bow. By candlelight, his yellow silk hussar costume seemed to glow. He looked more handsome than ever. "I have a message for you."

People were singing the "La Marseillaise" in the ballroom, singing it boisterously. I wasn't sure I'd heard him correctly. "A message for *me*?" I hoped he didn't know about what had happened with Rudé.

"Yes. The General would like you to play the piano during the refreshment break."

Play in front of this enormous crowd? I *couldn't*! "I thought Citoyen Jadin was going to." I hadn't seen him. Was he in disguise?

"He sent a request that you play in his stead. He is . . . unable to come."

Something in the hesitant way Christophe spoke puzzled me. "Why?"

"Would you care to sit down?" he asked, indicating an upholstered bench.

"Do you think I'm going to faint or something?" I was joking. "I'm not the fainting type." Well, not usually.

"Please?" he said, imploring.

I lowered myself onto the bench. He sat down beside me, close enough that our knees almost touched. He smelled sweetly of tobacco—tobacco and something citrus. Orange water, perhaps?

"I don't like having to be the one to say this," he began, staring down at the patterned carpet. People were milling about, coming and going. "The General and I were asked not to tell anyone, at least not just yet," he said, lowering his voice, "but your music instructor, Citoyen Jadin—I am so sorry, Citoyenne, but he . . . he died."

I stared at him. "*Hyacinthe* Jadin?"

He nodded regretfully.

"That's impossible," I said evenly.

"I'm sorry," he repeated, lifting up his hands, and then letting them fall. "He had consumption."

Mon Dieu. My stomach lurched. I thought of how ill Hyacinthe had been. I recalled his terrible cough. "But he's so young." *Was* so young.

"I know," Christophe said gravely. "It's tragic. Apparently he didn't want anyone to know."

We don't have much time, Hyacinthe had told me. Again and again. He must have known all along, *known* he was dying. *I won't always be here to encourage you*, he'd warned me at our last lesson.

Everything began to spin.

———

"What happened?" I heard a woman say.

"Did she faint?" a man asked.

"Citoyenne Beauharnais?" I heard Christophe's voice close beside me, but I could not respond.

"Stand back. She needs air," I heard him say.

He lifted me up. I felt light as a cork, safe in his strong arms.

He lowered me onto a divan in a sitting area between two columns. "I fainted?" I managed to say.

"I believe so," he said, pulling a wooden chair up beside me.

I struggled to sit up. Was I becoming one of *those* women, one of the silly, simpering ones who were forever swooning? And then it came to me again: Hyacinthe was dead. "Is it true, what you said?"

"One of his brothers came to tell us."

I choked down a sob. I thought of Nelly, my father. Death was so cruelly irrevocable. "He had faith in me," I said, taking a jagged breath. And now he was gone? *Forever?* "Have you ever had a friend like that? Someone who challenged you to become better than yourself? Or more fully yourself, even when you didn't think it was possible?"

Christophe leaned forward, his hands clasped. He nodded. "Your stepfather, actually."

I shouldn't have been surprised. I'd seen how the General encouraged Eugène—and me as well, I realized. He'd told me I was a composer, a *good* composer. My heart sank, realizing the mistakes I'd made. I'd been ungrateful. Worse, I'd been—*yes*—immature. The General might have been socially awkward, and he wasn't tall or handsome, but he had other qualities, qualities of the heart and mind that mattered so much more.

"The General trusts me," Christophe said.

Because Christophe was so very trustworthy. But I couldn't tell him that. At least not yet. "Then you understand how I feel," I said.

"I do," he said.

I wondered what it would be like to kiss him.

"I think I can stand now," I said. A march was in progress. Soon the dancing would stop and food would be served.

"Are you sure?" He offered his arm and helped me to my feet. I took a few cautious steps.

"Have you seen my daughter?" I heard someone ask.

Maman?

"Dear heart!" she said. "I've been looking all over for you."

I glanced up at Christophe. Did my mother know about Jadin? *No*, his eyes said, stepping back. *Don't say anything*.

"It's Maîtresse Campan," Maman said. "She's had a bit of a shock."

"Is she all right?" I sat back down on the divan, to be safe. There had been too many shocks that evening. It wouldn't do to faint again. "What happened?"

Maman sat down beside me, taking my hand in hers. The iridescent layers of her butterfly gown wafted out around her. "She saw our ghost," she said with a grimace. "The Queen."

Mon Dieu. I glanced at Christophe. He must think us lunatic.

"Might it have been someone in costume, Citoyenne Bonaparte?" he suggested.

"I wish it had been, Colonel, but no." She glanced over her shoulder. There was nobody close by. "I saw her too," she said quietly.

Aïe. "Maman, that's . . ." Ridiculous, I started to say, although I was beginning to think that anything was possible. "Is Mouse with her?"

"I can't find her. Could you see to Maîtresse? I would, but Bonaparte is expecting me."

A REQUEST

A maid in the cloak chamber gestured to the alcove, where I found Maîtresse stretched out on the chaise longue.

"I don't need that," she told an attendant, pushing away a tin—the tin of salts, I realized.

"Maîtresse?" I was alarmed to see her disordered, the layered skirts of her beggar costume knotted up.

"Angel! I saw her! I saw my beloved *Queen*. It was wonderful! Do you have the antidote with you?"

Oh no. The antidote Caroline had used, thinking it was scent. "You've been poisoned?" I asked, alarmed.

"No, not *me*," she said, sitting up, "but the Queen might need it. I'm to have it with me always, just in case."

I sat down beside her, perplexed. Maîtresse wasn't making sense, and she always made sense. She more than anyone. I repressed an urge to feel her forehead, to see if she was feverish.

"My beloved Queen!" She wiped her cheeks with the back of her hands.

I'd never seen Maîtresse weep. I put one arm around her shoulders, comforting her in the way she had so often comforted me. "Breathe," I reminded her, looking about for a handkerchief. The maid stepped forward with several, folded and pressed.

Maîtresse took a moment selecting an embroidered one, then patted her cheeks dry. She took three deep breaths. "Ah, that's better!"

"I'm sorry, Maîtresse Campan, but no—I don't have it with me."

"Have what?"

"The antidote."

"Antidote?"

"The one you—" I realized she didn't remember asking for it.

"Angel, I don't know what you're talking about," she said with a forgiving smile, straightening the ragged layers of her beggar-woman costume. "About this problem with the Marquis de Rudé—"

Aïe.

"He's so very generous. When I consider all the things he's donated to the Institute." She pressed her hands against her chest. "It's not easy, you know, keeping a school running."

"I can imagine." I thought of all the times Maman had been late paying tuition.

"I know he's close to forty—"

I was shocked. Rudé struck me as much, much older.

"—but do you think he might be a match for my niece?"

Mouse! I was speechless.

"She wears spectacles, but he might consider. She has a good dowry, after all."

"Maîtresse Campan, there is something I think you should know," I said, grasping her hand. It was not a good time, but there might never be another, and I dared not put it off. "I'm afraid—" I swallowed. What if she didn't believe me? "Citoyen Rudé is not . . . He's not a good man. He . . . likes little girls." The maid was hovering. "He likes them *too much*," I said, lowering my voice. "And in the wrong way. Do you understand what I'm saying?"

Maîtresse paused for a long moment before saying, "This is true, angel?"

I nodded, relieved that I did not need to spell it out.

"And you're *sure*?" She looked deflated.

"I'm not," I admitted, "but you taught us to trust our instincts. And Mouse thinks so too."

Maîtresse's nostrils flared. "He hasn't . . . you know . . . *done* anything? Has he?"

"No," I assured her. "Not that I'm aware of." I heard the clatter of china and cutlery. Soon it would be time for the refreshment break. I thought of Hyacinthe, the music he was to have played. How was it possible that he no longer existed?

"*Grâce à Dieu.*" Maîtresse struggled to her feet.

"Maîtresse Campan, shouldn't you . . . ?"

But she was already at the mirror, tucking her hair back under her peasant bonnet.

"Citoyenne Beauharnais?" An attendant gestured to me from the door. "There is a gentleman who wishes to speak to you. Colonel Duroc."

"Go, angel," Maîtresse said. "Don't worry about me. I'm tough."

A tough old bird, the General liked to say—and she had to be, I knew, to accomplish all she'd done, inspiring us with her intelligence and ambition.

"I never doubted that for a minute," I said, tearing up, kissing her powdered cheeks.

Christophe was waiting for me in the long gallery. "Is she . . . ?"

"She's had a shock is all," I said. Well, *two*.

"And you? How are you?"

"Better, thank you." I still felt a little light-headed, in truth.

"I hate to ask you this again," Christophe said, "but I need to let the General know. Do you think you could do it? Play the piano during the refreshment break?"

Play for this *crowd*? "I'm sorry, but I . . . I *couldn't*." The thought made me tremble.

"There's something I haven't told you," he said. "We were told that Citoyen Jadin requested that you play a particular piece. It doesn't have a name, but it's one you composed?"

I stared down at the floor. I knew which composition he meant.

"Is it true that you composed a piece?" Christophe asked.

I nodded. Few people knew.

"That's amazing," he said.

"Did *Hyacinthe* Jadin request this?" I asked. *Creativity is by its nature generous,* he had once told me.

"That's what his brother said. Just before he . . ."

Aïe. "Before he died," I said quietly, and Christophe nodded.

My heart was pounding. I was going to have to do it, I realized. "Very well," I said quietly, looking up at Christophe. His eyes gave me strength. *Safe now.* "I'll do it . . . for him," I said, my voice quavering. For Hyacinthe.

And for *you*, I thought, giving Christophe my hand.

I stepped onto the platform at the side of the stage, a little unstable. I positioned myself on the piano stool and looked out over the ballroom. A number of people were still on the dance floor, standing and watching. Those in the tiered boxes were talking amongst themselves. Maman and the General appeared to be laughing at something Eugène was telling them.

At the back, people were streaming into the dining hall for refreshments. I caught a glimpse of Mouse and Ém following Maîtresse, who was leaning on Caroline's arm. Mouse saw me and pointed me out to the others. They stopped, smiling with amazement. Mouse wiggled her fingers at her forehead. My Fearsome!

I saw Christophe appear behind Maman, Eugène and the General in their box. He bent down to say something to the General, who glanced my way. He nodded his approval and I gave him a tight, nervous smile. He touched Maman's arm. *Watch. Watch your daughter.* Maman, in turn, nudged Eugène, who glanced over with a look of surprise. "Chouchoute!" I heard him say.

Christophe stood behind them, regarding me proudly, his arms across his chest.

It was time.

I squared up the scores propped on the stand in front of me, but the sheets shook in my hands. They'd been intended for Hyacinthe. My eyes began to sting. I took a shuddering breath, lightly running my fingers over the smooth ivory of the piano keys. Could I do it? I closed my eyes for a moment, imagining Hyacinthe sitting on a wooden chair beside me, imagining his pale, all-seeing eyes.

Play as if your very life depended on it.

Play from your heart.

My heart ached, so full of love, so full of sadness.

We don't have much time.

Oh, Hyacinthe.

I began.

AFTERWORD

I wish I could say that Hortense and Christophe lived happily ever after. Such was not to be. Hortense's mother *and* Maîtresse Campan pressed her to marry Napoleon's brother Louis. Their reasons were complex. Considered to be an artistic and sensitive soul, Louis seemed to them to be a good match for creative Hortense. But Josephine had a strategic reason for urging this union. A child born as a result of the marriage would unite the Beauharnais and Bonaparte families and provide Napoleon with an adoptable, legitimate heir—a child Josephine was unable to give him. This issue of an heir became politically critical, and Josephine needed to ensure that Napoleon would not abandon her. Everything depended on Hortense marrying Louis—everything but Hortense's happiness.

And Christophe's, as it turned out. Hortense appealed to her stepfather, Napoleon, to allow her to marry the man she loved. Napoleon agreed, but stipulated that once she and Christophe were married they live far, far from Paris. Christophe balked at the offer. He was devoted to Napoleon, and accepting this "offer" would have meant the end of his career as one of Napoleon's most trusted aides.

Heartbroken over Christophe's refusal and pressured on all sides, Hortense relented and agreed to marry Louis. Their marriage was bitterly unhappy. Ironically, not long after the wedding, Hortense and her mother arranged for Christophe to marry an extremely wealthy, attractive but unpleasant young woman who succeeded in making Christophe's personal life miserable.

Sadly, Hortense's marriage to Louis ultimately did nothing to ensure either Napoleon's political stability *or* her mother's happiness. Unable to give Napoleon a child, Josephine was divorced by him after fourteen years of marriage. She died a little over four years later at the age of fifty—of heartbreak, her doctor said.

Concerns about safety once Napoleon took power were justified. Several assassination attempts were made on his life, including a plot to poison him. The most dramatic attempt was the explosion of a wine cask filled with gun powder and bits of iron—"The Infernal Machine," it was called—on Christmas Eve, 1800. Napoleon, and those with him (including Christophe) were unharmed, but the blast killed or injured over fifty bystanders and came *very* close to killing Hortense, Caroline and Josephine.

Hortense had three sons. The sudden death of her eldest at four years of age caused her to have a complete collapse. She stopped speaking, and it wasn't until she heard music being played that she "woke" from her emotional coma.

Her second child by Louis, Charles-Louis Napoleon Bonaparte, became Napoleon III, and ruled France from 1848 to 1870. Helping him was Charles de Morny, his unacknowledged younger half-brother. Charles was Hortense's third child, the result of a secret love affair she had while estranged from Louis, a child she gave up at birth.

One of the most tragic events of Hortense's unhappy adult life was the early death of her best friend Adèle ("Mouse") at the age of twenty-five. The two young women were visiting, exploring a neighboring property—with the thought of living side-by-side—when a plank walkway over a ravine gave way and Mouse fell to her death.

Ém's life, too, ended tragically. After Napoleon was defeated, her husband Antoine was imprisoned. Heroically, Ém enabled him to escape execution by disguising herself as a man and taking his place in prison. In jail for two months, she had a mental breakdown and never fully recovered.

Caroline and Joachim Murat became Queen and King of Naples in 1808, courtesy of Napoleon's generosity. Predictably, Caroline thrived in her new position as Queen, but both she and her husband later betrayed Napoleon for the sake of their little kingdom.

Hortense's easygoing brother Eugène consented to an arranged marriage with Princess Augusta Amalia Ludovika Georgia of Bavaria, with whom he fell in love. Theirs was a happy and fruitful union: of their seven children, six married into European and Brazilian royal families.

Eliza Monroe's father, James Monroe, became the fifth President of the United States, and Eliza often performed the duties of First Lady as well as acting as a spokesperson for the President. She and Hortense maintained their friendship through a long correspondence.

The one consistently fulfilling aspect of Hortense's life was her art: her music and painting. She published beautiful books of her musical compositions. The piece she composed in this story—"Partant pour la Syria"—is played today as one of France's national anthems. There are many recordings of it on YouTube.

Readers often want to know, "What is fact and what is fiction?" And my answer always is: it's hard to say. I try to keep to the historical record, but there are times when doing so interferes with the story. In writing historical fiction, it is often necessary to prune the family trees. Families were bigger in the past, and instead of refrigerators and stoves, they had servants, many servants, and all these servants had families as well. To include everyone would be overwhelming.

For example, Mouse had two older sisters, one of whom was at school with her. However, because Mouse was Hortense's closest friend, and because so much of this story focuses on their relationship, I decided not to include the two sisters. For the same reason, I've not included Maîtresse Campan's son Antoine-Henri-Louis, who was enrolled in Collège Irlandais, the school for boys next to the Institute. Simplifying a story often makes it stronger.

In addition to pruning and simplifying, I have sometimes created events where little is known. Concerning Citoyen Rudé's proposal, for example, all we know from a letter Maîtresse Campan wrote is that *someone* proposed to Hortense and that her negative response created a scandal. Thus, Citoyen Rudé is my fictional creation.

Hyacinthe Jadin was, indeed, Hortense's teacher. I've shifted the actual date of his death by a few months, but he was a remarkable composer who died tragically young of tuberculosis (or "consumption," as it was called then). I highly recommend searching YouTube for recordings of his enchanting compositions.

Most of the letters from Maîtresse Campan in this novel are authentic. (You can find the French originals online at bit.ly/MmeCampan.) I have both translated and edited them, and taken creative liberties in some instances. The "Meeting of the Vows" did happen, although we do not know what occurred.

Maîtresse Campan was, in truth, adored by the girls in her school. In public, she defended her intensively creative and intellectual curriculum as one that trained girls to become good wives and mothers. Privately, however, she aspired to raise girls who were capable of independence.

Most of the details about the Institute—a wonderful school by all accounts—are historically accurate, insofar as can be known. One deviation from fact has to do with the Rose of Virtue, which could not be awarded to those over fourteen years of age. I decided to extend that age range for dramatic purposes. Also, although there was a "Repentance Table" at the Institute, it was simply referred to as the "Wood Table" because it wasn't dignified with a tablecloth.

At school, Hortense shared a room with Ém and Mouse, but the room was also shared with Mouse's older sister and the daughter of one of Madame Campan's sisters. I chose not to include either in order to simplify the story. Did Caroline join the girls in that room at some point? We simply do not know, but I like to think so.

I have slightly changed the timing of Caroline's confession to Hortense regarding why she told Napoleon that Hortense tormented her at school, but the discussion between the two girls did take place, and, according to Hortense's memoirs, they became good friends after.

There are differing accounts as to how Caroline and Joachim came to be engaged. What we do know is that they were very much in love, that Josephine was instrumental in gaining Napoleon's consent, and that they married almost immediately after the engagement.

Ém did get the pox in the summer of 1799—that's fact—but Nelly and her death from that disease is fiction. Ém's unhappy arranged marriage to Antoine Lavalette is fact, as well, as is her infatuation with Napoleon's younger brother Louis. Although Antoine's role in bringing Ém's father back to France is fiction, it is true that Ém did come, in time, to be devoted to her husband.

Marie Anne Lenormand was, indeed, a famous fortune-teller during the Napoleonic era. She knew Hortense's mother Josephine well—well enough, even, to write and publish a fake "autobiography" of Josephine's life.

Most of the details about Josephine, Napoleon and his troublesome family are based on fact, including the "failed" dinner party Josephine gave in her mother-in-law's honor—the dinner the Bonapartes refused to attend. A few more people, in fact, attended, but it's unlikely that Jadin or Lenormand were of their number. On

Napoleon's return to Paris, he did move Josephine's belongings out of La Chantereine and lock himself into his room. It was Eugène and Hortense who succeeded in bringing about a reconciliation. Was Josephine faithless with Citoyen Charles? Not in my opinion, but historians do generally differ.

And last, a word about the ghost of Queen Marie Antoinette: Hortense's mother, Josephine, was convinced that the Queen haunted the Tuileries. I've also had it on good authority that Josephine haunts Malmaison. *Not* that ghosts exist, of course! ;-)

THE REVOLUTIONARY CALENDAR

✢

In an effort to break with the past, most everything was changed during the French Revolution: the names of cities, the measures, forms of address, holidays and even the calendar. For example:

—The New Year was celebrated in the fall, in late September.

—There were five "free" days leading up to their New Year: *jour de la vertu* (day of virtue), *jour du génie* (day of genius), *jour du travail* (day of work), *jour de l'opinion* (day of opinion) and *jour des recompenses* (day of rewards). Every Leap Year, a sixth day was added: *jour de la Revolution* (day of the Revolution).

—The names of the months were based on nature. For example, *Frimaire*, which started in late November, was from the French word *frimas*, meaning frost, which one would expect to see in November. *Floréal*, which started in late April, was from the French word *fleur*, meaning flower, because one would see flowers in France at that time.

—The week was changed from seven to ten days, called a *décade*.

—The days of the week were named *primidi*, for first day, *duodi*, for second day, *tridi* for third day, and so on. *Décadi* meant tenth day. It was the last day of their ten-day week, and was a holiday, similar to our Sunday.

CAST OF CHARACTERS

❧

(Ages and ranks are as of September 12, 1798,
when the novel opens.)

At *L'Institut National des Jeunes Filles* (referred to here as "the Institute"), a boarding school for girls an hour west of Paris in what was then called Montagne-du-Bon-Air (now Saint-Germain-en-Laye):

Hortense de Beauharnais, 15: daughter of Josephine Bonaparte, stepdaughter of Napoleon Bonaparte ("the General").

Émilie de Beauharnais ("Ém"), 17: Hortense's cousin.

Adèle Auguié ("Mouse"), 14: Hortense's best friend.

Caroline Bonaparte, 16: Napoleon's youngest sister.

Maîtresse Jeanne-Louise-Henriette Campan, 45: headmistress of the Institute and Mouse's aunt.

Fighting in Egypt:

Napoleon Bonaparte, 29: commanding general of France's Army of the Orient.

General Bonaparte's aides-de-camp:

Eugène de Beauharnais, second lieutenant, 17: Hortense's older brother.

Christophe Duroc, major, 25.

Louis Bonaparte, captain, 20: one of Napolean's younger brothers.

Antoine Lavalette, captain, 28: Émilie's husband.

Joachim (pronounced "Wah-keem") Murat, general, 31.

Other:

Josephine Bonaparte (formerly Rose de la Tascher de Beauharnais, and Yeyette, a nickname), 35: mother of Hortense and Eugène. A widow, she'd married Napoleon Bonaparte two years before.

Euphémie ("Mimi"), full name and age unknown: Josephine's housekeeper and companion, a former slave.

Marie-Euphémie-Désirée Tascher de la Pagerie ("Nana"), 59: Hortense and Émilie's grandmother, married to the Marquis de François de Beauharnais ("Grandpapa").

François de Beauharnais, marquis ("Grandpapa"), 84: Hortense and Émilie's grandfather, father of Hortense's father, Alexandre de Beauharnais, and Émilie's father, François de Beauharnais.

Paul Barras, director, 44: a politician during the Revolution and main leader of the Directory regime that followed, he was influential in helping Hortense's mother.

Hippolyte Charles, 25: a friend of the family and Josephine's business partner.

The Bonaparte Family (by age):

Signora Letizia (born Maria Letizia Buonaparte and later known as Madame Mère), 48: mother and widow.

Joseph (born Giuseppe), 30: the eldest child, a politician and, after the death of his father in 1785, the head of the Clan.

Napoleon (born Napoleone), general, 29: Hortense's stepfather.

Lucien (born Luciano), 23: a politician.

Elisa (born Maria Anna), 21: married.

Louis (born Luigi), captain, 20: an aide-de-camp.

Pauline (born Maria Paolo), 17: married.

Caroline (born Annunziata), 16: a student at the Institute.

Jérôme (born Girolamo), 13: a student.

Deceased or Disappeared:

Alexandre de Beauharnais, general, 34 at the time of his death: Hortense's father, executed by guillotine.

François de Beauharnais, about 33 when he fled France around 1789: Alexandre's brother and Émilie's father.

Adélaïde Genet Auguié, 35 at the time of her death: Mouse's mother and Maîtresse Campan's sister.

GLOSSARY

❖

Aide-de-camp—An officer assigned to assist a general.

Amourette—A love affair.

Apoplectic fit—A heart attack.

Apothecary—A person who prepares and sells medicines and drugs.

Bonnet rouge—A soft red cap with its peak pulled forward, modeled after hats worn in antiquity. It was worn by the more radical supporters of the French Revolution.

Bourrée—A popular seventeenth-century French dance consisting of fast steps on tiptoe. A number of pop and rock bands of our day have incorporated the bourrée in their pieces.

Calèche—A light, low-wheeled carriage with a hood.

Childbed—When a woman gives birth.

Consumption—A deadly wasting disease of the lungs, now known as pulmonary tuberculosis (TB). Even today, over eight million people die of TB every year.

Council of Ancients and Council of Five Hundred—The French Constitution of Year III, adopted in 1795, provided for two legislative chambers: the Council of Ancients and the Council of Five Hundred. The Ancients were similar in structure to the U.S. Senate, the Canadian Senate and the

British House of Lords. The Five Hundred corresponded to the U.S. House of Representatives, and the Canadian and British House of Commons.

Creole—In the late-eighteenth and the nineteenth centuries, *Creole* referred to someone of European descent who lived in the Caribbean. The Creole culture includes language, music and cuisine.

Décadi—The official day of rest in the Revolutionary calendar that replaced the traditional Sunday.

Domino (costume)—A robe-like costume worn at a masquerade ball. Large, with a big cape, a hood and wide sleeves, it could easily slip on over a dress.

Dowry—The money and property given by a girl's parents when she was formally engaged and then wed. In most cases, the understanding was that the daughter could then not claim part of the family inheritance. A dowry signified a girl's value in the marriage market. If sizable, it ensured that she would "marry well," for few men would consider marrying a girl with no dowry. An exception was Antoine Lavalette, who married Émilie, who had no dowry.

Eau de Vie—Literally translating as "distilled spirits," in 1800 it signified brandy of poor quality.

Émigré—Anyone who had fled France during the French Revolution. Most were aristocrats, and because they favored a return of the monarchy, they were suspected of supporting the overthrow of the Revolutionary government. Considered traitors, their property was confiscated and their names were put on a list of those forbidden ever to return to France.

Fantasmagorie—A form of theater using a "magic lantern" to project images of skeletons, demons and ghosts onto walls, smoke or semi-transparent screens. For more on this early form of the modern horror movie, go to bit.ly/EarlyHorrorShow.

Falling disease—Epilepsy.

Forcemeat quenelles—Poached meatballs made of a mixture of ground meat, seasonings and fat.

Gigue—A lively dance, rather like a jig.

Green sickness—Also called the Virgin's Disease, it was a type of anemia found primarily in young women. Symptoms Included a greenish tint to the skin, lack of energy, shortness of breath, headaches, a loss of appetite and the absence of a menstrual period. The most common cause of this kind of anemia was an iron and protein deficiency, but at the time it was blamed on laziness, lovesickness, the swamping of "humors" before menstruating or excessive masturbation.

Haberdasher—Someone who sells small articles such as caps, purses and sewing notions.

Hussar—A soldier who was part of a light cavalry squadron.

Institute, the—A boarding school for girls founded and administered by Maîtresse Campan. For details about life at the school, go to bit.ly/institute4girls.

Interesting condition—To say that a girl was in an "interesting condition" meant that she was pregnant.

La Fontaine—Jean de La Fontaine's poems are stories about animals used to illustrate human foibles. Hortense reads "The Dove and the Ant" (bit.ly/DoveandAnt).

Laudanum—One of the most common remedies for what was then called "female complaints," laudanum was a mixture of opium, alcohol and water. Sometimes saffron, cinnamon or cloves were added for taste or color.

Madeleine—A delicious traditional French cookie which is not hard to make. Google "how to make madeleines" for instructions.

Man-of-all-work—A handyman.

Masquerade ball—A ball where almost everyone wears a disguise. During the Revolution and for a period after, such balls were not allowed because crimes might be committed under cover of a mask.

Montagne-du-Bon-Air—The name of the city Saint-Germain-en-Laye during the Revolution. In proclaiming independence from the Catholic Church, anything having to do with saints—even a name—was changed.

Necessary, the—An outhouse.

Palais Égalité—Formerly the Palais Royal; during the Revolution, names with royal connotations were changed to reflect the new ideals.

Partlet—A decorative covering for the neck and shoulders worn by women.

Pianoforte—An earlier version of what we think of as the piano. The pianoforte had sixty-six keys, compared to the piano's eighty-eight. *Piano* means soft in Italian, and *forte* means loud, so *pianoforte* indicates an instrument that plays both soft and loud. See the YouTube videos bit.ly/pianohistory1 and bit.ly/pianohistory2 for an excellent history.

Place du Trône-Renversé—A square in Paris where Hortense's father was executed. The guillotine was moved there for about one month, during which time 1,306 people were beheaded, including sixteen nuns who were beheaded in one day. Before the Revolution, it was called Place de Trône, and now it is Place de la Nation.

Plombières-les-Bains—A village in the mountains of southeastern Paris. It has always been famous for its hot mineral springs, which are believed to cure certain ailments. Josephine was there to seek a cure for her infertility, but tragically had a fall when a balcony gave way—a fall that very nearly killed her.

Pockets—Old-style "pockets" were like tie-on cloth purses, worn under a hoop and skirt. This was one reason hoops were so big, to hide the bags of stuff women carried under them. Women could reach into their pockets through slits in their skirt. This system worked well for hundreds of years, until the "nearly naked" look came into fashion. The new style was slim; nothing could be tucked underneath. Instead, women began to carry a cloth sac, called a "reticule"—the first version of what we think of as a purse.

Pork crepeinettes—Small, flat sausages.

Post house—A house or inn where horses were kept or changed for travelers, often offering refreshments and rooms.

Prisoner's Base—A rambunctious running game often played at Malmaison. Enjoyed for centuries, it is still played today. Go to bit.ly/PrisonersBase for the rules.

Reds—An old expression signifying a girl's menstrual period. It was also referred to as the *flowers*.

Sal prunella elixir—Most medications were made in the home. The "elixir" (an old-fashioned word for *drink*) prescribed for Ém was made of sal prunella, which is saltpeter, a type of salt in cake form. Saltpeter had a number of uses, from curing meats to soothing sore throats.

Sarabande—A dance that possibly originated in Mexico, the sarabande was taken up in Spain, then Italy and then France, where it became a slow, balletic court dance. Initially it was controversial and was banned a number of times, in part because of its suggestive hip movements.

Scimitar—Originally from Middle Eastern countries, a scimitar is a short sword with a curved blade that broadens toward the point.

Shoe roses—Ribbon and other fabrics formed into the shape of a flower, used to decorate the point of a shoe.

Smelling salts—Used to "wake" someone out of a faint, something that seemed to happen rather often in times past, especially during dental and surgical procedures, which had to be done without any pain medication. The salts smelled strongly of ammonia, which irritated the nose and lungs, triggering inhalation.

Sweetmeats—Dessert delicacies made of sugar, including preserved fruit, gingerbread, sugared almonds and jelly.

Supreme Being—The name given for "God" by the Revolutionary government.

The Rights of Man—*The Declaration of the Rights of Man and of the Citizen* was written during the French Revolution in 1789. It was directly influenced by Thomas Jefferson, of the United States, and inspired by the American Revolution. The U.S. Constitution declared its citizens free and equal. The French *Rights of Man* took it further, declaring *all* men free and equal. *"Men are born and remain free and equal in rights."* It had a major impact on freedom and democracy worldwide.

Upsick—To vomit.

Urgency—An emergency.

Wax tablet—The eighteenth-century version of an electronic tablet. Made of a smooth, notebook-sized wooden board covered with a thin film of wax, the tablet was written on with a sharp-pointed stylus or pen. Later, the wax could be heated and smoothed, ready for new notes.

Wet-nurse—Babies were often sent to be breastfed by another woman, called the wet-nurse. This woman would continue to have a motherly relationship with her charge. Napoleon, for example, was very fond of his "milk-mother," as Hortense was of hers. Eugène was nursed by his mother Josephine, a practice inspired by a pre-Revolutionary "back to nature" movement.

Hortense, however, had to be sent out to a wet-nurse when Josephine was ordered into a convent by her first husband. The French word *nounou* means nanny, or nurse. Ém's *nounou* was her nanny, and also, likely, her wet-nurse.

Wheat cakes—Small wheat cakes (something like cupcakes) were the original wedding cake. Breaking the cakes over the bride's head ensured that she would get pregnant. Each guest ate a bit of the cake to bring good luck. If an unmarried woman put a piece of the cake under her pillow, she would dream of her future husband.

In order by mention in the novel:

1. The Institute in Montagne-du-Bon-Air (Saint-Germain-en-Laye today).
2. La Chantereine, Josephine and Napoleon's house in Paris.
3. Place du Trône-Renversé, where Hortense's father was guillotined. Formerly Place du Trône, today it is called Place de la Nation.
4. The Carmes, where Hortense's mother and father were imprisoned.

5. Malmaison.

6. The Petit Luxembourg.

7. The Palace of Kings, named Palace of the Government by Napoleon. Also known as the Tuileries, it was burned to the ground in 1871. Today only its formal gardens remain.

8. The fortune-teller Lenormand's house.

To see current-day locations, go to bit.ly/GameofHopeMAP.

THE GAME OF HOPE

The Game of Hope deck of cards shown here is the earliest Lenormand set known, dating from 1800. It is now in the British Museum. There are many books and websites, and at least one app, that explain how to use the cards, should you be interested.

| RIDER | CLOVER | SHIP | HOUSE |

| TREE | CLOUDS | SNAKE | COFFIN |

| BOUQUET | SCYTHE | WHIP | BIRD |

| CHILD | FOX | BEAR | STAR |

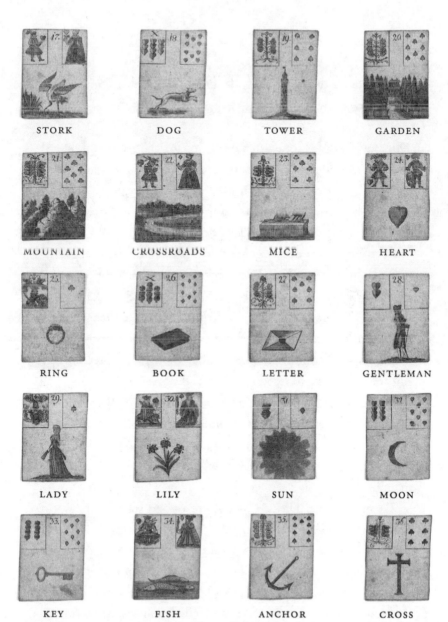

| STORK | DOG | TOWER | GARDEN |

| MOUNTAIN | CROSSROADS | MICE | HEART |

| RING | BOOK | LETTER | GENTLEMAN |

| LADY | LILY | SUN | MOON |

| KEY | FISH | ANCHOR | CROSS |

ACKNOWLEDGMENTS

❖

This novel would not exist were it not for the irresistible spark of an idea—wrapped in ribbons and presented deliciously with chocolates—from Nicole Winstanley and her team at Penguin Canada. Big thanks, as *always*, to my agent Jackie Kaiser for her enthusiasm, sage wisdom and support.

In editing, I am deeply grateful to my essential early-stage editors Alison McCabe and Fiona Foster, and especially to Lynne Missen of Penguin Random House Canada and Regina Hayes of Penguin Random House U.S. for their insightful feedback on what must have seemed an endless succession of drafts. As well, special thanks to Catherine Marjoribanks; her thoughtful, precise copy edit was a pleasure to read.

It takes a team to create a book, and if I knew, going forward, all the names of the dedicated book-loving professionals—the proofreaders, designers, printers and publicists—who will help bring this book into the world, it would be my pleasure to credit them here.

Thanks to Peter Hicks, Chantal Prévot and staff for the warm welcome at the Fondation Napoléon headquarters in Paris. I spent fruitful hours in their Bibliothèque M. Lapeyre Library. Grace Gately, Sarah Lawrence and Corinne Gressang all provided invaluable research assistance. A number of academics came to my aid through the H-France list server and The Napoleon Series forum, including Jennifer Germann, for her article on the painter François Gerard, a teacher at Madame Campan's school, and Lucia Carminati, who recommended that I look into the work of Abd al Rahman al-Jabarti for glimpses into the Egyptian perspective during Napoleon's Egyptian campaign. Special thanks go to Drs. Maureen MacLeod, Rebecca Rogers and Susan Howard for generously providing invaluable information about the Institute, as well as to genealogist Philippe Chapelin who dove into the Archives Nationales in Paris to find letters written by a student there.

Very early on, Marcello Simonetta, author of *Napoleon and the Rebel: A Story of Brotherhood, Passion, and Power*, provided fascinating unpublished notes on Hortense from Lucien Bonaparte's journals. Grateful thanks, as always, to Dr. John McErlean, who kept me informed of any and all Napoleonic news pertinent to Hortense; Monique Boulanger and Anne Challamel, for help with translations; Jana Anna, for guidance in spiritual realms; Bruce Backer, for working out a chess sequence for me (or, rather, for Napoleon and Hortense); Ann Coombs, for photos sent from a museum show at Malmaison; Ryan Naylor, for kindly taking me on a tour of the property in Saint-Germain-en-Laye that had formerly been the Institute; and Simon Kiskovski and his wife Jocelyne for generously showing me around Mortefontaine. *Special* thanks, as well, to Dominik Gügel and Christina Egli at the Napoleon Museum Thurgau, a charming museum devoted (largely) to Hortense in her Arenenberg Castle on Lake Constance in Switzerland.

My Napoleonic history consultant, Dr. Margaret Scott Chrisawn, saved my hide a number of times by pointing out errors. In deference to her reputation, I must make clear that she is *in no way* responsible for those errors that no doubt remain, both accidentally and willfully. Thanks, as well, to my other special consultants: P. A. Staes on historical medical details; Marcus Katz and (especially) Tali

Goodwin on Lenormand's Game of Hope; composer Jon Brantingham on eighteenth-century music composition; and Merilyn Simonds on what flowers might have been blooming in late October in a Paris garden in 1799.

A *very* special thanks goes to my amazing beta-readers: Astrid Mohr, Audrey Beach, Abby Brown, Emma Buell, Sierra Luce, Zoe Sklein and, *extra*-specially, Vanessa Van Decker. These astute, perceptive readers ranged in age from twelve to twenty, reminding me time and time again who this novel was for—and why I was writing it. Special thanks, as well, to Emma's mother, Patti Buell, an adult beta-reader who brought Emma to one of my readings when she was only a few weeks old.

For emotional support, thanks, as ever, go to the Fiction Writers' Co-op on Facebook, and to Jenifer McVaugh and Johanna Antonia Zomers of the WWW (Wilno Women Writers), my hometown writers' group.

A huge thanks (with hugs) to my Fearsome cheerleaders, to whom I owe *everything*: my husband, Richard Gulland, our daughter, Carrie Sudds, and our son, Chet Gulland.

At the last, I'd like to mention, in memoriam, François Marie René Héritier Combe, with whom I had delightful chats about this work and who would have been surprised and pleased to see his name mentioned here.

Also in memoriam, sadly, my dear friend and colleague, Paul Kropp, from whom I learned so much about writing for young adults, and who I pray forgives me in spirit for what happened to little Nelly.